SHIPMENT 1

Paging Dr. Right by Stella Bagwell
Her Best Man by Crystal Green
I Do! I Do! by Pamela Toth
A Family for the Holidays by Victoria Pade
A Cowboy Under Her Tree by Allison Leigh
Stranded with the Groom by Christine Rimmer

SHIPMENT 2

All He Ever Wanted by Allison Leigh
Prescription: Love by Pamela Toth
Their Unexpected Family by Judy Duarte
Cabin Fever by Karen Rose Smith
Million-Dollar Makeover by Cheryl St.John
McFarlane's Perfect Bride by Christine Rimmer

SHIPMENT 3

Taming the Montana Millionaire by Teresa Southwick
From Doctor...to Daddy by Karen Rose Smith
When the Cowboy Said "I Do" by Crystal Green
Thunder Canyon Homecoming by Brenda Harlen
A Thunder Canyon Christmas by RaeAnne Thayne
Resisting Mr. Tall, Dark & Texan by Christine Rimmer
The Baby Wore a Badge by Marie Ferrarella

SHIPMENT 4

His Country Cinderella by Karen Rose Smith
The Hard-to-Get Cowboy by Crystal Green
A Maverick for Christmas by Leanne Banks
Her Montana Christmas Groom by Teresa Southwick
The Bounty Hunter by Cheryl St.John
The Guardian by Elizabeth Lane

SHIPMENT 5

Big Sky Rancher by Carolyn Davidson
The Tracker by Mary Burton
A Convenient Wife by Carolyn Davidson
Whitefeather's Woman by Deborah Hale
Moon Over Montana by Jackie Merritt
Marry Me...Again by Cheryl St.John

SHIPMENT 6

Big Sky Baby by Judy Duarte
The Rancher's Daughter by Jodi O'Donnell
Her Montana Millionaire by Crystal Green
Sweet Talk by Jackie Merritt
Big Sky Cowboy by Jennifer Mikels
Montana Lawman by Allison Leigh
Montana Mavericks Weddings
by Diana Palmer, Susan Mallery

SHIPMENT 7

You Belong to Me by Jennifer Greene
The Marriage Bargain by Victoria Pade
It Happened One Wedding Night by Karen Rose Smith
The Birth Mother by Pamela Toth
A Montana Mavericks Christmas
by Susan Mallery, Karen Rose Smith
Christmas in Whitehorn by Susan Mallery

SHIPMENT 8

In Love with Her Boss by Christie Ridgway
Marked for Marriage by Jackie Merritt
Rich, Rugged...Ruthless by Jennifer Mikels
The Magnificent Seven by Cheryl St.John
Outlaw Marriage by Laurie Paige
Nighthawk's Child by Linda Turner

A CONVENIENT WIFE

CAROLYN DAVIDSON

H HARLEQUIN® MONTANA MAVERICKS

Special thanks and acknowledgment to Carolyn Davidson
for her contribution to the Montana Mavericks series.

ISBN-13: 978-0-373-41829-9

A Convenient Wife

Recycling programs
for this product may
not exist in your area.

HARLEQUIN®
™ www.Harlequin.com

Printed in U.S.A.

Reading has always been **Carolyn Davidson**'s favorite thing to do. She loves the written word, ranging from her early loves, Louisa May Alcott and Zane Grey, to present-day writers. Over the past several years, it's been her turn to compose books that bring pleasure to her readers. Carolyn loves to hear from her readers and no matter how busy she is, Carolyn always takes time to answer her mail. You can reach her at PO Box 2757, Goose Creek, SC 29445.

To a dear friend who cheered me on from the beginning of my writing career,
in those days when only a very few thought I would ever find someone to publish my stories.

A friend who listens and celebrates with me when things are going well in my life, and is still there by my side when troubles come along. A woman I call "warm and wonderful," who loves me unconditionally.

Tena Hoyle, this book is for you.

And, as always, to Mr. Ed, who loves me.

Chapter One

August, 1897

"I think I'm dying."

If her eyes had not been filled with tears, and her expression so woeful, Winston Gray might have smiled. As it was, he adjusted his spectacles and cleared his throat. Clearly, the young woman huddled in a straight chair on the other side of his desk was in dire straits. But dying? If clear skin, soft brown eyes and a full head of dark, waving hair gave any indication at all, he'd say she was in the best of health.

True, her form was slender, but not unduly

so. And yet there was a significant thickening of her waist and a suggestion of recent weight gain, if the fit of her dress was anything to go by.

"What's the reason for you to be so worried?" he asked, watching as her slender hand lifted to swipe at the tears on her cheeks. Concern was written all over the girl, and suddenly he lost his urge to smile. Rising from behind his desk, he moved slowly to where she sat, pulling a second chair closer.

She looked up at him, her mouth working as though she might burst into a full-fledged crying spell any minute. "My mama died from a growth in her belly," she whispered, and one hand spread across her own abdomen as she spoke. "I was only six years old, but I remember how she just got skinnier and skinnier, and her belly got bigger and bigger, till one morning she just stopped breathing."

Dr. Winston Gray knew heartbreak when it stared him in the face, and he sensed the girl's need for comfort. His large hand reached for hers, clasping it within his palm. "And you think you might have the same affliction?" he asked quietly.

She nodded, allowing the tears to flow now. "I've been feeling poorly lately, maybe for three months or so now. And my belly's getting bigger all the time."

And if his training had taught him anything, Win knew exactly what the girl's problem was. "Is there any chance you might be in the family way?" he asked.

Her eyes widened and her head shook with a violent movement. "Heavenly days, no," she blurted. "I'm not married, Dr. Gray."

"That doesn't always preclude a pregnancy," he told her. "Perhaps you…" How to phrase it delicately, so she would not take offense? "Do you have a gentleman friend?"

Her flushed cheeks lost their color and she wilted in the chair, tugging her hand from his grasp. "No." The single word was abrupt, and she straightened her shoulders. "Not anymore, anyway. Tommy Jamison used to come calling, but his folks moved back East a couple of weeks ago, and—" Her shoulders lifted in a telling shrug. "My pa didn't like Tommy anyway, and now, with me probably dying, it's just as well. His folks wanted him to go to college to get a good education."

And likely, the mother had taken a good look at Tommy's young lady and hustled her son as far away as possible from the problem he'd caused, Win surmised. He leaned his arms on his thighs and looked down at the wooden floor. How any young woman could be so ignorant was a puzzle he'd come across once before, and that time it had been solved neatly by a hasty marriage, aided by an angry father with a shotgun.

This particular situation didn't look as promising.

"How old are you?" he asked, glancing up to see her blinking back another deluge of tears.

"Almost nineteen," she whispered. "That's too young to die, isn't it?"

"You're not going to die." He hesitated, unwilling to speak further without at least knowing the girl's name. "You're George Mitchum's girl, aren't you?"

She nodded. "I'm Ellie. Eleanor, after my mama."

"Ellie." He tasted the name, liking its simplicity. "Do you have any female relatives? An aunt, maybe? Is there a housekeeper at your father's ranch?" From what he'd heard, Win was certain the man could afford to hire a woman to live in and keep up his ranch house.

"No, there's just me," Ellie said, dashing

his hopes. "I do the housework, and wash and cook for my pa and me."

Win cleared his throat. This was getting stickier by the minute. "Would you mind coming into my examining room, Ellie? I'd like to take a look at you and listen to your heart."

"My heart? What's that got to do with it?" she asked. "One of these days it's probably going to stop beating. Right now, it's doing just fine." She rose, and Win's gaze fastened on her slender form.

"Come along, Ellie," he said firmly, rising to his feet and grasping her elbow. "I'd like to check you over."

She nodded slowly. "All right. If you say so. But I can't imagine that listening to my heart is going to do much good," she said glumly.

Probably not, he agreed silently. But it was a beginning.

The examining room was small, centered by a black, leather-covered table, which Ellie approached as if she were heading for the gallows. "You want me to sit up on this thing?" she asked hesitantly.

"No," he responded. "I'd like you to lie down on it. On your back, please."

She took his offered hand and hoisted herself up, stepping onto the small stool, then sitting erect for a moment on the side of the table. "You sure you want me lying down?"

He nodded, taking his stethoscope from a drawer in his metal cabinet. He turned back to her, watching as she tucked her skirts neatly beneath her legs. "Let me help you," he offered, easing her head to the pillow he'd provided for his patients' comfort. "I'm going to unbutton two buttons, Ellie," he said easily, his fingers loosening the large black buttons from their holdings. Sliding the bell of his stethoscope inside the bodice, he pressed it to her skin, just left of center, where her heart tones would travel up the rubber tubing he'd attached to his ears.

Closing his eyes, he listened, aware of her hesitant breathing, as if she must take the smallest breaths possible, making herself shrink into the surface of the table in order to escape the pressure of his hand. Her heart was a bit rapid, but he'd expected that. And, as he'd also expected, it was strong and regular.

He slid his hand from her dress, noting the flush that tinged her cheeks with color. "I'm going to press against your stomach, Ellie," he told her, one hand judging the size of the fetus he was sure she carried. Indeed, it was a growth, one she would likely be carrying for a few more months, if he knew anything about it. Both hands measured her belly, pressing firmly against the expanded womb, and he wished he could perform a more accurate examination.

"You have a problem, Ellie," he said agreeably, offering a hand to lift her to a sitting position.

"I told you so," she muttered. "I knew it."

"Have you spoken to your father?" he asked.

She shook her head. "We don't talk much."

"I think you have something you need to tell him. And if Tommy were handy, you'd be telling him about it, too," he added.

Her eyes widened, their brown irises almost obliterated by black pupils. "What's Tommy got to do with me dying?"

"Ellie, listen to me," Win said slowly. "You're not dying, my dear. Not for many years. The problem you have will be solved in about four months, if my calculations are correct." He drew in a breath and tilted her chin with one long index finger, in order to look into her eyes. Bewildered eyes, he noted.

"You're going to have a baby, Ellie. I would

guess that Tommy is the father. Am I correct?"

"A baby? Tommy told me…" She halted, flushing deeply now. "He said if I loved him, I'd do what he wanted, and he was going to marry me anyway, so it would be all right." Her eyes squinted shut. "He lied, didn't he?"

"Maybe he intended to marry you," Win told her. "Maybe he would have if his folks hadn't taken him back East."

"Maybe," she agreed, and her eyes opened, a fierce anger darkening their depths. "I think I was a fool to believe him, Dr. Gray. I just needed somebody to love me." The words were an anguished whisper, and Win's heart jolted in his chest.

"We all need that, Ellie."

She lifted her head and turned to look out the window, where white curtains hung to ensure privacy from the outside. Through their gauzy fabric, his backyard offered a bleak landscape. Dried grass and clumps of bedraggled perennials dotted the dry ground, and at the back of the lot an unpainted picket fence delineated his property line. "You need somebody to tend your yard," Ellie said quietly. "Those flowers could use some watering."

"I suppose," he agreed, aware that she

struggled to face her dilemma. "What will you do, Ellie?"

She slid from the table. "Go home, I suspect."

"Will you tell your father right away?" He followed her from the room, through his office and to the waiting room, fortunately empty of patients this late in the afternoon.

"Maybe. I don't know. He'll probably figure it out for himself soon enough."

Win was surprised he hadn't already, given the tight fit of Ellie's dress. She was carrying high, and her waist had expanded enough to pull the buttons taut. "Will he help you?" Win asked.

Her shrug expressed doubt. "He don't much care about me, Dr. Gray. So long as I keep things up, he lets me be. But he's got a temper. I've seen him pretty near kill a horse that made him mad, and one day he beat the bejabbers out of a ranch hand who got drunk and didn't get out of bed the next morning. Sent him on his way afoot, just carrying his saddle and a bundle of his belongings."

"Are you afraid of him?"

She turned to face him, and Win saw the hesitant working of her mouth. "A little, maybe. Depends on how bad he needs me to work for him, whether or not I need to be dodging his fists."

His stomach knotted as Win noted the lack of color in Ellie's face. "Has your father abused you?" he asked.

She hesitated. "Not bad, no. He's smacked me a couple of times, but he pretty much lets me be. I just know he's going to be awfully upset when he finds out about this." Her hand touched her abdomen, fingers widespread as if she could somehow protect the child within.

And wasn't that a pretty future for a girl to face, he thought with a lump of despair in his throat. "If I can help in any way, Ellie, you know where to find me."

He held the door open for her and she walked out into the late-afternoon sunshine. Hesitating on the stoop, she looked up at the sky, where clouds floated on currents of air. Those same winds held birds suspended aloft, wings outspread as they circled high above the wheat fields outside of town. "Sure is a pretty day, isn't it?" she murmured, then, stepping to the ground, she trudged down the path to his gate.

"Come back to see me," Win called after her impetuously, waiting for her nod as she unhitched her horse and climbed into the buggy next to his gate. He watched the slow movement of the horse as Ellie turned in a half circle, heading toward the main part of town. The dainty mare picked up her feet in a trot as she moved toward the mercantile, where townsfolk were still moving in and out of the wide double doors.

Ellie slid from the buggy seat, and Win watched as she tied her horse, then stepped onto the wide boardwalk and into the store. Her hand on the door, she turned in his direction and hesitated, then lifted her other hand in a small salute.

Grim. Her prospects were grim, he decided, walking back to his house, where the small waiting room, office and examining room took up fully half of the downstairs space. He straightened a chair near the door, then walked on through to where his cluttered desk awaited his attention. Several files, yet to be noted with patient information, were stacked on the right side of his blotter, and he settled into his chair to do the jotting of symptoms and treatments he'd diagnosed and prescribed for each patient.

Paperwork was the bane of his existence, but it was a necessary thing, and he bent to it with a will, aware that he must make notes while his mind still retained the information from today's patients. Swiftly, he tended to business, moving the stack from one side of his desk to the other, noting with relief the absence of dire illness in the day's allotment of sickness. The usual chronic ailments were to be expected: dyspepsia, a cough that seemed to have no reason for being, a broken arm to be checked and sutures to be removed from a ranch hand's leg—the result of a horse's misplaced hoof.

A clean file was taken from his drawer, a clean sheet of lined paper inserted and a name written on the top line. Ellie Mitchum. He looked at it, then added, in parenthesis, Eleanor. Age, eighteen. The next line was filled in neatly. Heart tones normal, skin clear, eyes… eyes, brown, he thought, his pen held over the paper. Hair, dark and waving.

Abdomen, filling slowly, but surely, with a baby whose mother could find no joy in the news of its conception.

Tess Dillard cast Ellie a glance, then took a second look, her forehead furrowing into a puzzled frown. "I haven't seen you in a while, child," she said softly. "You haven't been to town lately, have you?"

Ellie shook her head. "I wouldn't be here today, but for some things my pa forgot when he came in last week. I usually just give him a list of what we need, but he left it home last time." And besides, she'd wanted to see the doctor. For all the good that had done her.

"Well, let me see what we can do for you," Tess said, reaching for the folded slip of paper Ellie held. Her fingers touched the back of Ellie's hand and lingered. "Are you feeling well?" she asked kindly.

Ellie stiffened, looking around for listeners. "Of course, I'm fine, Mrs. Dillard. I just have to hurry along today. I've got supper in the oven, and I need to be home before the roast gets overdone. Pa doesn't like his meat cooked all the way through."

Tess reached to the shelf behind her and lifted a metal container to the counter. "I've got spices in here," she said, sorting through the tins it held. "Here we go. Cinnamon, and there's another of nutmeg. Are you doing a lot of baking these days, Ellie?"

Ellie nodded. "I make pies for the men. Clyde does their meals, but I fix cookies and such for them. I only cook for Pa and me in the house."

"Well, let's see what else you need." Tess

placed the list on the counter and turned back to her shelves. "I've got liniment and a fresh supply of Dr. Wilden's stomach remedy." Her sharp eyes honed in on Ellie's face. "Is that for you? You're not feeling well?"

"Pa gets heartburn lately," Ellie said quickly, feeling the telltale blush rise to color her cheeks as she told the blatant lie. "Don't forget I need sugar, too, Mrs. Dillard."

"Yes, all right," Tess said, eyeing Ellie with suspicion. She leaned over the counter, her voice low. "If you need someone to talk to, I'm always available, honey. I know you've missed havin' a mama in your life."

"I'm fine," Ellie said, desperate to be on her way. "Just put my total on the book if you will. Pa will pay when he comes to town next." She gathered up the small pile of bottles and tins Tess had placed before her and held the assortment in both hands.

"Here, put that in this box," Tess said, reaching beneath the counter for an empty cardboard container. Adding the sack of sugar, she reached for a peppermint stick and placed it amid Ellie's purchases. "That'll settle your stomach, Ellie," she said quietly, pushing the box across the counter. "Just remember, I'm here if you need me."

And that was the second offer she'd had today, Ellie thought, lifting the box and heading for the door. Striding out onto the sidewalk, then stepping down to the road, she ignored the passersby, nodding only when the tall minister of the Methodist church spoke her name.

"Ellie, we haven't seen you in Sunday morning service for a long time. Don't be a stranger now, you hear?" Reverend Fairfax said with a wide smile. He tipped his hat and moved along the road, speaking to another of his parishioners as he made his way toward his own buggy.

"I doubt you'll be seeing me at all," Ellie muttered beneath her breath as she untied the mare from the hitching rail. The box with her purchases settled beneath the seat, she climbed into the buggy and turned the mare toward home. Although seeing the kindly minister would have been a logical move if Tommy had stayed here, instead of moving back East. If he'd told his mother that he wanted to marry Ellie.

She sighed, envisioning the event. Her with a new dress maybe. Tommy with his hair slicked back and his smile flashing just for her benefit. She frowned, closing her eyes, as his image eluded her, replaced by the tall, kindly man who'd just rocked the very foundations of her world.

Winston Gray. No problem recalling him, she thought with a flash of humor.

Now, as to Tommy… Ellie squinted as the buggy headed toward the setting sun. Funny, she could barely remember what he looked like. And he was supposedly the love of her life. Although, hard as she tried, today she couldn't come up with much more than lukewarm feelings for the man.

That she'd been a fool to listen to his palaver was a given. He'd played her like a shabby fiddle, plucking at her strings, telling her she was beautiful, just the girl he needed for a wife.

Beautiful, indeed. As if plain brown hair and eyes that matched were anything to talk about. But she'd listened, bewitched by the running on of his compliments, intrigued by his kisses that promised pleasure. But there'd been no pleasure to be had in his taking of her body, only a painful, embarrassing few minutes of prodding and thumping on her, while Tommy wheezed and groaned against her ear.

She'd been a fool. That fact recognized,

she set about working on a plan to get her future in order. The first thing would be to tell Pa. And to that end, she set her jaw and considered the best way to approach George Mitchum.

No matter what she'd done, the results would have been the same, Ellie realized. She crawled with effort into her bed, aching in every muscle, bruised from the blows she'd accepted as her due from the man who'd sired her. The man who'd told her in no uncertain terms that she was no longer welcome in his house.

"You've got till tomorrow morning to be gone from here," he'd shouted as she'd huddled in the corner of the kitchen. "I won't have a bastard in this house. I always knew you were just like your ma. You'll no doubt have a simpering girl child, just the way she did. Worthless females, both of you."

Supper forgotten on the table, he'd stormed out the back door, leaving Ellie to consider the condition of her body. Her face hurt from two sharp slaps, and unless she was mistaken, her eye was swollen. If the aching in her arms was any indication, there'd be bruises turning blue by morning, where great hammy fists had punched her as she'd sought to protect the child she carried.

Her backside throbbed from several kicks and her legs bore bloody scuff marks from George's boots, but there hadn't been any serious bleeding done, and for that she supposed she should be thankful. She'd thought at first that he would surely kill her, but his look of disgust had not included a gleam of hatred akin to murder in his eye.

She sighed, curling beneath the quilt. Maybe Tess Dillard would be the person to seek out. Perhaps she could use a hand in the store, at least until Ellie found a better solution to her problem. And that didn't seem likely, at least not for the next few months.

The house was quiet when she crawled from her bed, donning the same dress she'd worn yesterday. Her other two dresses, one she wore to do chores, the other her Sunday best, hung in the wardrobe and she gathered them, along with a spare petticoat and her good drawers, folding them all neatly into a small bundle. Two pairs of stockings completed her pile of belongings, and she stuffed the lot into a small valise that had been her mother's.

Her chest of drawers held extra bed linens and a shawl. The shawl she took, along with her comb and brush and a small bottle of scent Tommy had presented her with. Lily of the Valley, it said on the gilt label, and she smiled ruefully as she recalled her pleasure in the gift.

On second thought, she decided, she'd do just as well without any reminders of Tommy, and cast the bottle aside. It was about as worthless to her as the promises he'd made and broken. She surely didn't need to smell good for his sake anymore.

Damn Tommy Jamison, anyway. "I hope he rots in hell," she whispered, and then slapped a hand over her mouth as she muffled the curse word she'd said aloud.

The kitchen was empty, the coffeepot cold. Pa must have taken breakfast with the men in the bunkhouse, she decided, heading for the pantry. Last night's leftover beef and cooked carrots were on a platter, covered with a dish towel, and she wrapped a good portion in a clean napkin. It might be a long time before she found something else to eat.

Her final act was to take the sugar bowl from its place on the kitchen dresser. A handful of coins were in the bottom of the flowered china container. Pa didn't hold with fancy dishes on the table, preferring to take his sugar from a jar. Ellie had squirreled away all her meager savings in the last piece of china left from her mother's good dishes, and thankfully, George hadn't discovered the cache.

She dumped them into her small reticule and replaced the bowl. Then in a moment of rebellion, she snatched it back and settled it in the top of her valise.

"It's the last thing I have of yours, Mama," she whispered. "I won't leave it for him."

The faraway sound of men's voices came to her as she walked out the back door, looking toward the near pasture. The big farm wagon rolled across its width, filled with men holding scythes, her father holding the reins of his team of draft horses. One of the men, John Dixon, looked up, nudged another, and shook his head slowly in her direction.

Whether it was an expression of sympathy or a declaration of disgust she couldn't tell, and as she set off staunchly down the lane toward the town road, she decided she didn't care.

That she was a fallen woman was a fact she could face. That her father had turned on her with a vengeance beyond belief was more than a reality, as her bruised and battered body could attest. Her hips ached as she walked the length of the pasture fence. Her eye throbbed, and she squinted through its swollen slit as she turned onto the dirt track leading to Whitehorn.

The load she carried, her valise in one hand, her bundle containing food and every cent she owned in the world in the other, was heavy, yet not nearly so weighty as the pain of being an outcast. "He never loved me, anyway. I don't know why I'm surprised he wouldn't let me stay on and work for him," she murmured to herself. "If I'd been a boy like he wanted, he might have been different."

And wasn't that the truth. She wouldn't be in this fix if she'd been a boy. She'd have been the one doing the sweet-talking and taking advantage.

No. She shook her head. Even as a man, she wouldn't have done what Tommy did, hurting another human being the way he had. Running off back East with his folks, not even a goodbye issued in her direction.

Useless. Pa had called her that, plus a few other choice names, none of which she felt were fit to pass between her lips. Her chin lifted as she paced along on the side of the dusty road. It was only two miles to town. She could make it in less than an hour.

And then what?

Chapter Two

Winston Gray was a good doctor. He didn't need the opinions of the townspeople to recognize the fact, although they were ever ready with praise on his behalf. He'd filled a need in Whitehorn, and the men on the town council had been jubilant at his arrival.

They'd given him a house in which to live and set up his practice, and he'd been properly grateful, although they'd said it was just part of the package.

The rest of the parcel included a whole community of men, women and children who'd done without the services of a doctor for almost two years. Harry Talbert's wife had done her best, but being the wife of a barber did not automatically fit her for the role she'd been called on to perform.

"I'm sure glad you came to Whitehorn," she'd told him that first day when he climbed from the stagecoach. "I've had to sew up more cuts than you can shake a stick at, and deliverin' babies is not what I do best." Her grin had welcomed him, as had her unexpectedly firm handshake, matched by the dozen or so men who'd joined her to meet the stage.

He'd settled in nicely, awaiting the arrival of his office equipment, and the shiny, walnut desk he'd ordered from Saint Louis. For several months he'd spent time with the people of the community, tending to their problems, mending broken bones and stitching up their wounds, with an occasional delivery tossed in for variety. A box of medicine he'd brought with him kept his black bag supplied, and he'd ordered more as it was needed from a pharmaceutical outfit in Kansas City.

Now, his day half done, he polished the bell of his stethoscope with the cuff of his shirt sleeve, awaiting his first patient of the afternoon office hours. His morning and most of the night spent on house calls, he'd only just arrived back in town. He'd been at Caleb

Kincaid's ranch, setting a broken leg for one of Caleb's ranch hands who'd been thrown from a horse.

Called from his bed just past midnight, he'd ridden to the Darby ranch, where Matt's wife had delivered her fourth boy just after daybreak. She could have likely done it on her own, he recalled with a smile, but had gratefully inhaled the chloroform he'd dosed her with at the end.

Bone-weary, but willing, Win opened his office door, noting with thankfulness the dearth of patients. That would soon be remedied when the chill winds blew in from the north in the next few weeks, and folks began the usual run of pleurisy and other winter ailments.

He might do well to consider outfitting himself with a sleigh, once snow fell and the buggy could no longer traverse the open country. There were always folks needing house calls, those too old or infirm to make it into town. It was a part of the business he'd chosen, he decided, although *business* was too harsh and uncaring a word for the lifestyle he'd accepted upon finishing medical school.

Business best described the world of his father and uncles, the world of finance, where money was the god they worshipped, and his love of medicine and its benefits to humanity had met with scorn and derision.

"You'll come crawling back one day," his father had said, his voice harsh as he'd delivered his final thrust. There'd never been a word of admiration for Win's success in medical school, or a note of support for his choice of medicine as a career.

Win took off his spectacles, recalling that day when he'd turned his back on family and the social scene in Saint Louis to come to this small town in Montana, where a doctor was desperately needed, and fervently appreciated.

"Doctor?" The outer door opened and Tess Dillard stood on the threshold. "Are you busy?"

Win smiled. The storekeeper's wife was a lovely lady, friend to all, and one of his staunchest supporters, sending him all and sundry who complained of major or minor illnesses. "Come on in, Tess. I'm just wondering where all my afternoon quota of patients have gone."

"It's too nice out to be sick, Doc. This spell of warm weather won't last forever, and folks are taking advantage of it. School's started up early this year, but before you know it we'll have snow falling. Time enough then to be visiting the doctor." Her cheerful words only served to support his own theory, and Win motioned to her expansively.

"Come on in," he said warmly. "Did you need to see me for anything special or is this a social visit?" He eyed her suspiciously. "You're not about to offer me up another young lady on a platter, are you, Tess? I told you I'm not in the market for a wife."

She shook her head. "No, not this time, Doc, but one of these days, I'll come up with a woman you won't be able to resist." She crossed the room and sat on one of the straight chairs he furnished for waiting patients. "There's something going on I thought you needed to be aware of."

Win joined her, pulling a second chair from its place against the wall and scooting it closer to where she sat. "What's the problem? What can I do?"

Tess glanced out the open door. "I'm kinda keepin' an eye out for the girl, Doc. I'm afraid she's run out of choices, and I'm worried about her."

"What girl?" Win asked, and even as he spoke the words, his heart sank. *Ellie Mit-*

chum. As sure as he was of his own name, he knew the words that would fall from Tess's mouth next.

"It's Ellie, George Mitchum's daughter. I don't know if you're aware of her existence even, but she's gonna need a doctor before long, and I'm afraid you're elected. In fact, she could probably use some of your witch hazel and that arnica stuff you used on my boy's banged up leg when he got it bruised so bad last month."

"Tincture of Arnica," Win said distractedly, his mind racing. "What are we talking about here, Tess? Have you seen Ellie today? What's wrong with her?"

"You know her?" Tess frowned, taken aback by his recognition of the girl's name.

Win nodded quickly. "She was in here yesterday. Said—" He halted the words that would have spewed from his lips. "Well, let's just say she needed a bit of advice."

Tess slanted him a knowing glance. "She's going to have a baby, Doc. Don't tell me you didn't notice."

He nodded. "I noticed, all right. Did she tell you when she left here? I saw her stop at the mercantile."

"No," Tess answered. "I figured it out, once

I took a good look at her. She hadn't been in town for a couple of months, but I knew when I saw her comin' in the door of the store she was in the family way. Now today, just after noon, she came walkin' into the mercantile, and she's all banged up. Looks like somebody ran her over with a team of horses."

Win stood, his heart racing. "She was in an accident?"

Tess shook her head. "Not unless you call running into her father's fists accidental. She looks like he pounded her good."

Win felt his stomach clench, and anger rose to tighten his jaw. "She must have told him about the baby," he surmised, wishing for just a moment that he could lay his hands on the brute who had fathered the young woman.

"I expect so," Tess answered, her eyes bleak. "She came in to see me, asking if I could use her help in exchange for a place to stay for a while. Don't know where she's planning on going or what she'll do when she gets there."

Shoving his hands in his pockets, Win strode to the doorway. A vision of the young woman he'd seen yesterday appeared in his mind's eye. That her piquant beauty should be marred by a father's anger was not to be tolerated. And yet there would be no one to stand up for the girl. A father was the authority in today's society, especially here on the edge of civilization.

He turned abruptly. "Tess, where is she now?"

"At our place, stretched out on a bed. She was absolutely exhausted, poor child. I made her get washed up and showed her the bed. She didn't even have the energy to eat something first, just plopped down and closed her eyes."

Tess looked at him expectantly. "Will you do something to help?"

"You got something in mind?" he asked.

"I thought maybe she could come in by the day and do for you. You know, cook and clean, maybe." Tess surged to her feet. "No woman deserves to be an outcast, Doc. And I'm afraid that's what's in Ellie's future. There's certain women in town who will turn their backs on her once everyone realizes her condition. And there's others who'll sympathize, but keep quiet."

"Cook and clean." As if his mind had latched on to the phrase, he repeated it, almost absently. And then he cast her a penetrating glance. "This isn't one of your matchmaking projects, is it?"

Tess colored, shaking her head. "No, of course not. For heaven's sake, a doctor should have a wife above reproach in the community. That's why I've tried to get you interested in several of the young women from the better families."

"Ellie told me my yard needed watering," Win said, a smile coming to life as he recalled her words. "Send her over when she wakes up, Tess. I'll see what I can do."

The scraps from last night's roast lay heavy in the pit of her stomach as Ellie awoke. Sleeping the afternoon away wasn't something she generally did, and the undigested food she'd eaten on the long walk to town hadn't agreed with her. She struggled to sit upright, the bed having an unfortunate tendency to sag in the middle.

Once on her feet, she scooped her hair into a bun at the nape of her neck and sought out the hairpins she'd placed on the night table. It might not be neat and tidy, but it was as good as a hairdo could be expected to look when a day had gone as poorly as this one.

The scent of chicken cooking lured her to

the kitchen, and she crossed the room to the back door, opening it wide, inhaling deeply of the fresh air. Food was not at the top of her list right now, but Tess and John Dillard would be home from the mercantile soon, and if supper was ready, they would probably be most appreciative.

The oven held a whole roasting hen and from the looks of it, it only needed potatoes and vegetables added to complete the meal. Ellie explored the pantry, finding a bucket of new potatoes, and a bunch of carrots. Cooking gave her a sense of accomplishment, and she scouted out a paring knife, her capable hands readying the vegetables for the oven. A pan of stale bread, cut up into cubes, told her that Tess had plans for chicken stuffing, and in minutes, Ellie had cut up an onion and found spices to complete that dish.

She drained broth from the roasting hen into the bread pan and mixed the stuffing quickly, placing it in a greased tin to bake. Outside the back door, two little girls played in the afternoon sunshine, and waved in her direction when they saw her in the doorway.

"Mama said to let you sleep. She told us we wasn't to disturb you," the tallest of the two said cheerfully. "This here is my friend

Alice. And I'm June-bug. At least that's what my papa calls me. And sometimes he calls me an afterthought." She grinned widely. "I don't know what it means, but he always laughs and hugs me when he says it."

June-bug. Ellie smiled, even as a sadness descended over her. Imagine having a father who would designate his daughter as such, who would tease the little girl with a nickname, bringing smiles to her freckled face.

"June-bug sounds like a wonderful name," Ellie said. "I'm just Ellie."

"My mama told me. Is that what your papa calls you?"

Ellie nodded. But not lately, she thought, the memory of those hated appellations he'd shouted in her direction coming to mind. Not lately.

"Are you cookin' our supper?" June-bug asked. "I can smell chicken."

"Your mama had it in the oven. I'm just putting some potatoes and carrots in with it."

"She'll be glad," the child said with a sharp nod. "She's kinda tired when she gets home. And when my sisters got married last year, there wasn't nobody left to cook dinner, but me and Mama. And she won't let me touch the stove without her bein' here to watch."

Tess was more than glad, her words joyous as she followed John into the house less than an hour later. "You didn't have to cook for us," she exclaimed, eyeing the pan Ellie had just taken from the oven. "But I surely do appreciate it, Ellie. June said you were making biscuits when she looked in the door a while ago."

"We may just keep you," John teased, up to his elbows in soapsuds as he washed up at the sink.

Ellie smiled, forcing a pleasant look, as she caught sight of Tess's sympathetic glance in her direction. She'd looked in the mirror herself; knew the sight of a swollen eye and cheek would be causing talk around the town should she appear in public. It was enough that she'd paraded down the road with her head bowed, finding her way to the back door of the mercantile in order to see if Tess could use any help.

"You've got no need for me," Ellie said bluntly. "But I'll find something to do. Maybe I can get a job at one of the ranches."

"I may have something in mind," Tess told her. "I stopped by to see Doc Gray earlier. He might have need of you. Man never eats right, and he's having to send out his washing to be done. I'll warrant his floors haven't seen a scrub rag in a month, since he had Eula Peters in to clean up things."

"Dr. Gray? You want me to go clean his house and cook his meals?" Ellie closed her mouth with a snap of her jaw. "He can't afford to have a woman like me hanging around his neck. Folks would talk if I were to work for him."

"Just go and see what he has to say," Tess told her soothingly. "I suggested it and he didn't seem to take it poorly. In fact, he told me to send you over. He wants to talk to you."

Ellie gritted her teeth. "I'm going to need a place to stay. I don't think it'll work, Mrs. Dillard."

"Let's eat first," Tess suggested. "And then you can go talk to him."

Ellie wavered. "I'll walk over there a little later on. I don't want any more folks to see me than have to, with me looking like this." She bent to take the stuffing pan from the oven. "I hope you don't mind that I made this. I saw the bread all cut up and I thought it was what you intended."

"You're a gem, Ellie." Tess's praise was heartfelt as she sank into a chair at the table. "I'm not usually one to take advantage, but

I've had a long day. I thought I was doing well to come home long enough to stick a chicken in the oven. Hadn't even gotten as far as what we'd have with it."

"Well, if I can't do much else, I'm a good cook. At least my pa never had any complaints," Ellie said stoically. Her gaze scanned the table, where plates and silverware awaited. "I guess you can eat now."

"Aren't you going to join us, Ellie?" John asked, glancing at his wife with a puzzled look.

"I'm not hungry," Ellie admitted, sidling toward the door. "If you don't mind, I think I'll take a walk around the back way to the doctor's house. If he's willing to give me work, I can't afford to turn it down."

"Take some of this chicken with you," Tess offered, rising quickly and bustling to the cupboard for a container. "We've got more than enough. Unless I miss my guess, Doc will be thankful for a decent meal." She darted a look at Ellie, and smiled widely. "Maybe he'll be impressed if you tell him you did the cooking."

The bread was moldy and the milk had gone sour. All in all, supper looked to be a complete disaster, Win decided. Scrambled eggs didn't taste like much without a piece of bread alongside, and he'd lost his appetite for them anyway. With a shrug, he left the kitchen to stalk through the living room, and sat down on the front stoop, reaching to pet the stray cat who'd been hanging around lately.

"I'd give you the milk, cat, but you'd turn your nose up at it," he murmured. He glanced toward the hotel, where the dining room offered a decent meal. Somehow, it seemed to require too much effort, and he decided to settle for a can of peaches from the pantry.

A movement caught his eye and he turned his head to where a woman's slight form approached from around the corner of the house. "You weren't in the kitchen," Ellie said, "so I came around, hoping to find you." She carried a pie tin, covered with a bleached dish towel, and his hopes for a decent meal rose from the depths to a more palatable level.

"What's that you've got?" he asked, aware of an optimistic note in his voice.

"Mrs. Dillard sent over some of their supper, in case you're hungry," Ellie said. "I'd hand it over, but the pan's hot, and you don't want to burn your fingers. I suspect your patients would admire you more without blisters."

He grinned at her dry remark and hastened to open the screen door. "Come on in, Ellie. Go on through to the kitchen and put it on the stove." He followed her, lured by the scent of chicken, and watched as she lowered the tin plate to the back burner. Placing the dish towel she'd used for padding aside, she removed the covering.

"I made stuffing to go with Mrs. Dillard's roasting hen, and I brought plenty for you. I must have thought I was gonna feed an army, with the big panful I put together."

"Tell you what," he said hastily, reaching for a cupboard door. "I'll get out some plates. It looks like there's enough for both of us." He turned to look at her, dishes in his hand. "Or have you eaten already?"

She shook her head and he scrutinized her in the dim light, then decided against lighting a lamp. "I'm not real hungry," she said quietly. "But I'll be glad to dish you up some."

"Sit down, Ellie," he told her, and she sat on the nearest chair, then glanced up quickly, as if his firm tones might give way to anger. Placing two plates on the table, he lifted the meal she'd carried to his door and divided it, allowing himself the larger portion, knowing she would protest otherwise.

After retrieving two forks from the cutlery drawer, he approached her, then squatted beside her chair. His hand lifted to touch her swollen flesh and she flinched. "I won't hurt you," he said calmly. "I just want to see how much bruising you have."

She nodded, sitting quietly beneath his touch, and he silently cursed the man who had done this. "Is there more?" he asked as he rose and circled the table.

Ellie hesitated. "Some."

Win picked up his fork and took a bite, savoring the flavor of chicken and stuffing. "Where?" he asked after a moment.

Ellie looked up, startled, then replaced her empty fork on the table. "In places you don't need to see."

"I'm a doctor, Ellie." He took another bite, and nodded at her. "Eat now and we'll talk about it later."

She sighed and obeyed his dictum, bending a bit, perhaps to hide the damage done her face, he thought. The next problem would involve coaxing her to allow him to examine the full effects of her father's wrath.

The few bites of food left over from their

meal were scraped onto a small dish on the back stoop for Win's porch cat, and Ellie smiled as he described the stray who'd adopted him, taking occasional meals from his hand, although he didn't allow her entry into the house. The dishes were washed with hot water from the reservoir on the side of the big black cookstove, and Ellie dried them carefully, putting them back in the cupboard.

"Mrs. Dillard says you might want me to do some work for you," she ventured as she emptied the small dishpan and wiped it out with the cloth she'd used.

"That's right," Win answered. "I need someone to do up my washing. I've had the woman at the hotel doing it, but I fear she's partial to bleach, and my best blue shirt has blotches all over it. I'd thought you might take a hand and see if you could keep me in order."

"You need someone to cook?" she asked diffidently. "I'm pretty well able to keep a kitchen, and I've always been a good hand at housework."

"I think we could work something out," Win said quietly, watching as she wiped the table, then picked up the broom. "You don't need to sweep right now," he told her. "Come sit with me and we'll talk."

Her eyes darted in his direction and then back to the darkness that had gathered as the sun settled beneath the horizon. "I'll light a lamp," he offered. "It's getting too dark to see in here."

She nodded, settling in the chair across the table. Her hands were folded neatly before her, and he looked down as he lifted the globe of the lamp to light the wick. "Would you rather I lit a candle?" he asked. "I have a good supply of them."

She shook her head. "The lamp's fine. You can take a look at me and see for yourself I'm not hurt bad. You don't need to worry about my eye," she said with a wave of her hand "I've seen worse on men after a Saturday night on the town."

"Men from the ranch where you lived with your father?" he asked, sitting down again to face her.

She nodded. "I did a little mending when they got banged up. Used witch hazel and carbolic acid, and even stitched up a few cuts before you came to town."

He smiled, admiring her nonchalant description of the chores she'd been called upon to perform. "So I put you out of business, did I?"

Her eyes were warm as she turned them in his direction. "I didn't mind. I never much liked tending to the men. Sometimes they made me feel odd, like they were looking at me funny. You can have the whole kit and caboodle of them."

"They looked at you funny?" He caught the offhand remark and dwelt on it. "Like men do here in town? As if they admire your pretty hair or your smile?"

"I don't have pretty hair," she said firmly. "It's brown and gets all tangled up and in my way. My pa won't allow me to cut it, said the good book is against women having short hair."

And wasn't that the first thing he'd found to admire about the brute? Win nodded agreeably. "I like long hair myself," he said affably. "And whether you realize it or not, yours is lovely."

Ellie reached up self-consciously to smooth the stray locks from her cheek, tucking them behind her ears. "We need to talk about my working here," she told him. "I need a place to stay, first off. Is there any chance I can have a room out back? I see you've got a shed on the back of the house."

"You can have a room upstairs," he told

her. "There are three bedrooms there, and I have one down here. There's plenty of furniture that came with the house and more in the attic if the room you choose doesn't have what you need."

He held up a hand, gaining her silence as she would have spoken. "I know you think the folks in town will talk, but I don't think they'll trouble you. Once it's known that your father took out his anger on you the way he did, I'll be considered the man of the hour for taking you under my wing."

"You think so?" She sounded uncomfortable with the idea, yet the first sign of animation crossed her face. "You don't think they'll take it wrong?"

"Lots of single men have housekeepers, back in the city where I come from," he said firmly. *But none so pretty as you.* The thought flashed through his mind before he could snatch it, and he considered the idea.

If Ellie thought herself unattractive, she'd been looking in the wrong mirror. Dark hair with red highlights, gathered from the lamp overhead, tempted him to gaze in her direction, and velvet couldn't begin to describe the soft warmth of her brown eyes. Even the one that had a swollen lid owned a hopeful cast, and he smiled as her lips quirked just a bit.

"We could try it out," she ventured. "Maybe see if what I do is up to snuff."

He nodded, gesturing to the clean kitchen that surrounded them. "You've done just fine so far. I expect a meal on the table in the mornings by seven o'clock and maybe a bite to eat around noontime, when I get back from house calls. And then when my day is over, if you could have something hot on the back of the stove, I'd surely appreciate it."

"Do you have fixings for breakfast in the pantry?" she asked, her eyes looking toward the narrow opening on the opposite wall.

"Not much of anything. Just some eggs I got at Tess and John's place. My milk's sour and the bread I bought from Ethel Talbert, the lady next door, went moldy on me. I think there's some canned goods, but I eat at the hotel a lot, when I think of it."

"Can they cook good? At the hotel I mean? I've never eaten anywhere but at home."

"Not as good as what I had tonight," he told her. "I'll have to watch that they don't coax you to work there, once they find out I've hired the best cook in Whitehorn."

She smiled again at his teasing manner, and

he felt the warmth of her approval. "You don't have to say nice things about me, Dr. Gray. I'll just be grateful for a chance to rest in one place until I know what I'm going to do."

"You're welcome to do that here, Ellie. And while we're alone, I'd like you to call me Win, or Winston, if you'd rather."

She'd begun to look more hopeful and he flashed her a smile. "I think we're going to be good friends, Ellie. If you don't mind, we can begin by shaking hands and striking a bargain."

Ellie offered her slender hand in his direction, and Win took hold of it, cradling it in his palm as if it were a wounded bird and he must treat it with care. "What's our bargain?" she asked, color rising on her cheeks.

"We'll share this house, and you'll do what's necessary to make my life more comfortable. In return I'll pay you a good wage and tend to your bruises."

She tugged her hand from his. "My bruises are fine, all but a couple on my leg. If you've got some carbolic salve I'll dab some on. They're looking a little angry around the edges."

He stood and rounded the table. "Let me look," he said firmly, squatting before her.

His hands were warm and strong, and when he lifted the hem of her dress to expose her ankles and calves, she allowed it. Above the tops of her shoes, several scabbed-over areas took his attention, and he stifled the urge to curse aloud.

"Let me get my bag, Ellie. You sit right here and wait for me."

Chapter Three

"That should help these spots heal faster," Win said, eyeing the areas he'd cleansed and anointed with salve. "We'll just put on a bandage for tonight. By morning you can leave them open to the air." Each scabbed and scuffed area was covered with soft fabric, and held in place by a strip of cloth circling her leg.

He's a doctor. The words whirled in her head, rebuking her as she felt distinct pleasure in the touch of warm hands against her skin. His head bent over his work and she was afforded a bird's-eye view of his dark, crisp waves. Stunned by the sudden urge to place her fingers there, to know for herself the texture of those masculine curls, she clenched her hands into fists and buried them in the fabric of her skirt.

"There, that should do it," he said, easing her skirt down to cover her legs almost to her ankles. "Now, where else are you bruised?" he asked, standing erect to replace the roll of bandage in his bag. At her silence, he sighed. "I only want to help, Ellie."

Untangling her fingers, she unbuttoned her cuffs, rolling up the long sleeves she'd been careful to use as coverings for her arms. No matter how warm it became, she'd determined to hide the evidence she wore there from shoulder to wrist. Now, it didn't seem nearly so important that she admit defeat at her father's hands.

Win was silent as she revealed the purpling bruises, but his hands were tender as he bathed them with wool batting, dousing them well with witch hazel. "It's an old remedy," he said as he opened the bottle, "but it seems to work well. Mostly, the blood will have to dissolve back into your system. I fear there's no rapid recovery from bruising."

Ellie nodded agreeably. "I'll just keep them covered for a while."

Win cleared his throat. "Is there anything else I need to tend to? Your father didn't hurt your stomach in any way?"

She shook her head and grimaced. "No, that's why my arms got all banged up. I had them wrapped over my belly and when he was hitting on me, they took the brunt of it. My hip is sore where he kicked me, but there's nothing broken. I'll get over it."

He pressed the bottle of witch hazel into her palm. "Here, I've got lots more where this came from. Promise me you'll use it tonight. And, Ellie…" He paused, choosing his words carefully. "If you should have any pain or bleeding, let me know right away. Do you understand what I'm saying?"

Ellie looked up. "I reckon I've about got over the whole mess already." There was enough pain and some to spare, but she suspected it wasn't the sort of thing he was hinting at. "I expect I'll be fine. You don't need to be fussing over me, Dr. Gray. I'm the one that's supposed to be looking after you."

"Starting tomorrow," he told her. "Now, let's walk you back to Tess and John's place and get your belongings."

"You want me to stay here tonight?" The thought was daunting, that she should be given a room on the second floor of this big house, all for her own, with nothing more to do than keep the place clean and cook three meals a day for her keep.

"I don't see any reason why not," he said. "I'll want to explain things to the Dillards though, so folks will understand the arrangement."

Gathering her scant supply of clothing from June-bug's bedroom took little more than a moment, and Ellie walked back into the kitchen in time to see Winston Gray shaking John Dillard's hand. Win looked up as Ellie stood just inside the doorway, a question in his eyes.

"Yes, I'm ready," she said. Her valise packed full with all but her mother's shawl, she approached Tess. "Thank you for…" She looked around the kitchen, then back at the woman who'd come to her aid. "For everything," she finished lamely. "I appreciate your kindness, Mrs. Dillard."

"I think you might call me Tess." Her fingers touched Ellie's cheek and warmth flooded the area, as though affection gave healing to the skin she stroked. "I'll be over to look in on you tomorrow. Doc says you need foodstuffs, so just make a list and I'll carry it to you."

The immensity of her situation seemed staggering as Ellie considered the offer. "I don't even know what he likes to eat," she murmured.

"Most anything you cook will be better than what he's been puttin' in his stomach lately. I'll get some staples together for you tomorrow," Tess told her, turning her toward the back door. "You run along now. Things will work out."

Things will work out. The words resounded in her head as Ellie prepared for bed. Clean sheets and a worn quilt covered the feather tick, and its comfort tempted her as she blew out the lamp and glanced from the bedroom window. A light blazed from the house next door, and she caught a glimpse of a woman's form, silhouetted and unmoving. And then the shadow turned and the unmistakable burden of pregnancy altered the vision she watched.

A man entered the room and Ellie watched, unable to turn away, breathless as the tall, dark-haired figure approached. Bending to look into her face, he took the woman's hands in his and then drew her against his body. The image of tenderness she beheld brought tears to Ellie's eyes, and she turned away, feeling she had somehow violated a private moment.

Stunning in its simple beauty, the image beckoned, and she looked back. Only darkness met her gaze. The light was extinguished, the second floor room darkened.

She sank into the bed behind her. The feather tick welcomed her aching body, and she curled on her side, one hand pressing against the firm swelling of her belly. A movement deep inside caught her attention, and a gentle nudging pushed against her hand. She held her breath, and again the skin beneath her fingertips was rippled by the tiny presence within. With a sigh of delight, Ellie closed her eyes.

If there was truly a God watching over her, as the minister had said in a sermon on one of her occasional visits to church, then surely he must be taking a hand right now.

The woodstove was familiar territory, and Ellie peered into its depths to gauge the amount of kindling she'd stacked. She'd found a small case of sulphur matches in the pantry and placed a box of them atop the cookstove. Now with a scrape on the side of the box, she set a match ablaze, firing the kindling, then quickly added small lengths of wood. Watching as they caught fire and began to burn, she bent to the wood box, lifting three larger chunks, enough to make a good cooking fire.

In ten minutes she could begin breakfast, and to that end she scouted out the pantry shelves. A flour bin held enough for biscuits, and she found a can of lard with a good scoop left on the bottom. Sniffing it, she decided it had not gone rancid. But the addition of lard went on the mental list she was concocting as she worked.

A pot of coffee was the next detail, she decided, and a blue speckled pot sat on the back of the stove. She rinsed it at the pump and filled it halfway, then added a handful of coffee from a jar on the shelf. Cracking an egg, she dropped it into the water and placed the pot on the front of the stove, where the hottest fire would burn.

A knock on the back door caused her to tremble, and she looked over her shoulder, the thought of her father speeding to the forefront of her mind. A woman cupped her hand to peer through the screen door, and Ellie sighed with relief.

"Good morning." It was a cheery greeting

and Ellie hastened to open the door. "I live next door. He gets bread from me when he takes a notion, but he hasn't got a fresh loaf for pretty near a week," the neighbor said, her gaze sweeping Ellie from stem to stern. "I'll bet you're the young lady who's going to be doing for him."

"You've heard about me?" Ellie asked, astounded that the news had traveled so quickly.

"Tess Dillard told me late yesterday afternoon that he was thinking of taking on a housekeeper. The man needs looking after, sure enough." The loaf of bread she carried was placed on the table and then the woman headed back to the door. "If you need anything else, just call out. I'm Ethel Talbert. My husband, Harry, owns the barber shop."

She was past the screen door and halfway across the yard before Ellie caught her breath. Scurrying across the kitchen, she leaned out the door. "Mrs. Talbert, where can I buy some milk?" The biscuits could be put together with water, but they wouldn't be near as good, and, for Winston Gray, Ellie would beg, borrow or steal what she needed to serve him a decent meal.

"Land sakes, child. I didn't think about

that. I've got extra. Come along and I'll send you some back."

Patting her hair and brushing the flour from her hands on a dish towel, Ellie scampered across the yard, past the hedge of bushes and up to the neighbor's back door. A quart jar was being filled from a crock, even as she watched through the screen, and in moments Ellie was carrying it back to Win's kitchen.

"What's going on?" Win stood just inside the doorway, rolling up his shirtsleeves as Ellie scooted past him. "You out visiting already?" He reached to brush at her cheek. "You've got flour dust all over your face," he said, grinning at her.

"I thought I wiped it all on the towel before I went to Mrs. Talbert's house. I just borrowed some milk from her so I can make biscuits. I hope you have baking powder or soda."

"Both, I suspect," he said, entering the pantry. "Though I don't think I've used either. When I moved in, Tess brought over what she thought I needed to furnish my kitchen, but most of it is still just like it was that day. I'm not much of a cook."

He sat down at the table, watching Ellie knead the biscuits, then cut them into circles with a water glass and place them on the baking pan she'd located.

"You do that well," he said, sounding pleased. "This idea is gaining ground." He peered past her to the stove. "Is that coffee I smell?"

Ellie nodded and found a cup for him. "If you have something you need to do, I'll start the eggs in a few minutes. The biscuits won't take long."

He chuckled. "I'm enjoying this, Ellie. No one's cooked for me since I left home, and that was a long time ago." He sipped from the cup and placed it on the table. "Did you sleep well?"

"How could anyone not sleep, all cozied up in a feather tick?" she asked. And then remembered the neighbors in their bedroom. "Who lives on the other side of you, the house I see out my window?"

"That's the sheriff, James Kincaid, and his wife, Kate. She's been teaching school for a little over a year now. They say she's a crackerjack. Keeps the big boys in line. The kids all seem to like her. Word is she's a good teacher."

"And they're going to let her keep on teaching after the baby's born?"

"Yeah, I understand the town council has given permission for her to take the baby to school with her unless she's decided to get someone to watch it. They've really gone overboard to keep the sheriff happy. In fact, school was in session early this year. They figure to let the students out for a couple of weeks when Kate delivers."

The biscuits were golden and tender, the eggs scrambled and waiting, and Ellie poured a second cup of coffee for Win as he picked up his fork. "Aren't you eating with me?" he asked. "Get yourself a plate, Ellie. You cooked enough for both of us."

The intimacy of sitting at a breakfast table with a man was unsettling, Ellie thought. Her father had insisted on her staying by the stove to serve him while he took his meals, and she was left with whatever he chose not to eat. She'd taken to standing at the window with a plate or pot in her hand as a result, and decided quickly that the pleasure of sharing a meal was something she could get used to in a hurry.

"I'm going out on house calls," Win told her, placing his plate in the dishpan. "I should be back a little after noon. Maybe you can find something in the pantry for a sandwich for me."

He waved a farewell and vanished through the kitchen door into the long hallway that divided the lower floor into his offices and dwelling place. And then the front door closed and he was gone.

Ellie looked around the kitchen, then walked to the back door to look out upon the sadly neglected grass and flowers in Win's backyard. She smiled as she considered the joy of plucking back the dead growth, of watering and watching the flowers flourish, of tending the soil. Stepping out onto the stoop, she lifted her face to the morning sun and inhaled deeply, tasting the scent of freedom.

"Is Doc around?" Tess Dillard called through the back screen door and opened it at the same time. "Ellie? Are you here?"

Ellie clattered down the stairway, then hurried through the hallway to the kitchen, almost colliding with Tess in the doorway. "He's gone on house calls," she said. "Is something wrong?"

"Cam from over at the saloon asked me to locate Doc. Said one of his girls needs to be patched up." Tess grimaced. "I think a customer got rough with her. Cam said she's bleeding."

"Is she cut?" Ellie asked.

Tess shook her head. "I don't think that's what he meant." She looked past Ellie toward the door leading into the other side of the house, where the office was located. "Did he say how long he'd be?"

"No." With a shake of her head, Ellie walked into the kitchen. "He's been gone quite a while. Left right after breakfast. He didn't say where."

"Well," Tess said with a sigh, "I don't think an hour or so longer will make an awful lot of difference anyway. Just tell him Cilla needs to be looked at."

"Will he know where to go?" The thought of Winston Gray tending to a saloon girl didn't appeal to her for some reason, and Ellie swallowed her distaste. "Does he get called over there often?" she asked hesitantly.

"They're pretty sturdy females," Tess said with a chuckle. "They take care of themselves most of the time. But once in a while…" She pursed her lips and eyed Ellie thoughtfully. "There's men who don't care how they use a woman," she said.

And whatever that was supposed to mean,

Ellie assumed it didn't bode well for the ailing Cilla. "I'll tell him when he gets back. He said to have something ready for him to eat at noontime, and the sun's about overhead already."

"Are you getting along all right?" Tess asked, looking around the tidy kitchen. "I planned on bringing you a grocery order this morning, but I clean forgot when I set out to find Doc. If you can think of anything you need, write a list for me to take back."

"He likes eggs, I think. At least he ate three of them for breakfast. And I'll need some meat to cook for his supper. I don't know where I should go to get it."

"There's a side of beef hanging out back in the shed behind the store," Tess said. "I'll have John cut you off a piece for a roast and bring it over. You'll want some potatoes, and maybe beans or carrots to go with it. John can use the wagon and bring you a burlap sack of spuds and a bucket of carrots. I'll add everything to Doc's account."

"I know how to put stuff up if Doc has canning jars," Ellie offered. She crossed to the pantry and looked in the lower shelves. "Do you suppose there's some in the cellar?"

"This place was picked clean when the

Chambers family moved out last year," Tess told her. "I doubt there's anything left. I'll scout up some jars and lids and rubber rings for you and send them along."

"I saw some onions going to seed by the side of the house this morning," Ellie said. "Maybe they're still good."

Tess sat down at the table. "Let's just make a list. I think this is going to be a long, drawn-out project we got going here."

Ellie found a tablet Win had left on the kitchen buffet and located a pencil. Her heart raced as she considered the task ahead. "I may have more to do than I thought at first," she told Tess with a grin. "Here I was, thinking I'd just have to keep things redd up and put meals together. I think I'll be starting from scratch, won't I?"

"You've run a house before, haven't you?" Tess asked, scribbling one item after another in a rapid fashion. "Your pa never had a housekeeper, did he?"

Ellie shook her head. "No, and I'll bet he's up to his neck in dirty dishes by now. He was never much of a hand at cleaning up behind himself."

"You wouldn't go back out there, would you, girl?" Tess's hand stilled as she looked up, and her eyes narrowed as she waited for Ellie's reply.

It was quick in coming, a single word uttered with no chance of mistake. "No." Ellie shivered as she stood abruptly and wrapped her arms around herself. Her jaw was set, her shoulders squared as she paced to the back door and looked out onto the ragged patches of grass. "I'll never set foot on the place, not so long as I live. If I have to take off down the road and live in a cave up in the mountains, I'll do just that, rather than let him touch me again."

"I don't think that's going to happen. I've got a notion Doc talked to Sheriff Kincaid about you. I doubt your pa would stand a chance of making you go back home."

"He said I was his property, just like his livestock, and I had to do whatever he said." She grinned suddenly. "First time I ever enjoyed taking orders was when he said I had to leave by morning. I figured anyplace else was better than living there."

She turned back toward Tess and approached the table. "I'm going to do a good job for Dr. Gray. He won't be sorry he took me on."

"He's a kind man, Ellie. And you don't

have to worry about him ever taking advantage." Tess looked down at her list, then nodded briskly. "I think this will do it." She rose and pushed her chair beneath the edge of the table. "I'll run on over to the store and get things together. You're gonna need some clothesline and pins, too. I'll warrant Doc's got wash piled up."

She was gone in a moment, and Ellie took a deep breath. There was so much to consider, things she'd taken for granted, like a scrub board and washtub to be located, and a supply of dish towels to be made. It was almost like having a home of her own, she decided. Almost.

"Eat your dinner first," Ellie said as Win picked up his bag from the table. It had barely touched its surface when she delivered the news about the saloon girl, Cilla, and his hand had reached for it without pause. "I made you a pot of potato soup. Tess sent over a slab of bacon and I flavored it with that and a good big onion."

Win hesitated, one hand rubbing his stomach in a distracted motion. "Maybe I'd better," he said. "It's hard to say how long I'll be over at the saloon. And there'll be folks coming in for afternoon office hours before long."

He replaced his bag and turned to the sink. "I'll just wash quick while you dish me up some soup, Ellie."

She had it on the table in moments, slicing bread to go with it as he sat down and picked up his spoon. "Won't you eat with me?" he asked, watching as fragrant steam rose from his bowl. His spoon dipped in and he blew on the creamy broth, then bit down on a chunk of potato. His eyes widened as he chewed and swallowed, then dipped again. "You got some secret recipe?" he asked. "This is wonderful."

She shook her head. "I just scraped a little carrot in it, and thickened it up." Pleased by his response, she dished up a portion in a second bowl and joined him. "You don't mind if I eat with you?"

He glanced up, his brow furrowing at her words. "Of course not. I told you at breakfast time to sit down with me." He ate silently for a moment, watching her. "Didn't you share meals with your father?"

"He said it was a woman's place to wait on menfolk."

"He was wrong, Ellie, and don't you forget it." His tone was mild, but the look he bent in her direction was stern. His hand touched her arm, a gentle nudge that made her look up. "Women may get the short end of the stick when it comes to keeping a house in order and providing for the needs of her family, but it's a man's obligation to make her life as easy as he can. And that includes those to whom he pays a wage."

And wasn't that a different way of looking at things? Ellie thought with a start. That a man should be concerned about a woman's well-being was a concept she'd never heard voiced. And yet that seemed to be what Winston Gray was talking about.

She washed up the dinner things after he left for the saloon, his final words of instruction spoken as he walked out the door.

"Prop open the kitchen door and listen for the front door, Ellie. If patients come in, tell them I'll be back directly. They can wait in the outer office for me." He stuck his head back in the door. "If you have time, make a list of them as they come in and I'll take them in order."

So it was she came to be sitting at the small desk in his waiting room an hour later, talking to a young mother who held one sick child while Ellie amused another. Win's brow rose and a grin curved his mouth as he caught her eye. "Send my first patient in, will you, Miss Mitchum?"

"Yes, sir," she said agreeably, rising to settle the small girl on her chair as she picked up her list. "Mr. Taylor, you can go in now."

The room held only three remaining patients as Win leaned through the office door more than an hour later. "I can finish up now, if you need to see to supper," he told her quietly. And Ellie escaped thankfully to the kitchen, aware of the curious eyes that had watched her for the whole of the afternoon. No one had questioned her, yet all had paid her mind, and she felt she'd been on display, sitting behind the desk, calling out names, and trying to be as inconspicuous as possible.

The potatoes were ready for the oven and she placed them around the piece of beef she'd put in the roasting pan earlier. Carrots swam in the broth, and two onions sent a savory aroma upward as she opened the oven door. By the time the table was set, the last patient had taken his leave, and Win joined her in the kitchen.

"You were a big help, Ellie," he told her, washing at the sink, his shirtsleeves rolled above his elbows. "I don't usually have so many patients in an afternoon. I think they made up for yesterday." He peered over her shoulder as she stirred flour and water into the pan, watching as it thickened into gravy. "You'll have me spoiled."

She felt a warmth take hold of her, and she turned her head to look up at him. "I think it would be a joy to spoil you, Dr. Gray." And then she looked away, flustered at the words she'd spoken without forethought.

A flush crawled up his jaw and centered on his cheekbones. "Thank you. That's probably the nicest thing anyone's said to me in a long time." He turned away and sat at the table. "I saw the girl at the saloon, Ellie. I thought seriously about bringing her here for you to tend, but she didn't want to leave her friends there." He glanced up at her. "I didn't know if it would be the right thing to do, anyway. I wouldn't want folks to talk about having her here with you."

"What would they say?" she asked, dishing up the meat and vegetables with ease. Placing the platter before him, she poured the gravy into a deep bowl. "If a woman's been hurt, what does it matter who she is? If she needs taking care of, I reckon I can do it."

"I thought you'd feel that way," he said,

dishing up food onto his plate. "But Cilla said she'd be all right, and the other girls will look out for her. I told Sheriff Kincaid about the ranch hand who hurt her, and I believe he'll handle it. Not that most folks would think much of it."

"What can he do?" Ellie asked, sitting down across the table from him.

Win shrugged. "Not an awful lot. Just warn him to behave himself. I don't think Cam will let the fella in the place again anyway."

Ellie took up her fork. "Did he hit her?"

"It wasn't so much that, Ellie," Win said slowly. "Billy's set on stealing money that's hidden in the foundation of the addition to the saloon. He made the mistake of telling Cilla about it, and then decided he'd better convince her not to spill the beans about his plan to anyone else." His mouth was taut as he paused, as if he chose his words carefully. "Don't repeat what I just told you, Ellie. Cilla told me in confidence and I probably shouldn't have repeated it, but I'm certain I can trust you."

His head bent as he spoke and Ellie remembered Tess's words. *There's men who don't care how they use a woman.* What Tess had meant, Ellie wasn't sure, but good sense prevented her from asking Win. Maybe it was like when Tommy had hurt her, that day in the barn. She'd bled, and ached something awful for a couple of days, as if there was something all torn up way inside of her.

"Do any of those women have babies?" she asked quietly.

"Babies?" Win sounded surprised. "I doubt it, Ellie. At least, not that I've ever heard about. Those girls pretty much know how to prevent such things from happening."

And wasn't that a puzzle. If Tommy had given her a baby from his shenanigans that day, it made sense that… She halted that line of thought and bent low over her plate. There were things she needed to be asking Tess, that was for sure, and one of these days, she'd get up the nerve.

For the first time in months, Winston Gray went to bed with a full stomach and the sure knowledge that a good breakfast would be awaiting him in the morning. He grinned to himself as he lay in the center of the big bed, his hands stacked beneath his head. Ellie was working out well. His house was clean, his pantry organized, and she was planning on using a scrub board to do his clothes, first thing tomorrow.

She'd washed her hair in the new bucket after supper, out on the back porch where she couldn't be seen by those who might pass the house, and he'd watched from the doorway as she dried it with his newest towel. Her hands had been adept, brushing the length of soft, brown silken strands, then braiding them in a simple plait that hung down her back.

The sight bothered him, setting up a yearning he tried his best to dismiss. A woman was the last thing he needed in his life right now, what with his practice taking up all his time.

But Ellie was proving to be a complication. She felt grateful to him, trying her best to make his life an easier path, and his very masculine self could not help but wallow in the attention she gave.

That her soft eyes rested on him often was a fact he tried diligently to ignore. That his own gaze focused on her at times was to be expected. She was a lovely woman, a girl really, he decided. Pregnant though she was, she projected an aura of innocence that brought forth his male urge to protect and cherish.

And those thoughts needed to be banished, he decided abruptly, rising from the bed to stalk to the window. Ellie Mitchum was his housekeeper, and he'd do well to look upon her as a servant. His snort of laughter was swallowed as amusement followed that thought. She was like no servant he'd ever come in contact with, and there'd been plenty of them in his life.

None of them had followed him to bed at night, as had the woman who slept overhead. Not in physical form, certainly, but in his mind. And she'd only been here for two days. He shifted restlessly, stretching one long arm to rest against the window frame.

Taking Ellie Mitchum into his home had been a hasty decision. Taking her into his life would surely follow. Already, she was keeping him awake and on the edge of arousal.

His mind spun as he considered the state of his body. Damn. Having a woman in his bed was the last thing he needed to be thinking of.

Visiting the saloon today had given him access to several women, any of whom would welcome him into their presence. All but poor Cilla, that victim of a cowhand whose idea of persuasion involved brutality.

Ellie was another victim. Not as was Cilla, but certainly worthy of his care. And for all of her innocence and eagerness to please, she was a woman. A warm, needy female, sleeping in his house. And if Dr. Winston Gray knew what was good for himself, he'd get her youthful beauty out of his mind.

Otherwise, he was going to spend a sleepless night.

Chapter Four

"You think you've fallen into a soft bed, don't you, girl?"

George Mitchum's words were harsh and accusing, piercing Ellie's thoughts. Startled, she dropped the shirt she held into the dirt; then, gathering her courage to face the man behind her, she bent to pick it up.

"Drat," she whispered, aggravated at the mud that stained both the shirtfront and one sleeve. Carefully, she placed it beside the wash basket, then turned to look at her father.

"I'm working for my keep," she said quietly. "Same as I did at home."

"Does he know you've got a bastard under your skirts?"

Scornfully, he tossed the query in her direction, his eyes raking her figure with a scalding look, then seeking her face. With every speck of courage she possessed, Ellie met the gaze he turned on her.

"Doc Gray knows I'm going to have a baby, yes." Pain swept through her, that her own father could be so cruel. Yet what had she expected? That he would come to visit, seeking her out to ask forgiveness for his brutal actions?

Not likely, she thought, her lips tight as she fought the trembling that seized her. "I didn't get this way all by myself," she said curtly, wary of the clenched fists hanging against George's thighs.

"You flaunted yourself, just like all women, looking for—"

"Is there a problem here?" Win's voice was stiffly polite, his words reeking of a courteous inquiry as he spoke from the back door. Long strides brought him to Ellie's side and she straightened her spine, lest she be tempted to lean against his stalwart strength.

"This is my daughter," George said sharply. "I don't need you interfering. Seems like you've already stuck your nose in where it doesn't belong."

"All I've done is hire Ellie to be my housekeeper and tend to my kitchen," Win said quietly. "You're trespassing, Mr. Mitchum, and causing Ellie to be upset. I don't think you need to say any more to her."

"Well, well," George drawled, rocking back on his heels. "Looks like you got yourself a champion, girl. At least he won't have to worry about getting you in the family way, will he? Since you've managed to do that already."

Ellie shot a look at Win, noting the crimson streaks that lined his cheekbones. "He's my employer, Pa. Nothing else."

"You just keep tellin' folks that, girl. Not that anybody's gonna believe you."

"They'll believe her, Mr. Mitchum," Win said forcefully. "The truth always manages to win out in the end. And Ellie is being honest with you."

"I doubt you'll have much of a practice left when folks realize you're harboring a woman like Ellie under your roof," George sneered. "And I'll see to it that they know what's goin' on here."

"Why'd you come here, Pa?" Ellie asked in a small voice. "Haven't you already done enough damage?"

He shook his head, his eyes sweeping over her face. "Not near as much as you deserve, shaming me the way you have."

From the other side of the yard, near the sheriff's back door, a woman spoke. "Good morning, Doc. Does James need to walk on over there?"

Ellie gasped. It wasn't bad enough that Pa was giving Win a rough going over. Now the neighbor had to be privy to the shame of it all.

"I think Mr. Mitchum is leaving, Mrs. Kincaid. Thanks just the same."

"Good morning, Ellie," Kate Kincaid called cheerfully. "I heard at the mercantile that you were going to be my new neighbor. Why don't you step over, and I'll pour us each a cup of coffee."

Ellie turned slowly to face the neighbor. That the invitation was an escape route was all too obvious, and yet she hesitated leaving Win to face Pa alone.

It seemed Dr. Gray had other thoughts on the matter. His hand touched Ellie's shoulder. "That sounds like a wonderful idea, Ellie. Go on across and visit with Kate for a while. You can finish the wash later." More than a suggestion, his firm tone implied an order, and Ellie cast one quick glance at his stern profile.

"Yes, all right," she said breathlessly, and lifting her skirts, she turned and hastened across the yard to where the neighbor watched, a determined smile curving her lips. Kate Kincaid was definitely the woman in the window, Ellie decided, except that by daylight, she wore small spectacles. Her body heavy with advanced pregnancy, she was nonetheless a beautiful woman, her dark hair and delicate features only enhanced by the sunlight.

And with a soft word of welcome, she cast Ellie a lifeline she felt sadly in need of this morning. Behind Ellie, her father muttered a profanity and Win murmured an answering phrase, one Ellie could not decipher. It mattered little. If Win was willing to face George on his own, and obviously he was, Ellie was more than willing to let him. She stepped onto the low stoop as Kate opened the screen door wide.

"Come on in," she invited, waiting until her guest was over the threshold before she allowed one last look at the two men who faced each other some seventy feet away from her back door.

"Sit down, Ellie," Kate said quietly. "You look like you're about to pass out cold." A cup of steaming coffee appeared before her, and Ellie gripped it with both hands, craving the heat of the cup against her chilled skin.

"Thank you," she whispered. "I'm sorry you got involved in this, ma'am. But I surely appreciate you allowing me to escape my father. Maybe Dr. Gray can persuade him to go along and let me be." To her enormous shame, hot tears cascaded down her cheeks as she spoke, her voice choking on the words.

Kate settled across the table, easing her pregnant body onto a chair. "Well, I'm just glad he didn't call my bluff, Ellie. James is already gone to his office, and I'd have looked mighty foolish trying to call him home to take a hand. I figured your father wouldn't know I was lying through my teeth, insinuating that James was in the house."

Ellie lifted the cup and sipped at the strong brew. Her hands trembled, but she persisted, knowing that the warmth would penetrate and soothe her inner trembling. Kate watched silently as the cup was settled back on the table, and Ellie pulled a handkerchief from her pocket. Tears were dried and her nose attended to before she spoke again.

"Did Tess really tell you I was next door?" she asked. And then added in a hesitant whisper, "Did she tell you about me?"

Kate nodded. "She was pleased that Doc hired you on. It's a wonderful place for you to stay." She pushed a plate across the table. "Here, have a cookie, Ellie. I baked this morning. James loves Saturdays. During school months it's the only day I can devote to being a wife."

"And you teach at the schoolhouse all day, every day?" Ellie asked, reaching for a cookie.

"I've been there just over a year now," Kate told her. "I'm probably the first woman to teach during a pregnancy, and I'm still surprised that the town council agreed. I'll be taking a couple of weeks off when the baby comes, and then he'll go with me every day."

"They'll let you do that?" Ellie asked, stunned by such a thing being possible.

"It looks that way," Kate said. "They thought for a while that they had a man available for the job, but Will Kincaid gave him a job at the bank. Jonathan, the fella who came to take over my place, decided it was easier handling folks' accounts and sitting behind a desk than coping with a schoolroom. They're looking for another teacher now, but in the meantime, I'm it."

"When do you think—" Ellie faltered, her gaze resting openly on Kate's girth.

"Probably in a couple of weeks. Doc says babies have a schedule of their own." She leaned over the table and her eyes twinkled behind the round lenses of her spectacles. "I happen to know something Doc doesn't. And if I've got it figured right, my nine months will be up two weeks from today."

"Nine months. That's how long it's supposed to take?" Ellie asked. "I didn't want to sound foolish in front of Doc, and I never knew anyone before who was going to have a baby."

"You don't have a mother?" Kate's eyes were kind, her hand reaching to clasp Ellie's fingers. "No one to talk to?"

Ellie shook her head. "No, just my pa. And he's never been one to do much talking. At least not to me." She glanced toward the door. "It's quiet out there. Do you suppose Doc convinced my pa to leave?"

"He's gone for now," Win said from just beyond the screen door. "Didn't mean to eavesdrop, ladies," he said, opening the door and stepping inside the kitchen. "I'm afraid I made him angry, Ellie. He's determined to give you a bad name, it seems."

"I think I've already done that, without any help from him," Ellie said, resignation shadowing her words. She picked up her cup and held it between trembling hands.

"Is there any chance you might marry the baby's father?" Kate asked quietly.

Ellie shook her head. "He's gone back East with his folks."

"Sounds like a fine specimen of manhood to me." Kate's eyes flashed with scorn as she rose to find a cup for Win. "Have a cookie, Doc," she said. "It's good for what ails you."

"I thought maybe you could keep an eye on things while I'm out making house calls this morning, Kate. In fact, it wouldn't hurt for Ellie to keep an eye on you. Are you feeling all right?" He cast a measuring look at Kate, and she rested her hand atop the rounding of her belly. "You've dropped, haven't you?"

"It's easier to breathe, the past couple of days," she admitted with a grin. "Is that a good sign?"

"The best," Win said. "It won't be long now." He frowned at the coffee and shook his head. "I don't have time for this, but I'll take a couple of your oatmeal cookies with me, if that's all right."

Kate laughed. "There's more where those came from. Tess told me I'm nesting. I've been baking and cleaning house like a mad-woman this morning. James made me prom-ise to send for him if I have so much as a twinge, and now you're siccing Ellie on me. I don't stand a chance, do I?"

"Well, Ellie's worked hard ever since she got here. It won't hurt her to take a day off." Win headed for the door. "I'm going to stop by and talk to James. I'll let him know you're in good hands, Kate."

"Billy Barnes is Cilla's current flame, Doc." James leaned back in his chair and shrugged. "She's clammed up about the whole episode, so there's no use in you wor-rying about it."

"Has he pulled this kind of stunt before?" Win asked. He settled on a straight chair across from the sheriff's desk and crossed his ankles. "You know, I put in a nasty thirty minutes with her. There's no excuse for a man hurting a woman that way." His disgust re-flected in his voice and manner.

Win drew a deep breath. "It's bad enough

when someone gets shot up or falls off the roof, but to see a female used the way Cilla was makes my blood boil."

James nodded agreement. "I think they go back a ways. He's been hanging around the Double Deuce for over a year, and Cilla's the only girl he pays much attention to. Matter of fact, he used to do carpenter work around town till just lately. Now he's dabbling in ranching out at Caleb's place."

"Well, I don't like the man, and I've never laid eyes on him," Win said bluntly. "And I'm about half-mad at Cilla, that she's not willing to make a fuss over it, but…" He paused. "I guess I understand. She's afraid of him."

"Saloon girls are a breed apart," James told him. "I'm just happy I've got Kate. I never had much truck with the women in saloons. I think a man's got to be pretty hard up to…" He paused for a moment, and then a grin lit his face. "I didn't know how lucky I was gonna be the day Kate came to town."

Win sat up straight in his chair, another thought manifesting itself at James's words. "You know that Ellie Mitchum is living at my place, don't you?"

James nodded. "I heard. Her pa came by

here a few minutes ago and told me she was living in sin."

"And what did you say?" Win asked mildly.

"Not much I could say. It's none of my concern. Not unless George tries to force her back home. I heard from one of his hands that George roughed her up and sent her on her way. Seems like he's singin' a different song today. I'll warrant he's missing having regular meals and clean clothes. The talk is that he treated her like a servant. I don't think there's many folks would take kindly to him dragging Ellie back home."

"He's not dragging Ellie anywhere," Win said, rising and stalking to the doorway. His anger was quick, remembering the belligerent stance George had taken. "He thinks I've taken the girl to my bed, James."

"She's a good-looking young woman," James said quietly. "I think he won't be the only one with that opinion."

"It's not true."

James nodded agreeably. "Not yet, anyway."

"I won't take advantage of her." Win felt a heated flush rise to his throat. His thoughts had been roaming in that direction last night, he reminded himself.

"You need a wife," James told him. "Ellie wouldn't be a bad choice for you."

"You ever heard about falling in love with a woman first?"

"Yeah." James grinned. "But sometimes there's other reasons for marriage. And having a woman around isn't the worst of them."

"Wait till I tell Kate you said that."

James shrugged. "Kate knows I love her, and a lot of that came later down the line. Ellie's a good girl. There's never been a breath of scandal about her till the Jamison boy started keeping company with her. And then the whole damn family vamoosed and went back East. It's not too hard to figure out why, I guess."

"Well, her father's not going to drag her home," Win said harshly. "If I have to, I'll marry her myself. There sure isn't anyone else lining up for the job."

"Now, I heard that Tess has been scouting up women for you to consider ever since you came to town."

"That's true. The woman can't stand to see an unmarried man."

James leaned forward over the desk, looking up at Win. "All joking aside, Ellie would make a good wife, Doc. You could do a hell of a lot worse."

"How did we get into this discussion?"

"You brought it up," James told him. "I just pointed out a few facts. Just thought you might like to consider all the angles." He grinned up a Win. "I'm an agreeable sort, Kate tells me."

"Well, I've got a couple of house calls to make," Win said. "I just wanted to let you know that Ellie's keeping Kate company for a while. In case her father comes back, I'd just as soon she wasn't alone at my place."

"You going to church next Sunday?" James asked as Win stepped over the threshold, bringing him to a halt.

"You got some reason for asking?"

"If you take Ellie with you, it'll set folks talking, you know."

"They're probably already hashing me over," Win said defensively. "If Ellie wants to go to church, I'll take her." He stomped across the sidewalk and headed for the livery stable, where he kept his horse and buggy. And then paused midstep. He'd forgotten his bag with all the to-do about Ellie and her father.

It didn't look to be a wonderful day, he decided glumly, heading for home.

* * *

Church had been barely tolerable, Win thought, walking beside Ellie as they left the small white chapel. They'd been the focus of all eyes, even though he'd been as decorous as possible, speaking when spoken to, and ignoring the sidelong looks of the women in the congregation. Ellie, oblivious to the attention they'd garnered, had sung with a sweet soprano voice, and listened intently to the minister's sermon.

"Well, we managed to raise a few eyebrows," Win said gruffly, slowing his pace for Ellie's shorter steps. Hands shoved into his pockets, he knew he was being taciturn, but being the subject of gossip didn't set well with him.

"I know I'm not dressed for church," Ellie said quietly. "I probably shouldn't have gone till I could afford a new dress. It's just that Pa didn't take much stock in church-going and I didn't get to attend service very often. Only if he was in a good mood or one of the men had to go to town on Sunday and I could hitch a ride."

"He let you out and about with a ranch hand?" Win asked, his brow lifting as he considered the idea.

"They knew not to make advances," Ellie said softly. "Pa would have fired them on the spot if they looked crossways at me. Not that there's much to look at."

The girl honestly didn't know how pretty she was, Win decided. She wasn't a great beauty, but with decent clothes to wear and the healing of her bruised face, she'd be more than presentable. Her hair alone was enough to make a man sit up and take notice.

She'd brushed it early this morning, there on the back porch, while she thought he was still abed, and again he'd watched her through the screen door, his gaze devouring the heavy tresses that waved the length of her back. She'd been so unaware, so innocent of guile, her body moving in an unconscious rhythm, and Win had found himself yearning to bury his hands in the depths of those rich, brown curls. He'd warrant not another man alive, not counting George, had ever seen the sight, and a twinge of satisfaction brought a smile to his face.

"What's funny?" Ellie asked suspiciously. "Are you laughing at me?"

Win shook his head. "Far from it, Ellie. I'm just remembering how beautiful your hair looked when you brushed it, out on the back porch this morning." He met her gaze and his only thought was to banish the look of wariness she wore like a second skin.

"You're a lovely woman. Any man would be proud to have you in his home."

"You must be blind in one eye and can't see outta the other," she scoffed, and yet a blush tinged her cheeks with a rosy hue.

"I'm not blind, Ellie. I've seen more pleasingly arranged features than yours, perhaps, women who spent long hours to make themselves attractive. I've known females with elegant wardrobes, and the money to buy jewelry and pay for fancy hairdos." He hesitated at her stricken look, and then reached for her hand, squeezing it gently as he turned to face her.

"You don't understand, honey," he said quietly. "They don't hold a candle to you. None of them."

Doubt made her toss her head, and he recognized the air she assumed. "I know what I am," she said proudly. "A woman without means, having to work for everything I own. And that's all right, Winston Gray. I'm proud that I can work hard and earn my way. You don't have to try making me feel good with fancy words and—"

"Hush," he said quickly. "I'm not doing that. I'm telling you the truth, Ellie, and you're too stubborn to recognize it. You're a woman any man would be pleased to claim as his own."

"Oh, sure," she said curtly, her lip curling in derision. "I'm gonna have a baby, and I wasn't even bright enough to know the difference between being in the family way and dying of a tumor. I'm sure some handsome man is gonna come after me with a wedding ring in his hand." She pulled her fingers from his grip.

"You don't know what you're talking about, Doc. You sure don't know much about men, and the way they look at women like me."

She stalked down the road ahead of him, and he stepped double-time to catch up. "You're the one who's all wet, my dear," he said firmly, his hand circling her arm and slowing her pace. "I know exactly how men look at a woman like you." He stopped dead in his tracks and brought her to a standstill next to him.

"I'm a man, Ellie. Do I need to remind you of that?"

She shook her head dumbly, her eyes wide.

"And I know exactly how I'm looking at you." His jaw clenched as his eyes focused on her face.

She was pale, her mouth trembling, and even as he watched, a lone tear slid from each eye to dampen her cheek. "Don't be mad at me," she whispered. "I couldn't stand it if I did something to get you riled up."

Shame buried his aggravation, and he bowed his head. "I'm sorry, sweetheart. I didn't mean to upset you. I just can't stand for you to think of yourself in such a way." His fingers loosened their grip and his hand rose to her face, fingertips tracing the damp trails.

"You're a wonderful young woman, Ellie. You're strong and honest and worthy of any man in this town."

"I don't want any man in this town," she said quietly. "I just want to work for you and stay in that beautiful room you let me have, and make flowers grow in your yard."

"I'd say that's little enough to ask of life," he told her, bending to touch her forehead with a gentle brush of his mouth. Drawing her hand through his arm, he turned them in the direction of his house, aware of a buggy that passed, conscious of two families who walked on the opposite side of the road…and mindful of the lapse he'd just committed.

Kissing Ellie was like placing an item in the weekly newspaper. Dr. Gray To Marry Ellie Mitchum. He might as well have announced a forthcoming wedding while he sat among the parishioners in the community church just moments ago. That the word would spread like wildfire throughout the county was a given. He could no longer keep Ellie in his home without making her his legal wife.

Thankfully, the news took almost a week to reach Ellie's ears, and then it came from Win, himself. She'd spent long hours scrubbing floors and windows. Her arms ached from washing curtains and ironing starched ruffles, and her back protested the reaching to hang every blessed thing she could find to wash on the clothesline.

But the results were worth it. Winston Gray's house gleamed from top to bottom. His floors shone, his rugs had been beaten properly and every window was framed by freshly washed curtains. All but the living room, and those draperies had been shaken and wiped with a damp rag, before Ellie re-hung them.

Kate had ventured over once to see what was going on and declared that Ellie made her tired, just watching the momentum she'd developed. Admonishing the girl to slacken her pace, Kate had waddled back next door, and then set off for school for the afternoon classes.

Ellie smiled as she scrubbed, pleased at Kate's interest, touched by her concern. But pleasing Win was her first consideration, and though he cautioned her against climbing to hang the curtains, he'd obviously been pleased at the end results of her whirlwind of activity.

"I never thought this old place could look so good," he told Ellie, leaning against the doorjamb one evening as she dished up supper. "I just don't want you working too hard. Folks will think I'm taking advantage of you." And with those final words, his mouth tightened and he walked toward her.

"Has anyone been by, Ellie? Have you spoken to any of the ladies in town?"

She shook her head, intent on pouring gravy into a deep bowl. "I've been too busy to go to the mercantile. Tess brought me a chicken and a slab of bacon this morning, and we talked, but she was in a hurry. She just wanted to know if I was doing all right."

"And are you?" he asked, lifting the plate of fried chicken from the warming oven and transferring it to the table.

She cast him a questioning glance. "You know I am, Doc." Ellie halted midway across the kitchen and turned to him. "She sounded kinda funny, though. She asked me if we'd talked about a change in my status. And I said, did she mean from poor to well-to-do?"

"Your status?" Win snatched at the word, well aware of Tess's meaning.

"I suppose she was thinking how different my life is now, since I've been here. But I don't know exactly what she meant."

Win pulled her chair out and waited as she picked up bowls of vegetables from the stove. Watching him closely, she placed them on the table, then slid onto her seat. She'd eyed him curiously the first time he held her chair for her, but had come to accept the small courtesy without comment. He walked to his place and sat down, weighing his words carefully.

"I think she was referring to your status as a single woman," he said. "I have a notion folks are wondering about us, Ellie."

"What for?" she asked. "What is there to wonder about? I'm your housekeeper and you're the town doctor."

"Some folks saw me kiss your forehead on the way home from church Sunday morning, honey. There's been talk."

"People think I'm after you?" she asked, fingers lifting to cover her mouth as her eyes widened in horror. "I've never meant to—"

He reached across the table and clasped her wrist. "Don't, Ellie. Don't even think that. It's not you they're speaking of. It's me. They think I'm taking advantage of you." It wasn't the sum total of the gossip that was circulating, but not for a moment would Win allow Ellie to be privy to the words that criticized her presence in his home.

"You haven't," she gasped. "Not for a minute. You wouldn't." Her head shook from side to side as she spoke, and tears formed in her dark eyes, spilling onto her bodice.

"I didn't mean to make you cry," Win said, reproach gnawing at him. "But the truth is, I did kiss you, Ellie. And in so doing, I've compromised your..." Somehow, *virtue* wasn't the correct word to use here, he decided.

"Reputation," he finished with a nod.

"I didn't have much of a reputation when I

got here," she said softly. "I'm sure that little peck on my forehead didn't do a whole lot of damage."

"Well, it made folks talk. And I won't allow them to besmirch your name in any way."

"You can't go fighting any battles over me, Doc," she told him. "I'll just have to find someplace else to live."

He shook his head. "Not on your life, honey. You're staying here, where you belong." Releasing her hand, he motioned to her fork. "Come on, now. Eat your supper, and I'll tell you what I think we should do."

Obediently, she picked up the utensil and speared a piece of carrot, carrying it to her mouth and chewing it, her eyes never leaving his face. And then she leaned back. "I can't eat till you put me out of my misery, Doc," she told him. "What are you planning?"

"Well," he began, picking up a chicken leg and inspecting it. "You do fry chicken to a turn, Ellie," he said with a grin, then turned the full force of that smile in her direction. His teeth bit into the tender meat and he chewed for a moment, wondering how she would take the revelation of his plan.

There was only one way to find out.

"Your father has been making noises again, about you living here. And along with folks being curious about my intentions, I've decided we should get married."

Ellie dropped her fork, and it clattered against the thick china plate, then fell to the floor. "Oh, dear," she whispered. "Now look what I've done."

"I'll get you another fork," he said, rising quickly and walking to the buffet.

"Not that," she said, her voice breaking as tears formed. She looked up at him and anguish painted her features. "I've put you in a terrible spot, Doc. You don't want to marry me, any more than you want to…" She halted as if she could think of nothing horrendous enough to compare.

"Oh, but I do," he said, placing the fork in her cold fingers. "Now, sit up there and eat," he told her, circling to his own chair. He watched as she chewed and swallowed bites of potato and a forkful of green beans. Woodenly, she reached for a piece of chicken and ate it, her eyes fastened to her plate, as if something there was too marvelous to ignore.

"Ellie?" He spoke her name quietly, carefully, and was rewarded when she looked up at him.

"Doc? Are you funning me?" she asked, and beneath the scoffing words, he detected a note of hope.

"No." His head shook slowly. "No, I wouldn't do that, Ellie. You know me better than that, I'd think.

"I thought we'd go and see the preacher," he told her, mindful of her stillness. She'd eaten a bit of the chicken, but not enough to please him. "If you eat everything on your plate, we can go after supper," he said, his voice carrying a teasing lilt.

She looked down with a frown. "I don't think I have any appetite," she said. "My mind's just spinning around in a circle, and I feel dizzy."

"You're not going to faint on me, are you?"

Her color was good. In fact, he'd say she looked downright healthy. Except for the dazed look in her eyes, and that was to be expected, he supposed.

"No." She shook her head. "I never faint. I come from sturdy stock. But I surely do feel like I've been dreaming and somebody's gonna come by and pinch me awake any minute now."

"It's no dream," Win said. "And nobody's going to pinch you awake. I'm going to make a bride out of you, honey." And if he knew what was good for himself, and for Ellie, too, he'd save the *wife* part for later.

Chapter Five

A fist pounding on the door caught Ellie unawares as she cleared the table, and within minutes, Win had spoken to the visitor and was on his way, black leather bag in hand.

"I don't know how long I'll be," he called back over his shoulder. "Depends on how much stitching up I need to do." His response had been immediate, his mind set on the man who waited on a ranch outside of town, broken bone exposed, and in too much pain to be moved.

Ellie nodded in agreement, closing the door behind him, then set about cleaning up the kitchen. The visit to the parsonage would wait. Win's patient would not. A glimmer of what life would be like as the wife of a doctor made her pause in her work, the dish towel caressing the plate she held.

Win's face had been set in lines she was becoming familiar with, lines that bespoke his concentration on the task at hand. Nothing was as important to Winston Gray as the people who depended on him for the skills he possessed. A wife would come in second to that multitude, Ellie thought. And yet even that fact could not dissuade her from the notion of marriage.

She'd protested mildly, yet her heart had raced with joy as he declared his intentions. *Mrs. Winston Gray.* The sound of those words vibrated in her mind as she rubbed the surface of the plate she held, and she spoke them aloud.

"Mrs. Winston Gray." Her mouth curved in a smile as she repeated the title, drawing out each syllable with anticipation. She would walk by his side every Sunday morning from now on, march down the aisle of that small church and sit with him, her skirt touching his trousers, her hand occasionally brushing his as they shared a hymnal.

That a man like Win should consider marriage to Ellie Mitchum was not to be believed. And yet he'd said it was so, that they would talk to the minister and then speak their vows. She would hold her head up, no longer the cast-off daughter, but the chosen wife.

He was handsome. There was no doubt of that, yet it wasn't only his good looks that made her heart beat faster. Large, but well-formed, his hands were gentle. His body was tall and rangy, well put together, with not a trace of fat apparent. She knew the breadth of his shoulders, wide beneath the suit coat he wore, for only yesterday she'd ironed three of his shirts. They were tapered, by the looks of them tailored especially for him. Not for Win the merchandise from Tess's store. Rather, the fine broadcloth of clothing that spoke of city stores and handmade garments.

Yet there was more to Win than the outer trappings. Beneath the skin itself beat the heart of a man bent on helping those in need. *Kindness* was his watchword, Ellie decided, placing the plate in the cupboard and lifting another into the keeping of her dish towel.

He truly cared, and upon that quality hung his decision to marry her. She was only one in a long list of those he tended. In this case, he'd extended his helping hand to an unheard of magnitude, that of marriage to a nobody. And didn't that put her in her place.

She sighed, examining the plate she'd polished to a fine sheen, and then lifted it to the glass-fronted cabinet where his dishes were stored. A blurred reflection met her gaze, and she saw, within the waving glass image, a woebegone female who, but for the tender heart of a doctor, was bound for despair.

Ordinary. That's what she was. Ordinary, and in need. Without a doubt.

She bent closer to the reflecting glass. Surely something about her nondescript image must have appealed to the man. Not even Win would take a woman in marriage on the basis of compassion alone.

Ellie straightened, stiffening her spine. If he'd seen something worthy in her, then it would behoove her to seek out that same quality and shine it to perfection. She *would* be a credit to him, not allowing him to be shamed by her presence in his home.

"You need clothes. And you need them now. I don't know what I've been thinking of, not taking you to the mercantile. Tess is sure to have dresses that will fit." Win pushed back from the table and rose. "We'll take a walk over there as soon as I run next door to check on Kate."

The morning sun was high in the sky, and Win was in good spirits. The compound fracture had been set and the stitches put in place in record time, he'd told her. His arrival home, long after dark, had prompted her from her bed, and she'd poured him coffee from the pot left on the back of the stove, then sat with him at the kitchen table while he spoke of the house call.

And in all of that, she'd felt a foreshadowing of her life to come. Except for the moment when she'd rinsed his cup and turned it to drain, then left the kitchen. The stairs were long, her bedroom, for the first time, lonely. And below, she heard Win's footsteps as he walked through the hallway and into his bedroom.

Would she still be relegated to this room on the second floor, once the vows were spoken?

The memory of Kate and James, that stolen moment she'd glimpsed on her first night in this house, came to mind. A deep heat possessed her, one she was not familiar with, and she sighed, yearning for just such an embrace to be hers.

Now, Win waited for her, a quizzical look

on his face, as she hastened to prepare for the excursion to the mercantile. Just inside the kitchen door, he watched as she wiped the tabletop, then hung the dishrag over the basin.

"Kate is chipper this morning," he told her. "I found her on her knees, scrubbing the back stoop." An amused smile lifted his mouth as he spoke. "I don't think she'll make it much longer. That baby's about ready to make an appearance."

"Will the children just stay home when she has the baby?" Ellie joined him and walked out the door he held for her.

"There'll be enough for them to do this time of year. It's time for the threshing anyway, and they generally close classes down for that. Kate couldn't have planned this better if she'd tried."

"I've never heard of a teacher taking a baby to school with her," Ellie told him.

"Probably no one but Kate would do it."

Admiration shone through his statement, and Ellie felt a twinge of envy tug at her. What would it be like to have him speak with such confident pride on her behalf? And then she stifled the emotion that craved such a thing. Kate was more than deserving of Win's respect. Ellie had yet to earn it.

Tess waved a hand and beckoned them closer as Ellie stepped over the threshold of the mercantile, Win fast at her heels. "Come on in. You're my first customers of the day. I'll have to make a special effort to make a sale. My father used to say that if you made a paying customer out of your first visitor, your day would be a good one."

Ellie was swallowed in the warmth of Tess's welcome, and she approached the counter with a light step. "Win says I'm to have something new to wear," she said, her tone low, as if she confided a secret to Tess's ears.

"Well, isn't that fine?" Tess turned toward the shelves closest to her stockroom and lifted a stack of dresses from a bin. She eyed Ellie judiciously and nodded, turning to sort through another selection, pulling three from within a second cubbyhole. "Let's see if any of these please you, Ellie."

Dresses in a rainbow of colors were spread on the counter within moments, and Tess grinned at Win. "Just got in a new supply, Doc. Must have known you were coming by." She lifted one after another of the assortment, some of them striped, others flowered, all of them far beyond what Ellie had ever dreamed of wearing.

"I wouldn't know which to choose," she said with a sigh of pure pleasure. Her fingers caressed the fabrics, appreciating the smooth feel of percale, the ribbed texture of faille and dimity, the sheer elegance of batiste.

Tess leaned closer. "The garments in this stack are wrappers, Ellie. They'll be just the thing for you right now. You won't have to worry about them fitting properly, and they're perfectly respectable for you to wear around the house."

"They're so…fancy," Ellie said on an indrawn breath. "I can't imagine wearing something like this to cook in or when I scrub floors."

"Go ahead and pick out three or four for now," Win said from behind her. "Tess will probably know which will give you the best wear. And don't forget something nice to get married in."

"Married?" Tess spoke the word as if it were some magic incantation, breathing it past lips that quirked at the edges, trembling on the verge of a smile. Then with a burst of laughter, she leaned across the counter and hugged Ellie, able only to clutch at the girl's shoulders, what with over two feet of counter space between them. She whispered the

word against Ellie's ear. "Married? I'm so pleased."

Ellie fumbled for words, and came up feeling tongue-tied. She should have known that Win would spill the beans, and yet to have him voice aloud his plans somehow made them more valid. Made the idea of being his wife almost a reality.

She blinked away moisture that clouded her vision, gritting her teeth, lest she make a spectacle of herself, right here in the middle of the mercantile. "Win just decided, actually," she said quietly, then chanced a look in his direction.

His arm settled across her shoulders and he squeezed gently. "I think I took Ellie off guard, Tess. This has been in the making for a couple of days. I'm sure that's not a surprise to you. I finally realized that I didn't want to take any chances on some other young man coming along and snatching her away from me."

"You work fast, Doc," Tess murmured. "But I'm not surprised."

"He feels sorry for me," Ellie said wretchedly. "And he's making it sound as though…" Words failed her, and Win filled the gap with a ready retort.

"Ellie's the one who's taken a tremendous responsibility. I'm just lucky to have her. I never knew how wonderful it could be to have a woman in the house, tending to things and giving me someone to share my life with."

He turned Ellie to face him. "I guess I didn't make it clear how I felt, sweetheart," he said quietly, ignoring Tess, who had backed away at his words. "I'm not doing this for your benefit, although that comes into it somewhat, but for my own.

"I've made you cry again," he said softly, his index finger sweeping tears from beneath each eye. He held her gaze, forcing her to recognize the sincerity of the words he spoke. "Don't think I'm doing you a favor, Ellie. You'll meet yourself coming and going in my household, helping in my office, and making my life easier."

"Well, now that you've got that settled," Tess said brightly, "let's get this child something to wear." She picked up a blue-flowered print. With puffy sleeves and narrow cuffs, it was the height of fashion, and Tess allowed the skirt to fall in generous folds as she held it in front of her own ample form. "This will be nice for when you sit in Doc's office and keep track of his patients," she said, folding it and placing it to one side.

Win backed away as Tess lifted another choice from the stack. "You two just go on and make a decision, Tess. I'll run across the road and talk to James for a few minutes. Take what you want, Ellie," he said, smiling into her eyes. "The sky's the limit today. And don't forget something nice for the *wedding*." He whispered the final word, with a cautious look over his shoulder.

Two ladies had entered the store, and both were moving quietly and carefully within earshot as Win nodded and tipped his hat in their direction. He paused a moment to speak to one of them, and she greeted him warmly.

Tess shot a look at the new customers and smiled. "I'll be right with you. Ellie here is choosing some new clothes."

A striped percale was added to the first selection, and Ellie squirmed, knowing she was being scrutinized from top to bottom. In her drab wash dress, she felt like an interloper, sharing counter space with two upstanding members of the community. Both ladies looked familiar, one was certainly Caleb Kincaid's wife, Ruth, the other perhaps a lady from Sunday morning church service, she supposed.

When Tess suggested a green taffeta dress, cut with fullness in the skirt, and a high waistline, Ellie nodded, desperate to flee the confines of the mercantile.

"I'll just add a couple of petticoats, and two nice vests for you. Oh, and some pretty drawers," Tess murmured, writing down figures with the nub of a pencil. She wrapped the chosen items, snatching fine lawn undergarments from another shelf to add to the purchases.

Ellie nodded dumbly, her eyes fixed on the countertop, her tongue glued to the roof of her mouth. She managed a quiet thanks in Tess's direction, then shot a look of agonized shame at the two women who stood nearby.

"Good day, Ellie," one of them said kindly, while the other snorted a muttered word beneath her breath. A nudge with a quick elbow silenced her, and the first patron stepped forward. "I'm Ruth Kincaid," the woman said softly, her dark eyes kind as she held out a hand to Ellie.

Ellie grasped it as if it were a lifeline, and she about to drown. "Pleased to meet you, ma'am. I thought I recognized you," she whispered. Ruth nodded, her dark hair straight and heavy, bound into a bun at the nape of her neck.

"I've got to go," Ellie said, backing away.

"Don't forget your things, child," Tess reminded her, handing the package across the counter.

"No, ma'am." It was a heavy bundle, but Ellie took it with ease, lifting it to her breast as she headed for the door. She'd heard about Ruth Kincaid, known that the woman was from the Cheyenne tribe. George had made remarks about Caleb's good sense when he'd married the woman, seeing as how he had a child to raise from his first wife. She was apparently welcome here in Tess's establishment, and Caleb being one of the area's most prosperous ranchers certainly couldn't hurt any.

Best of all, Ruth seemed to be warm and friendly. Probably, she decided, due to her own problems with acceptance among the Anglo community. No matter the reason, she'd felt gracious approval from the woman, and that alone was enough to lift her spirits.

"I'll carry that," Win said, taking the bundle from Ellie's grasp. Outside the sheriff's office, he and James had watched as she crossed the street, and James had murmured a few words of approval.

"She's holding her head up these days," he said quietly. "I'd say you'll do well together, Doc."

With a quick glance of thanks, Win stepped down onto the road and greeted Ellie. Relieving her of the parcel was an automatic gesture for him, and he noted her quick look of surprise.

"I can carry it," she protested swiftly. "You don't need to be waiting on me."

"Ah, but I do," he told her, denying her words. "You're going to be my wife, Ellie. I'll treat you as a husband should."

"Well, I appreciate it," she said, shoving her hands into the pockets of her enveloping apron. She skipped once, catching up with his longer stride, and he grinned at her.

"I keep forgetting how short you are." He nodded at the occupants of a buggy, swinging the bundle from the string Tess had bound it with, then whistled a jaunty tune.

"You're in a good mood," Ellie said. "Did James brighten your day?"

"No, you did." He smiled at her look of surprise. "You've managed to be a bright spot in my life these days, honey. I'm just feeling fine, in general." He sobered, looking down at her. "But as a matter of fact, James and I talked about Cilla, over at the Double Deuce saloon. She told James that Billy promised not to ever hurt her again. Not that I believe it. The boy has a hold over her. Maybe she's hoping he'll locate the treasure and share it with her. James says they've been thick as thieves for a while."

"Does she have other—" Ellie cleared her throat. "Never mind. It isn't any of my business."

"Yes, she does," Win told her. "It *is* her business, honey. I'm afraid if she didn't have *other* men, she'd be out on the street. And that's a tough place for a woman to be."

"Don't I know it," Ellie said fervently. "And not all women are as lucky as I am."

"Don't ever compare yourself to Cilla," Win said fiercely.

Ellie looked up, stunned by the harshness of his voice. "Doc, I just meant—"

"I know what you meant," he said, interrupting her without apology. "There's nothing alike about the two of you, and don't you ever forget it."

"You're the one who's forgetting," she said

quietly. "I'm a fallen woman, even though I won't lay claim to all those other names my pa called me."

"You're a girl who was set upon by a man who should have known better. Who no doubt did know better, but managed to get past your defenses anyway." he told her. "It's not the same thing. In fact, you'd never get a job in the Double Deuce, honey. You're pure as the driven snow, compared to the women there."

Her heart lifted at his words, and her step quickened, as if a load had been removed from her shoulders. "I thank you for your kind words," she said primly. "And now, if you'll move along, I'll have time to try on one of my new wrappers before I start dinner."

They turned in the gate, and Win held it open for Ellie to walk past him. "I expect to see you wearing your new wrapper while you cook my dinner. That garment you have on is only fit for scrubbing, from now on."

The doorknob turned readily and Ellie walked the length of the hallway toward the kitchen at the back of Win's house. From the waiting room door, a voice beckoned, and she hesitated, hearing the note of pain it held.

"Dr. Gray. I've got a boil that needs lancing."

She turned back to Win, taking the bundle from his grasp. He was gone from her already, she realized, his mind concentrating on the man who needed him.

And so it should be. Winston Gray was a doctor, first and foremost.

"I like the outfit," Win said, drawn to the kitchen by the scent of food. He walked to the stove, peering over Ellie's shoulder at the kettle whose contents she stirred. "Is that soup?"

She nodded. "I used up yesterday's vegetables, along with a piece of beef. I'll thicken it a little, and maybe put dumplings on top. What do you think?"

I think you're about to be set upon by a hungry man, Win almost said aloud. And then decided against it. Not for anything in this world would he speak words she might take offense at. Maybe in a few weeks, he thought wistfully, when he'd prepared her for the intimacies of living in the same house, sharing their lives.

Sleeping in the same bed.

And at that thought, he winced, aware of a new set of problems he'd best set aside for now. "Do you think we can plan on getting married tomorrow?" he asked. "I thought I'd see the preacher for sure this evening. Maybe he'd even do it for us today."

"Today?" Ellie stiffened, the spoon held aloft, her left hand still pouring a thick white sauce into the soup. "Oh, drat!" she muttered, glancing down at the kettle, and wielding her spoon vigorously. "I'll have lumps."

Win attempted to stifle the smile that tempted to curve his mouth. "Lumps?" he asked. Then he backed away and made a pretense of scanning her from top to bottom.

She glanced over her shoulder. "In the soup," she said patiently. "The flour and water need to be stirred in gradually, or it will make dumplings I hadn't planned on."

Properly subdued, Win settled at the table. "Shall we ask James and Kate to go with us when we get married?" he asked.

"I don't know." That the thought had not occurred to Ellie was obvious, but she considered it for a moment. "Do we need somebody along?"

"We need witnesses, honey."

"Witnesses." She pondered that thought, and then shrugged. "I guess you can tell I've never had anything to do with folks getting married." The spoon she held was placed on a small plate atop the warming oven, and she paced to the back door, one hand pressed against her belly.

"At least they both know why you're marrying me. It won't be like having strangers there, will it?" Her fingers moved in a gentle massage as she spoke, and James caught her eye.

"Is the baby moving?"

A flush crept up from her throat to cover her cheeks. "Yes. I'm sorry. I didn't mean to call attention to it."

"Ellie." He spoke her name with patience, and then rose, approaching her slowly. "Do you mind if I feel it, too?"

Her eyes widened, wondering that he would seek out such a thing, but she nodded. His hand covered hers, then moved beneath her fingers, pressing more firmly against the bulge of her pregnancy. He closed his eyes and she sensed his concentration, holding her breath as the tiny life within her body responded to the pressure of his touch. It jerked once, then again, and as if the unborn child rolled over, she felt the movement radiate to Win's hand.

"This must be old stuff to you," she said, biting at her lip, astonished at the intimacy of the moment.

"This time it's new, Ellie. This will be my child."

Win's eyes opened, and a flood of love for the man before her invaded Ellie's very being. With those simple words, he took on the responsibility for her child. With that unvarnished phrase, he accepted her child as his own. And there was a wealth of difference in the two.

Responsibility was one thing. Acceptance, another.

"You'll make me cry," she whispered. "I never thought to know a man like you."

"You'll know me better before we're done," he promised.

Leaving Ellie to clean up the kitchen, Win walked to the parsonage and spoke his plans to the minister. Aside from a startled look, that gentleman was totally accepting of Win's solution to Ellie's problem.

"It's more than a marriage of convenience, sir," Win said upon leaving. "I've had a chance to know Ellie a bit, and I think we'll do well together. She needs me, and I certainly will be happy to have her in my home."

"Will you invite her father?" Issued without any hint of the parson's druthers, the query was met by an immediate negative reply by Win.

"No, sir. He hasn't been kind to Ellie. I don't want her upset."

"I understand." And indeed, he appeared to, not seeking Win's compliance.

"We'll return before dark," Win told him. "I need to locate James Kincaid and bring him and Kate along to stand with us."

He paused by the sheriff's office on his way home, but found it empty. "Sheriff's gone home early," Harry Talbert called from the door of his barbershop. "Nothin' much doin' today."

Oh, but there is. With a smile and nod, Win hastened on his way, eager to seal his intentions with vows and a ring. *A ring.* He halted in the middle of the road. He didn't have a ring. Except... He looked down at his right hand, where a heavy gold crest, signifying the degree he'd earned, decorated the band he'd worn since the day he graduated from medical school. A gift from his anatomy professor, the ring was a keepsake he'd vowed never to remove.

But for Ellie, he would give it as a pledge to his bride. It could be replaced later on, when there was time to order such a thing.

For now, for this day, the ring he wore with pride would do double duty.

If Ellie was hurt by the gesture, he'd explain it to her, apologize if necessary for the lack of forethought. And yet in the town of Whitehorn, there was no place to purchase a ready-made ring, such as he wanted his bride to wear. Cheap, narrow bands were available from Tess's mercantile, probably not even gold, through and through, he thought.

Cheap wasn't good enough for Ellie.

"I can't believe you'd give me your ring," she whispered, much later that evening, when James and Kate had made their way home, when the vows had been spoken and the sedate kiss exchanged before the kindly minister.

"I'll get you a better one, as soon as we can order it," he promised her.

"You'll want this one back, I know," she said. "But in the meantime, I'll be ever so proud to wear it, Win." The gold glistened in the lamplight, and she turned her hand, careful to hold the ring in place. "It's a little big. Kate said I should wrap it with yarn to make it fit, for now."

"I don't have any yarn," he said solemnly,

watching as she breathed against the gold, then polished it on her bodice.

Her eyes were startled. "I didn't expect you did, but I'm sure Kate does, or I can ask Tess for a short length." She held the ring before her, and he was thankful for the notion that had brought such joy to his wife.

His wife. He'd thought never to speak those words. At least not in the foreseeable future. And now he was married, all legal and binding. His wife. Ellie was his wife.

"Would you have liked to have your family here?" she asked softly. "I never thought of it before, but I suspect your parents will be hurt that they missed seeing you on your wedding day." A frown gathered her brows. "Though, I can't imagine they'd be thrilled to death over your bride."

"I'm the only one who needs to be thrilled over that part of it," he said firmly. "And, no, I didn't plan on inviting my parents to my wedding, no matter when it took place. They turned their backs on me when I chose the practice of medicine instead of being in the family business. If it hadn't been for the support of my uncle Gregory..."

She looked up at him unbelievingly as his voice trailed off. "I can't imagine folks not being proud of a man like you, Win. And being a doctor is a fine choice to make for your life, though I doubt you'll ever make a fortune at it."

"I don't need a fortune," he said bluntly. "I've got money inherited from my grandparents, enough to set myself up in practice and keep me solvent for a long time to come."

"I didn't know you were well-to-do," she said, her teeth sinking into her bottom lip as she considered the idea. "They'd have even more reason not to appreciate you marrying me, with them probably hoping you'd find a fancy lady someday."

"You're fancy enough to please me," he told her. "You're pretty as a picture in your new dress." His hand touched her shoulder, then lifted to caress her cheek as he cleared his throat. "I know we kissed before the preacher and our witnesses, Ellie. Do you suppose we could repeat it now, just for ourselves?"

She lifted startled eyes to him, her mouth forming a circle, as if she thought to breathe a reply, then decided against it.

He waited, unwilling to push her beyond the boundaries she might have set in place, but a small, slight nod put his mind at ease, and he reached for her. One long arm circled her waist, the other held her nape. The heavy weight of hair pressed against the side of his hand and he thought again of the length of silken tresses that would cascade down her back, should he remove several pins from place.

Fingers that were agile, that had formed stitches in torn flesh with precision, now turned to the simple task of taking down the hair of a woman. And he found, to his amazement, that those self-same hands were trembling. He tilted her head forward, resting it against his chest, and then began the mission he had set for himself.

Heavy, dark bone hairpins filled his palm... seven... eight...then the last of them. Nine in all. He reached past Ellie to place them on the kitchen table, then felt her soft, warm breath as she lifted her head and looked up at him.

His fingers separated the strands, tangling in the heavy treasure he'd managed to set loose. "I'm not very good at this," he murmured. "But I appreciated you allowing me to indulge myself. I've wanted to touch your hair ever since the morning I watched you brush it on the porch, Ellie."

She caught her breath and blinked, biting

at her lower lip. "I feel almost naked, Win. I've never…"

"Never let another man see your hair?" he asked.

She nodded. "It's just hair," she said uneasily, as if she sensed his growing arousal. "I'll braid it before I go to bed."

"You forgot, Ellie," he said quickly. "We were going to share a kiss."

"All right."

He felt the tenseness in her shoulders as he gripped them in his palms, knew she was wary of his intentions, and in that moment recognized that he could not, in good conscience, consummate his marriage tonight. But he could kiss her. In fact, he was determined to kiss her, give her a taste of his desire, perhaps incite a little of that elusive emotion in her.

He bent low, tilting a bit, meshing his mouth with hers. One hand left her shoulder and cradled her head, turning it to one side, the better to fit their lips in a soft, undemanding caress. She inhaled, her mouth opening just a bit, and her breath shuddered against his face.

Again he blended their mouths, urging her compliance as he nudged at her upper lip, then brought his teeth to capture the lower, laving her sensitive flesh with his tongue. She gasped, and, congratulating himself on his gentlemanly instincts, he took no advantage, but kept his play to the edges of her mouth, inside her lower lip and then to her cheek.

That his breath was rapid, his body tense and his manhood more than erect was to be expected, he realized. But that Ellie should lean against him so willingly was a bonus he had not anticipated. Her eyes closed as she allowed his gentle exploration, as though the pleasure of his touch was more than welcome.

Numerous kisses blessed each part of her face and throat, and against her ear he murmured soft wordless sounds. Small whimpers deep in her throat gave him the response he sought, and he held her closer, moving against her restlessly, seeking some small amount of relief from the pressure of tight trousers and a desire he'd long ignored.

At that, she stiffened, shifting away from him, and a shivering indrawn breath made him aware of taut muscles and a shudder that racked her frame.

He bent his head, pressing his forehead against hers. "I'm sorry, sweetheart," he murmured. "I didn't mean to frighten you."

Ellie nodded, forgiveness implicit in the small gesture. "I just…just for a moment, I—"

She wasn't ready for this. Her only experience with a man had not left her with anticipation uppermost in her mind for the act of loving. Tommy Jamison had much to answer for, Win decided.

Yet he could carry her to his bed. He knew it, as surely as he knew his own name. She would not deny him, no matter that her wariness was apparent. But he would not try to persuade or force Ellie into a consummation tonight. Over the next few days he would woo her, coax her with kisses and caresses. And then when she was willing, when she came to him, he would make her his bride.

Chapter Six

"Well, it's been almost two weeks since the big day. Do you feel married yet?" Kate asked, her tone amused as she sat beside Ellie on the back stoop.

"I don't know how that's supposed to feel," Ellie admitted. "I feel like a wife, I suppose. I'm doing all the things every other woman does with her days."

Kate cast her a sidelong glance. "I don't think you caught my meaning, Ellie. And perhaps I have no business being so nosy, anyway."

"Are you talking about sharing a bedroom, like you and James do?"

"That's part of it," Kate told her. "And I'll have to admit, I've peeked over here. I've seen your candle lit every night this week. So either Win has moved upstairs or you're not ready for that part of marriage yet."

"Win hasn't…" Ellie bit at her lip. "I don't think he wants to do that with me. He hasn't mentioned it anyway."

"Oh, I'll bet he does," Kate said airily. "He wouldn't be a man if he didn't." She patted Ellie's hand and squeezed it gently. "He may be waiting for you to make the first move. Maybe he thinks you're not ready to accept him into your bed."

Ellie felt heat invade her face and she looked down at the scant leaves of grass surrounding the porch. "I'd do anything in this world for Win. I think he knows that."

"Maybe he doesn't want you to do it as a favor, honey," Kate told her quietly. "He may be waiting until you decide it's something you'll both enjoy."

"Enjoy?" Now that was a new idea, Ellie thought with a scowl. "I didn't find much that was fit to talk about when Tommy—" She bit at her lip. "I didn't mean to say that."

"And this again is none of my concern," Kate said, removing her spectacles, and polishing them with a fold of her dress. She pressed on, her own cheeks taking on a flush that might have been embarrassment. "Did Tommy only make love to you once?"

"I wouldn't call it by that name," Ellie murmured. "It was a lot of puffin' and pantin' and shovin' at me, and all I got was five minutes of pure misery." She looked down at herself and one hand pressed protectively against her belly. "And a baby."

She looked up at Kate then. "I don't really mind about the baby. Not now, anyway. Not since Win married me."

Kate's arm slid to enclose Ellie's narrow shoulders. "Things will work out for you, honey. And by the time the baby comes, you'll be tickled pink about having a husband and a child of your own." She sent a look across the yard as a screen door slammed.

"Are you ladies gonna spend the whole afternoon sittin' in the sun?" James came across from the back of his house, and his gaze was warm as it rested on his wife. "I came home early, Kate. Thought you might need some help in the kitchen."

"I just let the children out of school," she said with a sigh, "and then I managed to drag myself this far. I'm afraid I didn't even go into the house."

"We can walk over to the hotel and eat in the dining room if you want to," he told her. "Just give me a chance to wash up."

Ellie's mouth opened before she thought twice. "If you'd like some pot pie, I've got a big one in the oven. Win will be home soon. He went out to take a look at the ranch hand with a broken leg. He's worried about infection setting in."

"That fella's lucky he doesn't have a family to support. It's hard to collect anything on payday when you're laid up," James said, propping one foot on the stoop and reaching to touch Kate's head. "You doing all right?" he asked, as she looked up at him.

"Just a backache," she told him. "I've had it most of the day."

"Did you tell Win?" He shifted, his eyes narrowing as he peered intently into her face. "Maybe the baby's—"

"What kind of a backache?" Win spoke from inside the kitchen, and Ellie jumped at the sound of his voice.

"I didn't know you'd gotten home," she said, hastening to her feet.

"I just got here, honey," Win said, his gaze

still on Kate. "Does it come and go, Kate? Or is it a steady ache?"

She shrugged. "I don't know, Doc. Once in a while I get twinges...." Her voice trailed off as she bit at her lip. "This is pretty personal stuff we're discussing here."

"Having a baby's a pretty personal event," Win drawled. "And I wouldn't be surprised if you're heading for the first stages. Might even be well on your way. Anybody who keeps going the way you have for the past months probably won't be having a long, drawn-out time of it."

"Do we need to go home and let you go to bed?" James asked anxiously.

Ellie thought he looked very young for just a moment, his brow furrowed, his mouth pursed. His eyes swerved to Win, and as if he must touch her, reassure himself that she was all right, he reached for Kate.

Ellie's heart ached, sensing that James would suffer right along with Kate when the time came for her delivery. She spoke quickly, wanting to distract him from his fear. "Why don't you come on inside and get some supper first?"

Kate shot her a grateful look. "That sounds wonderful. James may need a good meal to fortify him if Doc's right." She clasped James's outstretched hand and he tugged, giving her leverage to rise from the stoop. Once on her feet, she lifted massaging fingers to the small of her back and then eased her way to the door. "Come on, Ellie. I'll give you a hand."

With a fervent hope that there was more than enough food to go around, Ellie held the door for Kate, then hurried toward the big iron stove. "It's hot in here," she said, fanning the air with a dish towel as she opened the oven door. The crust was browning nicely, she decided. It had turned out well, and wasn't that a good thing, being the first time she'd had company for supper.

"There's potatoes in the pie," she told Kate. "I think just some tinned peaches and cookies for afters will be fine."

"James isn't fussy these days," Kate confided. "I've been pretty lax lately. By the time I get home from school, I haven't felt much like being a cook."

"I don't know how you do it," Ellie told her. "And yet I'm so happy that they haven't made you stay home and gotten someone else for the school."

"I'm the talk of the town, you know." Kate

lifted four plates from the kitchen buffet and placed them around the table, then turned to the drawer for silverware. "Half the folks are pleased as punch that our town council is so forward thinking, letting me teach, when the other half of the ladies think I should be secluded behind the doors of our house."

"Well," Ellie said sagely, "you can't please everyone. And James is happy with what you're doing, so I don't see that much else matters.

"Win said the threshers are coming next week. You couldn't have planned this better if you tried." Ellie checked the coffeepot, deciding to begin anew with a fresh brew, and poured the leftovers from earlier in the day into her slop bucket. Fresh water and a handful of grounds from the glass jar, followed by the egg she always added were put together quickly, and the pot was placed on the front of the stove.

"Why don't you sit down?" she said, watching closely as Kate's hands met beneath the rounding of her belly. And then her eyes narrowed as she watched the other woman's face settle into lines of total concentration. "Kate? Are you having pains?"

Kate nodded. "Not bad yet, but that's the

fourth one in the last little while." She looked toward the back door, where the murmur of men's voices could be heard. "I don't want James to worry."

Ellie shrugged. "He probably will anyway. He's pretty taken with you, isn't he?"

Kate nodded, and her smile was radiant. "Seems to be. He says he's going to be right there when the baby's born."

Ellie stepped into the pantry and returned with cans of peaches and a bowl of cookies. Knife in hand, she worked to open the tins, then poured the fruit into a bowl. "I could come, too, if you wanted me," she offered diffidently. "I've never seen a baby born. I guess I never knew anybody that was going to have one, till now. But I've helped with calves sometimes, and watched when the dog had pups."

She swallowed a bubble of laughter. "Not that those are anything to go by. I mean, I know having a baby is different. I just thought if you needed me, I could maybe stand by."

"I'd be pleased, if Win doesn't mind," Kate said agreeably. "He might not want you to be frightened by the process, what with you having to look ahead to the same thing, before too long."

Kate's fingers gripped the edge of the table as she spoke, and her eyes widened a bit. "I believe I'd better not eat very much," she decided. "This might be going faster than I thought."

Ellie walked to the back door. "If you'd like to come in, we're about ready to sit down at the table," she offered. Win opened the screen door, and in moments he and James had washed and were pulling out chairs. The pot pie was placed on a folded towel in the center of the table, and Ellie stuck her largest tablespoon through the crust.

"Coffee will be another ten minutes," she announced, "but we can go ahead if you want to." Looking at Win for directions, she placed small bowls near each plate, then brought the peaches and cookies to the table. "There's fresh bread, too," she said, remembering as she hastened back to the pantry.

"This looks wonderful, Ellie," James said. He reached to scoop a serving onto Kate's plate, and she held up her hand.

"Just a little. I don't think I should eat too much."

Win nodded. "I was about to suggest that." His eyes rested on Kate. "Do you want me to get Tess Dillard or maybe Ethel Talbert to help?"

Kate shook her head. "No. Ellie will be there. It's all decided."

If he had any objections, Win swallowed them, his glance at Ellie questioning. And then he nodded agreement. "If she's game for it, I can use a hand." He reached for the bread and slathered butter generously across the slice. "It's been my experience that husbands aren't much good, except for hand holding and back rubbing."

James ate steadily and quietly. Perhaps his worries had been soothed by Win's teasing, Ellie thought. It hadn't done much to ease hers. Her own stomach was in an uproar. She'd made the offer, and if Kate needed her, she'd do her best; but she was dead certain that birthing a calf and a baby were not really in the same category.

In fact, they were decidedly different. Settling Kate into bed at midnight, Ellie heard the low voices of James and Win in the kitchen, and glanced at the open bedroom door.

"Not yet," Kate whispered. "I don't want them just sitting in here, waiting for things to happen." Her eyes closed and her breathing became deeper, finding a new rhythm as she waited out the pain that gripped her.

"Maybe Win should check to see how you're doing," Ellie said.

"And maybe you should go home to bed," Kate told her, relaxing her hold on Ellie's hand, her whole body seeming to sag into the mattress.

"No, I want to stay with you." She reached to pull a chair closer and eased onto the seat. Kate appeared to be asleep, and yet Ellie sensed she was only a whisper away from awareness. It seemed only a moment until Kate stirred and her eyelids fluttered. A soft sound, uttered beneath her breath, signaled her discomfort and within seconds she was involved in another contraction. Her jaw was taut for a moment, and then she seemed to force herself to relax, inhaling deeply and releasing the captured breath through her lips.

Through the next hour, the pattern was repeated, with Ellie able only to sit by and watch, wringing out a soft cloth in cool water to place it on Kate's brow. Win came to the door twice and looked in, lifting an inquiring eyebrow in Ellie's direction. But Kate only grunted and waved him away, too intent on her labor to allow another participant.

And then, within a few minutes, the intensity of Kate's discomfort seemed to increase. Ellie had never felt so utterly helpless in her life. "Delivering a calf sure didn't prepare me for this," she muttered as Kate's muffled groan signaled the peak of the contraction. "I just wish I could do more to help," Ellie said fervently, reaching to clutch at Kate's hand, offering the only comfort she could. "Shall I get James?"

Kate shook her head, her eyes closing. "Don't call them yet. When it really gets bad, and the pains are closer together, it'll be time enough to—" Her words ceased and her grip tightened on Ellie's fingers, as another contraction followed.

"I think the time is now," Ellie decided. She rose from the chair and went to the doorway. "Win? I think something's different. Her pains are closer and a lot harder."

James was on his feet and halfway across the room before Ellie's words were spoken. He brushed past her and fell to his knees beside the bed. "You should have let me in sooner," he told Kate, his voice harsh with emotion.

"It wasn't necessary." Kate opened her eyes, her hand lifting to touch James's cheek. "You've always been a big distraction, sweetie. I needed to concentrate."

Win stood at the dresser, washing his hands in the basin, scrubbing his fingers with a small brush. "I have a notion things are underway, James. You sure you're up to this?" His tone was teasing, but his look was level as he turned to the bed. "Sometimes it's hard to see the one you love in pain."

"She stuck it out when Ethel took care of a gunshot wound in my arm a while back. The least I can do is return the favor," James said with a cocky grin. "I'm not leaving you, Kate. I was with you when this whole thing started, and I'll be here when the baby comes."

It seemed the pains would never cease, but Kate was uncomplaining, her body accepting the gradually increasing contractions that lifted and rounded the contours of her belly. Win's hands were gentle, carefully examining her. His words were encouraging, acknowledging her pain, assuring her of her progress. And in between each session, he walked to the window, looking out into the night, pacing to Ellie's side or across to where James murmured soft phrases against Kate's ear, his lips brushing her cheek and forehead.

Ellie's head rested on the mattress, her eyes closing in spite of her determination to remain alert, until Kate's urgent moan of distress brought her from the edge of sleep. Lifting her head, Ellie blinked and rose from the floor where she'd knelt for the past three hours. Kate gasped, groaning aloud, her breathing harsh.

"I don't think she can do this much longer, Doc." James sent a grim look in Win's direction as Kate once more sought his hand, her fingers tightening in a knuckle-whitening grip, as she turned awkwardly to her side, facing her husband.

"She's doing fine," Win assured him, his level glance at Ellie an unspoken request. Her lips were taut, her eyes were shadowed, and he almost regretted allowing her to be a part of this. And yet she smiled at him, her shoulders flexing as she leaned over the bed, applying pressure to the small of Kate's back, her strong fingers moving in a circular motion.

"I think we're about there, Kate," Win said quietly. "If James gets behind you, can you sit up just a little? I need you to push that baby into the world, honey."

From that point on, there was a feverish yet controlled atmosphere in the room. Kate, leaning against James, her face contorted as she labored. Win, easing the way with his capable, strong touch, until the slippery blue form of a baby boy lay in his hands. The tiny mouth opened and a soft mewling sound caught Kate's attention, and she strained to peer toward the source.

Win held the wriggling form higher, and Ellie watched as the infant's chest rose with an indrawn breath. An angry wail, accompanied by fiercely waving fists announced the babe's indignation at being wrenched from the warmth of his mother's body, and his skin began losing its dark tinge, turning pink, as if a magic wand had been waved over his tiny form.

Her eyes blurred by tears, Ellie bit at her lip. "He's beautiful," she whispered. "Oh, Kate. Your baby's beautiful."

"Here you go, Mama," Win said, placing the baby across Kate's stomach. He reached for a flannel cloth. "Hold this over him while I cut the cord, Kate. He's a slippery little fella."

Kate obeyed, her hands clutching protectively, her fingers encircling small legs and upper arms through the warm flannel. Three pairs of eyes watched as Win tied the pulsing cord in two places and then his scissors flashed as the connection between mother and child was severed.

"Wrap him up," Win told Ellie, tossing her another flannel square. "Let Kate hold him while I finish up down here."

Ellie's fingers trembled as she scooped the baby into the square of fabric, and then she folded it around his wiggling form, and Kate's arms were there, eager to accept her child.

"I'm proud of you, Ellie," Win said quietly, opening the back door to allow her entry to the kitchen. The moon was a soft glow at the horizon, and stars glittered overhead. "You must be tired," he surmised, closing the back door as Ellie lit a candle on the table.

She was silent, and he almost rued the fact that she'd had such a preview of the birthing process. It always looked to be harder on the mother than it really was, he'd decided after his first delivery. And Kate had been no exception. She'd pushed for almost an hour, working hard to bring her son into the world.

James, determined to stick it out, had come

close to tears when the red-faced, squalling babe was finally separated from his mother's womb. Win grinned widely, remembering. Kate had reached for her son, and James, kneeling by the bed, had enclosed them both in his embrace. It was a tender moment, and one Win cherished. It made the long hours of labor worthwhile, he decided.

Ellie was at the sink, and he went to her, hands grasping her shoulders. "You need to get to bed, honey. You've had a long night." She'd been quiet, all during the cleaning up and putting to rights, and still she was silent. Then with a whimper, she turned to him, and he was dismayed by the tears in her eyes.

"I don't know if I can be as brave as Kate," she whispered. "She barely made a sound, did she? Only a few groans at the end. And I wanted to cut loose with a yell, just watching her go through it."

"It's harder to watch sometimes," he said, "than it is to be the one doing the hard work." His hands slid to enclose her in a loose embrace. "You'll do fine when your time comes, sweetheart. And I'll warrant Kate will be here for you."

Ellie looked up at him. "I'm proud to be married to you, Win. I've never seen you do your doctoring before. At least not the way you were when you took care of Kate. It made me feel good to see how you were, helping Kate and handling the baby."

"Delivering a baby is the best part of my job," he told her. He bent his head and pressed a kiss against her forehead. "Come on, Ellie. You need to be in bed."

She swallowed with an effort and her eyes were anxious in the faint light from the candle. "Would you like to sleep in my bed, Win?" A rosy flush colored her cheeks, and she bit at her bottom lip.

"Sleep, Ellie?" His heart began a slow thundering beat as he watched her. If Ellie was thinking to offer herself because it was the expected thing to do, he wouldn't accept. And yet if he turned her down, it might put a real dent in her pride, and that would never do. Crawling into Ellie's bed was his aim in life these past few days. That was a given, considering his state of mind since they'd spoken their vows.

The single long kiss they'd shared had not been followed up by a second. He'd made a point of touching her frequently during the past week, a caress on her shoulder, an arm around her waist, and bending to press his cheek against her hair several times. She'd responded to his gestures with a smile, never turning from him. But gratitude was the last thing he wanted from a wife.

Desire was more to the point, and he wasn't certain that Ellie felt comfortable enough with him to allow that emotion to come to the surface.

There was only one way to find out.

"I'd like to sleep in your bed, honey," he said softly. "Or else you could sleep in mine. It's closer."

"My nightgown is upstairs," she said, her glaze flitting from his to rest on his shoulder, and then flicker to the wall beyond.

"You won't need it."

And at that simple statement, she turned away. "I don't look very good without my clothes on," she whispered. "I'm bulging in front, and my…" Her arms crossed loosely over her breasts as she struggled to speak. "I'm sort of big." Her eyes were apologetic as she forced the explanation from her lips.

"What makes you think that's going to bother me?" he asked with a grin. "Didn't you know that sometimes big is better?"

"I'm bigger all over than I used to be," she managed to whimper, her flushed cheeks seeming to require the presence of her hands. Wide-eyed, she looked up at him, and he clasped her hands in his, lifting them from her face.

"That happens when a woman is going to have a child, honey. It doesn't make you any less attractive as far as I'm concerned. I think you're lovely, Ellie."

"I'm not," she said, with a quick shake of her head. "I'm ordinary. I've got brown eyes and brown hair. My pa always said I'd never amount to anything." She closed her eyes. "He told me I was only good for one thing to a man, and Tommy'd already taken care of that. No one else would ever want me."

"When did he tell you that?" Win asked.

"The night I told him I was having a baby. And then he got really mad. That's why he hit me. He'd never done that before, Win. He'd never been real nice to me, but that was the first time he ever hit me. And then he told me to get out, after he called me a lot of names, and—"

Win's hand covered her mouth, and his words halted her spoken misery. "What he told you wasn't true. Making a mistake is only human. If he couldn't understand that, then it was his loss.

"And my gain," he whispered. He ran his index finger across her lower lip. "Look at me, sweetheart."

She obeyed, and he watched as tears flowed silently from dark eyes that doubted his words. Lifting his hand from her mouth, he wiped at the salty residue staining her cheeks.

"I want you, Ellie. I don't care that you're not slender anymore. That's not important. In about three months, you'll be as slim as ever, but I won't like you any more than I do now because of it. Yes, I want to go to bed with you. But not if you're doing me a favor. It has to be because you want to."

"Will you kiss me again?" she asked. "I'd like that, Win. It made me feel all soft inside when you kissed me the night we got married."

"Soft?" he asked with a smile. "I was hoping for warm, Ellie."

"That, too," she said with a nod.

He picked up a dish towel from the counter behind her. "Let me wring this out under the pump. I'm going to wash the tears from your face. And then we're going to bed."

And in the meantime, he needed to figure out how he was going to keep his randy self in line long enough to soothe her fears.

* * *

By candlelight the simple furnishings took on an aura of beauty. Ellie looked down at the oval, braided rug she stood on, aware that somewhere, sometime, someone had spent long hours in its creation. The windows, clad in white, sheer panels of fabric were open, and outside, the night sounds blended in a harmony that soothed her like a lullaby.

Win's bed was covered by a handmade quilt, fat pillows topping the soft muted colors that formed a large star. She pulled it back, folding it at the foot of the bed, then turned back the top sheet before she sat on the edge of the mattress. Her shoes left by the back door, she wore cotton stockings, held beneath her knees with ordinary garters, and she lifted the hem of her wrapper across her lap as she leaned to roll them down her legs.

Win watched from the doorway, lured by the innately feminine gestures, and wondered if all women were so graceful. His mother had used her hands, as did Ellie, with a minimum of fuss, yet telegraphing the silent message of elegance in their movement. Ellie's head was bent, her attention focused on the stockings she folded with precision, laying

them aside before she lifted her hands to unbutton the front of her gown.

It was made to fit women of varying mea-
surements, overlapping and tying at the waist,
and she worked slowly at the process. Beneath it he suspected she wore new undergarments, and if the glimpses of dainty, pale
bits of sheer fabric he'd seen fluttering on the
clothesline yesterday were anything to go by,
Ellie was clothed in fancies guaranteed to appeal to his masculine nature.

She'd hung them carefully between a row
of sheets and another of shirts and trousers.
Win had watched from the back door as she
pinned them to the rope line and touched
them with admiring hands.

His Ellie was filled with mysteries. Raised
without the benefit of a mother's care, she had
somehow achieved the womanly arts on her
own. Much of her upbringing had prepared
her for hard work, for the joyless chores of
keeping a house and providing for the menfolk who lived there. But somewhere, she had
gained a knowledge of the small touches that
proclaimed her femininity.

Her hands lifted to her hair, and she shed
the pins in seconds, allowing the dark mass
to tumble down her back. His loins tightened

at the sight, even as he felt the breath catch in his throat. And then she stood, her dress falling from her shoulders, sliding the length of her arms as she turned to place it over the nearby chair. She bent, and the upper curves of her breasts were full against the dainty fabric of the vest she wore, the darker shadows beneath it catching his eye.

A trace of guilt, that he should watch her as she disrobed, unaware of his presence, nudged his conscience and he cleared his throat, a soft sound that caught her attention. Her eyes met his in the candlelight, and he saw a trace of fear in the quick smile she assumed for his benefit.

Yet she stood before him, clad only in the form-fitting, long undergarment, with drawers in the same fabric beneath. They reached almost to her knees, edged with a lace ruffle, and beneath them were slim, curved calves and narrow feet.

"I didn't know you were here," she said quietly. "I thought you were locking up."

"I did. The cat was on the back stoop. Did you feed it tonight?"

She nodded. "Just leftover scraps. I think it's been mousing. Maybe it'll keep the mice from the house. They'll be looking for a warm place with the cooler weather," she said. "But I still take out bits and pieces for the cat, just in case. I can't bear to see an animal go hungry."

"I wasn't sure," he told her. "So I put out a bit of the pot pie for it."

"My pa wasn't much for having animals around the house," she told him. "He said they belonged in the barn. And I know you don't let yours in, either. I won't bring it inside."

Win shrugged. "I don't mind, Ellie. It's your house. You can do whatever pleases you." He moved from the doorway, approaching her slowly, unbuttoning his shirt as he walked across the floor. "Do I have a clean shirt for tomorrow?"

She nodded and stepped to his dresser. "I folded them and put them in the second drawer. Your small things are in the top. I hope you don't mind that I switched them around." He watched as the second drawer was pulled open and her fingers touched his garments with care, drawing forth a blue-striped madras cloth shirt. "Will this do?"

"That's fine," he said, looking over her shoulder at the drawer's contents. "My clothes have never been so well taken care of." He dropped his suspenders to hang loosely at his sides, then stripped from his shirt. "I may not tell you, but I do appreciate all you do to make my life easier."

"That was our bargain, Win," she said simply, placing the clean shirt atop his dresser. She closed the drawer and, watching him, motioned toward a clothes basket she'd placed in the corner. "From now on you can put your laundry there, if that's all right."

His nod was agreeable, and he did as she bid, scarcely able to take his eyes from her. Rosy cheeks drew his attention, and he carefully kept his eyes from sliding below her neck, aware of the embarrassment she felt at her scarcity of clothing. "If you blow out the candle, I'll finish up in the dark," he told her, unwilling to strip from his trousers while she watched. Frightening Ellie was the last thing he wanted to do, and one good look at his blatant arousal would likely be enough to send her flying up the stairs.

"All right." She walked back to the bedside, then bent over the candle, cupping her palm behind the flame to contain her small puff of breath as she extinguished it. As if she awaited further instructions, she stood quietly.

"I usually sleep on this side, if that's all right with you," Win said, sliding from his drawers under the cover of darkness, and dropping them beside the bed. Getting beneath the sheet was his first thought. Luring Ellie to join him, there in the comfort of his bed, should be no problem.

Coaxing her from her vest and drawers might be.

She sat down on the edge of the mattress and turned to face him. "I can sleep in my vest, if that's all right. It's long enough, I think."

"Whatever you want is fine with me," he told her, even as he considered lifting the garment over her head.

She lowered her drawers, then rose to step out of them. Her feet slid beneath the sheet and she rolled in his direction. "Maybe I should braid my hair. It'll be all tangled by morning."

"I like it down, Ellie," he said. His hand scooped it from her neck and brought it forward, allowing the heavy length to cover the front of her vest. "It's like silk, sliding through my fingers." The cushion of soft flesh tempted him, and his knuckles brushed across the fullness of her bosom.

"You're a tempting creature, sweet," he murmured, bending to press a tender caress against her forehead.

"I don't mean to be," she whispered, as though it were a flaw. "My pa said women get in trouble when they flaunt themselves in front of menfolk."

"You've never done that, honey," he assured her. "You only tempt me because you're pretty and feminine and, best of all, you're my wife."

"I like being married to you," she admitted quietly, tilting her head a bit as his mouth moved across her temple and down the length of her jaw. "I've enjoyed helping in the office and fixing meals for you."

"You're going to enjoy this even more," he promised, his hands careful as he cupped her breasts, his fingers sliding the soft fabric against the skin beneath. "I'm going to slip this over your head," he warned her, noting the quick catch in her breathing. Gathering the length of the garment, he slid her out of its folds. He turned back the sheet, exposing her shoulders, smiling as she would have gripped it against herself.

"I'm all naked." She crossed her arms across the generous curves and he tugged gently at her fingers, lifting them to his mouth, where they relaxed as he brushed countless kisses across her palms.

"How can I tell?" he whispered, a smile apparent in the soft sound. "You don't need to cover up, Ellie. Your beautiful body is nothing to be ashamed of."

Indeed, she appeared as a figurehead on a ship, he thought, full-breasted, with flowing locks of hair spread across her pillow and shoulders. "I told you I was too big," she muttered beneath her breath.

He lifted her hands to his neck. "Why don't you hold on to me like this?" he murmured, pleased as she clutched her fingers together at his nape. And then he turned his attention to the full curves she'd tried in vain to conceal. His hands caressed gently, his thumbs brushing across the dark crests, causing them to pucker and tighten.

She whimpered, shifting against him, and he whispered coaxing phrases against her lips, his voice husky with desire.

"You're beautiful, honey." And she was, he decided. Soft and womanly, modest and unaware of her appeal. He bent then, his mouth open against her flesh, his tongue tasting the sweet flavor of feminine skin, enchanted by her swiftly indrawn breath as he traced the edges of dark, crumpled morsels, touching the peaks with the tip of his tongue.

He suckled gently, and her hips lifted, her legs restless. Soothing her, gentling her to his touch, his hand traveled the length of her body, over the rounding of her hip, coming to rest against the firm curve of her bottom.

"I didn't know it would feel so…" Her voice was choked and her fingers slid through his hair, as if she would hold his head in place against her breast. Replete with wonder, her words were a sigh, and she shivered, an involuntary movement.

"You like it?" he asked, blowing against her damp skin, pleased as she laughed softly.

"Uh-huh." It was a softly breathed response, as though her voice could not form words, and she bent her head a bit to kiss his temple, her breath warm as she brushed her mouth across his forehead, whispering his name.

His palm slid the length of her thigh, across her knee, and then back up her leg, to follow the crease where her hip joined her body. She stiffened, trembling as he cupped the soft curls, brushing gently between her thighs.

"Let me, Ellie," he whispered, exerting the smallest bit of pressure.

Her hesitation was minute, and then he felt the relaxing of muscles as she allowed the intrusion of his hand into her most private place. He was gentle, careful with the tender, feminine folds, seeking out that small bit of pleasure-giving flesh. Ellie jolted as his fingertip touched there, and then she was still, her breathing shallow, as if she waited for some great discovery to take place.

He lifted over her, his mouth seeking hers, teeth and lips taking possession as she opened to him. Her tongue met his, darted back, then forward again, to be welcomed as a worthy opponent in the play of flesh against flesh. Whimpering, she inhaled sharply as his touch became firm, bringing her hips into motion.

Win's lips curved. His Ellie was a passionate woman, and he yearned to bring her to fulfillment. He listened carefully, gauging her pleasure as he felt the movement, pacing his caress to the agile thrusting of her hips. And then he felt the hot wash of her release as she whimpered into his mouth, her body arching, seeking the firm pressure of his hand.

She curled against him, capturing his fingers and he enfolded her, there where her woman's flesh throbbed in a final pulsing of pleasure.

"Win?" It was a whisper of inquiry, a sigh of unloosed passion, and he was exalted by the knowledge that he had brought her so easily to this place.

His mouth pressed a multitude of kisses against her face, and his words were murmured phrases of admiration for her feminine charms. Smothering himself in the plush beauty of her breasts, he nuzzled them, inhaling the scent of arousal and tasting the salty flavor of her skin. Her hands touched him, fluttering against his shoulders, clutching at his back, and he whispered encouragement as he shifted to lie between her thighs, pleased with her acquiescence to his every coaxing whisper.

Firmly, he lifted one of her knees, and she obliged, sliding it up the length of his leg, then matched it, without prompting, with the other, caging him effectively as he pleasured himself. His breathing harsh, he lifted a bit, allowing his manhood to nudge the soft folds, seeking entrance in the damp sheath.

So carefully she seemed almost unaware of his intent, he pressed into that narrow channel, inhaling sharply as it gloved him, squeezing him as she tightened the muscles that surrounded the firm length of his arousal.

"It doesn't hurt," she whispered in surprise, and he groaned against her throat, awed by the simple phrase that told him she had expected pain.

"I'll never hurt you, Ellie," he promised, lifting over her on his forearms, looking down at the vulnerable beauty of the woman who welcomed him into her body. Tears trickled from the corners of her eyes, and a smile brought beauty to the features she had claimed were but ordinary. Now they shone with pleasure, and he bent to kiss the salty drops from existence, his tongue taking them from her temples.

"I'm not really crying," she murmured. "I'm happy, Win."

He could only nod in reply, acknowledging her words, since speech was suddenly beyond his capabilities. The beating of his heart was a vibration against the walls of his chest, his whole being consumed by the pure ecstacy of claiming the woman he held. Her hips rose to meet him, and he groaned, bending his head, his body bowed as he plunged within her now, without the tenderness he had promised himself to bestow upon her body.

And yet she did not flinch from him, only flexed her legs around him, whimpering as she rose to his need, offering herself up to him with a cry of exultation that vibrated from her slender body to the firm, demanding thrusting of his loins. He emptied himself, spasms of pleasure flexing him against her, and his groan was deep, dark with the fervent passion he could not contain.

He held her then, trembling in the aftermath of bliss such as he had never known. Rolling with her to his side, he cradled her against his damp flesh, as if she might escape, should he loosen his hold.

"Ellie…Ellie." His whisper was an incantation in her ear, and she slipped her arm around his waist, holding him with a yearning strength that refused to allow him escape from her grasp. And indeed, he was not willing to release her, craving the blending of soft curves with his male strength, and the warmth of her arms and legs that tangled with his in an embrace that melded their bodies into a single form.

And then he felt the small movement against his stomach, the nudging of a tiny fist or foot, the reminder that Ellie carried a babe within her. Easing her upward, he peered into her face. "You're all right? I wasn't too heavy for you?"

"Oh, no." She breathed the words, a quick denial of his fear. "You made me feel so good, Win. So warm. I didn't know I could feel such things." And her hips moved against his as she spoke, as if the mention of her response somehow ignited a small spark of desire within her.

"You made me forget to be careful," he admitted. "I should have known better than to be that rough with you." He clasped her close again, and rocked her in his embrace. "I'm so pleased that you came to me that day." His lips brushed hers, clinging to the damp surface. "I shouldn't have let you go back home, Ellie. I should have known better than to let your father take out his temper on you."

"You couldn't have known," she said quietly. "And it's all right now. He can't touch me anymore." She lay quietly, and he felt the movements of the child she carried, softly shifting against her flesh, the minute ripples of her skin telling of each twist and turn of the life within.

"This will be my child," he told her. "As if I had put it there, Ellie. No one will ever dispute that. No one."

Chapter Seven

"You had no right to marry the girl. She's going to have my child."

The young man's handsome features were marred by a sullen look that drew his mouth up in a sneer, and the older woman by his side was obviously nudging him along as he laid claim to Ellie.

"I had every right," Win said mildly, leaning back in his desk chair. Keeping an ear tuned to the soft, subtle noises in the house, he prayed fervently that Ellie would remain in the yard, tending her drying laundry, until he was able to settle this mess. With heavy frost the night before, she might not last long in the cold and this was something he hoped to keep her from hearing.

Tommy Jamison paced to the window and turned to face Win, his hands clasped behind his back. Darting a quick glance at his mother, he began another diatribe. "Ellie doesn't love you. She's always loved me. It was a mistake, our moving away when we did. If you weren't afraid of losing a housekeeper, you'd give me five minutes alone with her. That's all it would take to convince her to leave here and go back to Philadelphia with me."

His jaw jutted forward and his eyes narrowed, as if he had been coached in presenting a threatening posture. And then his eyes shifted uneasily. "I had no idea she was carrying my baby."

Win watched as crimson streaks stained Tommy's cheeks, proclaiming his words a downright lie. The boy, and he was a boy, Win had already decided, was under his mother's thumb. He needed to stand on his own two feet and grow up before he went looking for a wife.

It made no matter. Whatever reason the woman had for this jaunt, it was doomed to failure. With a resigned sigh, Win aimed a direct look in Marie Jamison's direction. "I don't know what makes you think you have any claim to Ellie or her child, ma'am. But you're sadly mistaken in your pursuit."

Mrs. Jamison inhaled, increasing her ample bosom in generous increments. "There's no mistake, sir. We've come to take the Mitchum girl home with us. She and Tommy can be married after we reach Philadelphia." She sniffed, holding a handkerchief to her nose, as if the odor of medicine and disinfectant lingering in the office was abhorrent to her.

"We have *family* back East." She waved a hand in a grand gesture. "Eleanor will be exposed to society."

Absolutely the epitome of success, Win thought dourly, thinking of his own beginnings. But he smiled, his mouth forming a polite grimace. "I'm sure that's important to you. However, I'm not certain that Ellie is much interested in such things." He'd almost…almost lay odds on it, he thought, especially after the past several weeks, during which she'd found her place in his bed on a nightly basis.

And then his attention snapped back to the woman who presented a threat to the young woman he'd taken as his bride.

"I'd rather not get the law involved," Mrs. Jamison said, leaning forward, her tone denying the claim. "But I will if it becomes necessary."

Win cast a puzzled look at the woman. "Now, just how do you propose to find any legalities to pursue in this matter? Ellie is my wife, all neat and tidy. We were married almost two months ago, by a minister, and with witnesses. And I have a marriage certificate that will validate my claim."

He rose from his desk, his gaze level as he turned to Tommy. "You kept company with my wife over a short period of time, didn't you?"

"You know damn well I did," the young man huffed. "Ellie won't deny that."

"No," Win answered mildly. "I don't think she will, although I'm sure she regrets the fact."

"If she'd told me she was having my child, I'd have married her right off the bat," Tommy blustered.

"Really?" Win drew out the single word in a disbelieving tone, and then his glance sharpened and touched on Marie Jamison. "Why did you move from here so quickly, Mrs. Jamison?"

"There was an opportunity for my husband in Philadelphia," she announced, as if the words had been part of a script. "An opening in the family business was offered and he accepted the position." Her eyes darted from Win to Tommy, her eyes flashing a warning to the younger man.

"And now," Win began slowly, "why did you come back here?"

Mrs. Jamison lifted her chin in an imperious manner. "Tommy realized he'd made a mistake in not marrying the girl. He persuaded me to come with him, to make the trip as a chaperon for Miss Mitchum on the return trip."

Something was not on the up-and-up, and beyond the fact that both his visitors were telling tall tales, Win was certain some ulterior motive drove them to their actions. The slamming of the back screen door reached his ears, and he ignored the sound.

Not so the woman before him.

"Is that the girl?" she asked, shooting a silent command in Tommy's direction.

"Don't move," Win commanded, his steps long as he blocked the doorway. Tommy stood hesitantly in the center of the office, peering back at his mother as if awaiting instructions.

"That *girl*," Win said, "is my wife. She has a name. I believe you've labeled her as *that girl* half a dozen times in the past fifteen minutes. And that," he said firmly, "is an insult to the woman I married."

"I want to see her," Tommy said, stalking across the room to stand before Win. He had to look up a considerable distance, and his brow furrowed. "You can't stop me from talking to Ellie."

"How old are you, son?" Win asked, a sense of pity overcoming his growing anger. The boy didn't stand a chance, but it was obvious he was wriggling on the end of strings, and his mother held the controls.

"Thomas's age has nothing to do with this," Mrs. Jamison said coldly. "He has the right to speak to the..." Her pause was significant. "To Eleanor," she said, obviously recalling Win's accusation.

Win shook his head. "No," he said, his voice deepening as he surveyed the woman. "He has no rights at all. This is my office and my home. You are both trespassing on private property."

"Win?" From the back of the house, Ellie's spoke his name, and he clenched his jaw.

"That's her now," Tommy said, his cheeks again flushing with emotion as he pressed closer to Win. "Ellie?" He called her name loudly, and from the back of the house there was only the echo of his voice to be heard.

Win clamped one hand in Tommy's shirt and lifted the youth to his toes. His words snarled past bared teeth, and he knew an anger such as had never possessed him in his life. "Listen to me, boy, and listen well. You walk out that front door and you keep your…" He hesitated, unwilling to speak the words that begged utterance.

With exaggerated civility, he lowered Tommy to the floor, and brushed one hand over the front of his shirt. "Take your mother and leave. I won't tell you again."

His jaw clenched tightly as Win backed from the office and pointed toward the paneled entrance door. Through its glass panes, the sun shone and the last leaves of autumn fluttered past, blowing on the wind that promised a wintery blast before morning. A facsimile of that chill breeze touched Win's spine, and he was frozen by the fear that clutched at his heart.

Tommy and his mother walked from the office, across the hallway and out the door, and still Win stood poised in the center of the wide corridor. What if…? He could not bear to consider the thought of Ellie turning from him to the man who had fathered her babe. And yet—

"Win?"

He turned to face her, and his heart melted. Fear etched her features, leaching the joy from her eyes, turning her cheeks pale, and she fought tears, rubbing one fist against her mouth. He held open his arms, and then was struck by the fear of rejection. It wasn't fair to her, he realized, not to allow her the choice. And so his hands dropped, sliding into his trouser pockets, and he watched as she stepped toward him, then halted.

"That was Mrs. Jamison, wasn't it?"

His answer was stark. "Yes."

"What did she want after all this time?"

"You." He watched, noting the pinched expression she wore. "Tommy was with her," he said. "Didn't you see him?"

She shook her head. "No, I came out of the kitchen as she stepped through the door, onto the porch. I thought I heard voices, heard someone call for me…" Her words trailed off and her eyes were wary.

"They came to bring you an offer, Ellie."

"An offer?" She looked puzzled. "What sort of offer?"

"Tommy came here to see you. He wants to marry you and take you back East to Philadelphia with him. Introduce you to *society*." The final word was spoken as if it were distasteful in his mouth.

"Society?" She repeated the word. "I can't seem to think straight, Win. What are you talking about? I'm married to you."

Her hand curved against the rounding of her pregnancy as she took one step toward him, and then she faltered, her eyes enormous. "I don't—" She swayed and he realized with a jolt that she was on the verge of collapse.

Two long steps took him within touching distance, and he caught her as she fell, watched as her eyes rolled back, and her breath left her lungs in a soft sigh. She was slim, but solid, and he lifted her carefully, shifting her in his arms, angling her through the doorway into the kitchen.

Easing onto a chair, he held her limp form against himself, whispering her name. "Ellie."

He bent his head, brushing his mouth across her forehead, his lips touching the dewy perspiration dampening her cold brow.

At the back door a knock sounded, James called Win's name, as he opened the door. "What's going on?" he asked. "I thought I—" And then, as he caught sight of the scene before him, he pulled the door open and stepped inside. "Is she all right?" He moved closer and bent low over Ellie's still form. "What's wrong with her, Win?"

"She's had a shock. Can you dampen a towel for me?"

"Yeah, sure," James said, moving quickly to do as he was bid. "Why don't you take her on into your bedroom or the parlor? I'll be right behind you."

Win stood, lifting Ellie carefully, and walked through the dining room, turning to his bedroom. He placed her atop the quilt, tugging a pillow beneath her head.

"Here you go," James said, offering the towel. "Is there trouble?" he asked, his attention on Ellie's face.

"I'd say so," Win told him. "Mrs. Jamison showed up here, with young Tommy in tow. It seems the boy had a change of mind, and decided he wants to be a father after all."

"What did Ellie say to that?" James asked carefully, his tone level, as if he withheld judgment.

"I didn't give them a chance to talk to her." Win sat by her side, wiping her forehead, brushing her hair back from the clean line of her brow. "Maybe it wasn't fair of me not to let her listen to what they had to say."

"Don't be a damn fool," James said bluntly. "That boy walked out and left her holding the bag. She'd have been up the creek without a paddle if you hadn't stepped in."

"Yeah. But he's back." He turned to look up at James. "She must have cared for him once. And now I've settled it without her making a choice. Do I have the right to make that decision for her?"

"I can't answer that," James said. "I think the bigger question is, how do you feel about the whole thing?"

Ellie's head swam with voices, and she struggled to call out, her words captured in her throat. Her fingers refused to obey her will, as did her eyes as she tried to open them. Stirring, she shifted her head, wincing against the sunlight streaming through the window.

James was there. She knew his voice, heard

a harsh note in the words he spoke, and held her breath as his query vibrated through her mind. *"How do you feel about the whole thing?"*

Beside her, the mattress sagged and she sensed the nearness of a warm body, the touch of a hand against her face. And then Win spoke.

"I won't stand in her way. It has to be what Ellie wants."

She sucked in a breath. If those were the words of a man smitten to the core with his bride, she'd eat her hat. Her eyes fluttered, then opened, and she met Win's gaze.

"I think I'd like a drink of water, please," she whispered.

He nodded, rising at once. "I'll be right back, Ellie." With a look in James's direction, Win walked from the room.

"I'd send Kate over," James said, "but I've just taken the baby in for her to nurse."

"She doesn't need to be coming here, James," Ellie told him. "She's due at the school before long."

"I'll leave you in Doc's hands then," he said. Offering a grin and a two-fingered salute as he backed from the room. "Take care, you hear?"

She nodded, and frowned, trying to organize her thoughts. The voices had been strident, catching her attention as she left the clothes basket inside the back door. Like a bad dream, she'd caught the sound of Tommy's voice, that petulant sound he'd affected more than once when things weren't going as he pleased.

The dim light in the kitchen had caught her off guard after the bright sunshine in the yard, and she'd felt a wave of dizziness sweep through her. Opening the kitchen door into the long hallway, she'd called for Win, needing his presence, her heart racing as if some great calamity were hovering overhead.

And then she'd faltered, ears buzzing, eyes blurring as again her name was spoken. The sight of billowing skirts and a woman flouncing out the door had confused her, as had Win's face as he turned to her.

What had he said? Mrs. Jamison came to make her an offer? Was that it? And Tommy? He'd been there, too?

She closed her eyes, recalling Win's words, his answer to James. *"I won't stand in her way."*

Perhaps Win would be relieved if she left, taking the burden of another man's child with her. And yet he'd been so— What was the right word? she wondered, remembering the nights since he'd taken her to his bed, claiming her body with tenderness, his arms holding her throughout the night hours.

It was his right, she knew that. He'd married her, and so had the right, by law, to lay claim to her person. And why shouldn't he?

"Ellie?" Win stood by the bed, and she lifted weary eyelids to focus on his face. He bent to sit beside her again. "Here, honey. Drink some water. You look like you've been run over by a horse and wagon."

"Well, that's flattering," she managed to whisper. She sat up unsteadily and reached for the water glass, her hands trembling. Win helped her, one hand on her back, the other offering the cold water, his hand covering hers as she drank.

She lay back on the pillow, shaking her head in refusal as he would have offered more. Closing her eyes, she felt weariness sweep through her. Win's hands loosened her shoes and drew them from her feet, then returned to strip her stockings from her legs. He lifted a quilt from the rack in the corner and covered her, and she was grateful for the weight of it.

* * *

He brought her a tray, and she roused from a restless slumber, her eyes heavy. A lamp on the dresser illuminated the room, and she watched as Win placed the tray on the night table beside her. Fluffing the pillows, he stacked them behind her, lifting her to sit against the headboard.

"I want you to try some of this soup. It's what we had for supper last night, and there's enough of it to warm you up." He'd spread butter on a piece of bread from this morning's baking, and cut it in small pieces. A cup of pale tea completed his offering and she nodded her thanks.

"I appreciate this," she told him, feeling a strange distance from him, even though he was only inches from her side.

"Do you need me to help you?" he asked softly, and she shook her head, looking up at him with a shaky smile.

His eyes were dark with worry and she sought a way to relieve his concern. "I don't want to be a burden on you, Win. You do too much for me."

"You're my wife, Ellie."

It was a simple statement, one she might have taken at face value a day or so ago. Tonight it seemed only to be a reason for his kindness, and she needed more than kindness from this man.

He'd loved her body, and loved it well, teaching her how to please him and bringing her untold pleasure with each encounter on this wide mattress. And yet there had been no words of love, only whispers of admiration for her face and form. She'd held back her own avowal of that deep emotion, fearing to place the burden of her need on his already overloaded shoulders.

Winston Gray carried the weight of the well-being of untold numbers of townsfolk and ranchers. He was the only doctor within a hundred miles, and over the past weeks, she'd seen his practice grow and almost double as his reputation spread across the territory surrounding Whitehorn.

If she could help make his life more pleasant, she would do it. If taking his ease with her body pleased him, she would gladly be available to him for the comfort only a woman could give.

But if he was tiring of her, wearying of the responsibility of a wife, with a baby on the way, she would not impose on his kindness. Going with Tommy and his miserable excuse for a mother was not an option. Her flesh crawled when she remembered those grasping hands and the greedy fashion in which Tommy had misused her.

There would be another way. And in the meantime, if Win… She could not bear to think of it. The bread was without flavor, the soup choked her, and she pushed the tray aside.

"I can't eat any more," she told him, apologetic as she realized the trouble he'd gone to for her benefit.

"I'll leave the tea, Ellie. Try to drink some, will you?" He bent to take the tray and she nodded, then watched as he left the room.

He was a handsome man, tall and strong, his shoulders wide, his hands gentle.

And she loved him. With all her heart, she yearned for him, and tears slid from her eyes, blurring her vision as she turned away and buried her face in the pillow.

Win held her throughout the night, an undemanding, loose embrace, his arm across her waist, careful not to brush against the fullness of her breast, as had been his wont on other nights. The morning light awoke Ellie, and she found him gone, the house silent. Stumbling to the kitchen, she found a note on the table.

He'd been called away. Would Ellie please watch for patients during the morning hours and explain that he might be gone until late afternoon? And then his name, the letters firm and masculine, scrawled across the bottom of the paper.

She made a cup of tea, forgoing the coffee he'd left on the back of the stove. A piece of bread made up her breakfast, and she sat at the table, wrapped in Win's paisley-cloth dressing gown, her hair tangled around her shoulders and down her back.

A sound at the back door caught her attention and she rose to answer the knock. Tess waited on the stoop, her eyes anxious, and she scanned Ellie from top to bottom as she stepped inside the kitchen.

"Win asked me to stop by and check on you," she said. "He had to go clear past Matt Darby's place to tend a family that's laid low with whooping cough. A neighbor came by to fetch him early this morning. One little fella died last night, and the rest of them are in bad shape."

Ellie felt a shaft of shame pierce her. She'd been feeling a bit neglected, what with Win's not being here, and it was about time she realized that there were others more needy than she. "I didn't know where he'd gone, Tess. He left me a note, and I just got up a while ago."

"That old biddy, Marie Jamison, was in the mercantile first thing this morning, asking around about you and Doc," Tess told her. "She wanted to know just how long you'd been married, and was trying to discover if you were living as man and wife. As if it was any of her business."

"What did you tell her?" Ellie asked, lifting her cup of tea to sip at the lukewarm brew. She wrinkled her nose at the taste and settled the cup back on the table.

Tess watched, her eyes alert to Ellie's mood, it seemed, for she rose and snatched the tea, dumping it into the slop bucket. "You need a fresh cup, girl. Let me fix it for you." Her quick energy made Ellie wince, and she offered no protest as Tess found the tea cannister and filled the dainty teapot with hot water. Wrapping it in a heavy towel, she brought it back to the table, then sat with a sigh.

"You need one of those tea cozies. I'll have to get a couple for the store next time I place an order. Keeps your tea nice and hot till it's brewed." She bent forward to look into Ellie's eyes. "You look kinda peaked. Doc said you'd been upset yesterday, what with those two coming here and causing a ruckus."

"What did you tell Mrs. Jamison?" Ellie repeated her question, sensing that Tess was putting her off.

"I told her it was none of her business, but that Doc was looking mighty happy these days."

"Why would she want to know that, anyway?" Ellie moved her cup, daubing at a puddle of tea on the table with the edge of the towel. Looking into Tess's eyes was not an option. The fine flush of embarrassment was climbing her cheeks, and the thought of someone speaking so casually about her intimacies with Win was not to be believed.

"I suspect she figured if Win hadn't consummated the marriage, they could arrange for an annulment and haul you off to Philadelphia with them."

"I'd think I'd have something to say about that," Ellie said quietly. "I'm not interested in spending a moment with Tommy, let alone my whole life."

"Maybe that's what you need to tell them, then." Tess reached to pour tea into Ellie's cup, and they both watched the golden liquid, waiting until the leaves settled in the bottom of the cup. "If I had second sight, I could tell your fortune, Ellie," Tess teased gently.

"And if *I* had second sight, I'd never have gotten tangled up with Tommy," Ellie retorted. "Right now, I just wish Win had never put himself into this mess. It isn't fair to him to be burdened with a wife and child he never planned on."

"I don't hear him complaining," Tess said. "And I wasn't joshing about him looking pretty content lately. You're good for him, child. He needed someone to take hold here and offer him a home instead of a place to hang his hat."

Ellie grunted her disagreement. "Huh. He could have gotten that sort of service from a housekeeper. Instead he got stuck with me."

"You're not thinking of leaving him, are you?" Alarm etched Tess's words as she cast a quick, inquiring look in Ellie's direction. "Where would you go? And more importantly, why would you do such a thing?"

Ellie felt tears close at hand. Her eyes blurred and she looked down, unwilling to cry in front of Tess. "I've brought trouble to Win, and all he's ever done is to be good to me. Maybe if I wasn't here, he'd be rid of the hassle with Tommy and his mother."

"Win'll scalp you if you run off and make him worry," Tess predicted. "He cares about you, Ellie. You ought to know that. A man doesn't marry a woman without reason."

"He's kind," Ellie said, blinking back the threatening flood. "And I don't want the Jamisons pestering him." She rose and tightened the belt of Win's robe that had been handy when she arose. "I'm going to speak my piece to them."

Clad in the dress she'd been married in, and wrapped warmly in her coat, Ellie walked into the hotel. Behind the desk, Amos Carlton lifted a hand in greeting. "Good morning, Ellie. What can I do for you?"

"Are Mrs. Jamison and Tommy staying here?" she asked, looking around the lobby. It was her first venture into the hotel, and her curiosity was appeased as she took in the plush furnishings in the lobby and the cut-glass chandelier hanging overhead.

"Why, yes, they are," Mr. Carlton answered. He looked at Ellie cautiously. "Are you sure you should be seeking them out, ma'am?"

Apparently the whole town was in on yesterday's events, Ellie thought glumly. She approached the desk and nodded firmly. "I want to talk to them."

"I believe they're in the restaurant, having a late breakfast," he said, nodding to the wide double doors leading into the eatery.

Ellie nodded and turned, walking across the wide lobby. She hesitated at the doorway, searching out Tommy's familiar figure. He was seated near a front window, and even as she caught sight of him, he looked up and met her gaze. With haste, he placed his napkin on the table and rose, lifting a hand to her.

Her heart thudded unmercifully in her breast as she crossed the floor, weaving between tables, until she reached the place where Marie and her son waited. "I think we need to talk, Tommy," she said bluntly, ignoring the woman whose eyes were sweeping Ellie's pregnant form.

"I'm almost done eating," he said, glancing at his mother.

"Run along," she said quickly. "Unless you'd like to join us, Eleanor." Her smile was edged by white teeth, but her eyes were cold, Ellie thought.

She shivered as she felt the disapproval of

the older woman bent in her direction, and shook her head quickly. "I just want to talk to Tommy," she said politely.

He rose, leaving his half-eaten meal, and followed her lead as Ellie turned, walking toward the lobby. She cast her glance toward the arrangement of plush sofas and chairs in the center of the large room, and nodded in that direction.

"Can we sit down for a minute?" she asked, aware suddenly that her knees were trembling and her heart was beating in an irregular fashion.

"Yes," he said quickly, following her like an obedient puppy, she thought, smothering the laughter that welled up in her throat. Somehow Tommy had taken on a different, more boyish stature in the past months. Picturing him beside Win, she felt a moment of pity for the young man who had once seemed to be a candidate for her husband.

She sat and Tommy scooted the chair he chose closer to her. "We don't need anyone to listen in, do we?" he said with a nervous smile.

"This won't take long," Ellie told him. "I'm not sure why you're here, but Win tells me that you and your mother want me to go East with you. It's not going to happen, Tommy. I'm married to the doctor, and that's that."

"I could give you so much more," Tommy said quickly, his eyes lighting as he reached for her hand. "I'll have a good job. My grandfather wants to give me a position in the family business." He bent closer to her, his voice eager. "You'd like it there, Ellie. There's so much to see and do in Philadelphia, and we're going to be living in a fine house, with servants."

"You aren't listening to me, Tommy," she said patiently. "I'm already married. I'm not leaving Whitehorn."

His face took on a disdainful cast. "I'll match what I can offer against the doctor any day of the week. Besides, your pa might have something to say about it."

"My father?" Ellie was aghast at the idea. "He has nothing to do with my life."

"We can get you an annulment, Ellie," Tommy said, changing his tactics. "I'm the father of your baby. You owe me a certain amount of loyalty, I think."

"What I think is that you're out of your mind," she said sharply. "I don't owe you anything. You left me without a word, before I even knew I was going to have a child."

"My mother knew," he said. "She said you looked like you were in the family way."

"And that's why she hauled you away from here and left me holding the bag." She'd figured it out, and the realization stunned her. That a woman could desert the mother of her grandchild so readily only served to firm her opinion of Marie Jamison.

That Tommy would admit to his own desertion of her was the final touch. His handsome features were repulsive to her as he smiled, a deprecating twist of his lips.

"I know I was wrong, but the point is, I'm back, Ellie. Now that I know for certain we're going to have a baby, I want you to marry me."

Ellie rose, frustration overcoming good sense. "Go away, Tommy. Even if I weren't married to Win, I wouldn't take you. Not on a bet."

His face reddened and an ugly sneer narrowed his eyes. "We'll see about that," he told her spitefully. "I'd think a rousing scandal would make the doctor think twice about keeping you under his roof."

She backed from him, angry with her own stupidity. Why she'd thought she could untangle this mess by herself was beyond belief. Her first mistake had been in thinking she could send Tommy and his mother on their way.

No, she decided glumly. Her first mistake had been marrying Win. Now he was stuck in the middle of a mess, and his good reputation was on the line. Any chance of keeping Win out of the midst of gossip was gone.

Chapter Eight

A message from Win was stuck between the screen door and the jamb when Ellie arrived home. She shifted the package she carried as she spied the ragged piece of paper, and snatched it from its place with eager fingers. Win's angular penmanship scrawled a note, and Ellie's plans for the fresh side pork and dried beans she carried met with disaster. The beans could soak on the back of the stove, but it would be tomorrow before she prepared the meal for Win.

He wouldn't be home for supper after all. Apparently he'd found someone to carry a message to her. The family was sicker than he'd anticipated and he would not leave until a relative arrived to help out. She looked at his slanted signature, tracing the letters with her index finger, aching for his presence.

And wasn't that foolish? She wasn't his first obligation, and it was about time she got that into her head. Taking second place to his patients was a part of the bargain she'd struck with Win. He shouldn't even have to be concerned enough to send her word, she decided. She was splitting his attention, and it wasn't fair to the part of him that was, first and foremost, a physician.

Leaving this house for a while, at least until the Jamisons gave up and headed back to Philadelphia, seemed to be the best idea she could come up with, at least for Win's benefit. He didn't need the distraction of that problem, along with tending patients and making house calls, like the one that was taking up this whole day.

She went through the doorway into the hall and checked inside his waiting room. So far, so good, she noted. Folks were aware that he seldom was available in the hours before noon, and the room was empty.

Sliding a piece of paper from the stack he kept in his desk, she wrote a note. In large letters, she announced that there would be no office hours today, due to illness on a distant ranch.

A straight pin attached it to the screen on the front door, and she tucked the bottom of the paper inside the molding, holding it in place. She backed up a step and read it. Unless the patients had a problem with reading, it should do the trick. In any event, she had the rest of the day to herself, and she had some decision making to do.

Kate would be the one to talk to, she decided, and today being Saturday, she'd be available. Still wearing her coat, she headed out the back door, walking across the lot to pay a visit. Opening the back door, she announced her presence. "Kate?"

"I'm in the parlor," Kate answered. "Come on in."

Ellie passed through the kitchen, noting the breakfast dishes in the pan, and the laundry waiting Kate's scrub board. "I thought you might need a hand," she announced, entering the parlor, where Kate sat in the rocking chair, her son held closely to her bosom.

"Come take a look," she invited. "He's growing like a bad weed."

Looking less like a wizened old man, the

babe blinked up at Ellie, and she laughed spontaneously. "He's so tiny. How can you think he's grown any?"

Kate looked disgruntled. "He has. When I changed his diaper, his little legs weren't nearly so skinny, and his arms are filling out, too." She held up a tiny hand, the fingers wide spread against her palm. "Just look. He's gaining well. Even Win said so," Kate announced, as if that were the final word on the subject.

"I'm not much of an expert," Ellie admitted, bending closer to inspect the infant. Dark hair covered his head, and already he had taken on the look of James, his arrogance well in place as he yawned widely. Ellie's heart turned over in her breast as she felt a yearning heretofore unknown in her life.

That she would be holding just such a child in less than two months was a miracle she could barely believe. And yet with constant reminders from the kicks and nudges inside her belly, she knew it to be true. Hope rose within, and she felt joy cascade throughout her being. No matter how things worked out, she would hold her child, and cherish the tiny life she'd managed to create.

With the help of Tommy, a voice within

her said. What if he had those same feelings about a child of his loins? Was he right? Did she owe him anything at all? Or was she within her rights to deny him the privilege of being a father?

"Tommy and his mother are in town." Blurting the words before she thought twice, Ellie sat down on the sofa.

Kate's eyes widened. "Did they come to see you?"

"No. They talked to Win." Ellie felt the thump of a small foot against her side and her hand rested possessively against the spot. "I went to the hotel and talked to Tommy this morning, though."

"What do they want?" Kate's brow furrowed as she rocked, and Ellie drew in a deep breath.

"I don't want to worry you, but I guess you might as well know," she said glumly. And then she told Kate the whole story. "...Tommy said that Win would think twice about keeping me under his roof, when he was the subject of gossip," she finished, sighing as she contemplated the choice she had made.

"What are you planning?" Kate asked, suspicion alive in her voice. "I don't like the look on your face, Ellie."

"If I'm not here, Win won't be involved. I'm thinking I should leave for a while, until I can be sure that Tommy's given up his silly idea."

"Win will have a fit if you move out," Kate warned. "And I wouldn't blame him. He'll be hurt, Ellie."

"He's got enough on his mind without my problems making his life more difficult."

"You're his wife," Kate reminded her. "Don't you know that he'll come after you?"

Ellie sighed. "I don't know what else to do, Kate." She rose from the sofa and adjusted her dress, tugging at it to cover her stomach. "I need to change clothes and then I'm coming back here to scrub out your wash. I don't want to get this dress dirty."

"You don't need to do that," Kate protested. "James will help me when he gets home."

"Let me help. I really want to," Ellie answered. "It'll give me something to do." She waved her fingers in Kate's direction and left, the sound of mumbled agreement bringing a smile to her lips. It was wonderful to have a woman friend, the first in her life, she realized.

And then there was Tess, who was almost like a mother. It would be hard to turn her back on all this, even for a short while. But if it would make Win's life any easier, she'd do it. Maybe tomorrow she could decide where to go.

Kate's clothesline was filled with diapers and kimonos, along with James's clothing and the sheets Ellie had stripped from Kate's bed. They blew nicely in the cold wind and Ellie tackled the kitchen while she waited for them to dry. She looked forward to pressing out the tiny baby garments, but Kate would have to tell her how to fold the diapers into the right size.

It wouldn't be very long before she'd be doing these chores for her own child, and that thought brought a thrill to her heart. There was much to learn, she decided, her hands busy with hot soapy water and the dishes she'd buried in its depths. But between Kate and Tess, she'd have help to figure it all out.

Kate was tucked up on the sofa, with the baby in a basket at her side, her lap filled with papers she was grading. Ellie felt a shaft of envy for the life Kate had formed for herself. She was so certain of events, so well organized and capable.

And all I'm good for is housework, she

thought, rinsing the plates and setting them on the sink board. The soup she'd put on the stove for Kate's lunch was warmed through, and Ellie found a bowl in the buffet. Carrying it to Kate on a lacquered tray, she pinned a smile on her face.

"Oh, thanks," Kate said, holding out her hands to take the offering. "I could have come to the kitchen, but this is nice, having a day off and you here lending a hand."

Ellie glanced at the sleeping baby. "Do you think I could hold him when he wakes up?" she asked shyly. Her hands had itched to touch the precious bundle.

"Of course you can. You need to get in practice, anyway." She dipped bread into her soup and closed her eyes as she ate the moist morsel. "You do make good bread, Ellie. I didn't realize the difference till I ate yours the first time. Now I realize how hungry I've been for this. I've even sent James to buy a loaf from Ethel Talbert, but it's not as light as what you make."

Ellie's hands were deft as she flew through the work Kate had been unable to accomplish throughout the week. The washing was dried, folded and put away, James's shirts pressed and folded and his trousers neatly creased.

Ellie felt a sense of accomplishment as she surveyed the results of the afternoon. Kate's kitchen sparkled, and on the stove a pot of beef stew awaited James's arrival for supper.

"I can't thank you enough," Kate said from the doorway. She had dressed, complaining mildly that her dress was still snug, and Ellie had rolled her eyes, refusing to be sympathetic.

It was the best part of neighboring, she decided, walking across the backyard to her own kitchen, being with Kate, holding the baby. Even working in someone else's kitchen was a pleasure, when it was for a friend. The sun was sinking low in the sky as she opened the kitchen door and stepped inside, blinking against the gloom.

An unseen hand closed the door behind her and she jolted, turning awkwardly to see her father there, a grim look turned in her direction. "I come to get you, Ellie. Get your things together. You're comin' home with me till we get things straightened out. You got an obligation to the Jamisons, and I intend to see to it you do right by them. That boy came all the way from Philadelphia to make things right with you, and you're gonna take him up on it."

She shook her head. "I'll do no such thing, Pa. This is my home. You have no business being here."

His hand rose, and his palm cracked against her cheek, sending her reeling. She caught a chair and sat down, feeling the nausea rising from her throat. Lifting trembling fingers to her face, she looked up at George. "You have no right to touch me. I'm Winston Gray's wife, Pa."

"You're my daughter, first and foremost, and everybody knows that Doc Gray only married you 'cause he feels sorry for you." His grin was a leer and she felt her stomach churn. "I'm just gonna take you off his hands and see to it you come to your senses."

"What are you talking about?"

"Your bastard's got a daddy right here in town, ready and willing to marry you. All you need to do is tell the doctor you don't want to be his wife. Mrs. Jamison said she can take care of getting things fixed up so you can marry Tommy. And that's the right thing to do," he said judiciously. "He's the father, and he's got rights."

"I'm not marrying Tommy." Her head whirling, she rose, backing toward the hallway door. "Win is my husband."

"Mrs. Jamison is gonna fix everything," her father insisted. "Now you come on with me. You don't need any fancy fixings from this place. There's enough of your old things at the ranch for you to wear." He hauled on her arm, taking her off guard, and dragged her to the back door.

Twilight had fallen, the sun setting behind the far-off mountains in the southwest, and Ellie breathless and confused saw no one in sight to offer her a helping hand. Her father's wagon was around the side of the house, and he forced her to walk by his side, his fingers digging into her arm as he muttered threats beneath his breath.

She staggered and would have fallen, but for the wagon before her. Her hand gripped the wooden sideboard and she felt a sliver jab beneath her nail, the pain barely catching her attention, so great was the ache in her heart. She'd thought to leave, but not this way. Not by force, and certainly not in order to give Mrs. Jamison control over her life.

Win wouldn't even know where she'd gone, she thought. Then, from the corner of her eye, she caught sight of James walking down the road, heading for home. Her mouth opened and she inhaled, but only a small shriek left her lips before George slapped his hand over her mouth, then cuffed her with his other fist.

She sagged to the ground, head swimming, and he picked her up like a sack of oats, and rolled her onto the back of the wagon. His kerchief was called into service as he bent over her, jamming it between her teeth and tying it at the back of her head.

Pieces of her long hair caught in the knot and she winced, tears rushing to her eyes as he tugged roughly, jerking her head back. It was no use fighting, she decided, her body going limp as he knotted a rope around her wrists and tugged them to her back. The wagon bed smelled sour, but she could not hold her head erect, and waves of darkness overcame her feeble protests, as she was wedged between long pieces of lumber and a bale of straw.

Lionel Briggs was a most accommodating man, having slept at the livery stable in order to greet Win's return. "Knew you'd be back sometime tonight, Doc," the man had said in the midst of a yawn. "You'd better get on home. Your missus will be wondering what happened to you."

Win had nodded and obeyed.

The house was dark. Ellie was in bed, he decided, opening the front gate and approaching the house. A piece of paper hung from the screen door, held in place by a straight pin, and he removed it. She must have written a note to let his patients know he was away. Stuffing it in his pocket, he tried the knob, and it turned in his hand.

The door wasn't locked, though that wasn't unusual. He frequently forgot to latch the doors at night. One advantage to having the sheriff living next door, he thought with a wry grin.

The floor creaked beneath his feet as he traveled the length of the hall, with only a short detour to his office, where he deposited his black leather bag. No light shone beneath the kitchen door either, and he frowned. It wasn't like Ellie not to leave him a meal on the back of the stove. He'd thought the lamp over the kitchen table might be burning with a low flame on his behalf. But no scent of cooking met his nostrils, and he shrugged.

It was too late, and he was too tired to eat anyway. With five patients in various stages of whooping cough, he'd spent a long, wearisome day. The arrival of a maiden aunt had relieved him of their care, and with instructions he doubted the woman was in need of, from the way she'd taken charge, he'd left and headed for home.

Now Win sought out his bedroom, opening the door quietly, so as not to disturb Ellie's sleep. He stood just inside the room, blinking as his eyes adjusted to the dark, and listened for the soft sounds she was wont to make as she slept.

Silence greeted him, and he made his way to the bed, frowning as he discovered the quilt still in place, pillows unused, and no trace of his wife. "Ellie?" He spoke her name in the stillness, even as he recognized her absence. The room was empty.

"Ellie?" The bedroom door slammed against the wall as he threw it open, and his feet pounded through the parlor, then across the dining room, skirting the table as he raced to the kitchen. Moonlight traced a path across the floor, shining through the window, and the faint scent of food caught his attention. He moved to the stove where a pot stood on the back burner, almost cool to the touch. Probably the remains from supper, yet she hadn't banked the fire, and that was not like Ellie.

Opening the back door, he stepped out onto the porch, glancing toward the house next door. Perhaps she'd been called over to help Kate, and at that thought he shook his head. Ellie wouldn't walk out the door without leaving him a note. Unless there was an emergency.

He hastened across the yard, almost stepping on a toad that leaped from his path, startling him into a nervous chuckle. And then he stood on James's back stoop, feeling foolish as he rapped on the door. There had to be an explanation for Ellie's absence, but he'd be doggoned if he could come up with one. And waking James was the least of his worries. He'd rather be thought impetuous and a worrywart, than to sit alone and ponder her whereabouts.

A candle glowed beyond the kitchen, and a tall figure stumbled across the kitchen floor, heading in his direction. James swung the door open and peered through the screen door. "What the hell's goin' on?" he asked, reaching to scratch his head. "Something wrong, Win?"

"Ellie's not here, is she?" It lacked the note of inquiry to be posed as a question, and before James responded, Win knew his words were in vain.

"Ellie? Isn't she home?" James shoved the

screen door open. "Come on in. Kate said she was here till the sun went down, doing up the laundry and cooking supper for us." He deposited the candle on the table and in its flickering light, his face took on a look of concern. His jaw clenched as he turned to Win.

"Let me get some clothes on and I'll help you look for her." Trousers half-buttoned, and shirtless, he left the kitchen, and Win sank into a chair at the table.

His mind spun in relentless circles, and there was no rhyme or reason to his thoughts. Behind him, fabric rustled and soft footsteps brushed the bare wooden floor.

"Win?" It was Kate, dark hair caught up in a long braid, her spectacles perched on the end of her nose. "James said Ellie's not in the house." She approached him, placing a hand on his shoulder. "She was here with me, most of the day in fact. She did up the wash and cleaned the kitchen for me. Gave me a whole day to myself. Even cooked supper. But she sure didn't give me any reason to think she was going anywhere else when she left here."

Win reached to cover her hand with his, squeezing gently. "I don't know where to look first," he admitted. "I'd hoped she might…"

His shrug spoke of defeat. "Did she say anything at all to you? About…anything?"

Kate's hand clenched into a fist beneath Win's palm and his gaze shot up to her face. "What? What is it?"

"She told me about Marie Jamison and Tommy coming to see you, Win." Her eyes closed, as if she sought to recall the details. "She said something about not causing you trouble. She thought if she wasn't there, they wouldn't bother you anymore."

"Bother me?" He shoved the chair back as he rose, and it fell to the floor. "She left me because she thought she was too much trouble?" He felt anger surge in a wave of fury. "Where the hell would she go?"

Kate shook her head. "I can't imagine. Maybe to Tess? She'd know this would be the first place you'd look." Her arms hugged across her waist as Kate shivered. "I didn't think she'd leave without any word, Win. She was just upset because Tommy and his mother were making threats."

"Did they come back to the house? Were they bothering her?" And if they had, he'd see to it they were on the next stagecoach to Butte. His jaw was clenched, and his pulse pounded in his throat.

"She went to the hotel to see them," Kate told him. "Marie is talking about getting an annulment of your marriage. And Tommy was insisting on Ellie going back to Philadelphia with them."

Win gripped the back of the chair. "Does Ellie want to do that? Does she care for the boy?" And if she did, how could he let her go? "Damn, they can't get an annulment anyway, Kate. The marriage has been well consummated." That he would blurt out such a statement was a measure of his anger, he thought, but Kate took it without blinking.

"I'd figured as much," she said quietly. "Ellie didn't say, but I haven't seen a light on in her bedroom upstairs almost since you were married."

"She's my wife," Win said, each word forced between his teeth as if he would do battle to prove it. And he would, he realized. Ellie was his responsibility. More than that, she was the best thing that had ever happened to him. He cared for her, deeply…almost beyond measure.

James stalked through the doorway, bending to touch his lips to Kate's forehead. "I'll be back, honey," he said. "I don't know what we can do in the middle of the night, but we'll take a stab at it anyway."

"All right," Kate answered. "Win?"

He turned back, hopeful that she'd thought of something else that might lend a clue in his search.

It was not to be. Kate's eyes glittered with unshed tears, and she shook her head mutely. In two strides he was in front of her, and he hugged her, lending his strength and accepting the embrace she offered.

"Be careful," she said softly, and her gaze swept to her husband. "Check with Tess first."

Tess, wrapped in a dressing gown, answered the door in moments. "I just woke up out of a sound sleep," she said, "and then I heard you rappin' on the door and calling. What's wrong? My heart's goin' a mile a minute. There's something gone awry. I can tell."

"Ellie's not here, is she?" Win heard the hope that laced his words, and watched in despair as Tess shook her head.

"Heavens, no," she said quickly. "Haven't seen her since yesterday morning when she came by the store for a piece of side pork and some beans for your dinner, Win. What's happened?"

"She's gone," James said bluntly. "Win came home to an empty house, and there's no way of knowing where Ellie is. We just took a chance that she might have come here."

"Wish she had," Tess told them. "I know she was upset about Marie Jamison making such a fuss. And madder than a wet hen that Tommy was being led around by the nose."

"Kate said Ellie went to the hotel to see them." Win tamped down his banked anger, and forced himself to consider his next move. "Maybe that's the place for us to go, James. Do you suppose they had anything to do with this?"

"I doubt Amos will let us go stompin' around, waking his guests up in the middle of the night," James said with a frown. "I could do it as a lawman, but I'm thinking we'd might as well wait till morning. If she's there, she'll still be on the premises at daybreak."

"It's almost five o'clock now," Tess said. She pushed open the screen door. "Why don't the two of you come on in, and I'll fix you some coffee and make some breakfast. By the time you finish eating, it'll be time enough to shake Amos out of bed."

She lifted a hand as Win opened his mouth.

"Don't give me an argument, Doc. You probably didn't eat all day yesterday, and if you're plannin' on scourin' the countryside for Ellie, you need something in your belly."

"She's right," James said, and placed a hand on Win's shoulder. "Let's go on in and make some plans."

The rooster crowed twice, paused a moment, then sounded his arrogant message again. Ellie rolled over in the narrow bed and sat up, pushing her hair from her face, her aching arms protesting the movement. She'd spent a couple of hours with her hands tied behind her back, and bouncing around on the flat bed of her father's wagon hadn't helped any. She felt bruised from one end to the other, and as she got clumsily to her feet, she found her legs hurting in numerous places.

Her index finger throbbed unmercifully and she peered down at it in the dim light from the window. A splinter was pressed into the quick, just a bit of it protruding beyond the edge of her nail, and she gripped the bit of wood with her front teeth, easing it from the tender flesh. She was clad in the wash dress she'd worn to scrub out Kate's laundry, and it sagged like a shapeless, dark shroud around her weary body.

Win would be frantic. The thought battered her mind, and she snatched on her coat from the floor, then hastened to the window, thinking to slide it open and climb through to the yard. Too late, she recalled her father with hammer and nails, pounding long spikes to secure it against just such an event. For a moment she was tempted to smash the glass and take her chances with the jagged edges, and then thought better of it. Getting all cut up would be a foolish move, and Win would scold her roundly for such a choice.

Win. She closed her eyes, visualizing him as he must have looked, coming home late last night and searching for her. He would think she'd left him, and the words she'd spoken to Kate rushed to her mind. *I think I need to leave for a while.* She'd said it aloud, and Kate had discouraged her from the idea.

Leaning her head against the cool windowpane, she closed her eyes. He wouldn't know where to look, and if he thought she'd left on her own, he'd be hurt. And hurting Win was the last thing on earth she ever wanted to do. Her love for the man welled up within her and she hugged it to herself, a keening whisper escaping her lips as she thought of his pain.

"Win…" His name was a soft murmur and she pressed her fingers against her lips. "I love you." She hadn't told him, had been afraid of forcing her affection on his already burdened shoulders. He'd taken on so much, marrying her, accepting her child. She couldn't bear to make him feel obliged to return a declaration of love, when his feelings ran more to pity and heartfelt concern.

Now she wished she'd said the words aloud. During one of the nights when his hands had come to know her body, and his mouth had searched out secret places to give her pleasure untold. He'd held her throughout the long night hours, his embrace giving comfort, his kisses bringing her to a knowledge of passion. Maybe he knew. Perhaps his heart was attuned to hers, in some strange way able to sense the deep emotion she nurtured on his behalf.

Behind her the door opened, and her father stood on the threshold. "Get yourself out in the kitchen, girl," he said harshly. "Long as you're here, you might's well make yourself useful."

"I want to go home, Pa," she said quietly. "You had no right to treat me so."

"I told you last night, I got every right in the world. I gave you life and I can make you do as you ought. That boy wants to marry you, and as soon as his ma gets things in order, you're going to behave yourself and do what they want you to."

There was no use in arguing. She'd wait for a chance to escape and run for it. In the meantime, she needed to eat, and if fixing breakfast for her father would keep him off her back, she'd make enough for both of them.

And Win would come. As surely as she knew her own name, she knew he'd find her.

Chapter Nine

"Come on over to the office and we'll decide which area to cover first," James said. They'd eaten, though Win thought it a waste of time. But being rude to Tess Dillard was something he could not bring himself to do, and his good sense told him that she was right on this count.

"I'm all for calling out a posse," Win said, watching as a wagon rumbled past. Both men stepped onto the road and crossed quickly.

"Not enough to go on," James told him. "There weren't any signs that Ellie had been taken against her will, were there?" At Win's quick grunt of denial, James shrugged. "Kate said she talked like she might move out for a while. Maybe she went home last night and decided to stay somewhere else till all this mess gets straightened out. Sometimes women get things into their heads and there's no arguing them out of it."

"She'd have left a note," Win said stubbornly. "I know Ellie well enough to know that." He followed James into the sheriff's office and watched from the doorway as James circled the desk. "If you're going to sit there and plot out a plan, I'll start asking around town, see if anybody saw her after she left your place last night."

"Don't leave yet, Doc. I need to see you first." A voice from behind him took him unawares, and Win looked over his shoulder. Henry Morris was out of breath, his face flushed, and he cast a quick look at the hotel before he prodded Win back into the office. "Best no one sees me with you right now," he said quickly.

"What's up?" James asked, leaning forward over his desk. "You look like you're steamed over something, Henry."

"I don't know if this is against the law or not, and I suspect it could get me into a whole heap of trouble, but I think the two of you ought to know what's going on." Henry caught his breath and aimed his attention at Win. "There's something funny about that woman and that boy."

"That woman?" Win's mind clicked into gear as he heard Henry's words, and he spun toward James. "Marie Jamison," he said abruptly.

James's chair hit the wall and he let loose with a muffled oath as he rounded the desk. "Marie Jamison. You're talking about Marie Jamison, aren't you? And that fancy-pants son of hers."

"Yeah, you betcha," Henry said. "I sure don't want to get in trouble, Sheriff, but I think that woman's up to no good. And I'll warrant the doc don't know what they're tryin' to do."

"Have they done something with Ellie? Do you know where she is?" Win asked abruptly. "Do they have her?"

"Don't know," Henry said, "but I don't think so. They sent a telegram to Philadelphia to some lawyer fella, askin' about gettin' an annulment. That was yesterday, and I wasn't thinkin' what it was all about, till the answer came this morning first thing."

"Annulment." Win spat the word from his

mouth as if it were a vile assortment of syllables. "What lawyer fella in Philadelphia are you talking about? Do you know his name?"

"I didn't pay that much attention yesterday, but when the answer came back it was signed by somebody named Guy Wilson, Attorney at Law."

"Attorney." Win swallowed, willing his breakfast to stay where it belonged. "And they asked him about an annulment?"

Henry nodded, his eyes wide. "He told Mrs. Jamison that he needed a statement that the marriage hadn't been—" His mouth worked as if he could not bring himself to speak another word.

"Consummated." Win had no such compunction. And his anger rose as he contemplated the absolute gall of the woman. "He named me? And Ellie?" he asked.

"Well, the Jamison woman named your wife, Doc. Said that Eleanor wanted an annulment from a man she'd married."

"That's a lie," James said firmly. "You and I both know that, Win. I doubt Ellie left on her own hook. Something's happened. You were right on that account." He adjusted his gun belt and settled the pistol into its holster. "I think we need to hustle over to the hotel."

"Should I deliver the telegram to Mrs. Jamison?" Henry asked.

"I'll take it," James said.

Henry clutched the paper to his chest, and his face reddened as he defied the lawman. "I can't rightly let you have it, Sheriff. By law, I have to deliver it to the person it's intended for." Henry looked like he wished for the floor to swallow him, and Win felt a pang of pity for the man.

"It's all right. I appreciate you coming here," Win said. "Why don't you walk on over and deliver your message and we'll be right behind you?"

"That'll work," James agreed. "And don't you be putting your hands on Tommy, Doc. We can't have anything happening to you."

"If he's hurt Ellie, he's a dead man," Win said, the words calm and chill. Fury cascaded through him like a river of fire, and his fists clenched at his sides. "You coming along?" he said over his shoulder as he followed Henry from the building.

"I doubt if they want her damaged, Doc. They're obviously planning on taking her back East with them." Even as he spoke, James grasped Win's arm, halting his headlong pace. "Just hold on."

"You hold on, James. This is my wife we're talking about." His strides were long, and Henry double-stepped as he scurried across the road, ahead of the two men. He pulled open the hotel door, and, ignoring Amos Carlton, hastened across to the wide, curved staircase.

Behind him, his followers shot through the hotel lobby and up the stairs, James taking two at a time, attempting to move ahead of Win. And then they stood at the door of room 211 and watched as Henry raised a fist to pound against the wooden panel.

"Mrs. Jamison," he called loudly. "I got a telegram for you."

The door opened wide and Marie's mouth gaped as she was confronted by the three men. With a swift shove, she attempted to close the door, but James inserted his boot neatly into the opening and leaned his considerable strength against the woman's lesser weight.

"Don't you want to read your message, ma'am?" he asked in a deceptively quiet tone. "Hand it to her, Henry."

The paper rattled as it exchanged hands, and Marie's face paled, her mouth pinching tightly as she viewed her visitors. "This is my room, Sheriff," she said harshly. "You have no right to cross the threshold."

"Maybe not," James said agreeably. "But then, I think we need to talk about your telegram."

"It's private business." Her chin thrust forward and her eyes glittered with anger, her disdain evident as she clutched the telegram in her fist.

"It's monkey business, is what it is," James said flatly. "You're breaking the law, ma'am."

"I'm protecting the rights of my son," Marie blurted. "That man," she stated, her index finger pointed at Win, "forced my son's fiancée to marry him. We've come to right the wrong and take Eleanor back to Philadelphia with us, where we can have a real wedding, and Tommy can claim his child."

"You weren't so quick to admit the baby was Tommy's when you hauled buggy out of Whitehorn a while back," Win said, his words a savage growl.

"It was a mistake," she said sharply. "One we intend to rectify immediately."

"I don't think so," James said, his words slow and distinct. "I want to know where Ellie is, Mrs. Jamison."

"I don't know what you're talking about,

Sheriff," she blustered. "How would I know her whereabouts? Tommy is gone right now, trying to locate her. I understand she's not at the doctor's home."

"Damn right, she's not." Win's words were a snarl. "What have you done with her?"

Marie smiled with a show of teeth. "Maybe she's left you," she said spitefully.

"I don't think so," Win said, denying her suggestion. "She had no reason to leave." And yet she'd spoken of it to Kate, he thought, and his heart sank.

"What makes you think you can get an annulment?" James asked, and Win watched as the query slammed through Marie's composure.

"You had no right to read my private business correspondence," she lashed, crumpling the telegram into a ball.

"Is Tommy trying to force Ellie to sign a statement of some sort?" James asked.

"Shouldn't be any force involved, I would think," Marie said firmly. "An annulment is the best for all concerned."

"You won't get one." Harsh and firm, Win's words denied her claim.

Marie's eyes widened, and a triumphant smile twisted her lips. "Are you claiming you've consummated the marriage? Do you expect anyone to believe that? The girl's having another man's child."

Win smiled back, his own mouth curving with satisfaction. "The day I married Ellie, I claimed her child. She's sleeping in my bed. Has been for two months."

Doubt colored Marie's expression. "No decent man would…" Her voice trailed off and she shook her head. "I don't believe you."

"You think I care what you believe?" Win asked, his hands itching to shake the woman's arrogance from place. "I want to know where my wife is. And I want to know right now."

James cut in quickly. "Before you deny it, you'd better think again, Mrs. Jamison. You don't want to spend the day in jail, do you?"

Her nostrils flared, and her bosom rose as she inhaled sharply. "Don't try to threaten me, Sheriff. I have connections you wouldn't want to deal with."

"I don't give a damn about your fancy connections, ma'am," James said harshly. "In Whitehorn, I'm the law. And if you don't want to spend the day cooling your heels in a cell, you'll tell us what you've done with Ellie."

She tilted her head imperiously. "*I* haven't

done anything with her. She's obviously left the doctor and gone on her way."

"Where's Tommy?" James asked, scanning the room as he spoke.

"I told you. He's gone to look for Eleanor."

James studied her a moment, then shot a glance at Win. "I'll have Amos keep an eye on things here," he decided. "We'll start with George Mitchum's place."

"Come on, Ellie." Tommy's words were coaxing, and he'd put his best smile in place. "You know you love me. We'll get married and live in a fancy house. My grandfather is intending to give me a good job. He's made an offer, and I'm going to be the one to win the prize. I've got three cousins who think they've got it over on me," he said harshly, "but I've got a head start, with a baby already on its way. All I have to do is prove I'm a family man."

Ellie looked around the deserted farm-yard. She'd guarantee her father was within hearing, but for the moment he'd left her to Tommy's persuasion. "You're not a man of any sort," she answered. "I don't love you, Tommy. I thought I did, back a few months ago, but when you headed out of town and left me holding the bag, I discovered I didn't even like you."

"My mother can make you marry me," he blustered. "She's got a big-city lawyer working on it right now." He stepped up onto the porch where she'd taken her stand, unwilling that he should enter the house.

"She can't make me do any such thing," Ellie told him, refusing to back away. "I'm already married to Winston Gray, and I've got a certificate to prove it."

Tommy grinned. "Maybe so, but the lawyer is checking into an annulment, and we'll be hearing from him today." He reached for her hand and she snatched it from his grasp, jamming it into her apron pocket.

"You can't force anyone to get an annulment, Tommy." Ellie shook her head, exasperated at his foolishness. "I don't want to leave Win. Having my father kidnap me last night was a mistake. When the sheriff finds out about it, you'll all be in hot water."

"Your pa has a right," Tommy insisted. "He knows what's best for you."

"You're crazy, do you know that?" She turned her back on him, and his hand clamped tightly to her shoulder.

"Don't do that, Ellie. Don't turn away from

me. You know I love you." A hint of desperation entered his voice, causing it to tremble.

"That's not true," she said, jerking from his touch. "You don't love me. You never did. You lied to me and made up stories about us getting married, and then walked away." She turned her head and shot an angry look in his direction.

"Your mother figured out I was in the family way, and that was why y'all left town in such a hurry."

He flushed an unbecoming red and shook his head in denial, his gaze refusing to meet hers. "No, certainly not. It just worked out that way. My grandfather had a good job for my father, and we had to move to Philadelphia."

"And now your grandfather has set up some sort of contest? He's offering you a job and a nice house if you can get somebody to marry you and have a baby for you?"

"That's not exactly what's happening." He shifted from one foot to the other. "It's just that he doesn't believe in having people in the bank who aren't settled. This is the opportunity of a lifetime for me."

"Well, you'll have to look in Philadelphia for a woman foolish enough to want you,

Tommy," she said firmly. "Because I'm not going with you."

From the corner of the house, just beyond the porch, George stepped into sight. "You'll do what the Jamisons want, daughter. Or you'll wish you'd never been born."

"Don't you touch me, Pa. I'm a married woman, and you've got no rights over me."

George's eyes narrowed, and his chin jutted forward as he climbed to the porch. His fingers curled into a fist and Ellie ducked, her arms crossing over her belly. In two swift strides, George reached her, thrusting her against the side of the house. With a loud thump, she hit the wooden siding, her head bearing the brunt of the blow, and she blinked, her senses reeling.

"Now get on in the house, and get your things together. If Mrs. Jamison says she needs you to write down your name on a piece of paper, you'd better do it."

"I don't know what you're talking about," Ellie cried, her tears of frustration vying with the pain in her head.

"You have to say that you didn't sleep in the doctor's bed," George said. "That'll solve the whole problem."

"It would be a lie." Ellie's chin lifted as she glared at him.

He hooted, jeering at her with a look of derision. "No man in his right mind would touch you, with you carryin' a bastard like you are. That doctor's got himself a fancy education. You think anybody would believe he'd ever put his hands on you?"

"I just know I won't sign anything," she said stubbornly. "You can go and tell your mother I said so, Tommy." The door slammed behind her as she went in the kitchen, and on the porch, George laid his hand on the youth's shoulder.

"You tell your ma I'll take care of Ellie. She'll sign anything I tell her to."

Ellie watched as Tommy rode away, and then her father turned to enter the kitchen door, and her heart sank within her breast. "I'm gettin' you outta here before Kincaid shows up with his fancy guns and his silver badge."

They'd ridden from town in virtual silence, James leading the way, Win searching his mind for an answer to Ellie's disappearance. "You think she's out there?" Win asked. As they neared the Mitchum ranch, he began second-guessing James's idea for setting up a search. "Maybe we should have split up, headed in opposite directions."

James shook his head. "It makes sense to me that someone took Ellie last night, and the logical person is her father. Don't know why I didn't think of it right away. I suspect I was thrown off by what Kate said, thinking that Ellie was afraid to stay and cause you trouble."

"Here I thought everything was going so well," Win said. "She seemed happy with me, and... Damn, will you look up ahead, James. Is that that young fool coming this way?"

The horse and rider were headed in their direction, and Win felt a surge of anger as he recognized Tommy, although to be absolutely honest, he'd been in a temper for the past several hours. It wasn't a good time for the boy to appear in front of him.

James dug in his heels and rode ahead, halting Tommy in his tracks. "Where you off to, boy?" he asked.

Tommy eyed the two men and tugged at his horse's reins. "Been out lookin' for Ellie."

"You find her?" James asked mildly.

Tommy's gaze veered from the sheriff, and red splotches appeared on his cheeks. "No, I don't know where she is. I was hopin' she was at her pa's ranch, but she isn't there."

James frowned. "Don't lie to me, boy. If George took her against her will, he'll end up in jail."

Tommy shook his head. "You can't do that. He's her pa. He's got rights."

"She's my wife," Win said, his fingers itching to grab hold of the youth and shake the stuffings out of him.

"Not for long," Tommy jeered, hatred flaring in his expression. "My mother has a lawyer workin' on it right now."

"Working on what?"

"I'm the one who should have married her," Tommy said stoutly. "It's my baby she's going to have."

"You should have thought of that a long time ago," James told him. "You're a little late on the draw, son."

"Way too late," Win chimed in. "And for the life of me, I can't figure out why you and your mother came all the way out here to get her. Aren't there any girls in Philadelphia? You didn't treat her right when you were keeping company with her. Why on earth do you want to cart her clear across the country now?"

"I'm not sayin' any more about it," Tommy muttered. "I'm heading back to town. Mr. Briggs let me take this horse, but he said he needs it back this afternoon."

Win looked after him as Tommy sent his mount into a gallop. "You going to let him leave?" he asked James, exasperation roughening his voice.

"Don't have much choice," James said. "He hasn't done anything for me to nail him." He lifted his reins and his horse set off at a trot. "We need to check out the Mitchum place, Doc. If she's not there, we'll put out the word and notify all the ranchers in the area to be on the lookout for her."

George was suspiciously welcoming, allowing them to search the house without a word of protest. "I told you she wasn't here," he said, his leer triumphant as James and Win exited the back door. "You're wastin' your time, Sheriff. The girl's no good. Probably ran off with the first man that looked cross-eyed at her."

Win held his tongue, his every sense alert to Ellie's presence. Even the room upstairs had held a faint scent he identified as hers, and it had obviously been hastily straightened, the quilt askew on the bed, the rug rumpled. "She's been here," he said quietly.

"Yeah," James agreed. "But she's not here now."

"How about the barn?" Win glanced toward that huge structure.

James stepped off the porch. "We can check it out."

"Where you headin'?" George asked, rounding on them as they set off toward the barn.

"Just going to take a look out back," James said. "You got some objection?"

The man shook his head. "Look all you want. She's not here."

And Win felt, with sudden conviction, that the man was telling the truth. "He's moved her," he said. "He's had someone take her off somewhere."

"Where are your hired hands?" Win asked.

"Out on the range, most of them," George said, waving a hand to the north, where open range held hundreds of head of cattle. "They're roundin' up the calves, bringing them closer in for the winter."

"They staying out in your line shacks?" James asked, and George grunted a reply.

Win swallowed his query, willing to let James be the spokesman here. Was a line shack somewhere a young woman might be held against her will? The idea festered as he gave the barn a perfunctory once-over, climbing the ladder to the hayloft, even though he was dead certain Ellie would not be found there.

James made the rounds of tack room, empty stalls, and even the bunkhouse, where empty cots and the odor of stale food told Win that the men were long gone. "You here alone?" Win asked George, who'd followed them with a smug expression on his features.

"Just me and a couple of my men, enough to tend to chores." His chest puffed out like a banty rooster, and his fingers slid into the back pockets of his trousers as he grinned, an evil expression that turned Win's blood cold. That this man had Ellie in his power was almost too much for him to tolerate.

"Come on, Win." James tugged at his sleeve, his face seeming carved of stone from the mountains. Win obeyed, helpless in his anger, yet aware that James would not give up on their quest. "We'll ride out, and talk later," James muttered, checking his stirrups as he readied himself to mount his horse.

Win followed his lead, lifting into his saddle with an easy movement, catching up the reins in his hand and turning the gelding to the east, where the road to Whitehorn stretched like a narrow ribbon past the fields and pastures of the area ranchers.

"I'm sorry, Miss Ellie." Tall and sinewy, Al Shrader lifted Ellie from the back of his horse and held her firmly as she attempted to catch her balance. "I have to do what your pa says. And he wants you kept out here for a while."

"You'll end up in jail for this," Ellie threatened, although even to her own ears, her voice was a tenuous thread, her weariness causing her to stumble as she wrenched from his hold. "Don't touch me." She shuddered as he ignored her protest and bent to lift her, carrying her into the rude line shack.

It was small, with a potbellied stove, a wide set of bunks and a table with three mismatched chairs. She remembered it from her childhood, when, as an adventure, she'd ridden out to play house in it, during a hot summer afternoon. And then been severely berated by her father for making him search for her. Now it was even more dilapidated, the furnishings ragtag and worn by years of hard use by a series of cowhands during roundup time.

She slid from Al's arms, aware that he treated her with unaccustomed care. "You gonna be all right?" he asked, standing in the doorway, watching as she slumped onto a chair. "I'll get some water from the stream for you."

He snatched up a bucket from the corner and stepped out the door, then turned back. "Don't try to leave, Miss Ellie," he said, his voice reeking with apology. "It'll be worth my scalp if you run off. I don't want to tie you up, but I will if I have to."

She couldn't run anywhere right now if her very life depended on it, Ellie thought glumly. Her arms and legs ached from the harsh treatment at her father's hands last night. And now she'd survived a ride behind Al's saddle, and her thighs were sore, abrasions burning where her bare skin had rubbed the sides of the horse.

Yet all of that paled next to the pain she bore in knowing that Win might think she'd left him on her own hook. *I think I need to leave for a while.* She'd spoken the words to Kate, voicing aloud the fear of bringing shame to Win. And Kate, being the honest soul she was, would no doubt repeat those words, maybe gentling them for Win's hearing. But nothing could buffer the pain such a statement would bring him.

Maybe he wouldn't be looking for her, Ellie thought, her head lifting as fear settled deep. Maybe he'd think it was good riddance. And she couldn't blame him if he was angry with her. She probably appeared to be ungrateful, after him being so good to her. The fact that he'd even taken her to his bed must be making him feel like he'd made a terrible mistake, claiming her as his wife. No doubt his pride was stung....

Surely it must be. The whole town would know she was gone by now. And Win must meet and greet them with full knowledge that his wife had left him.

"Here you go, Miss Ellie." Al toted the bucket of water inside, placing it on the floor near the table. "If you want to wash up, I got a towel in my pack."

His feeble attempt at comfort did not go amiss, and Ellie nodded her thanks, grateful for the man's eagerness to please.

"Just don't try to leave, ma'am." Al stood in the doorway, hesitating as if he must gain some small measure of assurance from his captive. "Your pa holds a tight rein, you know that."

"I know." Ellie spoke the words dully, unwilling to antagonize the man who had at least offered her a small amount of kindness. Al cast her a last glance before he went outside, and she looked around the small room. A supply of firewood stacked against the wall assured her of warmth against the coming hours when the winds from the mountains blew across the acres of open range.

Surely there was food here. Even her father would not expect a woman to survive with no sustenance, she decided. Rising, she opened a heavy chest, built from rough wood and equipped with the necessities of life for whatever stray cowhand might require its contents.

A small kettle and a chipped coffeepot comprised the cooking supplies. A tin of coffee and an assortment of cans assured her she would not starve over the course of the next day or so. Several plates and cups nestled in one corner of the box and spoons were scattered amid the supplies. A large knife had been left to open the cans with, and Ellie wiped it off on her skirt before she placed it on the table.

"I'm gonna see if I can roust up a rabbit for you, ma'am," Al said, entering with a dingy towel and a bedroll from his pack. "I brought you some matches, in case there's none here. We ain't used this shack all summer, but there's enough stuff to do you for now."

"Thank you," Ellie said, limping to take Al's offerings. "I'll put on a pot of coffee if you'd like some."

"Yes, ma'am," he said agreeably. "I'd appreciate that." He turned away, and then spoke quietly, as though the confidence he shared was better said without peering into her face. "I won't be sleeping in the shack, ma'am. I'll bunk outside."

He stepped from the building and Ellie watched him go, aware that she could have done worse with several others of her father's hands. Al was the best of the bunch, and it was pure dumb luck that he'd been the one forced into bringing her here. With no warning, he'd been presented with an unwilling woman, and told to get her as far from the house as he could.

She'd shed her coat and her shawl lent a certain amount of warmth as she pulled the door closed, keeping the chill air outside the shack. The stove door swung open readily, and she piled kindling atop the ashes, then added small sticks of wood before lighting a match. It caught, flaring up and she watched for a minute, then added larger pieces, thankful that the wood was dry and plentiful. The damper was open, and the fire drew well as she closed the door on the blazing warmth.

Hopefully, it wouldn't be too cold once the sun went down. Perhaps Al had an extra bedroll to keep him warm. If not, she'd invite him in by the fire. The beds were stacked atop one another, and she spread Al's bedding on the bottom shelf. It left a lot to be desired, she thought, remembering the lovely quilt and the clean, crisp sheets she'd slept on in Win's house.

Win. Her heart ached as she whispered his name, and she closed her eyes, wishing she could send a message, let him know she had not left of her own accord. He was a city man, although he'd said he could ride a horse. Surely James would begin a search, but on his own, Win would have no way of searching out her whereabouts, no knowledge of the countryside. And perhaps not even the urge to seek her out. A shaft of pain struck deep inside as that thought entered her mind.

"Ma'am? I didn't see any sign of game nearby, but there ought to be enough provisions in that box to keep you fed till tomorrow." Al stood in the doorway huddled within his coat, and a draft of cold air swept past him. "I'm gonna make a fire and set up camp out front. If you have anything extra to eat, I wouldn't mind a bite."

"The coffee is beginning to boil," she told him. "I'll open a couple of cans and see what I can heat up."

He ducked his head, pulling the door shut behind himself. And she was alone.

Chapter Ten

Win's fingers held the stethoscope against Birdie Watkins's chest and he closed his eyes, determined to listen intently to the sound of a heart beating in an irregular rhythm. And succeeded only in remembering the first time he'd seen Ellie, when he'd pressed the bell just where the swell of her breast began.

Ellie. Her face swam before his closed eyelids and he blinked, erasing the vision.

"What do you think, Doc?" Birdie was peering up at him, her wrinkled cheeks and rheumy eyes giving away the advanced age she attempted to conceal with powder and touches of rouge. She was a dear, and he made no attempt to conceal the affection he felt for her.

"I think you're pretty spry for a forty-year-old woman, ma'am," he said dryly, and then waited for her cackle of laughter.

She didn't disappoint him, her eyes squinting nearly shut as she swatted at his hand. "Never mind the shenanigans, Doc," she chortled. "You know as well as I do that I'll never see eighty again."

"Would you want to?" he asked, grinning at her cheerful countenance. "You're not in any worse shape than most women your age, Miss Birdie. And a lot better off than a good share of them."

"Still gettin' around," she bragged. "Don't even use the cane some days."

"You need to get your feet up, several times a day," he admonished her. "Elevating them will relieve the swelling. And don't forget to take your medicine."

She wrinkled her nose. "Makes me run to the outhouse."

"That's the idea," he said, patting her shoulder.

"Doc?" Birdie looked up at him, her good humor held in abeyance for a moment. "I heard your new wife's come up missin'. Is that the truth?"

"Bad news travels fast, doesn't it?" He folded the stethoscope and placed it in its case. "Since night before last," he admitted.

"She's a good girl, that Ellie. I knew her ma. Old George's a hard man, Doc. I wouldn't be surprised if he had somethin' to do with it." Birdie lifted herself from the chair, and grasped her cane with both hands. Her jaw firmed as she met Win's gaze. "That Jamison woman came back to town, didn't she?"

Win nodded, then turned aside, unwilling to bare his pain. Marie Jamison had ridden down the road in a buggy only an hour ago, with James not far behind.

"She's a conniver, that one," Birdie said. "And that boy of hers ain't fit for hog slop."

A grin twisted Win's mouth as Birdie spewed her opinion. He turned back to face his patient and rested his palm on her narrow shoulder. "We'll find Ellie," he said quietly. "I appreciate your concern, Miss Birdie."

She nodded and turned to the door. Win held it open for her and watched as her grandson lent an arm, helping her from the office and leading her down the path to the road.

Frustration rode him hard, and he slammed his fist against the doorjamb. *"Damn."* Folks needed him, and in all good conscience he couldn't close his office. Yet working at the job of doctoring while Ellie might be in dire straits was almost more than he could tolerate.

A flash of color caught his eye, and he watched as a woman entered his gate and walked with a stilted gait toward his front door. Through the glass her appearance was blurred, but he recognized the untamed curls and voluptuous form. Cilla, the woman he'd tended at the Double Deuce saloon, come to call.

The knob turned and she entered the wide hallway, blinking as her gaze encountered him, there in the office door. "Hey, Doc," she said, her words overlaid with a seductive tone.

"Good morning, Cilla," he answered. "Problems?"

She hesitated, peering past him into the waiting room. "You got patients in there?" she asked.

He shook his head. What Cilla wanted was a puzzle he wasn't willing to explore this morning. He'd done all he could for her, and she'd be fine if she steered clear of the man who'd misused her.

"Can I talk to you?" Her laugh was low, a husky sound, and Win caught a glimpse of feminine beauty beneath the carefully applied powder and paint she used. "There's something you oughta know about."

"Sure. Come on in," he said, resigning himself to her confidences. He led the way into the waiting room and waved at a chair. "Sit down, Cilla. What can I do for you?"

"I owe you, Doc. That's why I'm here."

He shook his head. "No, I was paid for my services when I tended you. You don't owe me anything."

She looked at him, her mouth crooked, her smile restrained. "You were nice to me. Even knowing… Well, you know what I mean. I'm not fit company for decent folks in this town. But you treated me like a lady, and I appreciate it."

"I believe all women should be treated fairly," Win said. "You're a woman."

"Well, nevertheless, I heard about your wife takin' a hike, and I thought you ought to know that she had some help."

Win jerked, as if a branding iron had seared his flesh. "How do you know that?"

"A fella told me." Her mouth compressed. "I can't say any more about it. But I thought you oughta know that she didn't run off on her own."

"Who?" Win demanded. His heartbeat was rapid as he stalked across the room, reaching to jerk Cilla from the chair. "Who spoke to you about Ellie?"

She shook her head. "It's worth my neck if I tell you that," she whispered, her eyes wide as she beheld his fury. "I can't say, Doc. I shouldn't even have come here, but I wanted you to know that she's all right. Nobody's hurtin' her."

Win loosened his grip on Cilla's arm. "Did her father take her?"

"I don't know." Stubbornly, her chin jutted out. "And that's the God's truth."

He looked down at his hand, and deliberately opened his fingers. "I'm sorry. I hope I didn't bruise you."

"That's nothin', Doc." She bit at her lip. "I wish, just once in my life, somebody would've cared about me the way you do about that girl." With a flourish of skirts, she rose and turned to the door. "I've got things to do. I just wanted you to know—"

"Thanks, Cilla," Win said quickly. "I appreciate you coming by."

He watched her leave. James needed to hear

about this. Whether it would do any good or
not, every scrap of information needed to be
funneled in the sheriff's direction.

"Marie Jamison went out to the Mitchum
place to see George," James said bluntly. "I
watched and waited till she left, and it didn't
take long, only about ten minutes. She was
madder than a wet hen when she climbed
back in that buggy. Hollered at that boy of
hers, and that buggy shot out of George's
place like a bat outta hell."

"Then what?" Win asked.

"I just stayed in that grove of trees about
halfway up his lane and watched him ride
off."

"You didn't follow him?"

James shook his head. "He had a couple of
his men with him, and I had nothing to go on,
Doc. I don't think he'll hurt Ellie with that
many men looking on. And if he's got her
hidden somewhere on his ranch, we could
look all day and half the night and not come
up with any answers."

"So now what?"

"Now," James said, adjusting his gun belt,
"I go talk to Marie." Grimly, he pointed a finger at Win. "And you stay put, Doc."

"Do you think Cilla knows what she's talking about?" Win asked.

"Those women hear most everything that's going on. You'd be surprised what secrets they know."

"They're gettin' real antsy," George said, watching Ellie with a malicious grin. "I want you to sign this here paper, daughter," he said, approaching the table, slapping an envelope before her.

"I'm not signing anything, Pa. I already told you that." Today was the second day in this hellhole, and the misery and boredom of her stay had only served to stiffen her backbone. But Ellie knew the signs of George's anger well. She had only to deny him her obedience and he would attempt force.

Still, she could not betray Win or the vows she'd made before God and the minister in Whitehorn. Her mouth tightened, even as she clutched her hands together to still their trembling. "I'm not going to swear to a lie."

Her father hooted with derision, his face reddening as he thumped a fist on the table. "That man wouldn't take you to his bed. He's not that desperate for a woman, not with half the females in town givin' him the eye."

George's voice was harsh and strident, and he bent closer, mocking her with jeering words. "You can't make me believe he'd take a second look at you."

"He married me, Pa." Ellie's whispered reply was a small measure of defiance. George had ever been capable of making her feel small and worthless, and today was no exception as he focused his hateful gaze on her. And yet Win had thought her worthy of his attention, and she clasped that knowledge to her bosom like a talisman of hope.

"He just needed somebody to cook and clean," George said shortly. "Now you got a chance to go to Philadelphia and live in a nice house and wear fancy clothes, and you're turnin' your back on it. What's the matter with you, girl?"

"I don't want to go anywhere but home to my husband." It was the cry of her heart, and Ellie felt tears well up as she gave it voice.

"I've been about as nice as I'm gonna be, girl. I'll tell you this. Either you sign that paper, or I'll see to it you don't have a baby. One good kick in the belly oughta get rid of the bastard for you."

"What's in this for you?" she wailed. "How much money is Mrs. Jamison going to hand you if I sign her paper?" She wrapped her arms protectively around her unborn child and faced George with tears running down her face. "How can you be so ready to sell your own flesh and blood, Pa?"

"You're not worth anything to me, girl. You're about as useless as your ma. She couldn't even give me a son, the only time she ever carried to full term." He stepped closer and Ellie cringed from the sight of his uplifted fist. "You'll sign that paper, or I'll settle your hash right now."

From the doorway of the shack, Al Shrader's voice added persuasion. "Go on and write your name, Miss Ellie. You don't want to stay out here, do you?"

She looked up at Al, whose face was troubled as he glanced back and forth from George to his daughter. "Miss Ellie?" He nudged her with a nod, and George looked back at his cowhand, dismissing him with a glare.

"Get on outta here, Shrader. This is none of your concern." Shoving the envelope closer to Ellie's hands, George took a pencil from his pocket and slapped it atop the document. "Sign it…now," he said softly.

The tone bore more threat than his shouts and curses, and Ellie picked up the pencil.

With trembling fingers she opened the envelope and slid the folded sheet of paper to rest on the table. Holding it open, she scanned the carefully printed words. Simply, it stated that her marriage to Winston Gray had not been consummated, and even as she watched, George's thick index finger pointed at the bottom of the page.

"You sign it right there," he ordered, then watched as she obeyed. Snatching it from her, he folded it and replaced it inside the envelope, then tucked it into his shirt pocket. "Now just behave yourself, and you'll be outta here by tomorrow."

Ellie watched him leave, heartsick at the thought of her own father hating her so much. Simply because she had not been the son he wanted. Her hands spread wide across the rounding of her belly, and she felt the movement of her child. No matter the outcome, she would love this babe. Of that she was certain. Whether boy or girl, it was her child.

And, God willing, she would find a way to outwit the man who'd forced her into this predicament.

The moon played tag with the clouds and Ellie watched from the single window the shack boasted. Al Shrader lay in his bedroll close before the campfire, and she focused on his long form, wondering how long she dared watch and wait. He'd been silent after her father left, gathering wood for his own use, apparently satisfied that Ellie's supply was adequate.

She'd opened beans and watched as he heated them in the can, atop hot coals in the circle of his fire. Offering to share them with her, he'd only shrugged at her refusal and returned to sit cross-legged on his blanket. Now she wished for something warm in her stomach to ease the ache of hunger.

The wooden box offered another can of beans and she opened it with a knife, then ate the cold, congealed contents with the single fork the shack boasted. Tasteless in her mouth, they served to fill the void in her stomach, and she forced herself to eat the entire contents before shivering and setting aside the can.

A crust of bread was left, wrapped in a dingy towel, and she closed her mind to thoughts of where it had been and whose hands had touched it, biting into the stale chunk and chewing it into a wet paste in her mouth.

Still watching from the window, she calculated the distance to the small stand of woods just south of the shack. If she could open the door noiselessly, and if Al slept soundly, she could reach the trees within a minute. The cold wind was her only deterrent, and Al had reminded her quietly that a storm was coming on, with snow likely by morning.

"Don't try runnin' off, Miss Ellie," he'd said, accepting the beans from her hand. "You'll only freeze out there tonight, and it's a long haul to town. Farther than you could walk in a day and a night."

She'd nodded and looked aside, unwilling for him to read the thoughts that must certainly be rampant in her gaze. If there was any way that her signing that document of Marie Jamison's would put her in a bad spot, she'd take her chances with the cold and wet, rather than allow herself to be dragged across the country with Tommy. And how they'd manage that was something she didn't want to face.

If there was a way to force her into it, Tommy's mother would find it.

And if Win knew she'd signed that blasted piece of paper, he'd probably wash his hands of her. Not for anything in the world would she have that happen.

The blanket was warm, and she carried it, rather than wrapping it around her shoulders. Time enough for that once she got away from the shack. Her shoes were sturdy, her dress heavy, and her heavily knit shawl would keep her head and shoulders warm.

Her final trek to the bushes before dark had made her more than aware of the cold wind, and she shivered as she thought of the discomfort she faced. There was no help for it. She'd die before she put herself in Pa's hands again. And with that thought, she gathered her meager belongings and worked at opening the door.

It swung wide with barely a creak, and she stood framed in the doorway, watching as Al's motionless form gave assurance that he slept soundly. Pulling the door closed, she stepped from the shack, careful to stay on the course she'd plotted earlier, before the sinking sun had cast the ground into deep shadow.

She stepped cautiously, avoiding a windfall of leaves, detouring past a fallen tree limb, then gliding into the darkness beneath the stand of trees. Barren limbs overhead offered little protection, but the pines to the south would give her shelter once she crossed the next open area. Shivering, more from fear of discovery than cold, she set off, careful to walk where the ground seemed clear, pausing only to untangle herself from an occasional bush that snatched at her skirt.

Her breath became puffs of vapor as she hurried into the grove of pine trees and she cast a look over her shoulder to where the glow of Al's fire cast crimson shadows on the rough walls she'd escaped. He'd be angry with her, once he woke to find her gone, and she knew he'd set off in pursuit. His horse was staked near the creek, and she wished fervently that she'd been brave enough to make a circuit of his camp and steal the animal.

There was no use in regrets. Now she must try her best to head toward town, and to that end, she focused on the range of mountains whose peaks gleamed white in the moonlight. To the west, clouds gathered, and she ignored their portent, trudging forward, keeping the highest peak directly before her as she made her way.

With the blanket in place around her shoulders, covering her coat and with the shawl over her head, she was warm. She walked at a steady pace, sighting a herd of cattle to the west, following the contours of the land, over dried grass and around clumps of underbrush. The moon sank below the horizon and still she walked, stumbling over rocks, falling twice before she could catch herself.

Her hands stung from the second fall, when she'd landed on scrubby, rough ground, and she forced her aching legs into a regular rhythm, counting out the paces in her head. The glow of a small fire caught her eye, and she detoured a bit to the east, lest she be seen against the horizon, should a cowhand be on watch and cast an eye in her direction. The men were on the open range, and she knew her chances were less than zero if they should discover her.

Perhaps she should find a place to rest. Once the sun came up, the cold would abate. Only walking at a steady pace had kept her from falling prey to the freezing temperatures, and even at that, she could barely feel her fingers, so intent were they on holding the blanket closed over her coat.

Beneath a tree, she found a windfall of leaves, and she gathered them around herself, curling on the ground, covering her body as much as she was able. She buried her face within the warmth of the blanket and drew her legs up. Beneath her the ground was cold, but she huddled next to the wide trunk and felt her eyes close, unable to hold off the deep weariness that seized her.

"Win." She breathed his name softly, taking comfort from the single syllable, and then repeated it in a sighing whisper.

"Win."

"George's in town." James strode up the path to Win's front door, halting at the foot of the front steps. "I'm glad I caught you before you left. I just saw him ride up in front of the hotel."

"I've got a woman in labor, clear the other side of Caleb's place," Win said. "Her husband just left." His jaw clenched as he drew in a deep breath. "I'll send Ethel Talbert out there. She can hold the fort. It's Mary Beth's third baby. I doubt she even needs me, as quick as she told me she delivered the last one."

He opened the door and carried his black bag into the inner office, then returned to where James waited. "Give me a minute to talk to Ethel, and I'll be with you."

"I'm on my way to the hotel," James said. "I just wanted to catch you, in case you were heading out this morning. Come on over and wait in the lobby. I'll find out what's going on."

Win made short work of alerting Ethel. "I know it's late in the day, Ethel, and I wouldn't ask you to make the trip if it wasn't important for me to stay here."

"You go on, Doc," Ethel said quickly. "Do whatever you have to. I'll use the buggy and head out there. Mary Beth won't take long, and I think her mama's there, anyway." She grinned widely. "I'm not the best at the business, but I can still catch a baby, I guess. Driving the buggy at night isn't a problem for me. I can always leave a note and have Harry ride out there on his mare and wait for me."

Her smile faded and her brow furrowed as she took a step closer. One hand touched his arm and she squeezed gently. "You'll find her, Doc, and everything's going to be all right. I get feelings about such things once in a while, and I just know that Ellie is gonna be back here before you know it."

Win attempted a smile, and knew he'd failed miserably as Ethel's eyes filled with tears. "If we knew where to look, it'd sure help," he said quietly. "I feel like I'm fighting the wind, with nothing to go on and not a clue to work with."

"I'll guarantee her pa's got her hidden someplace," Ethel told him. "He's always been a hard nut to crack, that George. And tough to work for, they tell me. But I've never known him to be downright mean before this." She shook her head. "I remember El-lie's mama. We grew up together, and Eleanor just kinda faded away after she married up with George. He took all the joy out of her."

Win's mind filled with the image of Ellie, and as if she were beside him, he heard the words she'd spoken. *I think I'm dying....* It wasn't hard to understand what Ethel's mem-ories consisted of. Ellie had lacked that vital ingredient, had been empty of the joy of liv-ing. Until she'd moved, bag and baggage, into his upstairs room.

Yet even those days of contentment waned beside the vision of her awakening to desire and the pleasure of their coming together in his big bed.

The thought of never loving Ellie again brought unexpected pain to dwell within his chest, and he was torn by the knowledge that he'd come to love her, only to regret that she was unaware of his discovery.

"You all right, Doc?" Ethel peered up at him, her gaze so full of sympathy he could hardly bear its warmth.

"Yes." He drew back, forcing a smile to curve his lips, nodding a reinforcment of his affirmation. "I'm fine, Ethel. Tell Mary Beth I'll stop by to see her as soon as I can."

He turned away, closing the gate behind him as he headed toward the hotel. The wind had turned sharp during the past hours, and he thought anew of Ellie, his mind dwelling on her comfort, praying that she not be alone in the cold. Wherever she'd been stashed, surely there was a stove or fireplace for her comfort. The idea of Ellie in distress tore at him, and he ached, the pain sharp as he strode alongside the road.

Wagons and buggies were sparsely lined up along the boardwalk, their owners occupied with the late-day order of business. Most of the townsfolk were busy with the supper hour, but several men called out to him and lifted a hand in greeting as Win stalked almost the length of town. He barely noticed, aware only of the confrontation to come.

The Hotel Carlton wore its elegance well, with fresh paint outlining the windows on the second floor, and scalloped trim edging the roofline. It was wasted on Win, his eyes focused on the wide double doors that opened at his touch. Amos's head tilted and his eyes narrowed as he watched Win enter his lobby. "Good evening, Doc," he said amiably, coming from behind the desk to halt Win's progress.

"Where'd the sheriff go?" Win asked tersely.

"He's in the dining room," Amos told him. "Maybe you ought to wait here till he finishes talking to those folks."

Win cast him a scornful look. "They're talking about my wife," he said quietly.

Amos nodded. "I figured that, Doc. But it won't do any good for James to be worrying about you when he's in the midst of that mess."

"Is George Mitchum in there, too?" Win's glance took in the archway beyond which white tablecloths covered with glass and china waited for diners to appear.

"Mrs. Jamison and her boy are having a late supper, and George just got here a while ago. Give James a few minutes, Doc." Amos laid a hand on Win's coat sleeve, and his words were coaxing. "This whole thing is the talk of the town, and there isn't anybody gives two hoots and a holler about anything

but getting your wife back where she belongs.
I heard a couple of men in here last night,
talking about facing George down, but I don't
think it's going to do any good."

"You think he's got her, don't you." It was
a statement of fact, and Win felt the helpless-
ness wash over him again as he thought of
Ellie being held against her will.

"If he has, James will have him up on
charges, I'll guarantee you that," Amos said
bluntly. "Right now, I'm thinking he's treading light, lest Ellie get caught in the middle."

Raised voices erupted as Amos spoke,
and Win jerked from the older man's grasp,
stepping to the archway, and turning his gaze
across the dining room. James's hand was
clenched in the front of George's shirt, and
the man was half out of his chair, his face red,
his voice booming.

"You got no right to demand anything of
me, Sheriff. Ellie's my daughter, and I'm responsible for her welfare. She's signed that
paper of her own free will, and I'm going
to see to it that she marries the father of her
baby."

"The hell you are," Win said, his voice
quiet, yet strong enough to reach the four per-
sons who were silenced by his words. James

released his grip on George's clothing and spun to face Win.

"Take it easy, Doc," he said quietly, but with no effect on the man who strode across the dining room, skirting the elegant table settings, his footsteps silent against the fine carpets. If Winston Gray looked the part of an avenging angel, that impression was nullified by the savage words he spoke, phrases a heavenly body would never utter.

Even James appeared taken aback by Win's outburst, and three ladies at a nearby table made a hasty exit within moments of his entry. Amos Carlton watched in dismay as Win shoved the sheriff to one side and flattened his hands on the table, bending to speak directly into George's startled face.

"If you've hurt my wife, I'll kill you, Mitchum. If I hang for it, I'll see you dead and burning in Hell for what you've done. And you two…" He turned as if on a swivel, and his glare flattened Marie Jamison where she sat. Tommy scooted his chair back from the table and would have risen, but Win reached across to grasp his shoulder, shoving him back into his seat.

"Don't move. Not one inch," he grated. "I don't care what kind of fancy lawyer you have. I don't give a damn how many documents George makes Ellie sign. The bottom line is still the same. She's my wife and she's gonna stay my wife. You two can get your butts back on the next train east out of Butte, and forget about making any more trouble here. I've got access to more lawyers than you can shake a stick at, Mrs. Jamison."

Marie's face whitened at his words, but her bluster was undaunted. "You can't threaten me and get away with it. You're nothing but a two-bit, small-town quack."

Win's smile was cold, and his eyes pierced beyond the woman's facade of elegance. "This two-bit, small-town quack has more influence than you have any concept of, madam. One telegram to Saint Louis will settle your hash in no time flat."

Marie's nose tilted upward. "If you were so almighty influential, you'd have been in touch with your Saint Louis contacts before this," she challenged.

Win's mouth twisted and his words were loaded with contempt. "I left this up to the law until now, but that's finished. Besides, I didn't think you were worth the effort. But you've gone too far. If George has forced Ellie to swear to a lie…"

He turned toward George, his gaze fastening to the envelope beneath the man's broad hand. Without hesitation, Win grasped George's arm, gripping it tightly and lifting it to snatch the envelope.

"Here, you can't do that," George shouted, wrenching from Win's grasp.

"I just did." Stuffing the paper into his pocket, Win turned to James. "That's it, Sheriff. You can do whatever you have to. I'm going after my wife, and this bastard—" he pointed his index finger at George "—this bastard is going to tell me where she is."

George's face turned ashen as Win pulled him from his chair. "You going to let this man break the law, Sheriff?" he blustered. His hand slapped against his side, and he looked down quickly as Win's fingers wrapped with cruel force across George's hand, and then peeled it from his holster, gaining possession of the weapon.

"You won't need this," Win said, thrusting it into his pocket. "I have mine, and one's enough."

"You're carrying a gun, Doc?" James asked mildly, his look disbelieving. "I never knew you to be a violent man."

"I'm from a big city, Sheriff," Win answered. "A man isn't safe in some parts of town at night, and the hospital where I learned my trade was smack-dab in the middle of hell, as Saint Louis knows it. Every man with any respect for his own skin carried a weapon."

George looked from one man to the other, his eyes narrowing, as if he gauged the sheriff's influence over Win. "He can't just haul me out of here," he told James. "This is against the law. I'll swear out charges."

James shrugged, stepping back from the table. "I can't see that the doctor is doing anything illegal, Mr. Mitchum." His gaze swerved to Marie, who had begun to rise. "I think I'd stay right there, if I were you, ma'am," he told her.

"I'd like you to do something for me, James," Win said, his eyes fastened to George, even as he spoke to the sheriff. "Send a telegram to Winston Gray, Senior, in Saint Louis, in care of the law offices of Gray, Gray and Annison. In as few words as possible, let my father know that I have need of a good lawyer. I'm sure he'll handle things from there."

He looked directly into George's face as he spoke. "Tell him to notify my uncle Stephen in Washington, D.C., that I'm in need of legal advice. I'm dead certain the senator will reply with no delay."

"Your uncle's a senator? In Washington?" George asked, and then snorted his disbelief. "That's a good one. Anybody with those kind of connections wouldn't be stuck in the wilds of Montana, takin' care of cowhands and patchin' up saloon girls."

"Really?" Win smiled, his teeth flashing as he considered the man before him. "We'll have to see about that, won't we?"

Chapter Eleven

James clutched Win's shoulder. The sun was well on its way below the horizon and the street was almost empty of vehicles, only John Dillard and Harry Talbert visible, standing on the sidewalk in conversation.

"I can't let you shoot the man," James said, a grin easing the tension on his face.

"I won't," Win answered agreeably, "as long as he cooperates."

George was silent, looking from one to the other of the men who spoke of him as though he didn't exist. And then he smiled, a triumphant leer that returned Win's anger full force. "I knew you wouldn't let him get away with his high-handed notions, Sheriff," George spouted. He jerked his arm from Win's hold, only to have James grasp his other elbow.

"Sorry to disillusion you, Mitchum," James said. "I'm with Doc all the way on this one. You're going to tell us where Ellie is, or spend the rest of your life in a jail cell. You've got a choice. I may not shoot you, but if you give me too much trouble, I just might turn Doc loose on you again."

George was silent for a moment, his glare including both the men. Although he was a strong, sturdy man, he was obviously bright enough to realize his position. James and Win were tall men, broad-shouldered and physically fit, and neither of them appeared willing to back down.

"You're on your way, George," James said bluntly, hauling the man in his wake as he strode across the road to where the jailhouse shared equal space with the sheriff's office. George blustered, but James, unheeding of his threats, hustled him into the building and across the shadowed office to where two cells waited, empty but for a cot and slop bucket.

Win watched from the doorway and James, after locking the cell door, turned back to him. "Why don't you go on over and send those telegrams. Tell Henry Morris to give them first priority."

Win nodded and turned, making his way to the telegraph office. The thought of wiring his family was distasteful, but for Ellie, he would do anything in his power to relieve the situation. The second wire was simple. Sent directly to his uncle, he issued a plea for legal intervention, citing Marie's lawyer by name.

"How long before I get a reply?" he asked Henry, who had been hauled from his supper table.

"Probably in the morning, Doc, I'd think. I'll let you know as soon as an answer arrives."

Win stalked back to the sheriff's office, the lantern lighting the square room, where James sat waiting for him. "What do you think?" Win asked in a low voice.

"Let's go and get a bite to eat," James told him. "Kate will be holding supper for me. I'll warrant she has enough for two."

They walked the length of the road, cutting across lots to the back street where their houses were located. "He won't last past morning," James predicted. "He was fuming about his men not knowing what to do without him there, and I told him he could go on home as soon as he led us to Ellie."

"Will there be trouble, you holding him this way?"

James looked at Win, peering through the darkness. "What the hell's the use of being a Kincaid if I can't have a little clout? You think anybody in town's going to listen to George's ranting and raving? He can holler all he wants to. They hired me for a job, and if they think I'm not doing a good one, they can hire somebody else."

He grinned. "Do I look worried?"

"No, I'd say not." Win kept pace with him as they walked past the silent house that contained his office and home. "It's been intolerable without Ellie there."

"I think you're in love with the woman," James surmised, stepping onto his back stoop and pulling the screen door open. He turned inside the kitchen to survey Win's weary countenance. "Am I right?"

"Does it show?" Win attempted a smile, but failed miserably. "I guess I didn't realize it until a little while ago. You know I care for Ellie. I have from the beginning. But when I think of my life without her, I can hardly bear it." He pulled a chair from the table, leaning heavily on the back of it.

"James?" Kate came through the doorway, her gaze seeking her husband. Then as if assuring herself he was safe and sound, she turned to Win. "Any news about Ellie?"

"Yeah," he said harshly. "Her daddy made her sign some sort of paper." With a quick movement, he pulled it from his pocket. "I forgot I had it," he said, opening the envelope and unfolding its contents. His hand groped in his shirt pocket, retrieving his reading glasses.

It was simple. A document written in hand, signed by Eleanor Gray. Win's heart clenched in his chest as his index finger touched the rounded script that formed her name. This was the second time he'd seen Ellie's signature, he realized, the first being when she'd signed their marriage certificate. That had been a joyous occasion, with her eyes alight, and her fingers trembling on the pen. Now those rounded letters that spelled her name attested to a lie.

"Here it is, James," he said, tossing it on the table as if it were a detestable object. As so it was. "If George doesn't agree to take us to her in the morning, I'm going to pound it out of his hide," he said harshly, sliding the wire-rimmed spectacles back into his pocket.

James picked up the document and cast a warning look at Win. "You'll have to steal the keys to his cell first, Doc."

"I can do that," Win told him, and even as he spoke, his hands clenched into fists.

"I know where James keeps them," Kate said quickly, moving around the table to clutch at Win's arm.

"Kate…" James spoke her name quietly, and she responded with a flash of dark eyes through her round spectacles. And then he grinned. "The problem is, you know all my secrets."

She nodded, then stood on tiptoe to kiss Win's cheek. "Sit down," she told him. "And you, too, James. I kept supper hot."

The front door vibrated like someone's horse had gotten loose and tried to kick it in, Win thought, stumbling through the hallway to answer the summons. The sun was bright and he shaded his eyes as he opened the heavy door, recognizing Henry's eager face.

"Got news for you, Doc. You got a reply from Saint Louis, another one from Washington. First time I ever got a wire from the nation's capitol," Henry said in awe. "And from a real live senator. He said you're his nephew and his godson. How about them apples?"

"I am both of those," Win agreed, opening the screen door to reach for the sheets of paper. Henry handed them over and rocked on his heels, a wide smile telling of more good news.

"Mrs. Jamison got a wire from her lawyer. Came in just as I was leavin' to deliver these. Wanna see it?" He waved a third piece of paper between two fingers, and Win looked up, his attention divided as he absorbed the message he'd just read.

"Marie got a wire?"

"From her *attorney-at-law*," Henry said, drawing out the syllables. "Said he could not be a part of her illegal actions. He didn't even try to save any cost on words. Told her she was treading on thin ice."

"My uncle interceded," Win said. "And..." He scanned the second reply quickly. "My mother is coming here, probably before Christmas, it says." He looked up, his heart beating rapidly, his mouth dry as he considered the impact of his own words. "My mother is coming here, Henry. I haven't seen her in over a year."

"Hope that spells good news, Doc," Henry told him. He backed from the stoop and waved the third message. "I got to deliver this one to the hotel to Mrs. Jamison. She's gonna be hoppin' mad, I'll betcha." With a final wave, Henry hurried through the gate, headed toward the hotel.

"Win? Is there news?" James strode across the yard from his house, one hand touching the top of the low fence that divided their front yards, as he scissored its height easily.

"Yeah, I'd say so." Win handed him the two messages and James read quickly. "I don't think there'll be any doubt of George's co-operation this morning," he surmised. "He knows he's way out of his depths, and this should cinch it."

Within an hour, three horses were moving at a steady gallop, George in the middle, his face set in lines of stoic anger as they approached his ranch. Several men hurried across the yard as the horses approached, and George hailed them.

"What's wrong? Don't any of you know how to do chores without me here to give orders?" And then he looked sharply at the tallest of the men. "Why aren't you out at the line shack?"

"We were just gettin' ready to ride out, boss," Al Shrader said. "I lost her trail, and I came back for a couple of hands to help."

"What are you talkin' about?" George said sharply. "What trail?"

"Ellie left the shack last night. I went to sleep and she got away." Al looked shame-faced as he gave the bare details. "I tried to pick up her trail this morning, but I lost it in the woods. Figured I'd better get some help before I wasted any more time on my own."

"Ellie ran off?" Win's words were harsh, and his flesh felt the chill of winter air as he thought of Ellie, alone in the far reaches of the ranch. "Was she warmly dressed?"

Al shook his head. "Yeah, she had a shawl, I think and her coat, and she took a blanket. But damn, it was cold last night. There's frost all over the ground, hid her footprints real well."

James took charge, and Win allowed it readily, his own thoughts circling as he visioned Ellie, frozen beneath a tree. Inhaling deeply, he put the image from his mind, catching James's orders as he shot them in rapid fire at the men.

"...every man available. Spread out and check every hollow, every bush. You, Al, take us to the shack and we'll go from there."

She was cold, so cold, right to the bone. The blanket was stiff, damp from the harsh temperatures, and she shivered beneath its weight. Her toes were aching, her fingers unfeeling, and she tucked her hands beneath her armpits for warmth. Rising was a problem, her legs cramped, her body weary.

The birds were singing though, and through the bare tree branches above her, the sun cast a filtered warmth to where she'd slept. Ellie lifted her face to its light, inhaling the cold air, and then coughing harshly as it caught in her throat. She stood, leaning against the tree trunk, more weary than she'd ever been in her life.

"I've got to find Win," she whispered, as if the words were a talisman that would enable her to take one step forward, then another, until she found her way from this stand of trees, and across the open range to Whitehorn. "Win..." She whispered his name, remembering that she had done so as sleep claimed her during the night.

How long had she slept? she wondered.

Surely not more than a few hours. It was hard to recall how long she'd walked, stumbling through the brush, across what seemed like miles of rangeland. Win would be so worried. Her heart ached as she thought of his concern. If only he knew that she had not left of her own accord.

Surely he was searching for her. Certainly he would not believe her father's lies. And in that moment she recalled signing the document. "I had to do it, Win," she murmured, as if he were there to hear her denial of choice.

"I love you, Win. I'm coming home." The words were spoken in a slow cadence, her feet matching the rhythm she set, and she spoke them over and over. She bent almost double several times as harsh bouts of coughing beset her, and her tangled hair fell around her like a shroud. Her chest ached now, and she slowed her pace, every indrawn breath an effort.

The sun traveled higher in the sky and the frost covering the ground melted, making the grass slippery beneath her boots. She stumbled, fell, and rose again, casting the blanket aside as warmth welled within her. Her shawl went next, Ellie dragging it behind her for almost a mile before her fingers loosened and she dropped it on the ground.

"I'm warm," she whispered, her hands touching hot cheeks. "My hands are cold, but the rest of me is so warm." The words were mumbled, as she shrugged from her coat, and she staggered as she wove her way toward the range of mountains in the southwest. It seemed she'd been focusing on them for hours now, so long she couldn't keep track of the time. They faded in and out of her vision, and she halted for a moment, shading her eyes as she blinked, attempting to concentrate on the snow-capped peaks.

"I think I'm sick, Win," she said calmly. "I think I'm really sick."

A voice called her name and she stopped. "Now I'm dreaming that you've found me," she said with a rusty laugh. "I must be hearing things."

Her slender form swayed in the sunlight. Win cursed beneath his breath. The blanket had been found first, a crumpled heap of wool, and Al Shrader had identified it as the one he'd left for Ellie's use. Her trail had been simple to follow, small boot prints in the frost, and then the white covering had thawed in the sunshine, and they'd relied on Al's tracking ability.

The shawl and then her coat had been discovered only fifteen minutes ago, and both were draped over Win's saddle. He clutched at the shawl's woven strands, as if by so doing he could feel Ellie's warmth. Without it, she had to have been cold. The air carried the chill of winter, and he feared for her life.

The sight of her in the distance brought her name from his lips, and she turned. His horse obeyed his command and Win surged ahead of the three men he accompanied. James was with three others, spread out across the range to the east. Al Shrader lifted his rifle, pointing the barrel to sky, and fired three shots. The prearranged signal would alert the rest of the men.

They'd found her.

She was a small bundle in his lap. Even with the added weight of her pregnancy, Ellie fit across his thighs, and he turned her carefully, her face buried against his chest. His right hand left her hip and slid to her belly, his sensitive fingers pressing through layers of dress and blanket against the mound that was her child. A small movement nudged his palm and another lifted his index finger.

It was enough. The baby was active. As for the woman he held, she had collapsed into a small heap of dark dress and long, tangled hair as he approached. Al Shrader had signaled his intent, leaping from his horse to lift her into Win's arms.

"Here, Doc." His muscular build had made it simple, lifting the woman to lie across Win's lap, then his hands had gathered the long length of dark hair and bundled it under her head. "I'll get my bedroll," he'd said gruffly and in moments had wrapped the rough fabric around Ellie's limp form.

Now they headed for town, James and Win riding abreast, George and his ranch hands on their way back to the Mitchum place. "George's going to appear before the judge," James said, breaking the silence. "I'm going to charge him with kidnapping."

"Will he go to jail?" Win asked the question, but his heart wasn't in it. Ellie was safe, and in his arms. His anger at George had been put into the back of his mind, once his hands had touched her, once his mouth had brushed against her forehead. Now his concern was that she be put to bed, where he could treat her. The heat from her body radiated to his own flesh, his legs and chest warmed from the fever that claimed her.

She coughed and the rattle in her lungs

sent shards of fear through him. Pneumonia was almost certain. Pleurisy would complicate things, and surely she would need every ounce of strength she possessed to fight the fever. He clutched her closer and she moaned, her whisper calling his name.

"I'm here, sweetheart," he said, bending to press his lips against her temple.

"Thirsty," she murmured, restless now in his arms.

"You got a canteen, James?" He should have brought his bag along, he thought, but even that didn't hold a container of water. Besides, his instincts already knew her condition. The stethoscope wouldn't tell him anything he didn't already surmise.

"Yeah." James loosened the thong holding his canteen to the saddle horn and reached to place it in Win's outstretched hand. They slowed their horses by mutual consent and Win lifted Ellie's head a bit, loosening the canteen lid with his teeth, then tilting a bit of water onto her lips. She swallowed and licked at her lips.

"More," she whispered, her eyelids fluttering.

Win brought his horse to a halt, his left hand controlling the reins. He shifted Ellie in his arms and offered the canteen again. She drank, long, deep swallows, then shook her head and sighed. He handed it back to James, along with the cap, and bent low to whisper his wife's name.

"Ellie? Can you hear me, sweetheart?"

She nodded, just a faint movement of her head, and her voice sounded raw, rough and harsh. "I knew you'd find me, Win. I prayed."

"So did I, honey," he told her, rearranging her in his embrace. "We're on our way home. I'll take care of you."

"My father." The two words were barely audible.

"I know," Win said quickly. "I know what happened, honey. Al told us. He felt bad that you'd gotten away. He was afraid he'd be responsible if something happened to you."

"No." She shook her head, a minute movement, as if she would deny Al Shrader's blame.

"Hush, honey," Win said. "We'll be home in no time." And she relaxed against him, her breathing harsh now, her body burning with fever.

"Let me take a turn, Doc." Ethel placed her hand on Win's shoulder, and he shook his head.

"Thanks, Ethel," he said, "but I can't leave her." His big hands plunged the cloth into a basin again and he squeezed the fabric, then placed it on Ellie's forehead. A small towel lay in the basin and he wrung that out, then wiped her slender arms with its rough texture.

She was so warm, so feverish, he despaired of an end to the watch he'd taken upon himself. That Ethel would be vigilant, that her hands could tend to Ellie as well as his own, was a given. But walking from this room was not possible. Hovering over his head was the fear that she might slip from him, that her illness might take a final toll if he should look aside, even for a moment.

And so he lingered, dozing fitfully for long minutes at a time, only to rouse with a jolt and bend once more to his task. He exposed her legs, lifting the gown to her knees, and washed the blotched skin with the towel, worried by the heat that rose from her fevered flesh. For those few seconds she was cooled, and her skin was pale, until the fever returned in full force, and her body lay lax and limp before him.

"Let me bring you something to eat, Doc," Ethel coaxed, kneeling beside the bed, taking Ellie's hand in hers. She bent her head to kiss the slender fingers, and a tear fell against the palm. "She's such a sweetie, Doc. This just isn't fair, that she should be so sick." She looked up at Win. "Do you suppose the baby is safe?"

He nodded. "It's past the point of formation a long time ago. Now he's just growing, sapping Ellie's strength with his demands on her system. Babies are selfish little creatures, Ethel. They don't care about anything but the nourishment they require to live and grow. We need to control the fever if we can. That's our worry now, so that the baby won't be harmed."

"You need to eat, Doc. I've made some good soup, killed one of my laying hens this morning."

"I appreciate that," Win told her, tearing his gaze from Ellie to focus on his neighbor. "I never did ask you about Mary Beth's baby."

Ethel laughed softly. "She's fine. That little girl just squirted right out into my hands, like she'd been waiting for me to walk in the room. Mary Beth laughed at the look on my face. I had her all cleaned up in no time, and when I left she was nursing real good. I looked over the afterbirth, and it was all there."

Win nodded. "I appreciate your help. I figured it would be an easy birth. And from what I've heard, you're pretty good at it."

"So long as it all goes according to plan, I do just fine," Ethel said. She bent her gaze on Ellie again. "I'm anxious for this one to come to term. I'd like to be here to help you, Doc. She's a fine girl." Her eyes met his and her smile trembled. "You think she's gonna be all right?"

He nodded wearily. "I have to believe that, Ethel. It's all I've got to lean on right now."

"The folks over at the church have got a prayer vigil going on for Ellie. They've been taking turns at the altar since yesterday afternoon when you rode in with her. There's a couple of the ladies who had something to say when you married Ellie, and they're right there with the rest of them, taking a shift, even during the night hours."

"I'll never be able to thank folks enough," Win whispered. "Now, if their prayers are answered, I'll be forever grateful."

"I'm prayin', too," Ethel said gruffly. "Even when I was stirrin' the soup. I figure when she wakes up enough, we'll need to have something ready for her to eat. She's lookin' scrawny already, like she's been doin' without food."

"I don't think she's eaten since she was taken from here. Maybe something that night at her father's place, but then she was hauled out to a line shack for a day and a half before she got away. I suppose there was food of sorts there, but she's looking peaked, all right."

His hand measured her cheek, and he felt and saw new hollows where there had never been any sign of laxness in her flesh before. Her hands were fragile seeming, her nails holding a bluish tinge. "She's had a hard time breathing today," Win said. "I've propped her up to help a little, and I was thinking to set up a pan of water, so the steam would ease her lungs."

Ethel stood quickly. "I can do that, Doc. I'll bring a wide basin in and add boiling water every so often to keep the steam rising. We'll just empty it when it fills up and start over." As if she were pleased to have a task assigned, she hurried from the room and Win bent his head, his hands holding one of Ellie's in his clasp.

Her fingers twitched, then stilled, and he opened his eyes, shaking his head. He'd dozed off for a moment, and yet… Her fingers twitched again and he inhaled sharply. "Ellie? Are you awake?"

Her eyelids fluttered and she moaned, a soft sound of distress that tore at his heart. "Win? Where are you?" Her eyes opened, the soft brown gaze meeting his, and he felt tears spring to blur his vision.

"I'm here, honey. I'm right here." He lifted her hand to his lips and pressed a kiss upon the hot skin. "Are you in pain?"

She looked puzzled and then shook her head. "No. Just so hot, Win. My mouth is dry."

He lifted her and offered water from a glass he'd had ready. She sipped, swallowed and gasped. "Hurts to swallow," she whimpered, but opened her mouth for more of the cool water.

"Drink as much as you can," he told her. "The fever has dehydrated you, Ellie. You need all the fluid we can get into you."

She nodded, wincing as the water slid down her throat. "Baby?" She murmured the single word, but it spoke volumes to his ears.

"The baby's fine," he assured her. "The heartbeat is strong, and he's been moving a lot."

"She." It was a soft whisper, but his lips curved in a smile at its message.

"You think you're going to have a girl?" he asked, his words teasing.

She nodded. "All right?"

Did he mind? "As long as you're healthy, I don't care what it is, Ellie," he told her firmly. He held the glass up to her mouth again and she obligingly swallowed, then turned away.

"Enough." She relaxed against his forearm and he bent over her, his embrace loose. The need to hold her went far beyond the urges of his body. She was precious to him, this slender waif he'd married. His very being yearned to come to her aid, to give her his own strength, to spread arms of comfort around her and infuse her with healing.

"I love you, Ellie." He'd waited too long to speak the words, but they begged utterance, and he repeated them again. "I love you, sweetheart. Can you hear me?"

Her lids fluttered open again, and a wistful smile curved her lips. "Really, Win? Do you really?" As though speaking those few words took every ounce of strength she possessed, her eyes closed again, and she was limp against him.

"Oh, God, Ellie. I've said every prayer I know, and made every promise in the book, if only you'll get better. I want to spend the rest of my life with you, sweetheart."

She sighed, nestling closer, and he lifted her, quilt and all, to hold her in his arms. His head bent and he placed his face against hers, then stilled as he became aware of dampness against his skin. Perspiration beaded her brow, and Win picked up the towel to wipe it from her flesh.

"Win?" A masculine voice caught his attention and he laid the towel aside.

"I think her fever just broke," he said, looking toward the doorway as James cleared his throat. "Now we have to watch for chills."

"How's she doing? Kate sent me over."

"This is the first she's been awake," Win said. "And she's lucid. But there's a lot of congestion. I'm going to have Ethel make up a mustard plaster to put on her chest."

"Let me pass, Sheriff." Ethel was behind James, and he stepped inside the room as she entered, a large pan of steaming water in her hands. It was heavy, and she carried it with care, depositing it on the floor on the far side of the bed. "I'll make a tent with sheets," she offered. "Thought I'd bring in a couple of chairs and sort of aim the steam in Ellie's direction."

"I'll help," Win said. "She needs to be closer to the steam anyway." He bent to place her in the middle of the bed, covering her with the sheet and light quilt. She opened her eyes again and smiled, then inhaled, coughing harshly. "I want you to lay on your side, facing the steam, Ellie," Win told her. He propped a pillow behind her back and she did as he asked, breathing heavily.

Within minutes, they'd formed the makeshift tent, and Win settled down to watch. "I'll bring some soup in a while," Ethel told him, and he nodded. Footsteps alerted him as James came closer, but his gaze was unmoving, and only the pressure of the sheriff's hand on his shoulder told him of the man's presence.

And then he was alone with Ellie, his breathing matching hers, his mind racing as he sorted mentally through his medicine, deciding on the best course to take.

The steam helped to ease her breathing. Ethel sliced onions thinly, and brought in a dish filled with the pungent vegetable, then dumped them in the water. "That'll make her breathing even better," she told Win. For hours she carried one panful after another of steaming water to keep the moisture rising.

Win coaxed Ellie to drink, offering the water he knew would be soaked up by her dehydrated body, water the child she carried would use with no care for the woman whose blood held the nutrients needed to sustain life.

At dark, Win lifted Ellie again in his arms and coaxed her to sip small amounts of broth from a spoon. Ethel had cut up the noodles, making it easier for Ellie to swallow them. It was an effort, but as though she recognized Win's concern, she accepted the spoon he offered and swallowed the warm broth, persisting until her eyes closed and she could no longer stay awake.

She slept then, and Win edged her over, lying on top of the quilt behind her. It was late in the night when she woke him, her body shivering, her teeth chattering and he rose quickly. Stripping from his outer clothing, he slid between the sheets and gathered her close, warming her with his own body's heat. The quilt was warm, and Ethel had built up the fire in the kitchen, allowing the heat to pour through the rest of the house.

Yet Ellie trembled with the dreadful chills

that would not release her body from their frigid tentacles. The sun was rising as she shivered for the final time, and settled in his embrace, relaxing against his warmth. He rose to pull on his trousers, wanting to be prepared should he need to call Ethel for help.

And then he slept, holding her, waking when she coughed, offering her water and keeping her covered lest the chills take her once more. He roused when Ethel came into the room to change the water in the steam bath, and assured her that she could leave and seek her own bed. And was not surprised when the woman shook her head in silent refusal, knowing Ethel possessed a bent to aiding those in need. Win slept soundly then.

But by full daylight, Ellie's temperature rose again.

Chapter Twelve

"Ruth Kincaid is here?" Win blinked, reaching for his spectacles, as if the close-vision strength of his lenses could somehow bring Ethel into focus. They only served to blur her pleasant features, and, feeling foolish, he placed them back on the table beside Ellie's bed. He'd read medical books, one after another, until the print blurred before him, and then, when the rooster crowed from behind old lady Harroun's boardinghouse, he'd placed his head on the pillow beside his wife and closed his eyes.

Now Ethel stood in the bedroom doorway, patiently waiting for him to gather his wits.

"She's come to take a look at Ellie, Doc," Ethel said softly. Her gaze settled on Ellie's face, pale once more after the battle against fever during the night hours. "She's not lookin' too good, Doc. I'd think you'd take any help offered."

"Yes." Win staggered to his feet, the weariness of sleepless nights making him weave as he retrieved his spectacles once more, tucking them in his shirt pocket.

"Shall I have her come in?" Ethel asked.

Win looked back at his wife, discouragement running rampant as he thought of what her illness might do to the child she carried. Certainly, he would welcome help, in any form, he decided.

"Send her in," he said quietly, then turned to rinse his face in the basin of water he'd used to bathe Ellie with during the night hours. His hands held the towel over his eyes for a moment, rubbing gently against the closed lids, before he placed it beside the china bowl.

Ruth Kincaid stood before him, her dark eyes fathomless as she watched him. A faint smile touched her lips, and she stepped closer, one slender hand reaching to touch his forearm beneath the rolled-up, wrinkled shirt-sleeve. Her fingertips brushed lightly across his skin, barely disturbing the pattern of dark hair, yet he felt a warmth against his flesh that radiated from within the woman herself.

Bowing his head, he spoke her name. "Ruth. I wasn't expecting you."

"I know," she answered, the soft syllables almost musical in their tone. "I came to help," she said quietly. "Will you allow me?"

Win felt ashamed of his hesitation of only moments past, nodding quickly, all too aware that Ruth's presence must often have been brushed aside as of little value. And even more so the healing hands she offered. Too many folks on the frontier gave little credence to the Indian way of life, understanding even less the worth of herbs and mystical knowledge that was pervasive in lives of the Native Americans.

Winston Gray was not one of them. He'd learned much in medical school. Even more in his short time in Whitehorn. The Cheyenne woman known as Ruth Kincaid was in fact the wife of Caleb, James's cousin, and Win had heard her described as a healer. If that was true, if she could somehow lend her talents and gifts to heal Ellie, he would gladly step aside.

Covering Ruth's hand with his own, he led her to the bedside, and together they watched Ellie, silence stretching between them like a bond. Her fingers squeezed his, a gentle farewell to his touch, and she knelt beside Ellie, a graceful movement that offered Win a view of dark hair, woven with wildflowers into a braid. The scent was refreshing, bringing a trace of meadow into the sickroom, and he wondered at its significance.

It mattered little, and he harnessed his roving thoughts, directing them to the examination Ruth began to conduct. Her hand picked up Ellie's and she wove their fingers together, palms touching, bending her head to lay her cheek against Ellie's breast. She was silent, barely causing a movement of the bedcovers as she listened to the heart tones.

They were slow now, Win knew, for he'd placed his fingers on Ellie's throat upon awakening. It was a welcome relief from the rapid pulse that had fluttered against his ear during the time of fever.

"Eleanor?" Ruth's whisper was sweet, melodic, and, as Win watched, Ellie's eyelids fluttered in response to the calling of her Christian name. A name he'd never used.

"Eleanor? I want you to come back to me,"

Ruth said quietly. "I'm going to give you some tea to drink and you must be awake to swallow it."

At the doorway, Ethel caught Win's eye, her hands wrapped around a cup, steam rising from its contents. "It came to a boil, Mrs. Kincaid," she said, a measure of respect obvious in her voice.

"Good." Ruth rose to take it from Ethel's hands, and she placed it on the small table beside the bed. Then she turned to Win. "May I be alone with her?" Her eyes were placid, as if she would accept the denial of her request, should it be given. And, indeed, Win hesitated, unwilling to allow Ellie from his sight.

"Doctor?"

He nodded, turning to the doorway, and Ethel stood aside as he walked from the room.

"Do you need me?" Ethel offered Ruth her assistance, and Win was not surprised to hear the negative reply she was given.

That Ruth was a healer no longer seemed questionable, not even to his educated mind, which automatically rejected such a fanciful notion. That she insisted on being alone to perform her acts of healing, or magic, or whatever it was called, was not a surprise. The Cheyenne were a private people, proud and intelligent. He would take whatever Ruth was able to offer, and be thankful.

The kitchen was filled with fragrance, coffee blending with bacon, corn bread and soup beans—a tempting aroma that brought his empty stomach to immediate attention. "I think I'd better eat something," he told Ethel, who had followed him from the bedroom.

She bustled from cupboard to stove, then to the table, bearing a bowl of beans and a plate of corn bread. Bacon edged the golden offering, and beside it she placed a full cup of coffee. Steam rose and Win inhaled its scent. "I didn't know I was so hungry." He smiled at Ethel as he picked up a fork she'd provided.

"Stands to reason," she said shortly. "You've been in there for a long time, Doc. If you don't take care of yourself, you'll fall sick, and then where will Ellie be? Not to mention the rest of the folks who depend on you."

"It's only been since yesterday," he said, inhaling the scent of coffee, eager for its effect on his body. He would be renewed by eating, refreshed by the coffee, able to stay awake for the rest of the day.

From the doorway, Ruth spoke softly to

Ethel. "Will you take this basin and empty it out?" she asked. "Then I'd like you to boil water on the stove and add the herbs I'll give you. The steam from them will help."

Ethel moved quickly, eager to do as she was bidden. "It won't take long," she told Ruth. "I've just built up the fire real good, and the teakettle is full already." She lifted the heavy, iron container, hefting it to gauge its contents. "Won't take long at all," she assured Ruth again, placing the teakettle atop the hottest portion of the stove.

Win glanced back at the doorway, unsurprised at Ruth's absence. The woman walked on wind, he'd heard. What did surprise him was the warming of his heart with the knowledge of her presence in his home. Bending over his plate, he ate, even past the point of the assuagement of his hunger, knowing he would take little nourishment throughout the day.

A knock at the back door drew his attention, and he pushed from the table. No doubt this was a call for his services, and he was torn by the conflict. Whether to leave Ellie and go to help some other patient, or refuse his helping touch to another in order to stay by her side. A rancher stood outside the screen door, hat in hand, an anxious look on his face.

"Doc? My boy fell from the hayloft and it looks like his leg is broke."

Win shook his head. "I can't leave my wife," he said quietly, and though it pained him to issue the blunt refusal, he was adamant. "You'll have to bring him here."

The rancher, Clive Madison, nodded briefly. "I heard she was pretty sick, Doc. So I brought my boy on the wagon. Will it be all right if I carry him inside?"

Win nodded, stepping toward the hallway. "Come this way," he said, holding the door open. "Bring the boy in the front way and I'll see you in my office." Clive walked past him, and on out the front door, leaving it open. The wind blew through, caught by the draft from the kitchen, and Win closed that door quickly, lest the heat disappear.

He made a quick detour to his bedroom, where Ruth knelt beside the wide bed, and his glance within was brief. Sensing his presence, Ruth looked up, and her smile was serene. "I'll be in my office with a patient," he told her. "Clive Madison's boy broke his leg."

Ruth only nodded in acknowledgment, and, satisfied, Win turned away, his mind filled with the image of Ellie's form beneath the quilt. Her eyes closed in slumber, her hands in Ruth's, she was safe, at least for now. And how he could be so certain of that was a puzzle he set aside to ponder after his immediate work was done.

The boy's leg was a simple fracture, and Win splinted it, wrapping it firmly, then gave instructions for his care to the anxious father, who hovered over the boy as though he would take the pain upon himself. Jeremiah was ten years old, a winsome child, determined to be brave in the face of the unknown, and Win's heart was captured by the freckled face and fiery head of hair.

"You'll be fine, son," he said firmly, his hand seeking the boy's shoulder for a final squeeze. "Your pa will carry you to the wagon, and I'll warrant your mother will be waiting for you at the door."

"She was scared, Doc," Jeremiah confided quietly. "She told me she'd make me some cookies, and we're gonna put a cot in the kitchen for me to stay on, so I don't have to be alone upstairs during the day."

Win could not suppress a chuckle. "I'd say she has it all figured out. You'll be spoiled rotten inside of a week."

"And I can't go to school, can I?" Hope lit his eyes as the boy waited for Win's reply.

"I think you need to stay off that leg for a month," Win said. "But if I know Miss Kate, she'll send you enough lessons to keep you busy. And no doubt your mother will be happy to see to it you work at it every day."

Crestfallen, Jeremiah sighed. "I was thinking I was too bad hurt to be doing school work."

Win relented. "No school work for three days, Mr. Madison." He exchanged a look with the father, and understanding lit Clive's eyes. "In the meantime, I'll tell Mrs. Kincaid about your injury, Jeremiah," Win told him. "She can put together a package to be delivered to you."

"My sister will probably bring it home from school," the boy said glumly. And then he brightened. "But I get cookies when we get home, don't I, Pa?"

Win watched as the father lifted his son, careful to support the injury, opening the outer door for them, then following as the boy was tucked into the back of the wagon. "He's going to be hurting for a few days," Win told the father quietly, passing a bottle into the man's hand. "Give him a dose of this in the evening. It'll help him sleep."

Before the wagon had turned in the road, Win was back in the house, shivering from the cold air, welcoming the warmth of the kitchen stove that permeated his living quarters…eager to return to Ellie.

He met Ruth at the bedroom door, and looked past her to where Ellie's still form lay curled up on his bed. One hand tucked beneath her cheek, she slept. Her breathing seemed normal, her face not unduly flushed, and he drew a shuddering breath. "Is her fever down?" he asked, knowing the answer even as he posed the query.

"She's resting," Ruth said quietly. "I think the herbs have helped. But she's very sick, Doc. My guess is she won't be up and about for several days."

His gaze left Ellie reluctantly to focus on the woman before him. "Will you come back?" he asked, feeling humbled by the woman's serene strength. "I won't even ask what you did, Ruth. I don't need to know. If it helped my wife, that's all that matters."

Ruth's mouth twitched and humor lit her eyes. "There are no magic chants or ancient formulas in my healing," she told him. "I only use methods that have come to me over the years from my ancestors. The healing must come from within, and Ellie has strength we don't recognize." She looked back at her patient.

"I would like you to use the steam if you think it helps. I've left several packets of dried herbs beside the bed. Ethel knows what to do with them." Ruth's hand touched Win's arm, and again he was aware of a strange, potent force that delivered its silent message in a way he could not comprehend.

"I'll do anything you ask," he told her. "Contrary to what my medical books tell me, I know there are forces within each of us that continue to confound the higher learning we teach in universities and medical schools."

"You must send for me if she does not respond well in the next day or so," Ruth said. "I would be careful of using anything to sedate her. The child she carries is strong, but susceptible to whatever we use to treat Ellie."

Win nodded, feeling almost as incompetent as he had in those long past days when he'd first encountered a professor in medical school. There was no doubt in his mind that Ruth truly deserved the reputation of a true healer. He'd seen evidence of her talent, heard stories of her quiet ministry. Now he looked to where Ellie lay asleep, not stretched out in unnatural stillness, but curled in simple slumber.

"Thank you," he said, almost beneath his breath, blinking back a mist that blurred his vision. Ruth's hand left his arm and she stepped around him, the soft leather of her shoes silent on the wooden floor. In moments, he heard the murmur of voices in the kitchen, Ethel's raised in inquiry, Ruth's a soft assurance.

His strides were long as he crossed his bedroom floor, dropping to his knees beside Ellie, fearful of disturbing her rest, yet needing to be near her. One hand touched her brow, unable to believe his eyes as he observed the natural color of her skin. No trace of fever met his fingertips, only the warmth he was familiar with, the scent of womanly flesh he associated with Ellie.

His mind closed to all else save this moment, when his wife and child were deeply involved in the healing process. He brushed aside a tendril of hair that teased his fingers, and was rewarded by a faint smile, lifting Ellie's lips and bringing to life a small dimple in her cheek.

"Win." She whispered the single syllable, turning her head to seek his hand, sighing as her temple settled against his palm. "The baby?" Spoken so softly, he might have missed her concern had he not seen her lips move, the question tore at his heart. And yet he rejoiced that he could ease her fear.

"The baby's fine, sweetheart. Just rest now."

And she did, falling deeply into slumber, her mouth open a bit, her lips soft, her breath sweet. No scent of fever defiled the air; yet he knew, without a doubt, she was not through with her ordeal. For now, it was enough that she rested, gaining strength before the rising of internal heat would once more sap her life force.

"How's the missus?" Standing in the hotel doorway, Amos Carlton called out to Win. "John told me she's pretty sick."

Win halted midway across the road and waved. "She's doing better. Thanks for asking, Amos. She's sitting up in bed this morning, eating scrambled eggs that Ethel cooked for her."

"Well, that's good news," Harry Talbert said, leaning on his broom, as he joined the conversation. "Ethel told me she was spending the morning at your house."

"I'm on my way to the mercantile," Win said. "I don't like leaving Ellie alone yet. I suppose she'd be fine for a while by herself, but I appreciate Ethel taking hold the way she has."

"We think a lot of the girl," Harry told him. "She's made herself a nest there, hasn't she? Even got the weeds pulled in your yard. Said she's plannin' on plantin' flowers, come spring." His grin was wide. "Ethel says she's quite a cook, too."

"Don't know what I ever did without her," Win admitted. "Never thought I'd get married, even with Ruth and Tess lining up the women for me to look over."

"Well, you couldn't have done better if you'd tried," James said, joining the men as they gathered in the middle of the street. "Kate's quite taken with her, you know. She's been worried sick that tromping around at night in the cold air would weaken Ellie's lungs. Do you suppose she'll come out of this all right, Doc?"

Win nodded. "Whatever Ruth put in the steam she used seemed to do the trick. I was steaming her, but Ruth brought some Indian remedy along and it worked pretty well." He thought of the night just past. "She's still coughing, but she needs to bring all the congestion up, get her lungs cleared out. It about wears her out, and then she sleeps it off."

He'd changed the bed early in the morning, then helped her into her second gown. "I'm on my way to the mercantile. Need to get some things for Ellie."

"I'll walk over with you," James said, sauntering beside Win as the other men went back to their places of business, Harry wielding his broom on the last bit of wooden walkway in front of his store. "I want to talk to you, Doc."

"Something wrong?" Win asked. "Is Kate all right? And the baby?"

James waved away the words, shaking his head. "They're fine. I just wanted you to know that I put Marie and Tommy on a train yesterday morning, heading back East. And then I went out and brought George into town. He's in jail."

Win halted before the mercantile. "He is? Doesn't seem right that the instigators in this whole mess are heading for home and George is holding the short end of the stick. You know, I'd forgotten Tommy and his mother. I'd downright put them and their shenanigans out of my mind. I'll be…" He shook his head. "Was there trouble?"

"No, not unless you count the hollering old George is doing, sitting in a cell. I think Marie was glad to hightail it out of town and leave that mess behind. Once she got the idea that all her plotting was a fizzle, she cut her losses and hauled buggy back to Pennsylvania." He grinned and tilted his hat back, leaning against an upright post. "Of course, the fact that some highfalutin lawyer showed up at the hotel might have had something to do with it."

"A lawyer?" Win repeated James's words and looked up the street toward Amos's hotel. "Is he still there?"

"Yeah, he's having breakfast in the dining room. He told me that he'd be by to see you this morning." James lifted a brow. "The name Gregory Gray mean anything to you?"

Win nodded slowly. "He's my uncle, my father's brother. There's four of them in all, every man Jack of them a lawyer. Uncle Gregory's the eldest." He hesitated and grinned. "My favorite, to tell the truth. I might have known he'd be the one to come."

"Yeah," James said with a chuckle. "I heard about the one who went to Washington, the senator from Pennsylvania. Well, your uncle Gregory spent a while in a private parlor at the hotel with Marie and Tommy. And after he got through with them they didn't offer much of a fuss when I suggested politely that they might want to leave town before I found a spot for them in the jail."

"My uncle's at the hotel?" Win was having a problem digesting James's story. He'd been so involved in the sickroom with Ellie that anything beyond the walls of his home held no interest. But now, if he'd heard James correctly, his uncle Gregory was just a hundred feet away, eating breakfast in Whitehorn's fanciest hotel.

"Yup, that's what I said."

"Why didn't you tell me before? I'd have paid him a visit."

James eyed him dubiously. "Would you? With Ellie so sick? I heard from Ethel that you haven't even made a house call since we found Ellie. I figured the man could walk to your place and meet your wife."

"I'll pay him a visit, as soon as I stop here and do a little shopping," Win said, opening wide the front door of the mercantile. Tess greeted him from the back of the store and he waved in reply.

"How's Ellie today?" She bustled out from behind the counter, greeting him halfway across the floor, reaching to pat his cheek. "You've had a tough row to hoe, Doc. It's got to be hard, watching your own wife just layin' there, and you not able to offer any miracle cure."

"She's doing better, Tess. Did you know Ruth came by day before yesterday? She's coming back, probably today or tomorrow, and I think she'll be pleased at Ellie's progress."

"You let her work her magic, did you?" Tess eyed him dubiously. "I wasn't sure you'd turn her loose on Ellie, being a doctor yourself, and all."

"I'll take all the help I can get," Win declared firmly. "And whatever Ruth did, it helped. I'll never turn my back on someone who offers a hand, whether it be someone from a medical school or a natural born healer. And I'd say Ruth falls into that category. She worked a miracle of sorts, with some herbs and who knows what all. I just closed the door and left her alone to do what she came for."

"She has the touch, that's for sure," Tess said. "There's folks who'd do well to acknowledge the fact, instead of looking down their noses at her. Of course, being a Kincaid helps a lot, but when her name was Ruth Whitefeather, she took a lot of guff."

"She's welcome in my home any day of the week," Win said quietly. "I've never paid much mind to skin color. Never saw many Native Americans back East anyway, at least not in Saint Louis."

"Now, what are you lookin' for this mornin', Doc?" she asked brightly. "Got a grocery list for me?"

"Mostly I need a couple of new nightgowns for Ellie. She's going through them lickety-split. Every time I turn around, I'm changing her. Her fever goes up and we end up with another set of sheets for Ethel to wash, along with her nightgown."

"I'll pick out a couple for you," Tess told him, rounding the counter and pulling a wooden box from the shelf. "How many you want?" She held up three, fancy gowns to his way of thinking, with lace and ruffles and bitty little buttons marching up the front.

"Those will do," he said. "Put together some cheese and a dozen or so eggs and a slab of bacon for me. Canned fruit if you have any, and coffee. I'll pick it up in a while. I'm making a stop at the hotel. James tells me my uncle is in town."

Tess nodded. "I heard he sent Marie packin'. You lettin' her get away with causin' a fuss?"

"She's gone, and good riddance," Win said fervently. "Ellie's pa is the one I blame. If he wasn't so ornery, none of this would have come about. He could have put a bug in Marie's ear right off the bat, and she wouldn't have had a leg to stand on. All her talk about an annulment went kaflooey once her lawyer heard the whole story."

James stuck his head in the door. "You about ready to head for the hotel, Doc?"

Win nodded. "Yeah, I'm on my way." He tipped his hat to Tess and stepped across the floor to where James waited. "Let's go, Sheriff. It's been a couple of years since I saw my uncle Gregory. He might not recognize me."

The staid, sober lawyer who rose at Win's appearance seemed to have no difficulty knowing his nephew at first glance. "My boy," he said heartily, crossing the dining room with hand outstretched. Win's fingers were buried within the huge palm and Gregory Gray's grip was strong. Then, with a muttered word that made Win smile, the older man reached for his nephew and held him in an embrace that threatened to crush the breath from him.

"You're missed, my boy," Gregory said bluntly. "Your aunt Elmira and I have wondered for months on end where you were and what you were doing. And then I get a message that you need the services of a good lawyer. I told you having the law in your background would be your salvation one of these days."

"So you did," Win answered, disentangling himself with effort. "It's good to see you, sir. Won't you come to my home, and spend some time with me."

Gregory's eyes were sharp beneath bushy brows. "Several folks have filled my ears with stories about your new bride, son. I'm eager to meet the young woman."

Win hesitated. "That might present a problem. Ellie's quite ill, still abed for that matter. She's recovering from pneumonia."

"I heard that from your sheriff. A fine fella, that one." He looked over Win's shoulder and his smile flashed. "There's the man now," he said, waving a hand at James.

He hadn't changed, Win decided. As bluff and hearty as ever, the direct opposite of his brother. That thought made Win think of his sire. "How is my father?" he asked politely. "And mother?"

"Ornery as ever," Gregory said bluntly. "Well, if I'm not to meet your wife this morning, come on over to my table and drink some coffee while I eat the rest of my breakfast."

"Join us, James," Win said, but was met with an uplifted hand and a quick shake of his head as James refused the offer.

"I've got to check on my prisoner, Doc, and then trot over to the school to give Kate a hand. She's up to her neck with students, the baby's fussy this morning."

"Baby?" Gregory looked intrigued at that revelation. "What's all that about?"

"Sit down," Win told him, "and I'll fill you in while you eat."

Ellie was not a good patient. And he didn't have it in him to be harsh with her, Win decided as she pouted at his decision to keep her in bed the next morning. "You still have just a touch of congestion in your lungs, sweetheart," he explained for the third time. "You need to rest. You had a low fever again last night, and I can hear rattles all the way to the bottom of your lungs."

He pulled her gown back down to cover her back, his fingers caressing the straight line of her spine, appreciating the soft skin of his patient. No other woman had appealed to him as she did, and at that thought, he recognized anew the degree of emotion she managed to elicit from him. He, whose claim to matter-of-fact attention to the sick had made him clear-headed and analytical in his diagnoses over the past years, was now totally at the mercy of feelings he could not control.

No wonder the medical profession decreed that a doctor should not treat his own family. And if he'd stayed in Saint Louis, he probably would have called in a consultant. Or more likely, would have put Ellie in a hospital where she would get the best care available. He thought of Ruth Kincaid, and smiled. Her brand of healing would not be accepted where he came from. Perhaps, for Ellie's sake, it was a mercy that this was not Saint Louis, but rather the frontier.

"Win?" Ellie watched him warily. "When can I get up? I want to be dressed when I meet your uncle. He's the first of your family to be welcomed into your home, and I'm not going to greet him from my bed." Indignantly, she made her claim, and Win sighed, aware that she had a valid point.

Yet her eyes were shadowed, her skin pale after the restless night she'd spent, and she was in no condition to put her feet on the floor for longer than a few moments at a time. Beyond that, she was indignant at being kept from her kitchen, and he was hard put to argue with her dogged determination.

He bent to her, pressing his mouth against her forehead. "Maybe tomorrow, if your temperature stays down another day and night." His fingers were nimble as they buttoned her gown, his palms curving as if they anticipated touching the firmness of her breasts beneath the white cotton fabric. And yet he would not press her for intimacies, though his male flesh responded to her as a man needful of sustenance would react at the sight of a meal before him.

He hungered for her. Not to simply possess her in the act of loving, but to cleave to her, making her one with himself. He ached as he acknowledged his need for the vibrant female he'd married. He'd held her through the night hours, bathed her fevered flesh and changed her gown and bedding. And in those hours he had not needed to restrain himself, for she was a woman in need, and his was the healing, caring touch that she required.

Now, in this moment, she was simply his wife, and his memory was filled with moments of tenderness and passion. During the short weeks of their marriage, he had come to recognize the sweetness, the innocent appeal of the woman he had taken to himself. It was love he felt for her, and for the second time, he recognized it fully.

Ellie looked up at him, her smile knowing, pale lips curving in a tempting invitation. "Would you like to stay with me for a while, Doc?" she asked simply. "I don't think Ethel's come in yet, has she?"

"I told her I'd take care of things this morning," he said. "She'll be over later on."

Ellie's hands reached for him, her slender fingers strong as they tangled in his shirt-front, and she tugged him closer. "I don't suppose I'm very appealing to you right now, but I have a powerful need, Win."

He relented, sitting beside her, then lifted her to his lap, careful to wrap her in the quilt. Leaning against the headboard, he gathered her to himself, his arms enclosing her, aware of the movement of the child that rested against his stomach. Possessive fingers spread wide across her belly as he mapped the form of her babe. She was growing rapidly, well into the eighth month, and he thought of the day to come, when he would deliver her of this baby.

She moved against him and his mind formed a decision, one he knew only too well he might regret, given the circumstances. Yet he would not wound her by ignoring her plea, for Ellie asked little of him. Delving beneath the quilt, he found firm, rounding flesh, warmth and the scent of woman. "I've missed this," he told her, his palm curved beneath the weight of her pregnancy.

She sighed, leaning against him more fully, her arm twining around his neck to draw his face against hers. He kissed her then, fully aware of her arousal as his fingers curved to cup her feminine warmth. Her lips were soft against his, and he cherished them, his kisses tender. Fever had dried them until they bled, then peeled, and the new skin was fragile.

"Did you put on the cream Ruth left for your mouth?" Her reply was a soft murmur.

"It tastes like wildflowers," he told her, and she sighed against his lips. Her breath was sweet, no longer tainted with the scent of fever and congestion. And yet he knew the ordeal was not complete, that she would need constant care for the next days. But for now, he was filled with a sense of yearning for that which would please her, and his head dipped lower to where her breasts were covered by quilt and gown.

Ellie's hand dropped to her throat, pushing aside the covering that kept him from her skin, her fingers agile as they undid the buttons he had so recently put into their casings. In movements he recognized as unfamiliar to her, she guided him to the firm flesh that awaited his attention, and he obliged. His tongue tasted her, reveling in the flavor of her skin. His nose pressed against the fullness as he sought the crest that pebbled between his teeth.

A whimper caught his attention and he was still. "Are you tender? Did I hurt you?"

She shook her head, a single movement of denial, and then her hand pressed against his head, guiding him. "Ah, Win." It was a sigh of contentment, a whisper of delight as he suckled the treasure she offered. His hand pressed against her feminine warmth, his fingers probing, silently urging her compliance, and she opened to him. Her hips rose as he sought and found the source of her pleasure, and he explored the folds with tender care.

Ellie sighed, a soft eager sound that grew into a moan of appreciation as he guided her toward the goal he had set. "Shh, just rest easy," he whispered, slowing the rhythm, anticipating her growing arousal, feeding the flames with gentle movements that shattered her composure. She inhaled a shuddering breath, whispering his name, her fingers clenching in his hair. Her head fell back, and he answered the unspoken demands of rising hips and pleading whimpers.

Slowly, carefully and with a skillful touch, he brought her release, an achingly tender pinnacle of joy that brought shivering, shuddering groans of pleasure into being.

She relaxed then, her body quivering with the satisfaction of his loving, and he soothed her damp flesh with soft caresses, easing from her slowly, his hand once more seeking the rounding of her belly. The babe moved against his palm, a thrust of some small limb, and he heard the giggle Ellie tried to smother.

"I think he's protesting my intrusion," Win whispered, lifting his head from the skin he'd cherished. He kissed her mouth then, aware of the resilience of the woman he held. She'd been almost at death's door, and though it was a morbid thought, he knew the truth of his mind's appraisal of her condition. Now so short a time later, she was once more in the land of the living, her senses alert, her body healing, even now replete in the aftermath of his loving.

"Win?" Her query held concern, and her hand slid into his hair, fingers tunneling through the heavy, dark locks. Her eyes held a question he could not ignore.

He met her gaze and his lie was spoken with barely a flicker of his eyelashes. "I only wanted to give you pleasure," he said. "I can wait."

She looked troubled for a moment, but a yawn overtook her concern and she blinked her surprise. "I can't be sleepy again. I only woke up an hour ago."

"I wore you out," he teased, holding her closely and rocking her in his arms. "Close your eyes, Ellie. Sleep. I'll stay with you."

She smiled, contentment softening her features, and her words were slurred, as though they tumbled from a mind already seeking oblivion in slumber. "I love you, Win. I'm..." Her eyelids fluttered open and she frowned. "Do you really love me?"

"Oh, yes, Ellie. I love you," he said, then watched as her smile erased the frown. "I love you." It was a whisper this time, a tender avowal of passion. "I love you." He repeated it once more, his heart filled to overflowing with the powerful emotion he could not contain.

Chapter Thirteen

"So you're the girl my nephew's so besotted with. Thought I'd never get a chance to make your acquaintance, what with him making me wait to meet you." Gregory's eyes twinkled as he offered Ellie his hand, and then stunned her by turning their joined palms and placing a soft kiss against her knuckles.

"Congratulations, young lady. You've managed to turn this levelheaded fellow into a doting husband. Couldn't have happened to a better man." He laughed at his own humor and slapped Win's shoulder, a thumping blow that made Ellie wince.

"I'm so pleased you were able to visit.

Win's never told me much about his family. You're a welcome sight." She stood before the tall, rotund gentleman and looked up into piercing blue eyes.

Her shoulders drew back and Ellie found herself speaking her mind, not daring to look in Win's direction, lest he wear a frown at hearing her blunt words. "I'm probably not what his family would have chosen for Win, but I'm doing my best to be a good wife to him."

"Bother the family," Gregory said vehemently, his eyes crinkling at the corners as he smiled. "They never understood the boy the whole time he was growing up. Never had a head for the law from the word *go*. Just dragged home every wounded creature he could find and tried to put them back together." He turned to Win, his smile reminiscent. "Do you remember the infirmary you had in the woodshed? I helped you make pens and cages on Saturday afternoons on the sly. Figured your mother would never dirty her skirts by going out there and you'd be safe."

"We were right," Win agreed, and Ellie was touched by the look of respect and affection he turned on his uncle. "Remember the night I told them I wasn't going to law school? You stood beside me and took the blame, as I recall."

Gregory chuckled. "My shoulders were wide enough to handle it. Still are, as a matter of fact. I reckon that's why your father sent me here. He thought I should be the one to clear up this mess." His gaze traveled to Ellie and became questioning.

"I don't know the whole story yet, Winston, but I'm sure you had good reason to marry this woman. Just be sure you don't leave any loose ends. She doesn't need to go through any more run-ins with her father or those scallywags from Philadelphia."

"I had good reason," Win affirmed quietly. "And the reasons have only become more valid in the past weeks." He drew Ellie to his side, his arm circling her waist, holding her close, as though he sensed her lagging strength.

The day had been her best of the whole recovery period. But after finally cooking a meal, all on her own, and then bathing and dressing for this visit, she was growing weary. Now the big bed she'd left with such energy early this morning seemed to invite her presence. She leaned against Win, and he shot a quick glance at her.

"I think Ellie needs to be off her feet, Uncle," he said. With a sudden move that had her clutching at his neck, Win picked her up in his arms.

"Will we see you again?" she asked as Win hesitated long enough for her to make her farewell.

Gregory's big hand touched her cheek. "You'll see me again, Ellie. Probably not this visit, but I'll be back one of these days, and I'll bring Win's aunt Elmira with me. Maybe you two can take a trip to Saint Louis after the weather breaks in the spring. The family will be anxious to see the baby."

"But…" Ellie bit at her lip. How to deny Win's fatherhood?

Gregory nodded. "I know…I know," he said. "But Win's going to be the only father your child will know, young lady. Let him begin as he means to go on."

"I have," Win told him. "And now Ellie needs a nap." He turned with her and left the parlor, and she sagged against his chest.

"I'm a little tired," she admitted. "I guess I'm not as strong as I thought I was."

"You're strong," Win said, as he carried her into the bedroom. "If you weren't, you'd still be flat on your back. All that hard work you've done all your life has given you the constitution of a man who's done hard labor for a living."

"That doesn't sound very flattering," she said with a small laugh. "Makes me sound more male than female."

"Now that's a long way from true," he said, bending to place her on the mattress. "You're the most womanly creature I've ever known." He lifted her foot, removing her shoe, then rubbed her toes through the heavy fabric of her stockings.

"Um...that feels good," she whimpered, closing her eyes as she snuggled into the pillow.

"You're spoiled, young lady," Win teased, working on the other foot. He placed her shoes on the floor, then lifted the quilt to cover her. "I want you to stay right there until dinnertime. Ethel is making soup for you, and you have time to take a nap."

She yawned, lifting one hand to cover her mouth. "I've never been so tired in my life, as during the past few days." Her eyelids threatened to close as she spoke, and she blinked, wanting to tell Win the thoughts that were swirling in her head. Somehow, it didn't seem she'd be able to, and she gave in to the delicious sensation of slumber, the warmth of the quilt luring her to nestle into the mattress.

"I'll be back," Win promised, bending to touch his lips to her forehead.

She murmured something, then heard his chuckle as he turned to leave the room. *I love you.* The words whispered in her head, repeating over and over in a litany that lulled her, and she sighed as the door closed behind him.

"That's cold," Ellie complained, as Win's stethoscope touched her belly.

"No, you're warm," he said, contradicting her with a teasing glance. He bent low, his eyes closing as he listened, then moved the metal bell to another spot, this time lower, nodding as if what he heard was satisfactory. "The heart tones are good," he said after a minute, removing the earpieces and folding the tubes.

A weekly event, one he'd insisted on during the past weeks, her examination took only minutes, with Win's hands firm against the solid rounding of her belly. And then came the listening, his patience limitless as he monitored the heart of her unborn child.

"You made a hit with my uncle," he said,

lifting his head after a moment. "He was sorry to leave, but he felt he'd stayed too long as it was."

"He loves you," she said simply. "I think as if you were his son."

"Probably more than my father ever did," Win said, a tinge of bitterness in his voice. "He and Aunt Elmira have no children. I think they've decided to concentrate on me. Especially when my family almost disowned me for turning my back on the family traditions."

Ellie watched his face as he listened again, then smiled as he removed the earpieces and folded the black rubber tubes in his hand. "Can I try to hear it, too?" she asked, wondering what he heard that pleased him, anxious to be as connected in that way, as he was to the child within her.

"Certainly," he said. "Here, sit up so it will reach. You'll have to bend a little."

"There's not much bend left in me," Ellie said ruefully. She propped herself against the pillows and sat erect, reaching eagerly for the instrument. The earpieces fit snugly and she placed the bell against the upper rise of her belly. A swishing sound was loud in her ears and her eyes widened. The distinct beat was muffled, another seeming to echo it in the background.

"I can't tell what I'm hearing," she said impatiently, moving the bell lower as she bent her head.

"Probably your own heartbeat way up there," Win told her. He lowered the bell to rest beneath her navel and pressed it against her skin. "Now listen. It's going to be faster than your heart tones. And you're listening through the amniotic fluid, too. That swishing sound is the noise it makes flowing through the umbilical cord."

"Amniotic fluid?" she asked, aware that this was a language foreign to her. She only knew that there was a lot of messy stuff going on when animals gave birth, and she'd seen the cord that attached the babies to their mothers. Now, through the sounds vibrating in her ears, came a rapid *thump-thump* she recognized as the beating heart of her child, and her eyes filled with tears.

"I know it's real, Win. I sure feel enough kicking going on. But to hear it and know it's my baby's heart that's making that sound... It's enough to take a body's breath away."

Win sat closer, removing the earpieces, aware that he'd put off this conversation long enough. "I think it's time for a lesson on childbirth," he told her. "Having a baby is essentially the same every time, and I know you didn't see the whole thing when Kate delivered, but there was a certain amount of fluid that was discharged before the baby was born."

"I was busy holding her hand and rubbing her back most of the time," Ellie agreed. "I knew there was a lot of washing to do afterward, with towels and sheets, and those pads she had ready."

"Well, we're going to make up some pads for you, too. In fact, I'm going to the newspaper office and get a stack of old papers and cover them with old pieces of sheeting. That way we can just throw them away afterward. It'll save on the washing."

"Will they know what you want them for?" Ellie asked, flushing at the thought of the newspaper editor being privy to such intimate details.

Win shrugged. "Maybe so, but it won't be the first time I've done it. Newspaper is about as close to a sterile sheet as you can get. Some folks still don't understand that childbed fever comes from unclean hands and instruments, and dirty sheets beneath the mother."

He folded his stethoscope and put it in his bag. "We're not taking any chances with you, sweetheart. I want a live, healthy baby." He bent to kiss her, more thoroughly this time.

"And, above all, I want this mother to come through with everything in working order, and no rips or tears to heal."

"Tears?" Ellie felt her skin crawl at that thought. "I'm not sure what you're talking about."

Win looked as though he wished he'd kept his mouth shut, his lips tightening as he considered her query. "Sometimes the baby is larger than we expect, and once in a while a doctor doesn't use proper care, and the mother tears when she delivers the head." He placed a hand against her belly, as if to reassure her. "That's not going to happen with you. I'll be extra careful, I promise."

Ellie inhaled deeply. "I didn't know there was all that much to it. Usually, when the animals have their young, they just pop them out and then get up and go about their business." She thought a moment, remembering Kate's ordeal. "But then, I guess it wasn't quite that simple with Kate, was it?"

Win hesitated. "I won't try to pull the wool over your eyes, Ellie. Kate had an easy delivery. Sometimes, it's much harder than that. But," he said quickly, "I don't anticipate anything going wrong with you. The baby is fine, and you're a strong woman, and on top of that, you're built just right for having babies."

She frowned. "So is every other woman."

Win shook his head. "Not true, honey. But you've got nice hips." And at that, his hand strayed from the high rounding of her belly to the fullness of her hipline, and his fingers squeezed gently. "Very nice hips."

She shot him a haughty look. "Enough of your messin' around, Winston Gray. You're supposed to be a dignified doctor, and here you are makin' eyes at your patient." She swung her legs to the other side of the bed, and slid her feet to the floor. "We've fiddled around long enough with this examination thing. I'm going to the kitchen, and you get to sit and watch while I fix supper."

"You're kinda feeling your oats, aren't you?" he asked, grinning as she slid into her house shoes. She rounded the bed and he encircled her shoulders with his long arm. "Let me give you a hand. I don't mind helping, and we'll be done sooner. How about fried potatoes and applesauce and the leftover meat loaf from dinner?"

She nodded. "Anything sounds good to me. I'm hungry all the time since I'm feeling better." They walked through the kitchen doorway, Win standing aside for Ellie to go before him.

"You're not totally back to your old self yet," he cautioned her. "I don't want you to overdo. In fact, I think Ruth is coming by tomorrow to take a look at you."

Ellie watched as Win reached for an iron skillet and placed it on the stove. "You don't mind that she comes?" she asked casually. She'd wondered at Win's ability to allow Ruth's medicine to supplement his own.

"I'll tell you the same thing I told her the first time she was here, honey. I'd do anything it took to get you back on your feet. Up to, and including the magic Ruth makes."

"You think it's magic?" she asked cautiously. "She didn't weave any spells as far as I could tell."

Win looked over his shoulder at her. "Not that kind of magic. Just the innate knowledge she has that has come down through the centuries from her people. The Native Americans know things the medical profession still has to learn."

"I'll slice those potatoes," Ellie offered as

Win brought a bowl of leftover boiled potatoes from the pantry, and he veered from his
path to place it on the table.

"Good. You can probably do it quicker
than I," he said agreeably. "I'll warm the
meat loaf." He poured a bit of bacon grease
into the skillet from the cup atop the stove
and Ellie heard it begin to sizzle. Settling in
a chair, she made short work of the leftover
potatoes.

"I'll just be another minute," she said. "That
pan sounds like it's ready." Win watched the
food as she set the table, and in less than ten
minutes, they were eating. Ellie leaned back
in her chair to watch as Win dove into his
food. "I thought I'd never get to sit at this
table again," she told him. "I was so sick of
eating off a tray, and dripping soup down
my chin. I'm not good at being a patient, I'm
afraid."

She ladled applesauce on top of her fried
potatoes and Win cast her a look of horror.

"What are you doing to those perfectly
good spuds?"

She looked up, then laughed at his expression. "I've always eaten my fried potatoes
this way. My mother used to make applesauce
and can it every year, and we always had it, at

every meal it seems like." Memories flooded her mind as she spoke.

"My father wasn't so gruff and angry all the time when I was real small. I remember he used to put me on his lap and tell me stories sometimes."

"He must have missed your mother dreadfully," Win said. "Something made him hard to live with, and I'm thinking it came about after losing his wife that way."

Ellie took another bite of meat loaf. "I guess I never thought of him in that light," she admitted. "I was so full of my own pain, missing her and crying myself to sleep at night. I didn't think about what he must have felt. Mama wasn't ever real happy, Win. My pa wasn't always nice to her, I remember that. But," she said slowly, "maybe he has a hard time being…kind, the way you are."

Win got up, then filled a glass with milk and brought it back to the table, depositing it in front of Ellie. "He's having a hard time being patient, right now," he said gruffly. "Drink your milk, Ellie. It's good for the baby."

Ellie's fork hit the table as her fingers lost their grip, ignoring the milk he'd placed before her. "What do you mean? Where is he, Win?"

"In jail, waiting for the judge to show up for a hearing."

"In jail?" She considered that thought for a moment. "Who's taking care of the ranch?"

"His foreman, I suppose. The man that took you to the line shack was here yesterday on his way to visit the jail. He wanted to make sure you were all right."

"Al Shrader," Ellie said. "He's a kind man, Win. He was only following orders, and he wouldn't have done anything to harm me."

Win nodded, and nudged the glass of milk closer to her plate. "I know. I figured that out right away. He helped us track you down."

She watched as his eyes grew somber, and wondered at his thoughts. "It must have been hard for you, not knowing where I was."

"I didn't know what to think at first," he said. "Kate said you were talking about leaving me for a while, till things got settled with Marie and Tommy." He paused and met her gaze, as if to judge her reaction. "All I could think of was that you'd gone without leaving me a note or letting me know where you were. And then when I realized that you'd not gone on your own hook, I felt guilty that I'd doubted you."

"I was probably talking through my hat," she said, remembering the day she'd spent with Kate, and the half-formed plans she'd confided to her friend. "It did seem like I was more of a burden to you than a help. But there wasn't anyplace to go, Win. And I'd never have gone back to the ranch, not willingly."

"Well, George has had a bit of time to think about things, honey. James says he's cooled off considerably. I think he just went off half-cocked when Marie started her spiel about Tommy marrying you and taking you back to Philadelphia with him. Maybe he really thought it was the best thing for you. Who knows?"

"Will we go to the hearing?" she asked, obeying his unspoken order as he pointed again to her glass. She picked it up and drank half, smiling as he nodded his approval.

"I doubt anything's going to happen to your pa, Ellie. The law doesn't provide for the rights of women the way it should. I have a notion the judge will dismiss the charges. James just wanted him to stew for a while."

"I want to go to the hearing," she said

firmly. "I want to make sure they don't send him away somewhere."

"Not much chance of that," Win assured her.

"Well, anyway, I want to be sure."

"You're more softhearted than I am, sweetheart. I'd be willing to see him sweat it out in a jail cell for a while." Win leaned across the table, and his eyes were narrowed and dark with anger. "He could have killed you, Ellie. If you'd died out there on the open range, it would have been his fault."

"But I didn't," she said quietly. "I'm here, and I'm getting better and he's still my father. I may not like him very much, but if it weren't for him, I wouldn't be here in the first place. And then where would you be?"

Her voice trembled, and she set her jaw. "I know I may not be the ideal choice for a wife, but I've come in handy once in a while. At least you have a wife, a cook and someone to wash and iron your shirts."

"Hell!" The single curse word stunned Ellie. Win was not given to coarse language and she watched, wide-eyed, as he rose from his chair and rounded the table. She was lifted from her chair with one swift movement, her hands flying up to press against his chest as his arms pinned her awkward form against his long, lean body.

"Don't talk like that, Ellie. Like I married you to be a kitchen maid." His hands were strong, his muscles powerful, more so than was apparent at first glance. He wore well-fitting trousers, usually a vest and coat, but beneath the attire of a gentleman was the strength of a man used to fending for himself.

She seldom thought of him in that manner. He was simply *Win,* the man who'd married her when it would have been simpler to keep her around as a cook and housekeeper. *Win,* the champion she'd never had in all of her growing-up years. And right this minute, that champion was upset over something. Maybe *upset* wasn't the right word, she decided as Win lifted her in his arms and crossed the kitchen to the hallway, and then on to their bedroom.

"What are you doing?" She breathed the words from lungs that seemed to have lost their ability to inhale air. Her throat closed in a spasm of coughing and she buried her face against his chest.

He sat on the bed, holding her in his lap, and his big hand rubbed her back, between her shoulder blades. "Inhale as deep as you can, sweetheart," he told her, his voice harsh. She obeyed and coughed again, gagging as the hoarse coughing threatened to bring up the meal she had just consumed.

"I'm sorry, honey," he whispered, regret lacing his words. "I shouldn't have grabbed you up that way." One hand brushed the hair from her face, the other held her firmly upright, and she caught her breath.

"Why...?" The single word was halted by his fingers touching her lips.

"I heard you list all those foolish reasons for me to appreciate you, and not a one of them mentioned the fact that I love you. I don't care if you never cook another meal or iron another shirt, Mrs. Gray. You're my wife because I need you in my life. I can't remember what it was like before you arrived here, but I know it was damn lonely."

She leaned on his arm and peered up at him, noting the frown that creased his forehead. A ruddy flush rode his cheekbones, and the feverish gleam in those green eyes told her he was about halfway to stripping her from her clothing and easing his aching need with the warmth of her body.

His voice was harsh, filled with pent-up

emotion. "I've been lonely in another way, Ellie. I'm afraid you've spoiled me. I've missed the comfort of having you in my bed for the past little while."

"I've been in your bed," she said, her mouth pursing as she teased him. "It wasn't my fault you were such a gentleman."

"I wouldn't take advantage of you, with you being sick, honey. You know better than that. I'm going off half-cocked as it is, and I'm supposed to be taking good care of you. You're married to a doctor, and I'm carting you around and upsetting you, and now I'm horny as hell. I'd give any other husband a good tongue-lashing if he treated his wife this way."

"You haven't taken advantage of me, Win. I was the one who coaxed you to—"

His fingers halted her words. "That was my pleasure," he said, his mouth twitching, as though he recalled in detail the moments they'd shared only yesterday.

"I'm here if you want me," she said simply. "I won't even have to wriggle. I'll just be here for you."

His eyes twinkled and he hugged her close. "You can't help wriggling, sweetheart. I'll consider your offer, but not right now. You're going to rest, and I'm going to clean up the kitchen." He moved her from his lap, and tucked the quilt around her. His lips were warm against her forehead, and then he was gone, only his cheerful whistle from the other room making her aware that he was close at hand.

She'd put the kitchen in order after the noon meal the next day when a familiar form appeared at the back door, and Ruth turned the knob. "I brought you some tea, Ellie. It's good for you and the baby when the time comes for the birthing. It'll ease your pain." Ruth stomped her feet on the rug inside the back door, and shook the snowflakes from the shawl she'd worn draped over her head.

"It's beautiful outside. The sun is shining and the snow from yesterday is beautiful. There's just a little bit falling now, and it glitters in the air. Come look." She waved at the backyard and Ellie stood beside her, looking out through the double-sashed door.

"I love the first snow of the year," Ellie said. "It's been late coming, and what fell just blew across the fields and settled in drifts along the fence lines. Win took his buggy out this morning on house calls, but I'll bet he'll have to have Lionel Briggs over at the livery stable uncover his new sleigh before long."

"I wouldn't be surprised," Ruth agreed. "I rode in on the wagon, and Caleb had a fit. He thinks there'll be more snow by nightfall, and he doesn't want me out in it by myself." She shrugged. "I told him I'd be back long before then, but he's a fussbudget sometimes. I thought I'd wait and take Zeke home from school with me."

"That gives you more than enough time to have a cup of coffee or some tea with me," Ellie said, pleased by the visit. "Heavens, we have half a day to squander, don't we?"

Ruth sat tall in her chair, and Ellie admired the dark beauty of her eyes and hair. "I'm so glad you came back," she said. Her gaze sought the small packet of tea Ruth placed on the kitchen table, and her mind sped ahead to the use she would make of it. "Will you need to be here when the time comes?"

"No," Ruth shook her head. "Winston can brew it for you and keep it hot on the back of the stove as soon as he's sure you're in labor. If Kate or Ethel are here with you, they'll help you drink it as you need it."

"I wouldn't mind if you were here," Ellie said, unaware of the wistful note in her voice, fearful of overstepping Ruth's generosity.

"If you want me, I will come," Ruth told her. "But be aware that there are those towns-folk who don't appreciate what I do. You wouldn't want the doctor to be thought less of by having me with you."

Ellie felt anger rise within her, and she rose from her chair, walking around the table to where Ruth watched her with patient eyes. "Win admires you, I thought you knew that. And if you'll be here when my baby comes, I'd be grateful for your help."

"Have him send for me." It was a vow, not given rashly, but with a certain amount of pride, and Ellie was content.

She reached for the small package, seeking a place for it to remain until the time came for its use. Her mother's sugar bowl sat atop the kitchen dresser, and Ellie's heart filled with love for the woman she'd barely known as she touched the flowered container. Her fingers trembled as they lifted the lid and placed the tea within.

"It was your mother's?" Ruth asked.

"Yes." Ellie turned back to her. "It's all I have that belonged to her."

Ruth shook her head. "That's not true, child. You have her strength and wisdom within you. And I sense honesty and goodness when I come into your presence. Half of your spirit is a gift from your mother. Don't ever feel that she left you nothing but a bit of china to contain her memory."

"That's part of the problem," Ellie told her. "I don't have any memories I can put my finger on, only bits and pieces of her. Sometimes I catch a scent and it reminds me of something in my childhood, and once in a while I recall something she did."

"When that happens, you must stop and dwell on it in your mind," Ruth said. "Let your heart explore the memory, and allow your thoughts to focus on those few details you remember. Sometimes the events that are seen and heard can be recollected if we let ourselves be caught up in the flow of energy we possess."

"I guess I've never heard of such a thing," Ellie admitted. "I just figured that those early years were too far back for me to remember." She felt her eyes fill with tears, and her whisper was forlorn. "I don't even have a picture of her, and I can only see dark hair and eyes and the form of a woman who was sick in bed for a long time."

"Can you put your vision on paper?" Ruth asked. "Have you ever tried to draw the things you see?"

"What makes you ask?" Ellie's heart churned as she remembered the drawings her father had snatched and thrown into the big cookstove, accusing her of lollygagging around instead of doing her chores.

"You have the soul of one who has many talents, child."

"And you are an observant woman," Win said from the kitchen doorway. He crossed the room to offer Ruth his hand. "I'm glad to see you," he said, holding her fingers within his palm. "My wife needs to hear the very things you've been telling her."

His gaze swerved to Ellie, and his smile was approving. "I was listening in," he said, without a trace of regret. "I think Ruth has you pegged, sweetheart." He circled the table and bent to kiss Ellie's cheek. "Are you feeling all right?"

"She's doing well," Ruth said, even as Ellie nodded her reply. "Her color is good and her breathing is normal."

Ellie smiled. "All that and you haven't even touched me."

"I've watched you," Ruth said, "and sensed your well-being." She looked up at Win. "Your wife is one of the chosen ones, I believe."

Win grinned. "Well, I certainly think so. She's the only one I've chosen, at any rate." And then he sobered at Ruth's reproving look. "I apologize, ma'am. And I do know what you mean. She has qualities above and beyond those I would expect of a young woman. Maybe she's been refined by the harsh fire of anger and impatience, perfected by the cruel life she lived, isolated from those who might have lent a hand when she needed one."

"I think you're both talking way over my head," Ellie said quickly. "I don't know what you're getting at. I'm about as ordinary as oatmeal, and I surely don't have anything special to recommend me." She turned to Ruth. "I do know how to draw, though. Like you said, I can put pictures on paper that I see in my head. But my pa didn't like me wasting my time at it."

"You can do all the drawing you want to now, Ellie," Win told her, his voice harsh.

She looked up quickly, but his expression

held only affection, though his eyes were moist, as though he was pained by some errant thought. "One of these days, maybe I will," she said quietly.

Chapter Fourteen

"I've something to tell you," Win said, sitting down at the breakfast table. "James gave me some news yesterday. The judge was due into town late this morning and the hearing is this afternoon." He gave her a measuring glance. "Do you still think you should go?"

"Yes." It was a definite reply, the single word firm, spoken with finality. "I've been thinking, Win. If I spend the rest of my life hiding from Pa, I'll never get out from under his heavy hand."

"You never have to see him again," Win told her. "And just being married takes you out of his control."

"It didn't help any when he hauled me off to the ranch." She set her lips firmly and turned away from the table, to stand before the stove.

"Ellie, don't walk away from me," he said. "I don't want you upset over this."

She spun to face him, and anger edged her words. "I'll really be upset if I never let him know how I feel. He's made me cower for the last time, Win. I can't live my life in fear. You're not always here, you know. I can't hide in this house just because you're not around to protect me."

"I thought you needed me," he said quietly.

Ellie shook her head, despairing of making him understand. "I do need you. But I need to depend on myself, Win. And I can't be frightened of my pa any longer."

She'd hurt him. And that was the last thing she'd wanted to do. He stood abruptly and shoved his hands into the depths of his trouser pockets. His eyes were hooded, his jaw firm, and he watched her without speaking. It would not do.

Ellie approached him, for the first time unsure if her touch would be welcome. One hand lifted to touch the taut line of his cheek, and he jerked back, a minute movement she ignored.

"Please don't be angry with me." Softly spoken, her words were simply a request. She would not beg for his tolerance. If he couldn't allow her this small degree of independence without tightening the bonds he'd set in place, she would mourn the loss of his regard. But somehow, this had become a more important issue than she'd expected.

"I'm not angry," he said tightly, and his hand rose quickly to grasp her wrist. Then his grip softened, and he lifted her fingers to his mouth. His lips touched them, a soft, unspoken apology. Yet his mood told her he was more hurt than he would admit.

"I need to make three short calls this morning, but I'll be home in time for dinner, and then we'll go to the hearing," he said. He paused, and she sensed he had not spoken his mind. "You will allow that, won't you?" he asked in a stilted voice. Hurt laced each syllable, and she could only nod in agreement.

The morning seemed long, and the fact that Win had not eaten his breakfast before his abrupt departure bothered her. Still, she dithered between forming an apology to him, and strengthening her resolution. The apology lost. For one of the few times in her life, she'd made a stand. The moment she had faced Tommy, issuing her ultimatum that day in the hotel, became as nothing, compared to the confrontation she'd survived with Win.

He arrived home, chilled to the bone, his eyes watering from the wind, and Ellie ladled him a thick mixture of vegetables and beef. Joining him at the table, she ate little, her apprehension as she thought of the afternoon ahead blunting her appetite.

"You need to eat, Ellie," he said quietly, and she was aware that he'd been watching her.

"I'll probably feel more like it after we get this over with," she said, tasting the soup and chewing slowly.

"All right," he said agreeably, and she nodded, grateful that he hadn't coaxed her.

The judge sat before a high desk, one seldom used in Whitehorn, since he only traveled this way each month for a two-day period. James stood before him, George at his side, and Ellie halted in the doorway, her gaze traveling the width and depth of the small room.

James looked over his shoulder and nodded, lifting one hand to motion to chairs against the wall. George's shoulders stiffened and he shifted his stance, but faced the judge without turning to see who had entered the room. Win's hand was warm on Ellie's arm and he led her to the designated seats, easing her onto the chair.

"I think we're ready to begin," the judge said, looking down at the desk before him. "Are these the charges, Sheriff?" he asked, looking through his spectacles at James.

"Yes, sir," James replied. "All down in black and white. Pretty straightforward."

"Hmm..." The judge read slowly, and Ellie found herself holding her breath, her eyes barely swerving from the figure of her father.

"He looks smaller," she whispered, leaning to speak directly in Win's ear. "Has he lost weight, do you think?"

Win shook his head. "Your fear made him seem larger than he really was, sweetheart." He looked directly into her eyes, and his words were low, barely audible to her listening ear. "You're really not afraid of him anymore, are you?"

She inhaled, shaking her head. And then the judge spoke.

"This seems to be a case of an impetuous father trying to right what he saw as a wrong done to his daughter." He looked up and directed his gaze at Ellie. "Are you Eleanor Mitchum?"

"No, sir. My name is Eleanor Gray. I'm married to Dr. Winston Gray."

"Did your father physically harm you, young woman?"

"He knocked me to the ground, and while I was dazed he tied me and threw me into the back of his wagon," she said quietly.

"Sir?" The judge shifted his gaze to George. "Is that true?"

"She wouldn't listen to me," George said harshly. "I wanted that baby to be born to his real father."

"What else happened?" the judge asked Ellie.

She stood, an awkward movement, and Win rose to hold her arm. "He made one of his ranch hands take me to a line shack the next day, and they held me prisoner there."

"You got away, I understand," the judge prompted.

"Yes, the second night I walked toward Whitehorn, and then slept under a tree. My husband found me the next morning." The memory of those hours consumed her as she recalled the cold that penetrated her clothing and the hours of curling on the ground beneath a single blanket. "I was sick for a number of days," she said softly.

"Probably should have stayed where you were. Kinda foolish to go running off across the open range, I'd think." He took off his spectacles and polished them on a white handkerchief. "Your pa was a little harsh, but I suspect he thought he was doing the right thing."

Win stepped forward and James turned to issue him a sharp look. Subsiding, he looked down at Ellie, and she felt his anger as a viable entity. Her hand reached for his and found his fingers curved into a tight fist.

"I think Mr. Mitchum has served a long enough sentence, Sheriff," the judge said briskly. "I order you to leave your daughter alone, sir. And I release you from custody." With a sharp rap of his gavel, the judge made his decision and rose from his seat.

"Release your prisoner, Sheriff." Without another look in Ellie's direction, he stepped down from the platform and marched from the room, only pausing for a moment to speak quietly to James.

Ellie was stunned. She'd been scolded as though she were a small child. And her father was a free man. Her conscience reminded her that she'd already told Win that George should be released, but to have it happen in such an unfair manner was beyond belief. She looked up at Win, and found him watching her, his face ruddy with the anger he'd managed to suppress.

"You ready to go home?" he asked, and she shook her head.

"No, I want to talk to Pa."

George stood unmoving as Ellie approached, and she spoke to him quietly. "Pa, I need to talk to you."

He turned his head, and she saw new lines in his cheeks, a frown on his forehead and a weariness she had never seen exposed on his features before now. "I don't know as we have much to say," he muttered.

"You may not, but I do," she persisted. "You're my father, and I don't want to have to avoid you for the rest of my life, Pa. I want you to know that I'm not ever going to be afraid of you again."

She looked him squarely in the eye, and for the first time in her life, she felt no fear for the man who had browbeaten and abused her. Strength entered her voice, and she rejoiced at the knowledge that her words were true. "It's not because I'm married to Win, and have him to protect me. I'm a grown woman now, and I have the right to live my life the way I see fit. I won't let you take out your anger on me anymore."

"I've given up on you, daughter," he said bitterly. "You made your bed. You're stuck with it. You've got that fancy Dan next to you usin' you for a slavey, and you think you're better off than you were at home? Wait till he gets tired of lookin' at another man's bastard. That'll be the day he throws you out and slams the door behind you." Spittle edged his mouth as he spoke, and his final words were harsh and cutting. "I hope you hear what I'm sayin', because I won't give you squattin' room on my ranch."

She felt a pang of sadness that it should come to this, yet she could not back down. "You don't understand the first thing about love, Pa. You never have, and I fear you never will. I'll have your grandchild and you won't even know when it's born. I feel sorry for you."

She turned from him, unable to look any longer at the man who had done nothing but ill-use her for as long as she could remember.

"Let's go home, Ellie." Win's warm hand

touched her arm and she looked up at him, his features blurring before her eyes. He bent to brush a kiss against her cheek. "Don't let him see you cry," he said softly. "Don't give him the satisfaction, Ellie."

And she didn't. Holding Win's arm, she stepped from the room, out the door of the town council's office and onto the sidewalk. From there, they walked slowly and cautiously toward home, Win careful to dodge the icy spots where snow had melted.

"Are you feeling better, Mrs. Gray?" A gray-haired woman approached, and Ellie struggled to plaster a smile on her face, recognizing the minister's wife.

"Yes, ma'am, I am, Mrs. Fairfax," she said hastily. "Thank you for asking."

"We prayed for your well-being in church," Mrs. Fairfax said, resting her hand on Ellie's shoulder. She leaned closer and her voice lowered. "You look like you should be close to your bed. I'm surprised the doctor, here, allowed you out in the cold air."

Ellie felt a blush color her cheeks. "I've really been feeling much better of late. And Win takes good care of me."

Mrs. Fairfax looked up at Win. "We'll look forward to having you come back to church as soon as your wife is able. I'm sure she's fortunate to have you."

"I like to think so, ma'am." His head bowed in a gesture of respect, and they took their leave. "I'm glad you think I take good care of you," he murmured softly. "I guess I do come in handy once in a while, don't I?"

She slanted a look upward and tried her best to read his expression. It was bland, his eyes resting on the horizon, but a smile twitched the corners of his lips. "More than once in a while, Dr. Gray," she answered.

"Wait up!" The call came from behind them and Win tugged Ellie to a halt, turning to face the man who hailed them. James's stride was long as he approached. "Are you all right, Ellie? I didn't like what the judge had to say to you, but I wasn't surprised. Women don't ever get a fair shake, it seems." He grinned as he thrust his hands into his coat pockets. "Kate's been doin' her level best to get me trained. You think it's working?"

"I'd say there's hope for you," Ellie said slyly. "And I'm not really surprised at the judge. He'd probably have sent me home with Pa if he'd had a choice."

"Well, don't worry about your father any-more, Ellie. I told him it was worth his next five years of freedom if he caused you any more grief. And he didn't have a word to say. Just took off for the livery stable to rent a horse to ride home on."

"You think he'll behave himself?" Win asked, doubt coloring his words.

"He didn't enjoy jail. That ought to have some influence on his behavior," James said with a grin. And then his look of easy humor faded and Ellie saw a different side of James Kincaid emerge. His mouth grew firm and his jaw tightened as he faced her head-on and touched her shoulder.

"He knows better than to cross the Kincaid bunch," James said bluntly. "I'm not only the sheriff of Whitehorn, I'm a member of a family that's been here for a lot of years, and the men tend to stick together when the situation calls for it. Your pa is smart enough to know he'll be walking on thin ice if he causes any more trouble for you."

And then he smiled, and the lawman became her neighbor once more, his grin genial, his eyes sparkling with good humor. "Thank you, James," Ellie said solemnly.

"And now we're on our way home," Win told James. "Ellie's probably been out in this cold long enough."

"Let me give you a ride," James offered. "I just got a buggy from Lionel Briggs so I could pick up Kate at the school. I don't want her walking home with Tyler in the cold."

"Sounds good to me," Win said. "Got room for all of us? Even Ellie?"

"There's room for all three of us," James said, his eyes fixed on Ellie's face as he took her other arm and led the way across the street to where the buggy was tied in front of the sheriff's office. In moments they were on the seat and on their way home. "Now, doesn't this beat walking?" he asked Ellie, lifting the reins and urging the mare into a slow trot. "You feeling all right?" he asked, peering down into her face. "You look kinda peaked, like Kate did just before..." His voice trailed off and he glanced at Win. "You think she's about ready?" he asked.

Win nodded. "Almost. Maybe another couple of weeks."

"Before Christmas?" Ellie asked. "I figured around the middle of December, if it truly takes nine months, like you said."

"He oughta know," James said cheerfully, as he turned the buggy toward the back street where his house sat between Win's office and the home of the lumberyard owner. He pulled

the buggy up to the front gate with a flourish. Win jumped to the ground and reached
for his wife.

"Here, hang on to my shoulders. You don't
want to take a tumble," he said, waiting until
she gripped him firmly. Then, grasping her
waist through the heavy outer garment she
wore, he lifted her carefully, settling her on
her feet.

"You doing all right?" James asked, bending to look down at her.

Ellie nodded, pleased by his concern.
"I'm fine as frog hairs," she said, lifting her
skirts as she stepped to the gate and opened
it. "Thank you, James. Tell Kate I said hello,
will you?"

"I can do that," he answered agreeably. "It's
gonna snow for sure, Doc. Don't get too far
from home."

"I've got a couple of calls to make," Win
told him. "But I'll get Ellie settled first."

"You go ahead," she told him. "I'll be fine.
I'm going to start supper so it'll be ready
when you get home."

It was more than two hours later when
Win came in the front door. Ellie heard him
enter his office, and she smiled, imagining
him leaving his black leather bag there. He

would shrug from his coat and hang it on the hall tree, then make his way into their living quarters.

"Ellie?" His call merged with the opening of the kitchen door, and she turned to greet him. "I met up with some men from town, out looking for one of Kate's students. The rascal ran off after school, and his folks are worried about him." He came to stand by the stove and held his hands over the heat that rose from the top.

"You all right?" he asked, leaning to brush a kiss across her cheek. "That's better," he said, flexing his fingers. "My hands are warm now." He stepped behind her and his arms encircled her, his fingers spread wide over her belly. "How's the little guy doing?" His breath was warm against the side of her neck and she leaned back against his solid form.

"Fine, I guess," she said, her thoughts churning as a vision of the child, wandering alone in the falling snow, filled her mind. "Do you think he'll be all right, the little boy they're out looking for?" Ellie asked, turning in Win's embrace to twine her arms around his neck. "All I can think of is how cold I was when I wandered across the open range, trying to get back to you." She sighed deeply as her forehead rested against his broad chest.

"Ellie? Are you all right? I'm afraid today was hard on you." he said, and she knew he referred to the hearing earlier.

"Yes," she said, lifting her head to meet his gaze. "Probably better than I've ever been in my whole life."

"Well, don't be worrying about the boy, honey. I'm sure he's a healthy youngster, and no doubt warmly dressed." Win tried to encourage her, but his eyes were dark as though he felt more than a measure of concern.

She turned back to the stove and he leaned over her shoulder. "You got something cooking?"

She laughed. "You know very well I have, Dr. Gray. It's ready for you. Come on, we'll sit down and eat." She opened the oven and lifted a pan of biscuits from the shelf, their tops golden brown. A kettle of chicken stew sat at the back of the stove, rich with vegetables, its scent rising as she lifted the lid.

"I'm sure glad you're a good cook, sweetheart," Win told her, rolling his sleeves up and heading for the sink. "You've got me ruined for any other sort of life. My uncle

Gregory told me marrying you was the best decision I've ever made in my life, bar none."

"Did he?" She slanted him a good-natured look, and ladled stew into his bowl. "I've got milk in the back room, and coffee in the pot."

"Both, please," Win said, sighing as he inhaled the rich aroma of his meal. He rose as she approached with a glass of milk in each hand, and waited until she placed them on the table, then pulled her chair out, waiting to seat her.

"You make me feel so genteel," Ellie told him, lowering herself gingerly into the seat. "I'll bet not another woman in town gets treated the way I do."

"You're a lady, Ellie." And as if that were the last word on the subject, Win sat down and reached for her hand. His words of blessing were brief, and they ate with relish.

Ellie lay awake late into the night, her mind churning with the day's events. Thoughts of her father saddened her, and yet she sensed that somehow, sometime in the future, they would come to terms. And then she thought of the child who might, even now, be in the cold. Thankful, once again, for her rescue at

Win's hands, her own ordeal put aside, she turned her head to see the shadowy bulk of his body beside her.

She turned, rolling against him, her arm resting on his waist, inhaling the scent of him. Fresh air and laundry soap, combined with the natural male aroma teased her nostrils and she leaned forward to rest her forehead against his back.

The baby squirmed, and Ellie bit back a chuckle, aware of the cramped conditions her child was being subjected to. Bad enough that she was all squashed into a little lump inside the confines of her mother's belly, now she was being squeezed between Win's backbone and Ellie's innards. "You poor little tyke," Ellie whispered. She eased from Win's body, her hands rubbing the taut skin that covered her swollen abdomen. Her skin itched, yet was sensitive beneath her fingers, and she massaged the reddened marks that marred her flesh.

Win murmured her name, his voice drowsy, and she lifted a hand to his shoulder and then to his hair. "Go back to sleep," she whispered, but he only sighed and turned his head to kiss her hand.

"Did you wake me on purpose?" he asked,

reaching a long arm behind him to pat her bottom.

Her fingers tugged at a lock of his hair and she grumbled, attempting to sound indignant. "Of course not. I was restless and you were handy to lean on."

"Handy, am I?" he murmured, stretching to his full length and turning in the cocoon of sheets and quilts to face her. He lifted her to rest on the curve of his shoulder and his hand found a spot on her lower back that needed the firm touch of strong fingers. "Having a hard time sleeping?"

"Um. A little. I've been thinking about things."

Win yawned, and inhaled a deep breath. His head dipped and he nuzzled against her cheek. "You wide-awake?"

She nodded. "The baby's feeling crowded, I think. She keeps trying to stretch out and something pokes my ribs and makes them ache."

His chuckle was muffled against her temple. "She? You're sure about that?"

"No. But you know I'd like to have a girl. What do you think? You're the doctor."

"I learned a long time ago not to make predictions I couldn't back up, honey. If you want a girl so much, I'll think good thoughts, but there's no guarantee. We won't know for sure till she makes an appearance."

Ellie nudged his chin with her fist, then spread her fingers against his cheek. "Ruth doesn't think it'll be much longer. And I think the baby's shifted during the past day or so. It feels lower. I can breathe better, but it's pressing on my innards and I have to…" She halted, unwilling to discuss her major symptom with him.

"Run to the outhouse?" She felt his chest move, and she knew he'd struggled to keep his laugh silent.

"You're not supposed to be amused at my expense," she said tartly.

"Sweetheart, your running to the outhouse is natural, just a part of having a baby," he told her. "And if you've really dropped, it won't be longer than two weeks." His hand slid around, past her hip to the rise of her belly. "Besides, that's why we have that chamber pot over in the corner. You don't need to be running outside."

He pushed her to her back and his fingers measured the length and breadth of the burden she carried, his palm massaging the stretch marks she bore. "Might be a bit lower," he said after a moment. "But I don't think it's too low for me to—" His hand moved beneath the curve to rest against the top of her thigh.

"Ellie? Would you mind if I made love to you? I'll be careful, sweetheart. I won't do anything to hurt the baby." His fingers inched the fabric of her nightgown up the length of her legs and he drew it higher, until his hand met bare skin and the soft thatch of curls he'd uncovered.

She shivered at his touch, barely suppressing a moan of pleasure. "I've missed you there," she whispered.

"I've missed being there," he returned, his words soft and coaxing. "Can I take your gown off?" At her nod, he helped her sit upright, and in moments she was wrapped against him, her skin warmed by the brush of masculine flesh, aware of the urgency of his need as his arousal flexed against her belly. He bent to her breast, his mouth gentle, his teeth and tongue careful as he pressed warm kisses across her swollen flesh.

She felt at once tender, yet aching for the firmer touch he was wont to give, and she wriggled against him. "Please, Win?" His murmur of understanding was immediate, and his mouth opened fully against the crest that firmed and pebbled at the urging of his tongue.

"We'll be very, very careful," he murmured, teasing her puckered flesh, kissing the curve of her breast and across the firm swollen skin of her abdomen. "I don't want you to move, Ellie. Just be still and let me pleasure you."

"I want you, Win."

"Not nearly as much as I need you right now," he said fervently. Rolling her again to her back, he knelt between her legs, drawing her knees up so that her thighs lay across his. "Let me know if you feel too much pressure," he said, his hands trembling as he fit himself to her body.

She was totally exposed to him and in the dim light of the moon, she watched as his hands traced the contours of her body. He lavished caresses on each needy part, and she was hard put to lie quietly as he'd instructed, her flesh coming alive at his touch. He was within her, yet not fully a part of her, and she lifted to capture his length.

"Shh. Don't move, honey. I don't want to come near the baby's head." And it seemed he could find a measure of satisfaction even in the slow, gentle movements that enticed her. His fingers touched her with tender care and she moaned aloud, her enforced stillness seeming to add substance to the intense pleasure he brought her. Her breathing was shattered by the force of her release and she cried his name aloud.

His hands found the pillow on either side of her head and he leaned over to suckle at her lips, swallowing the words she spoke between shuddering gasps. Barely increasing his rhythm, he groaned against her face, shivering in the grasp of delight as his seed was spent within her body. Rolling carefully from her, he gathered her in his arms and his mouth sought hers again.

"Ellie, Ellie." He whispered her name between deep, gasping breaths, and his hands held her against himself as though he could not bear to be separate from her warmth. "You bring me joy," he said quietly.

"I love you, Win." It was all she could offer, and as she lifted her face to receive his kiss, he smiled, and it was enough.

"I'd be glad to keep the baby," Ellie told Kate, cutting short Kate's efforts to sound her out.

"He's got a runny nose," Kate repeated.

"And I don't want you to get sick again." She rocked the small bundle in her arms and bit at her lip. "Maybe I'd better ask Win if it's all right for you to watch him."

Ellie grinned, throwing up her hands in surrender. "Go on down the hall to his office if you think there's going to be a problem. He's in with a couple of patients this afternoon."

Kate headed for the kitchen doorway. "It's only going to be for three hours or so. I'll let school out a little early. It looks like more snow, and the children will need to get a head start on it."

Ellie smiled as Kate strode down the hall to Win's office door. Keeping an eye on Tyler would be a pleasure, she'd already decided. She'd have a chance to rock him and practice changing diapers. And since Kate had just nursed him until he spit back the last mouthful, he was pretty certain to be content until her return.

The meat in the oven was beginning to brown nicely, and Ellie added water from the iron teakettle, then put the cover back in place. Once it was done, she could hold it on the back of the stove until Win was ready to eat his supper. A kettle of green beans simmered, and fresh bread was covered with a clean dish towel on the buffet.

Outside the weather was cold, with a strong wind blowing up from the mountains, but her kitchen was cozy and warm, and satisfaction with her lot in life filled her with contentment. Beside the rocking chair Win had brought home only yesterday, she'd tucked her bag of knitting. And deep within its assortment of yarn and needles and the unfinished scarf she was working on for James's Christmas gift, was a small tablet she'd found in Win's desk drawer.

She'd filled several pages with sketches of Win, trying from memory to reproduce his face, and somehow not achieving success. Perhaps later on tonight, if he brought his books into the kitchen to work, she might be able to watch him and draw without his notice. The need to capture his image on paper was causing her to waste more sheets in the tablet than she could spare. Tonight, she'd coax him from his office, and then, in the lamplight, she'd be able to watch him as she drew.

The scarf would only take another hour or so to complete, and she could place it in her drawer beside the pale-blue shawl she'd made for Kate. To finally have friends in her life was one of the multiple blessings of being Mrs. Winston Gray. And her heart sang as she stood before the stove, deep in thought.

"Win says it's all right," Kate said from behind her. Ellie turned quickly, her mind switching from one thought to another as she focused on the squirming bundle Kate held.

"Give him to me," she told Kate, holding out her arms. "I can't wait to get my hands on him. It's been forever since I've held him."

Kate grinned. "I only hope he doesn't make you wish me home early," she said. "If he gets hungry before school's out, give him his sugar teat. I've put it in the sack with his diapers. Just dip it in a bit of water and he'll suck on it." She looked back, almost reluctantly, Ellie thought, as she donned her coat, then wrapped her scarf over her head and around her neck.

"It's getting colder out there. I think it's good that Tyler doesn't have to be hauled around in the wind any more today. Oh, and Win said to tell you he's got enough patients to last the rest of the afternoon. Don't plan on seeing him till suppertime." With a last wave, Kate opened the back door, and scooted through, quickly pulling it closed behind her.

Ellie turned to the rocking chair and settled herself, unwrapping the outer blanket from the baby. His tiny fist flailed at the air, and his mouth puckered as the light made him blink. "I thought you might be asleep," Ellie crooned, lifting him to kiss the downy head. "You precious child." Her arms held him against her breast and she rested his slight weight against the rise of her abdomen.

The baby protested once, a sluggish nudge of knee or foot pressing against Tyler's backside, and Ellie laughed. "You'd better get along, the two of you. You're going to be friends, right from the start, if I have anything to say about it." A lullaby she barely remembered came to mind, and she alternately hummed the tune and sang snatches of the lyrics as she rocked Tyler to sleep.

It seemed Tyler did not like the wash basket she'd called into use as a bed for him, and Ellie picked him up for the third time, shushing his fretful cries, holding him against her shoulder as she poured water over the potatoes she'd peeled. With one hand, she pushed the kettle to the hottest spot on the stovetop and slapped its lid in place. Surely it was almost time for Kate to be home from school, she thought.

"Hush, little baby," she sang, her voice rising, finally gaining his attention. He sniffled, and she snatched her handkerchief from her wrapper pocket to dab at the tiny nostrils. Again, he shrieked, and his face turned crimson with his fury. One small fist batted at her chin, and she paused in her lullaby to laugh aloud at his antics. But not for long.

He suckled on that same fist for a moment, his mouth working eagerly, and finding no sustenance there, he screamed anew. "The sugar teat," Ellie exclaimed, frustrated that she had not thought of it earlier.

Lifting the stack of cloth diapers to the chair, she bent to locate the small pacifier. "Maybe you need changing again," she told him, muttering the thought aloud. His blanket made a pad atop the table and she placed him there, the sugar teat forgotten for a moment as she stripped him from a wet diaper and reached for a clean one from the sack.

He kicked and squirmed, wailing mightily, his fists clenched, arms thrashing in the air. The diaper pin between her lips, she brought up the bottom of the triangle to his tummy and matched it with the other two corners.

Finally. Carefully, she pressed the heavy pin through the flannel and latched it.

"There you go, dumplin'," she told him, bending to brush her lips against his tummy before she pulled his gown down to cover him. The extra small blankets Kate had included to pad his tiny bottom fit between his legs, and Kate looked down. "That doesn't look very comfortable," she told him, aware that her voice caught his attention.

He frowned intently and his face reddened, and then she heard the unmistakable sound of his diaper being filled again. "Oh, Tyler!" She could barely suppress the groan, as he looked up at her with his wise eyes narrowed, and opened his mouth to yawn.

A hissing from the stove announced that her potatoes had boiled over and she held one hand on the baby's tummy as she reached to tug the pan from the hot spot. It was a long stretch and she held the very end of the handle between her fingers, giving it a jerk to move it to a cooler place on the surface of the stove. Boiling water ran over the side of the pan, the pungent aroma of potatoes combined with the hot stove lid making her wince.

Unpinning the diaper, she wrinkled her nose. "I don't know which smells worse, you or the burned potato water," she grumbled. "Although I think you win the prize, sweetie." Both hands filled with dirty diaper, the cloth she used to clean him with and nowhere to deposit either item, she stood erect, her back aching from the strain of bending over the table.

Her hair had come loose from the braid and curled in the steam from the stove. Tendrils hung against her cheeks, and she blew one from in front of her eyes, and then stood in dismay as Tyler discovered his lungs were in good working order once again.

"Well, drat," she muttered, just as the kitchen door opened wide and a woman marched into view.

"I'd say you've let things get out of hand, young woman," her guest said, peering at Ellie through spectacles that rode the end of her nose.

Ellie gawked. Torn between depositing the soiled diaper and rag on the floor, and tossing them in the stove, she could only allow her gaze to sweep over the middle-aged woman who faced her. A finely made traveling suit looked to have been tailored by hand, and a dark feather swept elegantly across the top of her hat. With dainty gestures, she tugged her gloves from her hands, working at each finger, while the reticule hanging from her arm swung in rhythm with her movements.

"I beg your pardon," Ellie said, her voice rasping. She cleared her throat and tried again. "May I help you? Are you lost?"

"I don't believe so. Not if this is the home of Dr. Winston Gray." She looked around the kitchen and her sniff was audible. "Are you the housekeeper?"

"No, I'm his wife," Ellie said sharply. "Who are you?" And at just that moment, Tyler's naked male apparatus sprayed like a veritable fountain. Ellie dodged, and the woman lifted a diaper from the stack and covered the source with a swift movement. Then she stood erect once more and allowed her eyes to take Ellie's full measure.

"I, my good woman," she said majestically, "am Winston's mother."

Chapter Fifteen

"You're Win's mother." As a statement of fact, it left Ellie feeling less than capable of sounding the least bit intelligent. And when the elegant lady in front of her only nodded her head, then took a long look around the kitchen, Ellie was certain she'd awakened in the middle of a bad dream.

The soiled diaper in her left hand and the equally dirty rag in her right precluded any attempt to shake the woman's hand in greeting. And the half-naked baby in the middle of the kitchen table needed tending in the very worst way.

"Well, shoot," Ellie muttered, and then sum-

moned her most welcoming smile. "Would
you mind keeping your eye on Tyler while I
get rid of his mess?" Not allowing Mrs. Gray
the time to summon up a refusal, Ellie turned
away, snatching up a remnant of brown paper,
left over from her latest delivery from Tess
Dillard. She wrapped the offending diaper
and rag, then stashed it next to the back door,
where it could be taken outdoors and rinsed
in a bucket of water when Kate arrived.

Shooting a glance at Win's mother, she
turned toward the sink, seeking to hide the
hot wash of embarrassment erupting in crimson cheeks and watering eyes. What a way
to meet this specimen of Saint Louis society, with the kitchen filled to the ceiling with
the stench of scorched potato water and the
equally noxious odor of a dirty diaper.

She scrubbed her hands with a dab of the
soap leavings she kept beneath the sink,
rinsing well beneath the pump, and then
snatched at a handy towel. Her hands still
damp, she headed awkwardly toward the
table, reaching for the back of a chair to
balance herself. Tyler was awake and alert,
peering up at Mathilda Gray with his wise
gaze focused on her face, his mouth work-

ing at one fist, while the other waved energetically in the air.

"I'll just put on a clean diaper," Ellie said, her head bent to conceal the incipient tears she attempted to blink away. Her fingers trembled as she lifted Tyler's legs and slid a clean flannel beneath his narrow behind. The damp cloth Mrs. Gray had put in place, Ellie used to wipe his round belly and the creases where moisture had accumulated. And then she repeated the diapering process, pinning him neatly inside the last clean triangle Kate had provided for her use.

"You seem to have had a considerable amount of practice at that," Mrs. Gray said, her voice suggesting that Ellie might have done at least one thing right during the past few minutes.

"Not a lot," Ellie admitted. "This is the first time I've had Tyler all to myself. But I've certainly used up a stack of diapers in a short while."

"And, who, may I ask," Mrs. Gray said, in her cultured voice that grated on Ellie's ears, "is the mother of this child?" The woman was straight as a pine tree, her shoulders squared, her head erect, and Ellie felt doomed as those sharp, green eyes took her measure.

"He belongs to our next-door neighbor. Kate is the schoolteacher."

"A schoolteacher, with a child?" Mrs. Gray asked, as if the idea of such a thing were out of the question. "She is allowed to teach?"

Ellie felt her own backbone stiffen at the insinuation that Kate was not fit to be in a schoolroom. "Yes, of course," she said firmly. "The town council realized that Kate is too good a teacher to keep her at home just because she's had a baby."

Mrs. Gray leveled a superior look at Ellie, issuing a statement she apparently believed in firmly. "A woman belongs in the home, where she can fulfill her obligations and spend her time on the duties of a wife and mother."

And wasn't that about as straitlaced an observation as anyone had ever spouted, Ellie thought. "Well, Kate feels she belongs in the schoolroom, and that's where she is."

"And she considers you a fitting substitute, allowing you to care for her child?"

Ellie reached up to brush back the wayward tress of hair that insisted on blurring her vision. "She probably thought I needed practice," she said quietly. And for the first time, she wondered how she would cope when her own child filled her arms. She'd certainly made a botch of things over the past fifteen minutes or so.

The fact that Win's mother put her at a disadvantage was the only shred of hope she could find right now in the awkward silence that settled over her kitchen. Overly warm, tremendously clumsy and more ill at ease than she'd ever been in her life, she felt the heat from the cookstove overwhelm her suddenly, and she pulled a chair from beneath the table. She plopped down in it, pulling the baby, blanket and all, toward her, where she could wrap him securely in his lightweight swaddling cloth, and ready him for Kate's arrival.

Her hands seemed inefficient as she tucked him together, and she concentrated on bundling him as Kate had presented him to her just three hours earlier. Had it only been three hours? Tyler's fist was wet, the sleeve of his gown drenched where he'd suckled in vain over the past few minutes, and as Ellie's hand brushed his cheek, he turned to her fingers, his mouth open, seeking nourishment.

"I don't have anything for you, sweetie," she whispered, watching in abject horror as his lips attempted to fasten on her knuckle and he discovered that she offered nothing to assuage his hunger. His eyes squinted shut and he howled, a mighty blast that brought Mrs. Gray into action.

She stepped neatly to Ellie's side and issued her next barrage. "I don't know what your neighbor was thinking of, allowing you to tend the child. There's a perfectly good sugar teat going to waste while that child is raising the roof." Snatching it up, she went to the sink, pumped once and held the cloth-wrapped object under the flow of water for just a fraction of a second, long enough to dampen its surface. Then with purposeful movements, she stalked back to the table and deposited it into Tyler's open mouth.

He clamped down on it, his jaws working as he sought what little nourishment it offered. Eyes blinking, he concentrated mightily, and with a flourish, Mrs. Gray swooped him from the table to hold him in both hands.

It was at that moment that Kate opened the door and backed into the kitchen, carrying a casserole dish in both hands. "Ethel waved me over from her door and told me to bring this to you, Ellie," she said. A dish towel in each gloved hand, she placed the pottery container on the buffet and turned to face Mathilda Gray.

"Ma'am?" Never at a loss for words, Kate appeared speechless, her gaze moving from Mrs. Gray's face to the bundle she held on outstretched hands.

"I assume this is your child?" Mathilda asked.

"Yes, of course," Kate answered hastily, reaching to take Tyler. "Oh, did he get hungry?" she asked. "I see you had to give him his doo-doo."

"Doo-doo?" Mathilda made the term sound somehow obscene, Ellie thought.

Kate's reddened cheeks flushed even more. "My mother used to call it that," she explained. And then she bent her head to the child she held. "Are you starving to death, angel?"

Ellie's eyes closed in relief. Kate's arrival couldn't have come at a better time, as far as she was concerned. Cleaning up the mess in her kitchen was imperative, and with the baby in safe hands, Ellie was free to tend to that chore. "Sit down here and feed him," she offered, motioning to the rocking chair. "I'll sort things out."

"Introduce me to your visitor," Kate said blithely, seating herself and opening her coat. Her gloves on the floor, her scarf flung back, she was well on her way to providing Tyler with his meal.

"Kate, this is Win's mother. Mrs. Gray, I'd like you to meet Kate Kincaid, my neighbor. Her husband is the town sheriff, and Kate teaches at the school here in town."

"Yes," Mathilda said, looking at Kate through her spectacles. "So you said."

"I didn't know you were coming to visit." Kate looked up with a cheerful smile, deftly ignoring Ellie's discomfort. "I imagine Ellie was surprised."

You have no idea. Ellie turned away, listening as Mathilda gave a recital of her trip. Even the mundane details she listed sounded of great importance as she paraded the trials of travel before Kate's hearing.

"I took the train to Butte, a nasty experience, I must say. I assume they assign the most aged cars to any area west of civilization. Then a stagecoach to Whitehorn. The driver was uncouth, the other passengers riffraff of the lowest sort." She paused, as if she considered those lowly beings she had been forced to travel with, and shook her head, a slight shiver causing her mouth to pucker. "I must say the accommodations were not up to the standards I'm accustomed to. But then, when one attempts to travel on the frontier, I suppose one must be willing to make concessions."

"By all means," Kate replied dryly. "I well remember my arrival in Whitehorn. I managed to interrupt a bank robbery, and when the bandits attempted to confiscate the stagecoach for their getaway, I ended up in the middle of the road, sitting flat on my fanny in the dirt."

"A most illustrious beginning to your career, I'm sure," Mathilda said stiffly.

"I don't know about that," Kate told her cheerfully, "but it did get me a husband."

"Indeed?" Ellie had not known eyebrows could climb so high, and decided that Win's mother was most adept at that particular talent. "I take it," Mathilda added with a note of disdain coloring her words, "that the sheriff took pity on you?"

Ellie bristled on Kate's behalf. "I'm sure there was no pity involved," she said quickly. "James Kincaid was a fortunate man to find someone like Kate."

"Well," Kate drawled, glancing down at Tyler, "I'm not sure I was the most glamorous creature he'd ever seen up to that point in his life. But he did tell me it was his first glimpse at my knees that convinced him to marry me."

Mathilda apparently decided that remark did not merit her attention, and she began a slow perusal of the kitchen as Ellie stifled a burst of nervous laughter in her dish towel. And then she looked at Kate, willing her to continue with the conversation. Lifting her shoulders in a helpless shrug, Kate grinned, and bent low over Tyler, murmuring softly, one foot keeping the rocker in motion.

"If I'd known you were on your way," Ellie said pleasantly, "I'd have been better prepared." She scrubbed at the oilcloth that covered the kitchen table, determined that no trace of Tyler, his blanket or any scent of dirty diaper should remain there. Her next project was the diaper she'd left bundled by the back door.

Kate apparently was alert to the movement around her for she spoke up quickly. "Just leave that be, Ellie. I'll take it home with me and let it soak on the back stoop while I cook supper."

So much for that escape route, Ellie thought glumly. She was not to get a reprieve of any sort from the relentless stare of Mathilda Gray, and she could only wish fervently for

Win to appear from his office. And with that, she felt a jolt of inspiration.

"I'll just run down to Win's office and let him know you're here," she said brightly, dropping the dishcloth on the sink board.

"I doubt he would appreciate being interrupted while he is doing whatever he does in his *office*," Mathilda said. "Has he found any *customers* in this godforsaken part of the country?"

Ellie felt the hairs on the back of her neck stand up. "He prefers to call them *patients*," she said quietly, wondering how soon they could ship the woman back to Saint Louis. How Win had ever been birthed by this high-falutin female was beyond her.

"If he'd gone into law or banking, he'd have dealt with clients who were of his social stature," Mathilda said curtly. "He was raised to be a gentleman."

"He *still is* a gentleman," Ellie replied. "His reputation is above reproach, ma'am."

"Oh? Then why did it take him so long to marry you? Or wasn't he the one who got you in the family way?" The look was frosty, and Ellie felt chilled by icy-green eyes that held more than a trace of dislike.

"No, he wasn't," she said. "I would have

thought Win's uncle would have given you the particulars," Ellie said quietly. "Or didn't you see him after he was here?"

"He arrived in Saint Louis the very day before I left. I didn't speak with him, although he did manage time to talk to Winston's father. Geoffrey seemed to think we'd be pleased to welcome you to the family," she said, her mouth twisting as though the idea were making her ill. "Given your denial of Win as your child's father, I don't think that is remotely possible."

"Maybe not," Ellie agreed. "And I guess that's your choice to make. But Win's uncle didn't seem to be angry about it. Maybe he thought Win had good reason for what he did."

She edged toward the hallway door. "I'll just go and check on Win." The knob in her hand, she sent a pleading look in Kate's direction. "Tell Mrs. Gray about the school, why don't you, Kate?"

The knob turned readily and Ellie was in the hallway, leaning against the wall, her breath catching in her throat. She'd never been exposed to such blatant prejudice in her life. Maybe the woman felt she had just cause, considering the circumstances, but she ought to at least listen to Win's story first.

Social stature. Whatever those words were supposed to mean, they didn't describe anything much that Win was interested in. If there was ever a true gentleman on the face of this earth, Winston Gray was his name, and she'd defy anyone, including the creature from Saint Louis to say any different.

"Ellie?" Win stood before her, his hands resting on her shoulders, and she realized her eyes were squeezed tightly shut, her fingers were pressed tightly against her mouth, and her heart was beating at a furious pace within her breast. "What's wrong, sweetheart? Are you feeling sick? Do you have pain?"

He looked down at a tapestry valise that sat on a chair near the staircase. "Whose is that?" His words were taut with suspicion, and he looked toward the closed kitchen door. "Ellie, is someone here?"

His hands traveled the length of her arms to cup her elbows, and he drew her from the wall's support to lean against his chest. She felt the tender caress of long fingers against her nape, the warmth of his breath against her ear and throat as he bent his head to kiss the soft skin. And she could only nod her head, then shake it quickly, as though her thoughts were muddled.

"Who's upset you?" he asked, his voice hardening, his head lifting, even as his palm cupped her chin, forcing her face into his field of vision. "Is there someone in the kitchen, Ellie?"

She nodded then, and as he dropped his hands from her and turned toward the door, she reached for him. "Wait. Don't go in there yet. Let me catch my breath first." It would be all right. Win was here, he'd take care of her now.

And I'll stand behind him and let him protect me. The words shattered her pose, and her shoulders lifted, her fingers wiping at the single tear that had fallen from each eye. She would not cower before Win's mother. For the last time in her life, she'd been put down, allowed someone to use her as a doormat. No more.

"I'm all right now," she said, only the barest quaver in her voice betraying the fear she could not totally subdue. "Your mother is here, Win. She came in on the afternoon stage, and must have walked over here. Kate's in there with her."

"What did she say to you?" His words were like river ice, those chunks taken each winter from the river and stored in sawdust in

John's warehouse. Amos Carlton paid dearly, she'd heard, for the privilege of having his ice chests filled throughout the summer months, and John had made a tidy sum with his venture.

"Answer me, Ellie. What did my mother do to you?" His lips were thin, almost colorless, and she thought idly she'd never seen him so angry. Except for the morning he'd carried her back to town on the back of a horse and tucked her into his bed.

"She's not very happy with me," Ellie said carefully. "Kate's keeping her busy while I came to find you."

His eyes were glittering chips of green, and faint color rode his cheekbones. "Well, you've found me, sweetheart." His hand clutched the knob and the door was wrenched open.

"Mother? Why didn't you let us know you were coming to visit?" he asked, the polite words lacking any trace of welcome. He stalked into the kitchen, tossing a nod in Kate's direction and approaching the woman who stood at the table. "I'd have met you at the stage if you'd sent a wire." He bent and his lips touched the air an inch from her cheek.

"How is Father? I assume Uncle Geoffrey arrived back in Saint Louis safely?"

"I wanted to surprise you," Mathilda said cooly. "I certainly managed to do just that, as far as your wife is concerned."

Win's sharp gaze cut back to Ellie. "Did mother introduce herself nicely?" he asked.

"Why, yes," Ellie said. "She said she was Winston's mother, and then was gracious enough to watch Tyler while I cleaned up his mess."

Kate smothered a snort, turning it into a chuckle, and stood, holding the baby up to her shoulder. "I believe I'll just wrap up this young man and take him home now," she said, her grin wide as she turned it in Win's direction. "How about tossing his heavy blanket over him for me, Ellie?"

Ellie did as Kate asked, tucking the covering around Tyler so the wind couldn't get to him, then helped Kate ease her arms into her coat. The large garment covered Kate and the baby, too, without any trouble, and Ellie bustled about, gathering up the soiled diapers and Kate's tote bag.

"Here's your belongings. I'll see you later," she said, opening the door and holding it wide for Kate's exit. "If you and James would like to join us, I'm sure there's enough casserole to go around," she said hopefully.

Kate offered a blank smile and shook her head. "No, I think you have your hands full, Ellie. I'll just trundle on home and find something for supper." She peered back over Ellie's shoulder. "It was pleasant meeting you, Mrs. Gray. I'm sure I'll be seeing you again." And then she was gone, bent over the baby, heading into the wind as she crossed the yard.

"I think you and I have some things to discuss, Mother," Win said as Ellie closed the door. "Why don't you come down to my office while Ellie gets supper on the table."

"Win?" Ellie held her head high and met his gaze without faltering. "Your mother has had a long trip, and I'm sure your talk can wait until after she's had a chance to eat and freshen up."

His hesitation was minute, and he obliged her with a short nod. "All right. I'll take her upstairs to the room you had when you first moved in here."

"Take the teakettle with you," Ellie said. "There's plenty of warm water to fill the pitcher, and soap and towels on the washstand." She looked at Mathilda, aware of the faint signs of travel, the shadows beneath her eyes. She'd missed them at first, caught up in the disdain that glittering gaze had shot in her direction. Now she read rightly the weariness the older woman struggled with.

True, the shoulders were straight, the back rigid, but a sigh escaped from those prim lips as Win extended a hand to usher her from the kitchen. "Win?" Ellie called his name, and he halted as his mother crossed the threshold into the hall, turning his head to answer Ellie's summons. His eyes were grim, his jaw firmly set.

It would not do that Win's first encounter with his mother, after all this time apart, should be filled with conflict. "I'm sure your mother is weary, Win. Save the talk for later." She held his gaze and his mouth worked, as though he bit back words, and then he nodded abruptly and the door closed behind him.

She envisioned them climbing the stairs, Win carrying the valise, his mother's footsteps firm and square upon each step. The faint sound of movement above told her they were in the hallway, and she waited, catching the barest murmur of voices through the ceiling vent that allowed heat to permeate the upper floor of the house.

A similar vent allowed warm air to rise from the hallway at the front of the house. Ellie recalled nights when she'd heard Win's movements as she nestled in the bedroom, where even now his mother was looking at the simple provisions the room afforded.

She turned to the stove, lifting the coffeepot to sniff the strong brew. Win would no doubt want the most potent drink available when he came back to her, but this was beyond redemption.

Opening the back door, she tossed the dregs into the yard and shivered in the cold wind. "Ellie?" He was behind her, drawing her back into the warm kitchen, closing the door behind her, and taking the pot from her hands. "Are you all right?"

"Yes." She looked up at him, and her heart sank as she recognized the face of sorrow. "She can't hurt me, Win." Her words were barely a whisper, knowing how audible their voices were on the second floor. "I need you to back off and let me work this out. She's your mother, and you don't want her to leave here with bad feelings between the two of you."

"I won't let her be cruel to you." It seemed he'd taken a stand, and Ellie nodded.

"I won't, either. But she's disappointed in your choice of a wife, and it won't make it any better if you argue with her over it. Either she'll grow to accept me, or she won't. Nothing you say is going to make a difference."

A suggestion of hurt firmed his mouth and he backed away a step. "All right. Have it your way, Ellie. Again, I won't interfere. Unless she is downright rude to you, I'll stay out of it." He turned to the sink and rinsed the wash basin, then pumped the water to refill it. "I'll help you with supper as soon as I wash my hands."

Ellie moved the casserole dish to the stove, and opened the oven door. The fire was still hot enough to bake bread, she decided, so surely it wouldn't take more than ten minutes to reheat the meal Ethel had sent. She slid it onto the rack and closed the door, then sought out the assortment of crocks and bowls in the pantry.

By the time supper was finished, Ellie had been regaled with stories of balls and galas in Saint Louis. She'd heard more than she ever wanted to know about the ins and outs of society's most prestigious families, who had married whom over the past two years, and what had happened to each and every person Win had ever known. Especially the young women, the socially correct, beautiful creatures who inhabited the world Winston Gray had once dwelt in.

"…and the wedding was fabulous, with eight bridesmaids. Do you remember Dorothy Hastings? Of course you do. What was I thinking? Why, you were her escort at the Christmas gala the year you graduated from college."

Ellie rose from the table, gathering her silverware and plate, then halted beside Win, to lift his from before him. He glanced up at her.

"I'll help you, Ellie. Why don't you sit down, and I'll clean up."

She placed a detaining hand on his shoulder. "I don't mind, really. I need to move around anyway. I was tired of sitting so long."

Mathilda's eyes surveyed Ellie's length. "I'm sure you can't be interested in such happenings anyway," she said cooly. "I fear the life Winston left behind is beyond your understanding."

"I think you're probably right," Ellie agreed. "Around Whitehorn, the biggest social event of the year is usually a barn raising or a square dance at the Grange hall. I remember when the schoolhouse was built a couple of years ago, before Kate arrived in town. And then the townsfolk all got together to put up a house for them when James married her. Most everybody turned out for that."

"I didn't know about that, Ellie," Win said, rising to take the dishes from her hands. "It must have been before I got here. You mean the house next door?"

"That's the one," she said. "It was the only vacant lot on the street. Used to belong to the man who owns the lumberyard. Of course, Kate and James have worked hard to make it look like it's been there forever. Kate planted..." Her voice trailed off as she glanced at Mathilda. A look of utter boredom drew down the woman's narrow lips, and Ellie deliberately clutched at the plates that Win held.

"Give me those back," she muttered. "You sit down and let me take care of this." She'd done all the palavering she was going to for one night. Bad enough she'd gone and made such a disaster of a first impression on the woman. Now she was boring her to death. "Where's my teakettle?" she asked Win, glancing at the stove. "I can't make tea without it."

"I must have left it upstairs," he said. "Use a saucepan for now." His glance in her direction held a frustrated frown, and she hesitated, unwilling to make him uncomfortable.

"All right. Would you like a cup of tea?" she asked, turning to Win's mother.

"I don't suppose you have any sort of imported English blend, do you?"

"I believe it's imported from Saint Louis, as a matter of fact," Ellie said carefully, stifling a giggle as she reached for the flowered teapot she kept on the buffet. She ought to use the small packet of herbs Ruth had brought, she thought with a glimmer of amusement. That would guarantee the woman a good night's sleep at least.

"I don't like the idea of leaving you here alone," Win said, drawing his trousers on with haste as Ellie watched. Swathed in a quilt, she sat in the middle of the bed, sleepy-eyed and yawning.

"I'm not alone," she pointed out dryly. "I have your mother for company." And then at his frustrated look, she relented. "I'll be fine, honestly. And I'm sure you don't need to be worrying about me in the next few hours. You'll have enough to do."

"It sounds like a nasty situation," he agreed, sitting to pull on his boots. "Matt Darby said

the Kirkpatrick family lost just about everything they owned in the fire. Must have had a
blocked chimney or something. Anyway, the
two youngest children are burned, and Matt
said the mother is in bad shape, too."

"I'll get your bag for you," Ellie offered,
easing to the edge of the bed, her toes searching out the warmth of her slippers.

"Stay there," Win told her. "Matt's out in
the hallway, waiting for me to get dressed. I
can grab my bag on my way past the office."

"How about something to eat?" Suddenly,
Ellie felt a chill sweep through her at the
thought of Win being so far away in the middle of the night. "Can I make you something
to take along?"

He shook his head. "No, you stay in bed
and cover up. I'll put a couple of chunks of
wood in the stove and check the fire in the
parlor stove, too. Just leave the door open so
the heat will come in."

"All right." She tucked her feet beneath the
quilt and scooted to the headboard. "Be careful, you hear?"

"I hear," he told her, leaning over the bed
to kiss her lightly. And then he bent again
and pressed a longer, firmer kiss against her
mouth, his hand at her nape to hold her in

place for his caress. "Take it easy when you get up, Ellie. No cleaning house or washing clothes, you understand? Just sit in the rocking chair and work on those little flannel things you've been sewing."

She smiled up at him, watching as he bent to blow out the candle beside the bed. And then he was gone, his words to the man waiting in the hall barely audible, the sound of Matt Darby's deep voice holding a note of desperation. She heard the sound of the stove door in the parlor clang shut, and in moments the outside door closed, and Ellie snuggled in the depths of the quilt. The sun wouldn't be up for hours, and daybreak would only bring another session with the woman upstairs.

Her brave words to Win rang hollow in her ears as she recalled the sheer bravery of her statement. *She can't hurt me, Win. Let me work this out.* "She's already hurt me," Ellie admitted in a whisper, and then her shoulders stiffened. "But better me than Win."

Chapter Sixteen

Breakfast was a disaster. It seemed that coddled eggs were Mathilda's usual repast and Ellie had never heard of them. "I can do scrambled or fried, or boil 'em in the shell," she offered, willing to oblige. "We have bacon hanging in the pantry, or sausage fresh from the butchering out at the Henderson place. Win took care of their children when they had whooping cough a while back and they brought us half a side of pork."

"In payment for Win's services?" Mathilda asked. "Don't the people here pay in cash?" She looked toward the pantry, as if the meat in question might be hidden behind the curtain.

"Sometimes," Ellie said simply. "Other times, they pay him in produce or jars of canned fruit or vegetables, or sometimes meat. Once in a while, he comes home with eggs and butter, if his patients don't have any money on hand. At least we can eat well."

Mathilda seemed to find no trace of humor in Ellie's remarks. She folded her hands on the table in front of her and sighed. "And if they don't pay, I suspect he doesn't dun them for it, does he?"

Ellie hesitated, unwilling to admit her ignorance. "Doesn't *dun* them?" she asked.

"Send them bills. Ask for payment." Mathilda sighed heavily as if to emphasize Ellie's lack of knowledge. "It's the usual procedure."

"Not here, it isn't, ma'am," Ellie retorted readily. "Folks do the best they can, and when times are good, they pay in cash. Other times they make do."

"He wouldn't have this problem in the city," Mathilda said, watching suspiciously as Ellie took four eggs from the heaping bowl on the buffet. "What are you going to do with the eggs?"

"You said you wanted them coddled," Ellie said patiently. "If you'll tell me how to cook them that way, I'll do it." Placing them on the stove, she went to the pantry and took down the slab of bacon, wiping it with a clean cloth. Her sharpest knife made short work of the slicing, and she placed eight thick pieces in her large skillet. "Do you want bread plain or toasted in the oven?" she asked Mathilda, unwrapping the last loaf from baking day.

"Toasted will be fine. And fix the eggs however you wish." Like a queen overseeing her subject, she sat at the table and watched as Ellie prepared the meal.

"You're not used to pitchin' in, are you?" Bringing a plate with two fried eggs, half the bacon and a thick slice of toast to place before her guest, Ellie blurted out her thoughts.

"Pitchin' in?" Mathilda looked up from her plate. "Did you expect me to help?"

"Didn't you ever have to do for yourself?" Ellie asked quietly. "Or did you always have someone else to cater to you?" Not waiting for a reply, she settled herself on the other side of the table and folded her hands. "Win always asks the blessing. Do you want to do it instead, since he's not here?"

"I believe it's the place of the man of the house to say grace," Mathilda said.

"Well, we don't have a man in the house this morning, so it'll have to be one of us, I guess." Ellie waited a moment, and then bowed her head. Win always mentioned the hands that prepared the meal, but Ellie felt foolish asking God Almighty to bless her own hands, so she left out that part. The rest was easily said and she lifted her fork to pierce the yolk of her egg, watching as the thick, golden river ran toward her bacon. A bit of her bread sopped it up and she lifted it to her mouth, aware of Mathilda's eyes on her.

"Your manners are atrocious," the woman said simply. "I should have expected as much."

Ellie placed her fork on the table with a thump. "And just what does that mean?"

"I can't understand for the life of me why Winston married you in such a hurry." She waved a hand as Ellie opened her mouth to speak. "You were carrying a child, and Win seemed to feel his decision to give the family name to a child of unknown heritage was allowable. But I cannot condone such a thing."

Her gaze raked Ellie as she lifted her cup and sipped from its contents, and then she cleared her throat. "I understand you're a passable cook, and your house seems reasonably clean, but you obviously—"

"Hold on," Ellie said firmly. "Winston married me because of some of that. I'm a good cook, and I keep his house clean and his laundry done up. And my manners are just fine. Win has never complained about the way I eat."

Mathilda interrupted with a wave of her hand. "Perhaps he should. I think you took advantage of him. It was convenient for you to marry him, wasn't it? He provided a name for your child, and a place for you to live. And wasn't it handy that he turned out to be decent looking and the possessor of a tidy bank account."

"Convenient? I never thought of it quite like that, but I suppose that door swings both ways. I'm a convenient wife, I guess. I just happened to show up at the right time, when he needed somebody to hang around and serve his meals when he gets home and look after his office and wash up behind him."

She rose and bent over the table, aware that her face was flushed and her good manners were totally absent. "I don't give a good gol durn about his money. I've never asked him for a thing."

"I noticed you're wearing his ring," Mathilda said smartly. "And whether you know it or not, it's worth a tidy sum."

"Wives usually wear rings. And I'm his wife."

Ellie sat down with a thump, aggravated with herself at allowing the woman to rile her so. A noise at the door caught her attention and, as she watched, Ethel stuck her head in. "Just wanted to tell you that I'll be gone all day, Ellie. Mary Ellen Gladwin is having her baby, and they've asked me to come, since Doc is busy, out taking care of the Kirkpatrick family."

"Thanks for coming by, Ethel. And I'm much obliged for the casserole. We enjoyed it last night."

Ethel waved away her thanks and cast an inquiring eye at Mathilda. "You're Doc's mama, I understand. Did your trunk get brought by this morning? I heard that Mr. Waverly offered to drop it off. Tess told him it would do him good to get out of the emporium and let the stink blow off for a while."

"Yes, it came earlier," Ellie said. And with another wave, Ethel was gone. No hope of a respite for her today, Ellie thought gloomily. Kate was at the schoolhouse, Tess was at the store, and Win was on a house call, probably not coming home for hours, if the burn victims were as bad as he'd expected them to be. It promised to be a long day.

By noon, Ellie was facing the fact that snow might be a factor in Win's return from the his trip outside of town. Beginning before breakfast dishes were done, the flakes had grown to monstrous size, and the yard was covered with six inches of fresh snow, on top of four or five that had fallen in the past two days.

She rubbed at her back, aware of a nagging ache, and wished for a moment for Win's strong hand to press firmly against the spot. No sense in that, she reminded herself, punching down the bread dough, then covering the pan and setting it to rise again. He wouldn't be home for hours probably.

Contrary to Win's orders, she'd already baked coffee cakes and two pies and now was almost ready to put a pork roast in the oven for supper. There would still be room for two loaves of bread, she decided, slicing onions and readying the meat for cooking.

Mathilda had busied herself going through Win's office, looking at his books there and checking out his instruments. Then she moved on to the parlor, rearranging the shelves against the inside wall, where he kept the majority of his reading matter. Ellie heard her moving around, and several times, she made her way to that part of the house, asking if there was anything Mathilda needed.

The last foray had borne fruit, and Mathilda had allowed as she might like a cup of tea and a piece of coffee cake. For the first time today, Ellie thought she might have done something right, and her smile was genuine when she placed several slices on the plate and carried it to the parlor, where she placed it on the low table in front of the sofa. The butter was fresh from Tess's store only a couple of days since, and bore the distinct pattern of a daisy on its surface. Like a brand on cattle, that small bit of decoration let Tess's customers know who had churned this batch of butter.

Ellie leaned back, then sat up straight, finally propping a cushion at the small of her back. Nothing seemed to help, and the frequent pain was making her edgy.

"Do you always wriggle around so much?" Mathilda asked sharply, eyeing Ellie nervously. "You're not going to have your child this afternoon, are you?"

"Of course not. Win thinks I've another week, or maybe two, before that happens." Again the pain seized her, across the small of her back and finally edging toward the front on either side, to where the spasms met beneath her belly. "Besides, aren't labor pains supposed to be in the front?"

"I really couldn't say," Mathilda said. "Mine were, but then I've a notion if it can be done in a way that will cause disruption, you'll manage to discover it."

"You really aren't willing to give me a chance at all, are you?" Ellie asked, aware of the pain that shimmered in her words. "I thought I might be able to prove to you that Win didn't make a mistake when he married me, but you won't let me."

"I think you probably are doing the best you can, Eleanor. But we both know that Winston deserves better. A better home, a larger realm in which to display his talents, and certainly, a wife who will be a credit to him. If I had my way, he'd return to Saint Louis and set up a practice there, since he seems determined to remain in the career he's chosen."

"Well," Ellie said with a sigh. "I guess that put me in my place, didn't it?" She rose and lifted the tray, uncaring that Win's mother still held a cup in her hand, and had not finished her coffee cake. "I'll just find something to do in the kitchen," she said, walking from the parlor into the hall.

Halfway to the kitchen, she felt another aching, tugging pain take hold, and with it came a rush of fluid from between her legs. *"Win?"* She whispered his name, knowing it was futile. He was miles away, perhaps snowed in with patients who desperately needed him. And she was alone. Or might as well be. With only Mathilda to help, Ellie wasn't the least bit certain she could cope with what was to come.

Win's stack of wrapped newspapers waited in the depths of the wardrobe, and Ellie bent to pick up several. Covered with old sheets, they fit across the middle of the bed, and she placed two of them there, on top of the clean sheet she'd put in place. Of all the things Win had told her, the word *clean* rang a bell in her memory. Her wet wrapper lay in the clothes basket in the corner and she was garbed in her oldest nightgown, sitting with a towel between her legs to catch the residue of moisture that continued to flow.

"You're dressed for bed?" Mathilda stood in the bedroom doorway and her gaze was sharp. "Is there something wrong?"

"I think I'm beginning my labor," Ellie answered, aware of another pain wrapping her in its embrace. She closed her eyes and felt the steady rhythm of it, clenching the bottom half of her body in an ever increasing momentum. And then it eased away, one small increment at a time, until she was limp, gasping a bit as she caught her breath. "I'd say I am definitely going to have this baby." The words were spoken for Mathilda's benefit, and Ellie looked up to see their effect.

"Who shall I call to come?" Her brows were lifted, her mouth pursed as she eyed Ellie with an expression of horror. "How can we reach Winston?"

"We can't." Might as well tell her flat out, Ellie decided. "Ethel has gone to deliver a baby outside of town, and Kate is probably still at school. For now I think it's just you and me."

"I've never delivered a child," Mathilda said pointedly.

"Neither have I," Ellie said agreeably. "However, I don't have a choice." And then she was caught up in another series of con-

tractions, and she closed her eyes to concentrate on the slow, steady breathing she'd
watched Kate put into practice.

She walked. From bedroom to hallway to
parlor, then back, she paced the floor. From
front door to back, down the hallway, through
the kitchen, she walked, ever listening should
the sound of Win's voice pierce the stillness. As one pain after another came on, she
paused, leaning against the wall, or the newel
post on the staircase, or the kitchen table.
Wherever she happened to be, she waited it
out, and prayed for Win to arrive.

The force of her misery was centered in her
back, and she recognized that it was different
from Kate's labor. Knew that something was
not as it should be.

There was no sun in the sky, only gray,
hanging snow clouds, that alternately dumped
heavy, thick drifts on the ground, or hovered
low, bringing on early darkness. James came
to the kitchen door during one of her treks to
that room, Kate having sent him to check on
her. He returned moments later to announce
that she'd brought Tyler home early and he
was running a fever.

"I'd watch him for her, but I've got a situation going on that I have to tend to," he said

apologetically. "Will you be able to hold out until Win gets here?"

Ellie grimaced. "I really couldn't say, James. This is all new to me. I just know I'm about ready to climb in my bed and let this thing happen."

She'd done just that when she heard a commotion in the hallway. Mathilda's shrill tones spoke of anger and perhaps a smattering of fear, Ellie decided, but she was too caught up in misery to crawl from the bed and find out. The door opened with a bang and Mathilda's form shielded Ellie from whoever was attempting to enter.

"You can't come in here, you savage," she said harshly. "You have no place in this house."

"Ellie?" Ruth's soft tones caught her attention, and Ellie lifted her head from the pillow. "Tell your mother-in-law to let me in."

"Ruth!" It was a choked cry, and Ellie realized to her dismay that tears were gushing from her eyes. "Mathilda! Get out of the way," she cried, struggling to sit up on the bed. "Let Ruth in!"

With barely a sound, soft leather moccasins crossed the floor and Ellie felt hot tears spring to her eyes as she held out a hand in welcome. Ruth's fingers gripped hers with supple strength, their cold touch bringing a strange comfort to Ellie's heart.

"I had to take off my heavy boots in the hallway, and then hang my coat," Ruth explained quietly. "I thought I'd not be able to get past your watchdog out there."

Ellie laughed, then hiccupped as she wiped her tears. "She's not mine. And at this point, I'm not sure Win is willing to claim her, either."

"He's gone out to the Kirkpatrick place, hasn't he?" Ruth asked. "I felt your need, Ellie. Caleb gave his blessings and rode with me to the edge of town, then left to go back home. He was fearful of me being alone in the snow."

"You knew I was alone?" Ellie asked. "Did you hear that Ethel went out for a delivery, and Kate is at home with a sick baby? James had a problem to tend to, and Kate is upset because Tyler has a fever and she doesn't dare take him out in the weather."

"No," Ruth said, a strange smile curving her lips. "I had no way of knowing you were alone here. I only knew that your need was greater than the force of snow and wind. And so I came to you."

"Who is this heathen creature?" Her lips drawn flat by anger, Mathilda stood in the doorway, her glittering gaze casting contempt on the woman who held Ellie's hands in a clasp that was almost an embrace. "What right does she have to enter my son's house without a by-your-leave?"

"I am Ruth Kincaid, wife of Caleb," Ruth said with a dignity that must surely be apparent, even to Mathilda, Ellie thought. "I've come to help in the delivery of Ellie's child." She looked back at Ellie. "Do you have the tea I left with you?"

Ellie nodded, feeling the angry surge of pain surrounding her once more, her belly drawing forward as though the child within would burst through flesh to be born, rather than take the path nature decreed. She groaned with anguish, pushing at the taut rounding of her belly, her skin straining from the tension and swelling of her womb.

Ruth's hands were gentle, removing Ellie's clutching fingers and replacing them with her own firm palms and widespread clasp. She closed her eyes and measured the height and width of the child who was struggling to be born, and her head bowed as she pressed even harder, as if her fingertips could receive a message from the babe within.

Easing its bite, the pain left Ellie, and she shivered, the sweat on her body chilling her as she relaxed against the mattress. Ruth pulled a quilt to cover her and brushed dark hair from Ellie's face. "I ask you to go into the kitchen, Mrs. Gray, and find a package of tea leaves Ellie has placed in a flowered sugar bowl on the buffet. Heat water, if you please, and brew it in a large cup."

Without looking up at Win's mother, Ruth settled on the side of the bed beside Ellie. "I fear the child is breech," she said quietly. "Do you know what that means?"

"No," Ellie whispered, dreading the meaning behind the word Ruth uttered with such solemn pronouncement.

"The head has not come down as it should, or perhaps the baby has turned recently, and Win hasn't noticed. Has he checked you within the last days?"

Ellie nodded. "The first of the week, just like always. He listened to the heartbeat and felt for..." She halted. "I never know just what he's feeling when he moves his hands over me. He just smiles and tells me that all is well." She hesitated, and then a thought came to her. "I know I've felt some hard movements in the last day or so, as if the baby was turning around, trying to get comfortable."

Ruth nodded. "So impatient they are to be born sometimes, they try another way to seek the light." Her smile was tender, but Ellie felt the tension that darkened Ruth's eyes and brought her lips together tightly. "We'll take care of it, Ellie. When you have your next pain, I'll try to turn the babe."

Mathilda approached the bed, her head high, her jaw set. "Surely, there must be a midwife in this godforsaken part of the world. Is there no one we can send for?" In her hands was a large mug, steam rising to scatter a pungent scent through the air. "The water was almost boiling in the kettle," she told Ruth, placing the cup on the bedside table.

"Lift up a bit and sip at this," Ruth told Ellie, holding the cup to her lips, her other arm supporting her shoulders. The tea was spicy, with a distinct flavor, and Ellie, remembering Ruth's promise that it would ease her labor, held the hot liquid in her mouth and swallowed it as instructed.

"Are you worried about me?" Ellie asked Mathilda with an amused glance in the woman's direction. She eased from Ruth's grasp and lay back on her pillow, and her subdued laughter was sharp, as if such a thing were next to impossible.

"I don't like the thought of anyone suffering unduly," Mathilda said stiffly. "And I certainly wouldn't trust myself to the hands of a savage, if I were you."

"Ruth is a healer," Ellie said in a thin whisper as pain once more became her tormenter, and its arms circled her body with an agony she'd never thought to know. "Help me," she cried, her body lifting from the bed as she twisted in the throes of labor.

Ruth's fingers sought out the baby's head with one hand, there where it pressed upward almost between Ellie's ribs, and with the other gripped the rounded part that bulged just below her navel. A high, piercing shriek erupted from Ellie's throat, and she sobbed her distress as Ruth exerted pressure.

With a sigh, Ruth released her hold and gripped tightly to fingers that clawed for purchase. "Hold me," she whispered, seemingly uncaring of Ellie's fingernails that dug into her darker skin.

The pain receded once more and Ellie was limp, weary from the hours she'd spent in walking throughout the house before she'd taken to the bed that held her now. "Win?" she asked, her voice ragged, the tears again in evidence.

Mathilda bent to peer at her, her face strangely strained, her eyes no longer cold, but instead filled with a concern Ellie could hardly believe. "Are you certain there's no one I can look for?" she asked. Her gaze sought Ruth. "This girl will die if you can't take the babe from her womb."

"She's strong," Ruth decreed. "And I feel that Win will be here soon."

Mathilda snorted her disbelief. "Do you interpret dreams, too?" she scoffed. "How could you possibly know such a thing?"

Ruth ignored her, bending to wipe Ellie's brow. "I want you to drink more of the tea, and then we must try once more to turn the baby," she whispered. "I know it will be painful, Ellie, but I fear it's too large to be born with its bottom coming first."

Ellie nodded, and eased upright with Ruth's help, drinking the brew eagerly, hopeful that it would live up to its promise. Then, unable to utter a word, she slid to her back once more, as the contraction began anew and she was torn on the rack of agony.

Win hadn't prepared her for this. *You're*

built for having babies. She recalled the laughter in his eyes as he'd smoothed his hand over her waist and downward. *You've got nice hips*. And then he'd...

She caught her breath, and in the black vortex of misery that gripped her, she heard his voice, listened as harsh words spewed from his mouth. And then, he was there. Cold hands touched her face and he whispered a faint promise.

"It'll be all right, sweetheart. Let me wash, Ellie. I can't touch you until my hands are clean."

He left her then and she sobbed at the vision that had been taken from her. Until his voice called her again, and his hands, no longer cold, but large and firm against her flesh, brought reassurance. He spoke quietly to Ruth, his words terse and stark, their meaning lost in the mists of Ellie's pain, and then he placed a cloth over her face and she turned her head, fearful of it cutting off her breathing.

"Hush, sweetheart. Hold still. I'm giving you something to relax you. I don't want you to sleep, though. Just listen to what I tell you." More murmuring met her ears as she inhaled the sickly, sweet odor of chloroform deeply into her lungs.

"Your hands are smaller than mine, Ruth. It'll be easier on her if you do it. You'll have to push upward and then bring the feet down." Hands pushed at her, fingers worked her flesh, and Ellie floated higher on the relief given her by the dripping dose Win administered. Stretched almost beyond bearing, she groaned as Win called her back from the netherland that beckoned.

"Ellie, we need you to push now," he said urgently, holding her hands in his and rousing her with gentle strength. A pain that overwhelmed the relief she'd gained tore at her, and she opened her mouth to cry aloud. But Win was there, bending close to speak encouragement, his voice spurring her to do his bidding.

"Take a deep breath, Ellie. Now push hard. Push against Ruth's hands. Don't quit pushing, sweetheart. Just one more time."

If Win said to climb the mountains, she would do as he asked. And if bearing the pain one more time would bring the laboring to an end, she could do no less. In moments, another cry split the air, one that began as a weak, tentative wail, only to escalate into an angry squeal, and then a scream that brought sudden laughter from Ruth.

"You sassy little girl-child," Ruth said with relief and humor combined. "Look here, Ellie," she called out. "See your daughter." Holding high the small body, the cord still attached, Ruth reached to place the squirming babe on Ellie's stomach.

"Hand me that string and those scissors," she told Mathilda, and Ellie was only vaguely aware of the movement between her legs. Through tear-drenched eyes, she viewed the infant she'd delivered and watched as Win wrapped a clean flannel cloth around the slippery form, swaddling the dark-haired babe with practiced movements, leaving only the last fold incomplete.

He held the bundle closer to Ruth for a moment, watching as she cut through the thick tissue of the umbilical cord with a single stroke. And then he turned back to Ellie. "Do you want to hold her, sweetheart?" His hands completed wrapping the wriggling infant, and Ellie smiled and nodded as she watched.

His voice was soft, yet deep with emotion, and she searched his face, wondering at the expression of pure joy that lighted his features. He had eyes only for the babe, and his head bent as he blest the wrinkled forehead with a touch of his lips. Then he looked up to meet his wife's gaze.

"She's beautiful, sweetheart. Looks just like her mama." His eyes shining with pleasure, he placed the child in Ellie's arms. Then he lifted them both, until they were surrounded by his embrace.

Ruth muttered darkly as she disposed of soiled pads and replaced them with fresh linen. "You're supposed to be doing this, Doc. I'm just the helper."

Win laughed aloud. "You do that so well, you'll be taking my business, Mrs. Kincaid," he said, teasing the healer as readily as though they had not just passed through the travail of childbirth, as if Ellie had not minutes since survived the trauma of a breech delivery.

"I don't want your business, Doc," Ruth said, looking up with a smile. "Although I hope you'll note, I didn't allow her to tear."

Ellie felt euphoria take her, recognized the residue of the drug she had inhaled as it brought surcease from the discomfort of the tugging and scrubbing Ruth was initiating. "I told you it would be a girl," she whispered. Triumph tinged the words and she was suddenly exuberant, her mind ignoring the pain and misery of the past hours.

"So you did, Mrs. Gray. So you did." Win's kiss was gentle, his touch tender as he spent comfort on his wife. And across the room, Mathilda watched, her mouth pursed, her bearing regal, her eyes narrow as she viewed the aftermath of new birth.

Chapter Seventeen

"I'll be leaving in the morning." Mathilda's words held her usual reserve within each syllable, but Ellie chose to see beyond the facade Win's mother put in place. In the depths of her eyes, behind her habitual shield of control, lurked a spark of humanity Ellie had caught a glimpse of during her long night of labor. And so, she bridled the impetuous response that begged to be spoken, to focus on a softer reply.

It would not do for Ellie to bristle every time Win's mother ruffled her feathers and now seemed the time to make a new beginning.

"I'd hoped you'd stay for the baby's baptism," she said quietly from her perch on a kitchen chair. Mathilda sat across the table, her face a mask of indifference as Ellie spoke her wish.

"It seems you have enough women running in and out of my son's house without adding myself to the clutter," Mathilda said in a tone that appeared to demean Ellie's stream of visitors.

And Ellie listened to her heart before she replied. Closed her mind to the words and concentrated instead on the lonely woman who watched her with wintry eyes.

"I have some wonderful friends," she said finally. "And I appreciate them stopping by to see the baby and bringing meals for all of us. But I don't think you understand what it's meant to Win to have you here. Those other women are friends…but you're family."

Win cast her an unbelieving look from his position by the stove, but fortunately, his mother was not in a position to view the cynical twist to his mouth.

"Winston all but divorced himself from his family several years ago when he decided to pursue the practice of medicine." Mathilda's words vibrated with pain, and Ellie suddenly recognized the aching heart beneath the woman's stiff reserve.

"He only did what he had to," Ellie said. "And how you could be here and watch him, and know how much he cares about his patients, without recognizing that, is beyond me." She reached across the table, placing her fingers over Mathilda's delicately formed hand. It was slender, the fingers long and tapering. The hand of a lady, and Ellie mourned for a moment that she would never possess such elegance.

Mathilda's hand twitched, but it was a mark of her upbringing that she allowed Ellie's palm to rest where it lay. "I've certainly made note that Winston is in demand, and I'm sure he's more than competent. I only rue the day he decided to leave the streets of civilization to spend his life on the frontier."

"And I," said Ellie with a look in her husband's direction, "will be eternally grateful for the day he arrived in Whitehorn."

"I'm sure," Mathilda said, and then her mouth twitched as if the words within must be spoken. "He saved your baby's life, Eleanor. Possibly yours, too. For that I'm thankful. I would never wish you ill. I hope you are aware of that fact."

"I am."

"She'd have lived through it, Mother," Win said dryly. "It would have been harder for her to deliver a true breech baby, but Ellie's strong. I just made it a little easier for her. Or maybe I should say, Ruth did." He grinned at Ellie. "It seemed I was just an ordinary father at the last there. Ruth did all the work."

"You told her what to do," Ellie reminded him. "And I'm glad you were with me. I couldn't have gone through it without your help."

Almost imperceptibly, a slow flush rose to color Win's cheeks, and his eyes glistened as he fastened his gaze on Ellie's face. "I've never been so touched during a delivery as with baby Grace," he said. "She seemed to fit in my arms as if she'd been formed perfectly for such an embrace."

Mathilda scanned him with a look of surprise. "Well, I think you won't have a problem with accepting the child, Winston. And certainly, every infant born deserves a set of parents who have its best interests at heart." She glanced at the cradle in the corner of the kitchen, and Ellie noted a softening in her gaze.

"Our child deserves grandparents capable

of loving her, too," Win said. "It doesn't look like Ellie's father will be as accepting as you, Mother. And you'll be the only real grandmother Grace will ever have."

A sound of disbelief from Mathilda's lips stunned Ellie as the woman rose from the table. "She'll be surrounded by the women in this town, who seem to be totally besotted with her already."

"They're not true family, though," Ellie told her quietly, aware that her voice held an unmistakable plea.

Mathilda folded her hands before her and hesitated. "I will say that you seem capable of making a home for Winston, Eleanor. Perhaps in time, you will be able to persuade him to shake the dust of this town and return to his beginnings. And if you do, the child will be welcomed into our home."

Win moved quickly, ignoring Ellie's uplifted hand. Striding to his mother's side, he grasped her shoulders, turning her to face him. "Mother, you need to understand something. I thought I'd made it clear that Whitehorn is my home. Ellie and I will travel to Saint Louis to visit you and the family if we are welcome, but this will always be our home."

He released Mathilda and one long arm reached for Ellie, drawing her to his side. Together, they presented an oddly formed triangle, but the greater distance was drawn between the older woman and her son. "Ellie is my wife, and I love her," Win said, emotion softening his voice. "I love the child we delivered last week, and the two of them are my family."

He cleared his throat and his words were slow. "There's room for you and father inside our family circle, but not unless you are willing to accept my choices."

Mathilda's eyes wavered from Win's gaze and she cast a glance again at the cradle, where Grace was making soft sounds of awakening. "I suppose," she said, a tinge of pain softening her words, "what cannot be changed must be accepted."

Her back stiffened as she stepped back from Win and tilted her chin with a habitual mannerism Ellie recognized from the past few days. "I'll go upstairs and pack now, so that there won't be a rush tomorrow before the stage arrives."

Her footsteps were firm and measured as she crossed the floor to the doorway and onto the flight of stairs that rose from the wide central hall. "She'll come around, Ellie," Win whispered, turning her into his embrace. "One day, she'll understand."

And Ellie could only hope he was right.

"Everett gave me a telegram from my mother yesterday," Win said, watching Ellie as she traveled from stove to table, her hands filled with a pan of biscuits. "She arrived home safe and sound late last week and wanted us to know that her trip was long and miserable."

Ellie glanced down at him. "She said that? Long and miserable?"

"Words to that effect," he said with a grin. "Wished us both a happy Christmas, with her best regards. My mother doesn't believe in making it short and sweet, that's for sure. Everett said it was the longest wire he'd ever delivered to anyone in town." He reached for a biscuit and watched as Ellie spooned scrambled eggs from the skillet onto his plate. "I forgot to tell you about it after I got caught up with patients."

Ellie settled herself in her chair and watched as Win buttered his biscuit. "Do you miss being home for Christmas?" she asked quietly.

He shook his head, and delivered a smile that made Ellie's heart race. So easily he could make her feel loved, with just a glance, a crooked grin or a touch of his hand on her shoulder. "I've got all I want right here," he said, his gaze taking in the cradle in the corner, then resting on his wife's face.

"Will we have a Christmas tree?" she asked, flustered by his words, and Win's eyes narrowed as if he considered the thought.

"I suspect that can be arranged," he said, a touch of mystery adding to her delight. They left the table in a few minutes, and Win headed for the hallway. Ellie listened to the impact of his booted feet on the stairs, then the movement overhead that told her he was shifting things around upstairs. Before she had cleaned the kitchen, he called her from the parlor and, wiping her hands on a dish towel, she answered his summons.

Win stood near the wide front windows that looked out upon the street, and at his feet lay several boxes, apparently the result of his foray to the second floor of the house. "Birdie Watkins's grandson brought me a tree last year," he told Ellie. "And I suspect he'll do the same this Christmas. He's got an enormous grove of pines on his place, and Birdie picked one out specially for me."

"She loves you," Ellie said simply, barely able to snatch her gaze from the boxes she suspected held unknown treasures. "I could see it in her face when she came by the other day to see the baby."

"She's a dear," Win said agreeably. "And if she behaves herself, she'll be around for a while yet. She told me she'd be at church on Christmas Sunday to see Grace baptized."

"Did she?" Ellie felt a thrill of delight at the words. It seemed that the whole town, with a few minor exceptions, planned to turn out for the event, if the parade of visitors were to be believed. "Should we have a reception afterward, do you think?"

"If you're up to it, I'd like that," Win said. His eyes were tender as he held her gaze. "Do you know how much I love you, Mrs. Gray?"

Ellie felt the familiar melting deep within her inner being. The man had a knack of reducing her to a puddle of emotion, his tone soft and musing as he voiced the query she delighted to hear. "I think I'm the luckiest woman in the world," she said simply. Her arms lifted to circle his neck, and Ellie pressed a quick kiss against his mouth. "We'll have a wonderful Christmas. The best I've ever had, at least of those I remember. I think my mother probably made Christmas special when she was alive, but my pa wasn't interested in fixing up the house or having a tree to decorate."

Win's brow lifted and he looked down at her with surprise. "You've never had a Christmas tree?"

"Not that I remember," she allowed quietly. "I saw the one in church a couple of years when Pa let me go to the service, and I remember once going home after dark a couple of days after Christmas, and I could see through the windows into houses and there were trees all lit with candles."

"You'll have one of your own this year," Win promised. He nodded at the boxes he'd hauled from one of the rooms upstairs. "Sort through that stuff and see if you want anything else from the mercantile. Tess and John have a pretty good assortment of decorations."

"We used to make chains out of colored paper when I was in school, but Pa burned mine in the stove when I brought them home," she remembered. "Maybe I could do that for our tree."

Win thought of the magnificent specimens that had filled the bay window of the parlor back in Saint Louis and his heart ached for the girl he'd married. Not for her the memory of crystal ornaments glistening and tinsel garlands catching the glow of hundreds of candles that reflected in the windows. Only a childhood of neglect, and a father who wallowed in his own misery, to make up the images in her mind. That she could be so happy with so little saddened him, yet uplifted his spirits.

It seemed that no matter what he did for her, she was delighted beyond measure. From simple dresses to the blown-glass ornaments at her feet, his gifts had gladdened her heart, and she returned tenfold the pleasure he brought to her life. He slipped his hand into his waistcoat pocket and withdrew a small, tissue-wrapped package. He'd thought to wait until Christmas morning, that day when the shipment containing his gift had arrived, but now seemed a better time to present Ellie with this part of her Christmas present.

"Let me see your hand," he said, frowning as if he'd caught sight of a blemish on the flawless skin. Ellie glanced up at him quickly, then her gaze flew to her hands and she held them both up for his inspection.

He grasped the left one carefully and slid the signet ring from her finger. "I think it's time to replace this, young lady." She watched through tear-drenched eyes as he presented the simple diamond-studded band for her inspection. "Do you like it, sweetheart?"

She could only nod, biting her lip as he slid it into place, then dipped his head to kiss it, as if to seal it there, where it belonged for all time. "Merry Christmas, Ellie. I know I'm a few days early, but I wanted you to have it now."

Her hands touched his face, even as the tears she shed touched his heart, and then she was in his embrace and he clasped her against himself, his mouth seeking hers in a kiss that spoke more eloquently than words, of his love for her. And then he laughed, a joyous sound that brought an answering smile to her face.

"It's wonderful, Win. I love it, even though I'll fear losing such a costly ring. But I promise I'll take good care of it."

"And I promise I'll take good care of you, Ellie Gray." He cleared his throat and motioned to the boxes at their feet. "Now why don't you take a look at what I've carried down from upstairs."

Turning from him, she knelt, opening the lids carefully, as if she feared damaging their contents. "It's all wrapped in tissue," he told her. "I had Ethel put things away for me last year when I took the tree down." His mouth twitched as he recalled the moment. "She thought I wouldn't take the proper care of my things, and she chased me on my way while she organized the whole assortment for this year."

"Did you have a party?" Ellie asked, and he thought her voice was wistful.

"Didn't plan on it," he recalled with a grin, "but Kate and James came by, and pretty soon a bunch from church stood on the porch singing carols; and before you know it I had a houseful. Kate ran home and brought back cookies, and Ethel happened to recall that she had a couple of gallons of punch all made up."

"They planned it, didn't they?" Ellie's eyes danced as she looked up from her task. "They knew you were alone, away from family, and they didn't want you to be lonesome." She settled back on her heels and her fingers splayed wide on her thighs. "Folks just take to you, Win. Everyone in town likes you."

Not a trace of envy marred her smile as she spoke the words, and Win was struck by the urge to drag her to her feet and carry her off to the wide bed they'd only recently risen from. If only she were healed from child-birth, he thought. And then brushed the errant thought from his mind. It would be another couple of weeks before Ellie was fit for what he had in mind, and he'd best skedaddle from the house before he gave in to his masculine urges. Perhaps by Christmas....

His hands were tender as he bent to her, his mouth less than urgent as he kissed her, there amid the tissue and open boxes of ornaments and tinsel. And she responded with the eager-ness he'd come to expect from her, her hands clasping his forearms, her mouth returning the caress he offered. "Be careful today," she urged him, and then looked out the window where snow drifted in a lazy fashion past the frosted panes.

"Are you going to use the new sleigh?" she asked, and he thought she looked expectant as her eyes took in the wintry look of things outdoors.

"I had Lionel uncover it last week," Win said. "I knew we'd need it for going to church come Sunday." He drew on his coat and buttoned it, then searched in the pockets for his heavy gloves. "Are you sure you're going to feel up to it?"

Her head swiveled in his direction. "Of course, I'll be up to it. I've been planning this for weeks. Since before your mother left, in fact."

He fingered the brim of his hat, reluctant to leave her. "You'll be all right?" he asked.

"I'll be fine, once I have a tree to put this stuff on," she said, lifting a length of tinsel and admiring it in the light from the window.

"Today," he promised. "I'll stop by Birdie's place and leave a message."

The dining room table was laden with pies and cakes, the kitchen filled with the scent of roasting turkey and the pungent smell of dressing. Ellie took a last glance around and lifted the precious bundle from the cradle. "I think I'm ready," she said, her tone absentminded, as if her thoughts were scattered.

"You didn't have to make enough food to feed the whole town," Win said with a grin. "If I didn't know Ethel and the ladies from church had helped I'd be downright upset with you, Ellie. You've worked too hard at this." Kettles on the stove were pushed to the back, their contents simmering, and several loaves of bread waited on the buffet, wrapped in clean dish towels.

"It just kinda grew," she admitted, her cheeks flushed with pleasure as she eyed the preparations for the party. "I'm so excited, Win. And Grace looks so pretty in her dress."

"So does her mama," he said quietly, lifting his hand to brush a stray wave from Ellie's forehead. "Now let's be on our way."

He loaded her into the sleigh, tucking the lap robe around her legs and over the baby she cradled in her arms. The heavy cashmere cape he'd ordered from Tess had arrived only yesterday, and he admired the velvet trim again, noting the glow of Ellie's skin against the dark-blue fabric. On her feet she wore new boots, their patent leather toes shining almost as nicely as the buttons marching up the side of each boot. She was altogether stunning, he decided, climbing into the sleigh beside her.

Bells jingled in the crisp air as a passing sleigh, pulled by a prancing team of horses, caught his eye. His hand lifted in an automatic salute, as voices called greetings.

"Was that Caleb and Ruth?" Ellie asked, peering after the vehicle.

"Yup. Must be they're going to church,

too." As well he knew, he thought with a sense of satisfaction. Half the town would be dropping by to help in the celebration today, bringing gifts to honor the baby's baptism. Having Ruth there would make Ellie's day complete.

From the enormous Christmas tree at the front of the small church to the carols that rang from the rafters, it was a Sunday such as Ellie had never known. Grace endured the sprinkling of water on her tiny forehead with only a fluttering of eyelids to denote her surprise. The church was filled to bursting with excited children, who offered verses and poems from beside the tall pulpit, even as their admiring parents watched from the simple pews. And then the congregation listened as the kindly pastor told the familiar story for the benefit of his parishioners.

"There were in the same country, shepherds…" The resonant voice spoke the words with reverence, tinged with joy. Ellie felt Win's hand creep across her lap to grasp her fingers and she looked up at him, aware again of the rare beauty of the man she'd married. He was dressed as a gentleman, yet beneath the formal attire lay the strength and stature of a man fit for the frontier life he'd chosen.

And he belonged to her, to Ellie Gray. Her heart could barely hold the pure joy of this moment, and tears slid from her eyes to fall on the soft blanket she'd wrapped around the baby she held in her left arm.

Win's head tilted toward her, his lips brushing her ear. "Happy Christmas, sweetheart."

The house was filled with friends and neighbors, most of them holding plates of food from the bountiful supply in the dining room, all of them bearing gifts for the new baby. Ellie was given a seat of honor in the parlor, Grace ensconced in the cradle beside her, Ethel having taken over the kitchen. It was no use protesting, she'd found, for several others volunteered to help, and she was only to open packages and admire the assortment of tiny dresses and shawls, sweaters and small booties that filled the tissue-wrapped presents.

The sun had set before the last person departed, and she watched from the front parlor windows as they made their way down the snowy path to the gate. Heading in different directions, they waved, calling back greetings into the steadily falling snow. Win closed the front door for the last time and entered the wide parlor doors, pausing in the entrance as Ellie turned to him.

"I'll never forget this day," she said quietly. "It was perfect, wasn't it?"

"Almost," he said, and walked slowly to where she stood, his gaze admiring the newly slender form of his wife.

"What would make it better?" she asked, her gaze lifting to meet his.

"Holding you in my arms." Simply spoken, the words touched her heart as had no other gift on this day of bountiful giving. He drew her close and his breath was warm against her face. "Do you know that I have all I've ever wanted in life?"

"Have you?" she asked, tilting her head to one side, the better to see him. "I'm thinking one day we'll have another baby, Win," she promised. "A son for you."

His words were steady. "It won't be any more precious than the daughter I already have, Ellie."

"It will truly be your own child, next time," she said softly.

"Grace is truly mine." His words were a tender reproof, and his smile muted their impact. "I could not love her more if I'd been there when she was conceived, Ellie. Mine was the joy of watching her born. It will be the pleasure of seeing her grow, the satisfaction of being called her father. No other child could remove her from the place she's claimed in my heart."

She felt her throat close with emotion, yet the words begged to be spoken once again and she could not deny them utterance. "I love you, Winston Gray."

"And I love you, Eleanor Gray."

"I'm just Ellie," she said simply. "Just the woman who loves you."

"You're my whole world," he said, denying her words. His voice hitched as if his breathing were restricted and she sensed the tears he would not shed. When he spoke again, his words were softer, coaxing and seductive. "And now, if I'm very careful, I think we can celebrate in a special way."

Releasing her from his touch, he walked to the front window and pulled the draperies together, closing out the twilight. Making his way around the room, he brought the parlor doors together with a soft thud, then blew out the lamp, casting the room into shadows. Only the candles on the Christmas tree lit his way as he returned to her. Ellie watched, her heart quickening as his strong hands lifted her against himself, then lowered her to the carpet beneath the shelter of ever-green branches.

"Are we going to make love?" she asked in a hushed whisper, her hands already busy with the buttons of his waistcoat, and the shirt beneath it. "Will it be all right?"

His nod was her only reply, and then he was tugging at an afghan from the sofa, lift-ing her to place it beneath her. She did as he asked, turning away as his hands worked at the buttons on her dress, his fingers touch-ing the column of her spine and leaving soft shivers of awareness in their wake. So easily he slid the clothing from her, so gently he ar-ranged her before himself, she was lulled into his spell, could only gaze into the warmth of his eyes and inhale the scent of shaving soap and the male aroma his body exuded.

He slid from his trousers, casting them aside impatiently, then returned to her, his hands refuting the hasty gestures he'd em-ployed while stripping from his clothing. Now they were gentle, tender and unhurried as he prepared her for his taking. His mouth was warm and damp against her skin, his fingers careful as he handled delicate flesh, his words soft and persuasive as he coaxed her along the path he'd set for her to travel.

She followed where he led, more than willing to do as he bid, her legs enclosing him in their grasp, her hands searching out the places of pleasure she knew would bring groans and murmurs from his lips. It had been long weeks since their last coming together, and Win's heartbeat was heavy against her, his hands trembling as he formed her breasts with his fingers and palms.

And then he sought the source of her pleasure, the delicate tissues of her womanhood, and she lifted to his touch, her body eager for the fulfillment he brought to her needy flesh.

So gently he caressed her, so tenderly he led her, she was aware only of the witchery of clever fingers against delicate flesh. Her eyes opened as the captivating lure of ecstasy to come held her in its thrall, her body quivering with the delight he offered. The candles blurred in her sight, casting a nimbus of light around the head and shoulders of the man hovering over her, and she cried out, a high keening sound that shivered in the silence.

"Ah, Ellie," he whispered, his breathing harsh as he took her with slow, measured strokes, barely penetrating, yet filling her with the joy of his possession. He shuddered in her arms, bending to press kisses against her face and throat. And she clasped him against herself, unwilling to allow him escape from her embrace.

From the cradle, a soft whimper announced the awakening of her child, and Ellie felt the rush of warmth in her breasts as milk filled her to overflowing. Win chuckled against her throat.

"We woke her." His words were filled with satisfaction as he lifted himself on his forearms and looked down at the dampness seeping from Ellie's breasts. "You're ready to nurse, aren't you?"

She nodded. "All I have to hear is one peep, and I overflow."

Reluctantly, he rose, stepped into his trousers and drew them on, then reached for the cradle. The bundle was small, and he lifted her easily, holding her against his cheek. Grace nuzzled eagerly, and Win's chuckle warmed Ellie's heart. "Your mama has more to offer than I," he said, his lips brushing myriad kisses across the tiny face.

Ellie sat up, and Win shook his head, snatching a pillow from the sofa and placing it on the afghan. "Stay there and nurse her, why don't you?" He offered the babe into Ellie's arms, then reached for a clean diaper from the cradle. With gentle movements, he placed it where so recently his seed had been spent. Then his hands were deft, wrapping both woman and child within the colorful warmth of the knitted covering. "I'll sort things out," he murmured, "and then we'll go to bed."

Too content to protest, feeling pampered and well loved, Ellie could only nod her agreement. She turned to her side and looked down at the babe who had found the nourishment she craved. Her arms cradled the small bundle, and she allowed her gaze to rest on the packages Win had piled beneath the tree. She'd added her own assortment only this morning, and she thought of the precious moments they would share as they opened the gifts together on Christmas morning.

"Thank you, God," she whispered, her eyes closing in slumber. And never knew when she was lifted and carried from the parlor to the bedroom down the hall, only wakening for a moment as she watched Win pin a fresh diaper in place, then hold baby Grace over his shoulder for a moment before he placed her in the crib beside the bed.

She felt his arms surround her as he gathered her to himself, and she snuggled against his warmth, sighing quietly, repeating the words of thanksgiving again. His voice was a deep rumble in his chest, vibrating against her ear, and she smiled as he whispered his love in her ear.

Epilogue

Spring came early to Whitehorn. Not so every year, but in all of Ellie's memory, this was the soonest the flowers had made an appearance. With the threat of snow still a possibility, the tiny violets and patches of trillium beneath the trees at the back of Win's yard were bravely facing the elements. She pulled the pine needles from around them and admired the delicate blossoms, enthralled at the sight of such beauty.

"It's too early to be planting a garden," a voice said from behind her. "Must be you're on the lookout for the gold that's supposed to be buried hereabouts."

She turned and smiled, clasping the shovel she'd carried around the yard for the past hour. "I think that's nothing but hogwash, Sheriff," she said with a chuckle. "Anyway, nobody in his right mind would bury gold in my backyard. Ethel told me there's talk that it's somewhere around the saloon, although how she'd know that is beyond me.

"I just couldn't resist turning over a patch of dirt out here, but I'll admit finding gold never entered my mind. A few earthworms seem more likely. Win warned me I was ahead of myself with the gardening."

"Talk of that gold seems to rear its head every so often," James said nonchalantly. "One of these days it may surface. But I'm not gonna hold my breath."

Ellie looked beyond him to the house next door. "Kate's not home, is she?"

He shook his head. "No. I'm on my way over to the schoolhouse to take her some dinner. Thought I'd bring Tyler back for the afternoon. Things are pretty quiet in town, and I'm taking a couple of hours off."

"Why don't you plan on having supper with us?" Ellie asked eagerly. "I'm cooking Win's favorite, roast beef."

"You sure know all the right moves, young

lady," James said with a grin. "We'll be here with bells on. Kate's always ready for a meal at your table." He shoved his hands deeply into the pockets of his trousers. "Couple of things I need to talk to you about, Ellie. First off, Cilla over at the saloon has disappeared. Some say she ran off with Billy Barnes, but nobody seems to know. I need to hear, should Win catch wind of anything."

"I thought she was afraid of him," Ellie said, remembering the pain Cilla had suffered at the hands of the young man. "Do you suppose—"

James cut in quickly. "Not much sense in trying to sort it out, honey. Folks are wondering if the gold you're set on digging up here might not have entered into it." His grin belied the seriousness of his concern as he gestured at the beginnings of Ellie's garden plot.

And then he stuffed his hands in his pockets and rocked back on his heels. "I saw your pa in front of the mercantile a while ago, Ellie."

She moved the shovel restlessly, punching a slice of dried grass into the earth. "Did you now?"

"He asked me if I thought you'd be willing to see him, maybe talk to him."

An uneasy spasm touched her midriff and her hand flew there, fingers clenching as if she could halt the hope that blossomed like the flowers at her feet. "What do you suppose he wants?"

James shrugged, yet his posture told her he was not totally relaxed. "Who knows? You won't, unless you speak with him."

She tried for nonchalance, but her mouth quivered as the words left her throat, and she knew she'd failed, miserably. "I guess I wouldn't mind if he stopped by."

"I think he wants to see the baby."

"He told me there wasn't squattin' room for me in his life." Her tone was bitter as she recalled the man who'd scathingly mocked her.

"Sometimes folks change," James said quietly. "Maybe you ought to give him a chance, Ellie. See what he has to say."

Hat in hand, George Mitchum stood at the back door, and Ellie thought swiftly of the last time he'd entered her kitchen. Her heart pounded as he stepped past the threshold, and she stood aside, watching as he made his way toward the table, then turned to face her.

"Sheriff Kincaid said you agreed to talk to me, daughter." His eyes held a wary question in their depths.

"What do you want, Pa?" She thrust her hands deeply into her apron pockets and stood her ground.

"I have a hard time with sayin' certain words, Ellie," he began. "But I reckon sometimes it's easier to eat crow than live with it stickin' in your craw forever."

From the corner of the kitchen, a sound caught his attention and his head moved, his eyes scanning the area like a chicken hawk sighting prey. "That the baby?" he asked, his words gruff, his hands clenching into fists as he waited for Ellie's reply.

"Yes, that's Grace," she said simply. And then her tender heart relented. "Would you like to see her, Pa?"

He nodded, inhaling sharply, and pulled a chair from the table, sitting down with a thump. "I guess I'd like to. Maybe you'd let me hold her for a minute."

"Maybe." Ellie lifted the blanket-wrapped child and gazed deeply into dark eyes. So wise and wonderful she looked, this tiny piece of humanity. So precious and perfect, in her pink wrappings, with delicate features and a mop of dark hair that hung in ringlets across her forehead.

She crossed the floor to her father and placed the bundle in his arms, watching closely as he shifted the babe uneasily for a moment until Grace was settled in the bend of his elbow. And then his head bent and he inspected her small face, touched her arm and then watched with absorbed interest as one infant hand curled around his callused index finger.

"She's kinda little, ain't she?" he asked gruffly. "Grace, did you say her name was?"

"Yes." Ellie relaxed, leaning against the buffet, watching carefully.

"Your grandma on your mother's side was called Grace."

"I know. I named her after my grandmother."

"Your ma would have liked that," he said, nodding his head a bit as he scrutinized the rosebud mouth that opened, the delicate tongue that touched with dainty skill against a lower lip, then retreated. The small nose wrinkled, and a quiver touched the rounded chin as if Grace recognized that a stranger held her. Her mouth opened again and a muted sound that could have been a prelude to a cry came forth.

"Did I do something wrong?" George asked hastily, glancing up at Ellie and then back down at his granddaughter.

The brown eyes squinted suddenly and then opened wide as the pink lips opened again, this time in an unmistakable smile. Soft cooing noises accompanied the curving lines, and George looked up at Ellie in surprise. "I think she smiled at me."

"I think she likes you," Ellie said agreeably. "Listen to her, Pa. She's just learning to make noises."

It was a scene he would never forget, Win decided, standing in the hallway and watching through the kitchen door, aware that James had been right in his judgment. The thought of Ellie facing her father again was difficult to swallow, but if George Mitchum was truly wanting to mend fences, Winston Gray would not stand in his way. And so he'd come in the front way, to be there should Ellie need him, but willing to stand clear if things went well.

And it seemed they had.

Ellie looked up, as if her inner senses spoke his name, and her eyes lit with a familiar gleam as she caught sight of him. "Come in," she said, waving him forward. "My father came to meet his granddaughter."

"So I see," Win said amiably, pushing his coat aside and tucking his hand into his pocket. "And does he approve?" The words were aimed at George and held a challenge that was unmistakable in its strength.

The older man looked up, acknowledging Win's presence. "How could I help but approve. She looks like her mama, don't she?"

"And how do you feel about her mama?" Win asked quietly, aware of Ellie's stricken features as he spoke the words.

"I hope her mama's able to forget all the harm I did to her," George said bluntly. "It's lonesome out there on the ranch, and it was a long winter. I did a heap of thinking, sittin' every night by myself."

"And?" Win's voice did not waver, even as he cast Ellie a warning look.

"I come to make peace with my girl, Dr. Gray."

"And is she willing to accept your apology?" He looked at Ellie again, and his arms ached to hold her, even as he knew she must make her own choices. And so he waited.

"We need all the family available, Pa," she

said finally. "I guess I'm willing to put the past where it belongs."

"I'll settle for that," George said, inhaling deeply, as if a load had been lifted from his soul.

"Maybe you'd like to stay for supper?" Ellie asked. "James and Kate are coming over, too."

He shook his head. "Not this time, daughter. Ask me again, if you want to. I need to be heading home. We've got a whole herd of cows dropping calves right and left, and I need to be there."

"All right. I'll ask you again," Ellie said, looking to Win as if for reassurance that she'd done the right thing.

He nodded his agreement, and she smiled, a tremulous movement of her lips that touched him to the depths. "You're welcome here, Mr. Mitchum," he said, adding his own words of acceptance.

George cleared his throat. "Well, I'd better be on my way, I reckon. I'll stop by again, Ellie." His hands tightened a bit on the bundle he held, and then he looked up at his daughter. "Thank you."

Ellie took the baby and eased her upright, patting the small back and waiting as her father rose and headed for the back door. There were a few awkward moments as George pulled the door open and stepped onto the porch, then looked back at the couple who watched him. His nod was brief, his teeth biting into his bottom lip as he turned away, and Win stepped forward to close the door behind him.

"What do you think?" he asked Ellie, careful to keep his voice neutral, not wanting to influence her mind.

"I think my daughter has just met her grandpa," she told him, a hint of happiness lighting her features. "I don't have it in me to bear him a grudge, Win. I just can't."

"I know," he said, crossing to where she stood, baby held between them as he circled her with his arms and drew the two females he loved against himself. "I know, sweetheart. And I'm pleased for you."

"Spring is coming, Win," she said after a moment. "The wildflowers are blooming at the back of the yard. I think this is going to be a good year, don't you?"

His nod was brief, and he bent his head to press kisses against her temple. "The best yet, honey. The very best." As always, his body responded to her, to the scent and feel of the child-woman he'd taken to wife, and he groaned as he thought of the hours before he would take her to himself once more.

"Win?" she asked, her eyes twinkling as she peered up at him. "Do you have a problem? Can I help?"

He shook his head. "Nothing I can't handle, love." He glanced up as James knocked on the back door, Kate behind him, and his grin was wide as he bent to deposit a long kiss on her mouth.

"Just hold that thought till our dinner guests go home."

* * * * *

YES! Please send me **The Montana Mavericks Collection** in Larger Print. This collection begins with 3 FREE books and 2 FREE gifts (gifts valued at approx. $20.00 retail) in the first shipment, along with the other first 4 books from the collection! If I do not cancel, I will receive 8 monthly shipments until I have the entire 51-book Montana Mavericks collection. I will receive 2 or 3 FREE books in each shipment and I will pay just $4.99 US/ $5.89 CDN for each of the other four books in each shipment, plus $2.99 for shipping and handling per shipment.*If I decide to keep the entire collection, I'll have paid for only 32 books, because 19 books are FREE! I understand that accepting the 3 free books and gifts places me under no obligation to buy anything. I can always return a shipment and cancel at any time. My free books and gifts are mine to keep no matter what I decide.

263 HCN 2404   463 HCN 2404

Name	(PLEASE PRINT)

Address	Apt. #

City	State/Prov.	Zip/Postal Code

Signature (if under 18, a parent or guardian must sign)

Mail to the **Reader Service:**

IN U.S.A.: P.O. Box 1867, Buffalo, NY 14240-1867
IN CANADA: P.O. Box 609, Fort Erie, Ontario L2A 5X3

REQUEST YOUR FREE BOOKS!
2 FREE NOVELS PLUS 2 FREE GIFTS!

ⒽHARLEQUIN®

SPECIAL EDITION

Life, Love & Family

YES! Please send me 2 FREE Harlequin® Special Edition novels and my 2 FREE gifts (gifts are worth about $10). After receiving them, if I don't wish to receive any more books, I can return the shipping statement marked "cancel." If I don't cancel, I will receive 6 brand-new novels every month and be billed just $4.74 per book in the U.S. or $5.24 per book in Canada. That's a savings of at least 14% off the cover price! It's quite a bargain! Shipping and handling is just 50¢ per book in the U.S. and 75¢ per book in Canada.* I understand that accepting the 2 free books and gifts places me under no obligation to buy anything. I can always return a shipment and cancel at any time. Even if I never buy another book, the two free books and gifts are mine to keep forever.

235/335 HDN F46C

Name _____ (PLEASE PRINT) _____

Address _____ Apt. # _____

City _____ State/Prov. _____ Zip/Postal Code _____

Signature (if under 18, a parent or guardian must sign)

Mail to the Harlequin® Reader Service:
IN U.S.A.: P.O. Box 1867, Buffalo, NY 14240-1867
IN CANADA: P.O. Box 609, Fort Erie, Ontario L2A 5X3

Want to try two free books from another line?
Call 1-800-873-8635 or visit www.ReaderService.com.

* Terms and prices subject to change without notice. Prices do not include applicable taxes. Sales tax applicable in N.Y. Canadian residents will be charged applicable taxes. Offer not valid in Quebec. This offer is limited to one order per household. Not valid for current subscribers to Harlequin Special Edition books. All orders subject to credit approval. Credit or debit balances in a customer's account(s) may be offset by any other outstanding balance owed by or to the customer. Please allow 4 to 6 weeks for delivery. Offer available while quantities last.

Your Privacy—The Harlequin® Reader Service is committed to protecting your privacy. Our Privacy Policy is available online at www.ReaderService.com or upon request from the Harlequin Reader Service.

We make a portion of our mailing list available to reputable third parties that offer products we believe may interest you. If you prefer that we not exchange your name with third parties, or if you wish to clarify or modify your communication preferences, please visit us at www.ReaderService.com/consumerschoice or write to us at Harlequin Reader Service Preference Service, P.O. Box 9062, Buffalo, NY 14269. Include your complete name and address.

HSEDIR13R

REQUEST YOUR FREE BOOKS!
2 FREE NOVELS PLUS 2 FREE GIFTS!

LOVE, HOME & HAPPINESS

YES! Please send me 2 FREE Harlequin® American Romance® novels and my 2 FREE gifts (gifts are worth about $10). After receiving them, if I don't wish to receive any more books, I can return the shipping statement marked "cancel." If I don't cancel, I will receive 4 brand-new novels every month and be billed just $4.74 per book in the U.S. or $5.24 per book in Canada. That's a savings of at least 14% off the cover price! It's quite a bargain! Shipping and handling is just 50¢ per book in the U.S. and 75¢ per book in Canada.* I understand that accepting the 2 free books and gifts places me under no obligation to buy anything. I can always return a shipment and cancel at any time. Even if I never buy another book, the two free books and gifts are mine to keep forever.

154/354 HDN F4YY

Name _____ (PLEASE PRINT) _____

Address _____ Apt. # _____

City _____ State/Prov. _____ Zip/Postal Code _____

Signature (if under 18, a parent or guardian must sign) _____

Mail to the Harlequin® Reader Service:
IN U.S.A.: P.O. Box 1867, Buffalo, NY 14240-1867
IN CANADA: P.O. Box 609, Fort Erie, Ontario L2A 5X3

Want to try two free books from another line?
Call 1-800-873-8635 or visit www.ReaderService.com.

* Terms and prices subject to change without notice. Prices do not include applicable taxes. Sales tax applicable in N.Y. Canadian residents will be charged applicable taxes. Offer not valid in Quebec. This offer is limited to one order per household. Not valid for current subscribers to Harlequin American Romance books. All orders subject to credit approval. Credit or debit balances in a customer's account(s) may be offset by any other outstanding balance owed by or to the customer. Please allow 4 to 6 weeks for delivery. Offer available while quantities last.

Your Privacy—The Harlequin® Reader Service is committed to protecting your privacy. Our Privacy Policy is available online at www.ReaderService.com or upon request from the Harlequin Reader Service.

We make a portion of our mailing list available to reputable third parties that offer products we believe may interest you. If you prefer that we not exchange your name with third parties, or if you wish to clarify or modify your communication preferences, please visit us at www.ReaderService.com/consumerschoice or write to us at Harlequin Reader Service Preference Service, P.O. Box 9062, Buffalo, NY 14269. Include your complete name and address.

HARDIR13R

READERSERVICE.COM

Manage your account online!
- Review your order history
- Manage your payments
- Update your address

> *We've designed the*
> *Reader Service website*
> *just for you.*

Enjoy all the features!
- Discover new series available to you, and read excerpts from any series.
- Respond to mailings and special monthly offers.
- Connect with favorite authors at the blog.
- Browse the Bonus Bucks catalog and online-only exculsives.
- Share your feedback.

Visit us at:

ReaderService.com

RS15